The fiery brilliance of the Zebra Hologram Heart which you see on the cover is created by "laser holography." This is the revolutionary process in which a powerful laser beam records light waves in diamond-like facets so tiny that 9,000,000 fit in a square inch. No print or photograph can match the vibrant colors and radiant glow of a hologram.

So look for the Zebra Hologram Heart whenever you buy a historical romance. It is a shimmering reflection of our guarantee that you'll find consistent quality between the covers!

"Wade!" Her ⬛⬛⬛⬛⬛⬛⬛⬛⬛⬛⬛⬛⬛⬛⬛⬛ n embarrassment than a⬛⬛⬛⬛⬛⬛⬛⬛⬛⬛ stretched out in the middle of the floor?"

"I needed to get some sleep and thought if I bunked down on the floor, right behind the door, that if someone tried to . . ." Wade was unable to finish the statement as he realized that she indeed lay on top of him, and reacting on impulse, he pulled that magnificent mouth down to meet his.

Callie's eyes flew open with surprise at such a quick, unexpected change in their positions, but before she could protest, a strange tide of delightful sensations moved slowly through her body. For a moment, her mind was unable to concentrate on anything but the sudden wonder of his mouth on hers. Never had Callie felt such a startlingly strong response to anything or anyone in her life. It was as if a strange sort of fire now raged uncontrolled inside of her, and all desire to stop him grew gradually weaker until she had no resolve left at all. . . .

EXHILARATING ROMANCE
From Zebra Books

GOLDEN PARADISE   (2007, $3.95)
by Constance O'Banyon
Desperate for money, the beautiful and innocent Valentina Barrett finds
work as a veiled dancer, "Jordanna," at San Francisco's notorious Crystal
Palace. There she falls in love with handsome, wealthy Marquis Vincente —
a man she knew she could never trust as Valentina — but who Jordanna
can't resist making her lover and reveling in love's GOLDEN PARADISE.

SAVAGE SPLENDOR   (1855, $3.95)
by Constance O'Banyon
By day Mara questioned her decision to remain in her husband's world. But
by night, when Tajarez crushed her in his strong, muscular arms, taking her
to the peaks of rapture, she knew she could never live without him.

TEXAS TRIUMPH   (2009, $3.95)
by Victoria Thompson
Nothing is more important to the determined Rachel McKinsey than the
Circle M — and if it meant marrying her foreman to scare off rustlers, she
would do it. Yet the gorgeous rancher feels a secret thrill that the towering
Cole Elliot is to be her man — and despite her plan that they be business
partners, all she truly desires is a glorious consummation of their vows.

KIMBERLY'S KISS   (2184, $3.95)
by Kathleen Drymon
As a girl, Kimberly Davonwoods had spent her days racing her horse, per-
fecting her fencing, and roaming London's byways disguised as a boy. Then
at nineteen the raven-haired beauty was forced to marry a complete stranger. Though the hot-tempered adventuress vowed to escape her new husband, she never dreamed that he would use the sweet chains of ecstasy to
keep her from ever wanting to leave his side!

FOREVER FANCY   (2185, $3.95)
by Jean Haught
After she killed a man in self-defense, alluring Fancy Broussard had no
choice but to flee Clarence, Missouri. She sneaked aboard a private railcar,
plotting to distract its owner with her womanly charms. Then the dashing
Rafe Taggart strode into his compartment . . . and the frightened girl was
swept up in a whirlwind of passion that flared into an undeniable, unstop-
pable prelude to ecstasy!

*Available wherever paperbacks are sold, or order direct from the
Publisher. Send cover price plus 50¢ per copy for mailing and handling to Zebra Books, Dept. 2650, 475 Park Avenue South, New
York, N.Y. 10016. Residents of New York, New Jersey and Pennsylvania must include sales tax. DO NOT SEND CASH.*

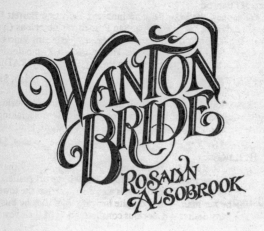

WANTON BRIDE

ROSALYN ALSOBROOK

ZEBRA BOOKS
KENSINGTON PUBLISHING CORP.

ZEBRA BOOKS

are published by

Kensington Publishing Corp.
475 Park Avenue South
New York, NY 10016

First printing: May, 1989

Printed in the United States of America

Dedication

This book is dedicated to that frightened young girl who gave birth to a chubby little brown-eyed, brown-haired baby girl on December 21, 1952 at Pilot Point, Texas. Because of her courageous willingness to let go, that chubby little baby is a happy, well-adjusted woman now, with a family of her own and two parents who opened not only their home to her, but their hearts as well. They raised that child as they would their own, taught her all about life and what it is to love.

So, to that young girl who so bravely gave up her baby when she knew she was in no position to care for it herself, I say, "Thank you!"—for not only did you give me life, you gave me happiness.

Special Acknowledgments

I would like to express my appreciation to the following people and organizations for helping me in times of true need: to Joan Boswell and Glenda Burt for their "fiery" criticism; to Jean Haught for taking my rope ladder away from me in Chapter One; to the Gilmer Fire Department for patiently answering what probably seemed like awfully dumb questions; to the Upshur County Library for service above and beyond; to my dad, Lowell Rutledge, for answering all my medical questions; to my editor, Lydia Paglio, who really puts up with a lot; and especially to my husband, Bobby, and my two sons, Andy and Tony, for their continued loyalty and undying support.

First printing: May, 1989

of the children back to the shooting-stage since they had
ridden the kennels two days with the heavy flails down most
of the time. As a result there had been very little breeze to

Chapter One

"Pine Fork!" Callie Thomas heard the deep, male voice call from overhead. Only a moment later the stagecoach slowed to a clattering halt near the right side of the deeply rutted, dirt and gravel street that ran through the center of the small East Texas town.

George Wilkins, an older man with thinning gray hair and alert blue eyes, reached across in front of Callie to pull the worn leather flap back away from the tiny coach window so she could catch her first glimpse of her new home. But the after-dust which had plagued them constantly the last hundred miles of their trip quickly swirled into the small confines of the coach. He quickly dropped the flap back into place.

"Looks like Pine Fork 'asn't 'ad any rain 'ere lately either," George said in his rolling Australian lilt, which Callie was just now becoming accustomed to. He raised a shaggy brow while he brushed at some of the dust that had collected on his pale green shirt and the dark brown moleskin trousers he wore. "Dry as a dust bowl, it is."

He then smiled wistfully before he reached for his handkerchief and mopped his damp face. Having preferred the enclosed heat to the choking stage dust, they had ridden the last two days with the heavy flaps down most of the time. As a result there had been very little breeze to

7

bring them any cooling relief. "Sort of reminds me of 'ome."

George came from one of the driest regions of Queensland, Australia, but was traveling through America to accumulate information for a book he wanted to write. He had caught the stage at St. Louis, Missouri, headed for Fort Worth, Texas, and had been a constant companion to Callie ever since.

Adamant that a pretty young lass barely twenty years old should not travel without an escort, George had immediately become her protector. And when he realized how little she spent on proper meals during their stopovers, he had quickly become her provider as well. During the days they traveled together, he had seen to it she had eaten three good meals a day, and provided her with a treat or two whenever they were to be had.

"Dust bowl is right," Callie commented while she too brushed at the pale-colored dust that had settled on her dark-blue traveling suit. She had already envisioned the dry, grassy plains and vast, almost-treeless terrain which would surely confront her the moment she stepped off the stage. For the first time, she wondered if she would be able to survive in a place so hot and dry. Having been born and raised in the North, she was unaccustomed to such unrelenting heat, and wondered exactly how hot the weather got in the South. It was only the beginning of June and she was well aware the hottest months still lay ahead.

"Not wot you are accustomed to, is it?" George asked, though he knew the answer.

"Not at all."

In the short time the flap had been back, she had caught a quick glimpse of the simple, wooden two-story structures that lined the far side of the street. Not at *all* what she was used to. And though the window had provided a view wide enough to see several buildings, she had not noticed a single person. The place looked deserted. No one was outside milling about. But in this heat, who could blame them? Yes, Pine Fork was indeed going to be quite a change from the tall, shade-giving buildings and the bustling city streets of New York, from which Callie had just escaped.

At that moment, while she was worrying over her hastily made decision to move to Texas, the stagecoach door swung wide on its squeaky hinges and the dusty face of the tall, slender driver who had been with her for more than half her trip appeared in the opening. The motion of the door caused a slight breeze to waft into the coach. It felt like a breath from heaven to Callie's heated skin.

"Pine Fork, Miss Thomas. I'll have your bags down in two shakes. Right now, though, you need to climb on out of there and get yourself a lungful of this fine fresh air," the driver suggested with a tired smile.

"Thank you," Callie responded while she reached down to gather the dark woolen folds of her indigo blue skirt so the bulky hem would be out of her way. Just before she accepted the driver's outstretched hand, she turned to George and smiled. "It looks like the time has come for us to say goodbye. I want to thank you for all your kindnesses."

"Think nothing of them, lassie. It was all my pleasure, I assure you," George replied with a wide smile and a gallant nod of his head as he finally lifted the flap out of the way and leaned gratefully forward for a breath of fresh air. "Just you take good care of yourself. And take good care of that new 'usband of yours."

"He's not my husband yet," she reminded him, then reached out to pat George's hand in a show of genuine affection. "But I intend to take very good care of the both of us, I assure you."

"Wot about those two daughters of 'is? Ya take good care of them too," George added with a firm shake of his head. Starting to become a little misty-eyed, he quickly turned his attention to refolding his gray and white handkerchief. "Young ones need special care."

"Oh, I'll take very special care of those two daughters of

9

his," she answered as she stepped out of the coach. It was the least she should do for a man who was willing to give her so much and ask so little in return. A man who knew her only through the letters she wrote in response to his catchy advertisement for a wife. A man she suddenly envisioned being a lot like George. Though George was not a genuinely handsome man, there was something in the gentle sparkle of his eyes and the deep creases around his smile that made him endearing.

Callie smiled and hoped that indeed Matthew would prove to be a lot like George. She already knew the two men were about the same age, late forties, and had the same kind and gentle heart. Now if they only had the same warm sense of humor and strong fiber of decency, Callie's future happiness would be practically assured.

Only a moment after Callie's feet settled onto the hard, dusty street, a cool breeze drifted past to welcome her to Pine Fork. Grateful for the cool respite, she closed her eyes and enjoyed the feel of it against her damp skin. She breathed deeply of the unfamiliar clean air and noticed, though there was a faint scent given off by the horses, there was none of the smoke and sewage smell that was present in the back streets of New York. It was a smell she had also noticed in St. Louis.

"I'll get your bags, miss," the driver assured her, then he spun on his heel and went to the rear of the stage. Callie turned back to the lone occupant of the stagecoach and, aware she would probably never see her newly found friend again, she quickly added, "I want you to promise to take good care of yourself too. And remember, if you come back this way, stop by the Circle T for a visit so you can meet Matthew yourself. Also, when that book of yours comes out, I want to know about it."

"Aye, I'll see that ya do," he said, and patted his shirt pocket where he had placed the slip of paper that had both her future name and the name of the local post office. "And don't you be too surprised if there's a golden-eyed beauty with long raven hair called Calico in the book. A pretty lass with fire in 'er eyes and an adventurous determination to make a good life for 'erself."

Callie's smile widened. Her pale brown, almost golden eyes glimmered with a sudden feeling of sadness. She was going to miss George Wilkins—a lot. He had shown her kindness, and that was something she had not known for a long time. Blinking back the moisture that collected beneath her dark, fringed eyelids, she waved one last time. Reluctantly, she turned away from the stagecoach when she heard the driver speak to her again.

"I put your bags on the walkway over there, miss. That's all you had, ain't it? Just the two bags and that one box?"

"That's all there is," she answered with a light shrug, and wondered why she felt apologetic for having so little when it was certainly not her fault. She glanced at the walkway where the driver had placed both threadbare valises with the small hatbox atop them, balanced at a precarious angle.

The amount of baggage did seem a mite scant, especially when considering all she owned was contained inside those two large bags and one small box. But then her step-aunt and her uncle had never been too generous when it came to providing her with clothing or shoes, or any other personal items for that matter. Her step-aunt was just too hateful, and possibly even a little jealous that her own daughters were not quite as pretty as Callie. And her uncle had proved to be far too weak in character to take a stand against the awful woman. If Matthew Tucker had not secretly wired such a generous amount of money to cover her traveling expenses, Callie would not have had even the one proper traveling outfit to wear on the trip— much less a decent pair of walking boots, boots that had *not* been handed down from one of her fat-footed older cousins.

Callie smiled and wished her cousins had somehow gotten a glimpse of her slender new footwear and the

11

store-bought fashionable dress before she stole away. Callie knew just how envious they would have been for the first time since her parent's death nine years ago.

Even during the four years she had lived in Pennsylvania with her grandparents, right after her parents were killed in the train wreck, Callie had not owned anything even half that grand. Though her grandparents had never mistreated her, they were always struggling to make ends meet on their small farm, and could not afford any special purchases for her.

The situation had gotten steadily worse when she was forced to travel to New York to live with her uncle and her step-aunt, soon after both of her grandparents died only months apart. Callie had worn nothing but hand-me-downs from then on, and it felt wonderful to have something brand new.

Though still extremely proud of the garments she had chosen, she frowned when she glanced down at the treasured outfit and wished now she had not bought wool. In the sweltering heat of the South, the dress proved to be very uncomfortable, uncomfortable enough to make her want to take the stylish jacket off and toss it over her shoulder. But when she remembered how very close to her destination she was now that she was finally in Pine Fork, and how she dearly wanted to look her best when she first met Matthew Tucker, she decided to keep the jacket on.

"Goodbye, lassie," she heard George call out only moments after the driver had returned to his position atop the sun-faded red stagecoach. "And ya be careful about who ya hire to see ya out to that ranch. There's a bad lot out there. Don't mistake them for the good."

"I know. I will be careful," she answered as the coach quickly lurched into motion. "Goodbye." Her voice was highly charged with many different emotions as she stood on tiptoes and waved as hard as she could.

Though she knew George could no longer see her after the stage had reached the far end of town, she continued to wave frantically until she no longer saw the movement of his waving hand. It was not until the coach turned and disappeared from her sight that she finally returned her attention to her surroundings.

During the days before she had finally gotten the courage to pack most of her things, hide them in the cellar beneath all the dirty laundry along with the three letters she'd received from Matthew, and then slip off into the night, Callie had wondered about Pine Fork. She wondered if Matthew's ranch would be as truly grand as he made it sound in his letters. But then it really had not mattered to her what the town or the ranch would be like. It would be a definite improvement over where she had been forced to spend the past five years.

In her step-aunt and uncle's small two-story apartment, where she was rarely allowed to go outside and see the light of day, she had only a small corner of the cellar to call her own. If ever anyone had been forced to live the life of the legendary Cinderella, she had. But instead of stepsisters and an evil stepmother, she'd had step-cousins and an evil step-aunt. Now her prince had finally come to save her, in the form of Matthew Tucker.

Luckily, she had been allowed brief moments of freedom — scant though they were — whenever she went to the neighborhood market for her step-aunt every Monday. It was during one of those market excursions that she had responded to the unusual advertisement she had read in the *Daily Times*. Thereafter, every Monday she had posted another letter to Matthew Tucker, and checked at the post office to see if she'd gotten one in return — which she'd read thoroughly before hiding it away at the bottom of the dirty clothes bin.

When Callie eventually had made up her mind to accept Matthew Tucker's offer, and written to him that she would gladly become his wife, all she'd really known about Pine Fork was that it was a small town located in the recently re-admitted Southern state of Texas.

Matthew had warned her about its small size in his letters, but she had not understood exactly *how* small until now.

There were barely enough businesses to fill even the one narrow street. But plenty of space had been left between the small clumps of existing businesses for side streets, and Callie decided the town's planners must at least have hopes for expansion.

While Callie quickly glanced over the buildings which faced her from both sides of the street, and read their brightly painted signs, she realized there seemed to be only one of every kind of store, except for the saloons. There were three of those. Yet three new buildings were going up at the far end of town. And one of the new buildings was obviously to be made of brick, a definite sign of progress, offering even more hope for strong future growth.

Callie studied the street further, wondering where all the townspeople were. Though there seemed to be no one about, she did notice that well over two dozen horses, along with five wagons and a buggy, filled the street. There were people somewhere.

While Callie looked toward the far end of the street where the stagecoach had eventually turned and disappeared, she noticed her first signs of human life. Two men had just fitted a large wooden beam into place near the roof of one of the new buildings going up, and began to hammer away at a lazy pace, in no real hurry to see their task done.

Her gaze was then drawn to the landscape surrounding the small town. She was pleased, and surprised, to discover East Texas was not at all the vast wasted plains and dry desert she had expected. It was truly beautiful to behold, with lovely pale-green rolling meadows in the near distance, which were dotted with an abundance of bright yellow wildflowers and stretched out to meet the tall wooded hills that lay beyond. Though the street itself was dusty, as if it hadn't rained in several weeks, and the heat was stifling whenever the light breeze proved unreliable, Callie was quite pleased with the area she was soon to call her home. Her spirits lifted. Maybe she had not made a

14

mistake after all.

Because she had become very eager to get away from the hateful clutches of her step-aunt, before the woman set her latest spiteful plan into motion, Callie had left days earlier than she had planned. As a result, no one was there to meet her. While she wondered what course of action she should take next, she walked over to the shady spot along the narrow boardwalk where the driver had been kind enough to leave her baggage.

Sighing outwardly, she glanced around for the livery. When she recognized the only building that could possibly accommodate both horses and large wagons—though there was a smaller building with a fenced area behind it—she smiled and pushed a damp curl off her forehead, tucking it back into the rest of her upswept dark brown hair. She was glad she had thought to style her long, heavy hair off her neck. It had not been an easy task to catch the thick mass at the back of her head, shape it into a manageable twist, then anchor it into place with the small, dark-blue satin hat and several sturdy hat pins.

Because of her unexpected arrival, and knowing Matthew's ranch was several miles out of town, Callie decided to hire a wagon or a buggy and a reliable driver to take her and her things to the Circle T Ranch. It was why she had been very frugal with the money Matthew Tucker had sent to her. She knew she would need to have enough left over to pay for a driver.

Gathering up her bags and starting across the street at an angle toward the livery, she heard the faint tinkling of a piano badly in need of tuning, and when she moved farther up the street, she became aware of loud laughter. It sounded to Callie as if there was a celebration being held somewhere, probably at the far end of the street where most of the horses and wagons stood.

When she neared the huge double doors of Gordy's Livery, she put down her heavy bags and flexed her numb arms and hands. The oppressive scent of horse manure and damp sawdust caused Callie only a moment's hesitation before she lifted her skirts and marched inside in search of the liveryman.

"Can I help you?" a young man, about seventeen years old, asked eagerly. He'd looked down from the overhead loft to see who had just entered, only to discover a pretty young lady, who looked to be very few years his senior.

"I hope so. I want to hire a carriage or a wagon plus a good, reliable driver," she said while she looked around, already aware there were no carriages or wagons inside the livery, just horses — and very few of those. She desperately hoped the conveyances were kept in another building.

"What rotten timin'," the boy said as he hurriedly climbed down a narrow ladder and came to stand directly in front of her. It was obvious by the gleaming approval in his eager green eyes that not too many ladies came inside that particular livery stable. "I just lent the wagon out. Not more than an hour ago."

"You only have one wagon?"

"That's it," he said with a shrug. "And if you'd come in before noontime, you might've got it." He frowned. "But I don't rightly know what you could have done about a driver. My pa is gone for the afternoon, had to make a trip over to Clarksville, and I'm the only helper he's got right now."

"Do you have any sort of conveyance that might do?" she asked, prepared to try to drive the thing herself. "It doesn't necessarily have to be a wagon."

"Conveyance?" The boy looked puzzled as he raked a hand through his thick, curly brown hair.

"A buggy maybe? Anything that would be able to carry both me and my things to the Circle T Ranch."

"No, only had the one wagon, and Wade Barlow just left with it less than an hour ago — like I just told you," the boy said with an apologetic shake of his head. "He just bought himself something over to the twice-annual unclaimed freight auction, and needed the wagon to haul it out to his ranch."

The boy's face lifted when a thought occurred to him.

16

"Hey, come to think of it, Mr. Barlow's ranch is just the other side of Circle T. Maybe, if whatever he bought doesn't quite fill up the wagon, he might have enough room left over to carry you and your belongings." Suddenly the boy's face drew back into a frown. "That is if you can convince him to make a stop on Circle T property."

"Where can I find this Wade Barlow?" she asked, more than willing to ask him for a favor, and willing to pay a very fair price for his help.

"Probably over to the Blackbird Saloon," the boy answered promptly. "That's the most likely place." He walked to the door and peered down the street, then turned back to face her. "Yep, that must be where he is all right. That's our wagon there out front."

"Which is the Blackbird?" she wanted to know, and joined him just outside the wide double doorway. Though she had never been inside a saloon before, and knew that no respectable woman would ever set foot inside one without a good reason, she was so eager to get to the Circle T that she'd consider it now. She'd do anything to reach Matthew Tucker's ranch before sundown.

"That one there, next to Miss Millie's Dry Goods, is the Blackbird," the boy said, pointing off toward a cluster of brightly painted buildings across the street. The building was at the opposite end of town where three of the wagons and most of the horses stood. No sooner had he pointed to the saloon in question than three disreputable-looking men came outside and leaned idly against the wall of the recessed entrance. None of the three looked as if he had bathed within a decade, and all had clearly failed to locate a usable razor in the past several days.

Callie looked at the three unsavory creatures. Suddenly, she was not as eager to go into the saloon as she had been, though she still wanted to find the man who had rented the only wagon.

"Are you sure he's in there?" she asked while she watched the three men ogle a young lady who had come

17

out of the dry goods store, and had had the grave misfortune of passing directly in front of them in order to reach her buggy.

"That's where he likes to spend some of his time," the boy assured her.

Callie looked again at the three men, who still openly ogled the poor woman while she stepped up into her rig, and knew they would treat her no differently. A sickly feeling ran through her when she considered they might actually follow her once she had entered the saloon. Suddenly, she was certain she could not enter that saloon—not if it meant passing those three.

Quickly, she presented one of her most winning smiles to the young man, who had rarely taken his eyes off her, tilted her head at a beguiling angle, and spoke ever so sweetly. "You look like a very helpful sort of young man. What did you say your name was?"

"David," he quickly supplied, his eyes so wide that they bulged.

"Well, David, would you mind going into that saloon for me and asking Mr. Barlow to step outside where I might have a word with him? I'll be waiting across the street."

The young man responded to her smile with a hard swallow. "I sure wish I could, ma'am. But I can't just up and leave this place unattended. What if Pa should come back while I was gone? He'd horse-whoop me for sure."

"Can't have that," she muttered aloud before she quickly took back her smile and replaced it with a tight-lipped frown. Chewing nervously on the inside of her lower lip, she continued to stare at the three unsightly men still standing outside the saloon. She then spoke with uncertain determination. "I guess I'll just have to go in there and find him myself."

"You can't go in there!"

"Looks like I have to."

"But you are a regular woman! Regular woman are not supposed to go into saloons."

18

"I'm aware of that," she snapped before she realized she had no reason to be irritated with the boy, for her predicament was in no way his fault. She spoke in a much calmer voice when she added, "But if I want to speak with Wade Barlow, it seems I have no other choice."

"But-but," David sputtered, still shocked she would actually do such a thing.

"David, will you at least keep an eye on my baggage so I don't have to drag it along with me?" she asked, and nodded toward where she had left her belongings just outside the livery.

The boy nodded, and watched with open-mouthed dismay when she suddenly turned and headed determinedly down the narrow boardwalk which ran along the store fronts.

The ordeal ahead horrified Callie—mostly because she had heard stories of all the sinful things that went on inside saloons, but partly because of the three grotesque men who watched her approach with noted interest. Still her steady footsteps never faltered, nor did she allow her determination to lessen.

When she crossed the street, directly in front of the saloon, she could see the movement inside. Through the wide spaces below and above the undersized saloon doors, she saw the dark shapes within, and when she got closer, she could hear a loud mixture of voices and glasses clanking—but nothing was clearly distinguishable at such a distance. She heard piano music again, but realized it came from another saloon three doors away.

To Callie's relief, the three men stepped aside and said nothing to her. They merely watched curiously while she marched up to doorway.

Still not certain she had the courage to step inside, Callie stood on tiptoe and peered over the tiny, cut-down doors. Already she smelled the unpleasant combination of stale tobacco, cheap perfume, whiskey, and unwashed flesh that filled the room. Even the constant movement of the overhead fans did little to clear the air of the offensive odors.

As if frozen to the spot, Callie continued to stare into the saloon, undecided. For the most part, the room was filled with more rough, unsavory-looking characters, much like the three who stood behind her now. But she noticed just enough decent-looking men inside to give her hope that one might come to her rescue should the situation get out of hand. Did she dare chance it? What if none of the men had that much sense of honor? What if no one was willing to risk the physical harm that might befall him should he try to come to the aid of a lady in distress, especially against the likes of some of those men? But then again, did she have any choice?

Bravely, she took one last deep, steadying breath before she pushed the brightly painted doors open and stepped inside. At first only a few of the men noticed her and fell immediately silent, but soon the hush spread through the room. She became only too aware that everyone's sudden wide-eyed interest was partly because of the way she was dressed and partly because of the manner in which she carried herself. She was obviously not like the other women in the room, who wore far skimpier garments designed in bright, garish colors and walked as if someone had released a whole colony of bees into their clothing. Suddenly, Callie was very glad she had decided to keep her jacket on, with its buttons securely fastened. She tossed her shoulders back another few inches, wanting to look as dignified as a lady could under the circumstances before she slowly moved forward.

Trying her best to ignore the many eyes upon her, she made her way through to the bar built along the far side of the room. Though she was eager to speak with the gaping bartender, her attention was quickly drawn to one particularly shady-looking character who nudged his two equally disreputable-looking companions with his elbows, then moved away from the bar to greet her halfway

"Hello, pretty lady, you look a mite thirsty. Can my friends and I buy you a drink?" he asked as he approached her with a bow that was a poor attempt at gallantry.

Callie stiffened. "No, thank you. I'm looking for a man."

"What luck. That's exactly what I am. Won't I do?" he asked, and gestured to himself with a wide sweep of the half-filled whiskey glass he held in his hand. His gray-green eyes glimmered with untold mirth when he winked at his friends, then looked back at her. "I assure you, I'd be plenty enough man for you."

By now they had the attention of the entire room, and the loud din of noise that had greeted her when she first entered had fizzled into a heavy, charged silence.

"No, you won't do," she said sternly, and tried to brush on passed him, but he and his two grinning companions moved to block her way. "Please, sir, I am looking for a particular man."

"Tell you what. I'll help you find him as soon as you've had a little drink with me," he assured her, then quickly grasped her by her arm to pull her to the bar. A low muttering swept the room, but no one came to her rescue.

"Let go of me," she demanded with a defiant toss of her head, hoping not to reveal her panic while she tried to wrench herself free from his grip. The din around her grew louder, some voicing protest, others expressing the humor they saw in the situation. Still no one moved to help her.

"Oh, I'll let go of you all right. After you've had a little drink with me and my friends," he assured her with a loud laugh, pulling her hard against him. "And maybe one little kiss. What say? Do you have a little kiss for old Gordon?"

The thought of this man's grimy mouth on hers made Callie's stomach knot, and the fact no one had come to her aid made her heart twist with fear.

"I said, let go of me," she demanded again, successfully dodging his poor attempt to kiss her, but still unable to wrench her arm free of his painful grasp.

21

"Gordon, I believe the lady has asked you to let go of her," a deep, authoritative voice said from somewhere just behind her. "I suggest you do just that."

To Callie's amazement, though the horrible man's face tightened in response to having been told what to do, he let go of her with no further hesitation. His gray-green eyes narrowed while he adjusted his rumpled collar. "I don't want no quarrel with you. I was only trying to have a little fun," he muttered in defense of his actions. "I wasn't going to hurt her none."

Callie released a shaky breath before she turned to face the man who had come to her rescue; but when she did, she found herself gasping for more air, for she was immediately affronted by a pair of the bluest eyes she had ever seen. Her heart stalled only momentarily before it resumed beating at the same wildly frantic pace as it had before, though for reasons far different from fear. She felt her own eyes widen while she wondered how she could have failed to notice anyone like him when she first entered. He had to be the most striking man she had ever seen.

Everything about the man exuded masculinity. He looked to be in his mid-to-late twenties, tall and lean, with noticeably wide shoulders. The faded blue workshirt he wore clung to a strong, muscled chest, and tapered down to fit against a narrow waist. His dark blue trousers molded perfectly to a pair of taut thighs and long legs. Her attention fastened momentarily on the worn black-leather holster fitted to his narrow hips. The holster held a large pistol—butt out. She wondered if he was a gunfighter of some sort, but let the intriguing thought pass when she returned her attention to his handsome face. Her heart fluttered like a caged bird wanting to break free.

He said nothing.

Callie next noticed the thick hair beneath his high-crowned work hat. The hair was dark brown in color and long enough to curl slightly at his nape and around his ears. Dark lashes fringed the uncanny blue of his eyes,

22

which had turned downward to assess boldly her feminine charms. Her breath caught at the base of her throat when his lips slowly curved into a sensuous smile of obvious approval.

Blushing, Callie pulled her gaze free of his and stared at his workworn boots for a moment, before finally finding the courage to look up again into the glimmering blue of his eyes — eyes that had a strange way of making her legs feel like they were suddenly made of hot wax.

"Thank you for your assistance," she finally managed to say, finding her voice weaker than she had intended it to be. But evidently he had heard her because his smile broadened to form long, curving indentations in his cheeks as he swept his hat from his head.

"Glad to be of help, ma'am," he said, then looked about the room in a confident manner before he replaced his hat. "You should be safe from harm now." Then he abruptly turned and walked away, moving with the easy grace of a powerful and extremely dangerous animal.

Callie watched with total amazement and a growing sense of dread while the man continued across the room and through the doors to the outside, deserting her entirely. Swallowing hard, she glanced around the room again and quickly noticed the many pairs of eyes, most of which remained trained on her paling expression. The room was deathly still. It was as if they waited for her to make the first move.

23

Chapter Two

Soon *every* man in the room stared at her, all but Gordon. Having shouldered his way back to the bar at the far end of the room, he riveted his attention on the drink he'd just poured for himself from a bottle he shared with his friends. He clearly wanted nothing more to do with her.

Callie felt certain the man's sudden disinterest had a lot to do with his fear of the man who had just left. She wondered again if the stranger who had come momentarily to her rescue was a gunfighter — or worse. But she did not have time to wonder about him for her present situation needed her full attention. Although Gordon offered no further threat, she could not be sure about the others in the room.

Unable to calm her hammering heart, she turned slowly and resumed her way toward the bar. The men who found themselves in her way quickly parted to give her plenty of room when she stepped closer to the bar. Evidently, *no* one was eager to find himself at odds with the tall, handsome man who had just left.

Slowly she released the breath she had held a little too long while she gently placed her folded hands atop the rough wooden surface of the bar and sought once more to still her hammering heart. Immediately, she became aware of the huge mirror hanging on the wall before her, where she quickly caught sight of her own reflection. Her face

24

was deathly pale and her eyes wider than usual; but otherwise, none of the inner turmoil she felt was evident. Or so she hoped.

Forcing a congenial smile to her almost colorless lips, she waited for the bartender to speak to her.

"C-can I help you, ma'am?" he finally asked, when he noticed everyone in the room was waiting for him to speak. He pulled in his burly shoulders while he waited for her response, clearly ill at ease over the prospect of having a lady stand before his bar.

"Yes, please. I'd like some information and I believe you are just the man who can supply it for me," she said quietly, aware of the low murmur of voices coming from the back corner of the room. She dared not look away from the bartender's craggy face to see who might have spoken, but knew it was in the general direction where the man called Gordon had gone.

"I'll do what I can," the bartender said agreeably, and stepped closer.

The low murmur of voices spread through the room.

Callie tried to swallow. "I'm looking for someone and was told he would probably be found in here. I'd be much obliged if you would point him out to me," she began. Her words came in a rush, for she wanted to get out of there.

The bartender's bushy black brows pulled together and his heavy mustache twitched while he considered everything she had said. "It depends on just who it is you want to find and what you want him for." If she was there to cause trouble for one of his regular customers, he was clearly going to have no part in it. "Just what do you want this man for?"

"I want to hire his services."

His bushy eyebrows shot up and a smile played below his brushy mustache. Several of the men who had been close enough to overhear the conversation began to hoot and howl with laughter. Others echoed what had been said for the men at the back of the room.

"What sort of services did you have in mind, ma'am?" he asked as soon as the laughter had died down. He struggled to keep his mouth straight.

Callie's cheeks flamed bright red when she realized what lurid thoughts had crossed these men's minds. She tossed her shoulders back in an unconscious gesture of defiance and answered in a strong voice, "Though I don't think it is really any of your business, if you really must know, I plan to ask him for a personal favor. And I intend to pay him handsomely for it."

The dying laughter rose again to a steady roar. Callie thought about what she had said, and tried to imagine how these men might have possibly misconstrued it. Then her cheeks crimsoned darker still.

Seeing a need to take pity on the innocent young thing who had shown the courage to enter his saloon to find whoever it was she sought, the bartender leaned forward so she could hear him over the loud peals of laughter. "And who is it you are lookin' for, miss?"

"A Mister Wade Barlow."

No sooner had the words left her mouth than the man's name was repeated back to those unable to hear the answer, and the laughter rose yet another degree.

"Ma'am," the bartender said, finally losing battle with his restraint and grinning broadly. "That was him who just left out of here."

Callie's eyes widened at the realization. That was Wade Barlow? *That* was the man she wanted to ask for a ride out to Matthew's ranch? Now that she'd seen what a powerfully attractive man he was, she wondered at the sanity of such action.

The bartender stared at her paling expression for a moment before his own expression filled with compassion because of the embarrassment the poor young thing was having to suffer at their expense. "What sort of favor do you have a mind to ask of him?"

Though Callie felt that was none of his business either, she was flustered enough to tell him, and set everyone's mind straight about her intentions. "Earlier, Mr. Barlow rented the only wagon at the livery for his own use. I want to rent part of his wagon space from him. I understand his ranch is just beyond the Circle T, and that he might be persuaded to leave me and my things by there on his way."

"Circle T?" the bartender repeated, his expression uncertain. "I doubt very seriously if you can persuade Wade to go anywhere near the Circle T."

"Why?" Why wouldn't he want to go near the Circle T?"

"Because the Barlows and the Tuckers don't get along. Can't recollect that they ever did. And because of that, Wade is not goin' to want to stop off there for *any* reason. You might better consider askin' someone else."

That sounded more than satisfactory to Callie, for she did not particularly like the thought of riding all that distance with a man like Wade Barlow—a man who, if it was at all possible, was entirely too much of a man. Her insides shook at the mere thought of being all alone with him out in the middle of nowhere.

"Do you know of someone else I could ask?"

"Several of these men came in wagons today because of the auction held earlier," he began while his gaze swept the room. "I'm sure any one of them would be glad to escort you out to the Circle T."

Callie felt the skin tighten along her neck while she also glanced about the room. The thought of being alone with one of those disreputable-looking creatures was even worse than the thought of being alone with an awesomely handsome man like Wade Barlow.

"I think I'd like to ask Mr. Barlow first. After all, as I understand it, the Circle T is right on his way," she stated, then brought her gaze back to the bartender's concerned face. "Do you have any idea where Mr. Barlow might have gone?"

"Insistent little thing, ain't ya?" the bartender said with a grudging smile. "Though I don't think it'll do you much good, I did hear Wade say he was headed back over to the freight office to pick up that brand new cookstove he bought. It'll take them awhile to get the thing loaded, so if you get yourself on down there, you'll probably find him still there."

"Where is the freight office?"

"Down the street, next to the stagecoach office."

Which was across the street from the livery and right back where she had started.

"Thank you," Callie said, then slipped her hand into the pocket hidden within the folds of her dark blue skirt in search of a coin. "How much do I owe you?"

The bartender crooked his smile to one side. "Awh, you don't owe me nothin'. I'm just glad to help. And if you find Wade won't oblige you — and there's every chance that he won't — you get yourself on back here and I'll see if I can't find someone who will."

Callie shuddered at the thought as she turned and headed back for the door. Though most of the men willingly stepped aside to allow her to pass, a few did not and she had to walk around them. But no one made a move toward her. When she finally neared the doors, she prayed that she would indeed make it to the outside without further incident. Her prayers were answered. Not only did she reach the outdoors unharmed, the three men who had been loitering near the door were gone.

Undaunted by the bartender's warning that Wade Barlow might turn down her offer, Callie silently rehearsed her deeply sympathetic plea for help while she walked along the dusty boardwalk. Though she had not thought it possible, the temperature had climbed several degrees from when she had first arrived. The woolen material of her dress trapped the stifling heat against her skin, and perspiration began to trail pathways between her breasts and under her arms. It was only her sheer determination to win Wade Barlow over to her cause that kept her from succumbing to her growing misery.

Irritated by the fact she had been needlessly forced to walk the length of the only street twice in the wretched

28

heat, Callie realized time was quickly slipping by. If she did not find transportation soon, she would be forced to stay the night in Pine Fork, and that would probably take the last of her money. Then she really would be in a bind.

Finally Callie reached the freight office. Entering, she discovered several men inside. All but one had their backs to her. While the others stood around a huge cast-iron stove as if trying to decide the best way to go about lifting it, the man who had noticed her came across the room to assist.

"May I help you?" he asked with a cordial smile.

Callie's gaze scanned the different sets of shoulders before her and tried to decide which one was Wade Barlow's. But to her dismay, none seemed quite virile enough, and none wore faded blue cotton.

"I'd like to speak to Wade Barlow," she said in a loud voice so he would hear her, if he was indeed one of the men who surrounded the stove.

"And why would you want to do that?" a deep voice called out from directly behind her.

Gasping at the unexpected sound, Callie whirled around. By the time her gaze rose to meet his, she already knew exactly what she would find—a pair of insolent, pale-blue eyes staring down at her. Wade Barlow.

Arrogantly, he pushed his hat back on his head with his thumb and waited for her reply.

But Callie found herself at an uncharacteristic loss for words while she watched those pale-blue eyes slowly sweep downward over the woolen dress, which was now so sweat-soaked it clung to every shapely curve of her body. She was well aware that his gaze lingered far longer than was necessary on the shiny buttons of the delicate Sicilian blouse visible between the narrow lapels of her two-button jacket. Unconsciously, Callie's hand moved to cover those tiny pearl-shaped buttons while she shifted uneasily beneath his studious gaze.

"Ma'am, you said you wanted to speak to Wade Barlow. I'm Wade Barlow."

Temporarily mesmerized by the slow, easy way his mouth moved when he spoke and by the deep, resonant quality of his voice, Callie was still unable to think clearly enough to respond intelligently. All she could do at that moment was stare at his splendid mouth—so full and so perfectly formed. Quite frankly, it was one of the most sensual mouths she had ever seen. She resisted the unnatural urge she had to reach out and trace the gentle curves.

"Sir, I'd like a word with you," she finally managed to say, but because her breath seemed caught in her throat the words were muffled. His gaze lifted to where her tongue quickly darted across her lower lip just before she cleared her throat and tried again. This time the words came out loud and clear—almost too much so. "Sir, please, I'd like a word with you."

"Any word you choose, darlin'," he said with a low drawl.

A slow, provocative smile sent her senses reeling faster still.

Callie heard the resulting chuckles, and knew that the other men in the room were clearly amused by what Wade had said and by her dim-witted reactions. And it was obvious Wade Barlow was just as amused as they were, as he lifted his brow and allowed his gaze to rake over her once again. It took every effort to remain calm and not allow his bold familiarity to ignite her explosive temper, which was already precariously close to erupting.

"Please, may we step outside?" Her hands curled into tight fists at her sides while she waited for his reply. She tried her best not to notice the way the other men in the room began to poke elbows at each other.

"Anything to please a pretty lady," he said, his cocky smile widening, again forming long, narrow dimples in his cheeks. He glanced back at the other men with raised eyebrows before motioning toward the door with a wave of his hand. Grinning wider still at the men's various reactions, he stepped back to let her pass. "After you, ma'am."

Many a sly comment was offered by the other male occupants of the room before Callie was able to make her hasty exit—comments that made her want to blush. Wisely she chose to ignore them, and waited until she and Wade were outside before speaking again. "I have a favor to ask of you. But before I ask, let me assure you I will pay you well for your services."

Wade's brow lifted. "And just who are you?"

"Callie. Callie Thomas. Please, Mr. Barlow, I need your help."

"Why? Did someone else in the saloon try to cause you any trouble? You really have to expect that. After all, it isn't every day a pretty young lady, such as yourself, decides to go in and make herself at home."

"I went in there looking for you," she explained, finding it harder and harder to keep her temper in check. If he would just quit interrupting her, she could get to her question.

"Me? Whatever for?"

"To ask you to help me!" she answered, exasperated.

"Do what?" His eyes sparkled with amusement while he glanced toward the freight window to see if his friends had moved forward to watch—and seemed pleased to discover they had. He was clearly enjoying himself.

"The boy at the livery stable told me how you had rented their only wagon so you could carry something home you'd bought at the freight auction—which I gather is that stove in there."

"Got a good bargain on it too," he conceded. "You thinking on trying to buy it off of me?"

"No." She sighed heavily. "If you will quit asking so many questions, I might have a chance to explain what I hope you will do for me."

"Explain away," he said with a shrug just before he stepped over to a tall, sturdy post and leaned his shoulder against it. A rougish smile still curved his lips while he waited for her to say more.

"I was also told that your ranch is just the other side of

31

the Circle T."

Wade quickly straightened. All humor left his face while he listened more carefully.

Callie realized the bartender had been right about Wade's reaction. Just the mention of Matthew's ranch had caused him to be on edge. "I had hoped to rent the wagon myself. I need transportation to the Circle T and I was hoping you might have enough room—"

"Forget it," he said, interrupting her, crossing his arms to show he was adamant. His blue eyes narrowed.

"But I only have two valises, my handbag, and one small box, none of which will take up much room. And I will pay you five dollars for your trouble."

"I said, forget it. Find yourself another man." Abruptly, he turned his back to her and headed back inside.

"But just a minute ago, you were more than willing to help me. You said as much yourself."

He spun around. "That was before you told me what it is you wanted me to do. I'm in no mood to set foot on Tucker's land. Besides, even as sick as I hear he is these days, that ornery old cuss would probably crawl right out of his bed, grab hold of his shotgun, and shoot me on sight if I was to get anywhere near his house. And I don't care much for being shot at."

"Why? What have you done to him?" Though she worried about Matthew Tucker being sick, she pushed that concern aside for the moment.

"Nothing. It's more what he thinks my father has done to him, and what he has done to my father in return. And I don't want to become involved in any of it."

"I'm not asking you to do battle for me, just drive me out there!" Her anger and frustration mounted.

"And I said forget it. Find yourself another man. I'm not getting myself shot for anyone." Again he turned his back to her and walked back into the freight office with long, steady strides.

"I can't believe you would refuse to help me. You yellow-backed coward. All I ask is that you let me ride

32

with you as far as the Circle T. You don't even have to get that close to the house. Just leave me and my things within walking distance."

"No thank you," he said without bothering to turn around. Then he walked up to the man who had spoken to Callie when she first entered the freight office, and asked, "Trey, have ya'll got it figured out yet how we are going to get that thing onto my wagon? I'm about ready to get out of here."

Callie tried again. "What if I offer you eight dollars? That's more than most men make in a week."

He did not respond. She curled her hands into fists and held them stiffly at her sides. For a brief moment, she considered making a try for his gun, forcing him at gunpoint to take her, but she knew she'd never get away with it. "All right. Nine dollars. But that's all I have left."

Trey hesitated to answer Wade's question, waiting to see if Callie had more to say or if Wade intended to respond.

Wade's gaze swept the room. "What about it? You men ready to get this thing loaded so I can be on my way?"

"Is your wagon out back near the loading platform?" Trey asked. His gaze moved uncomfortably from Wade's stern expression to the angry frown of the pretty, young woman who stood directly behind him.

"I got it within a bare inch of the side," Wade replied. "We should have no problem stepping over."

Callie's anger grew until she could hold it no longer. "You blackheart!" Then turning to the other men in the room, she asked, "Is there anyone else who could take me and what little baggage I have out to the Circle T ranch? I am willing to pay nine dollars. That's a handsome wage for only a few hours of your time."

When there were no volunteers, Callie became angrier still. "Well, thank you all so very much for your kind show of hospitality," she said angrily, then stomped out of the freight office and out into the street.

Once she was outside, her spirits sank further into despair. Pausing in the middle of the sunbaked street, she found herself at a loss over what to do next. Unaware Wade had followed her back outside, she turned to glare one last time in the direction of the freight office, only to find the recipient of all her anger casually watching her from the shadows. Quickly turning away, unwilling to be the object of his amusement yet again, she marched directly out of his sight and into the livery. This time to hire a horse. Although she knew absolutely nothing about riding the noble steeds, she intended to mount whatever horse was available and ride out to the Circle T on horseback. She would have Matthew send for her things with his own wagon later.

Within minutes, Callie had convinced David Gordy to saddle one of his father's tamest horses, and had followed him to the wide entrance of the livery, where he reluctantly handed the reins to her.

"Are you sure you know how to ride?" he asked with a cocked eyebrow, clearly doubting her ability.

"Not at all," she answered. "But there's no time like the present to learn." Then she smiled at the horse, and tried to sound confident when she patted its neck. "You aren't going to give me any trouble, are you, boy? We are going to get along just fine. Aren't we, boy?"

David tried to stifle his grin. "Uh, ma'am, *his* name is Shirley."

Callie felt the blood climb to her cheeks while she quickly apologized to the horse for her blunder. Then, turning back to David, she asked, "So tell me. How do I go about climbing aboard this animal?"

David's grin faded into serious thought. "Are you sure you want to try this?"

"Yes, I'm sure. Just tell me how to get up into that saddle, and then exactly how I steer the animal."

"Shirley's not a boat," David felt compelled to inform her. His grin slowly returned when he realized just exactly how green she was. "First you have to put your foot in that stirrup." To be certain she understood, he pointed to the foothold. "That's that thing there. Then you grab hold of the horn. Which is that leather padded metal thing up there."

Trying to ignore the fact that Wade Barlow still stood carefully watching her every movement from across the street, Callie first turned the horse so she would not have to lift her skirts toward the street. Then she grabbed a handful of the woolen material and raised it so she could try to put her foot in the stirrup. But the distance was impossible. With growing impatience, she raised her foot again. This time she got the toe of her boot in the wooden loop. Then quickly, before her foot slipped out, she reached for the saddle horn with both hands, and turned to face David, hopping on the one foot when the horse shifted its weight away from her. "Now what?"

"You gonna ride in that dress?"

"I have no other choice. Now what do I do?"

"Now you just boost up, swing your leg over, and you're all set," David told her, trying not to look at the bare expanse of leg her raised skirt had provided for his view.

Though the raised hem revealed only the few inches of the skin above her ankle-high boot, it was clear the boy was unable to pull his gaze away.

"Boost up?" Callie repeated what sounded like the impossible. "How?"

"I don't know. You just sorta pull on the saddle horn at the same time you straighten out that bent leg," David told her with a shrug.

Determined to prove she could do it, Callie tried again and again to straighten her leg while pulling herself up by the saddle horn, but it just did not work. Miserably hot and frustrated to the point of tears, she asked, "What if I can't?"

"I'll be right back," David said just before he disappeared into the livery, leaving Callie standing in the livery doorway with her foot caught awkwardly in the stirrup and her leg bent at an uncomfortable angle. It made her even more uncomfortable to know that Wade Barlow had not moved except to cross his arms. He still watched her, but she did not dare release her foothold for fear she might never get her foot back up there.

David returned in a blessedly short time with a small wooden barrel, which he set upright in the dirt beside the horse. "Here, climb up on this, then try again."

"Thank you," Callie said with open gratitude. She was certain the barrel would give her the advantage she needed to climb onto the horse. But when she tried to remove her foot from the stirrup to do as she had been instructed, she found her boot was too tightly wedged.

"Could you help me get my foot loose?" she finally asked in a very low voice, hoping to keep Wade Barlow from hearing the extent of her predicament.

"Me?" David asked, bemused at having to grab hold of the lady's boot to help her. "But what if someone should see?"

"Please!"

Reluctantly, David helped. His forehead broke out in a sweat as he touched the ankle of her boot to free her foot. Eventually, Callie was atop the small wooden barrel and able to swing herself into the saddle more easily. To her dismay, and David's mortification, her skirts were not wide enough to accommodate, and slid all the way up to her knees when she finally settled onto the saddle. Undaunted, Callie asked for the reins.

"They are right there in front of you," David pointed out, his Adam's apple bobbing noticeably when he attempted to swallow.

Spotting the two leather straps looped around the saddle horn, Callie immediately took them into her hands and inadvertently gave the reins a sharp tug, which caused the horse to take several quick steps backward—right into the tall, wooden livery door. Startled, the horse lurched forward again, only to send Callie reeling backward over the animal's rounded rump and onto the hard dirt-packed street with a dull thump.

"You hurt, ma'am?" David asked as he hurried to her side. His eyes were wide with concern when he knelt down

36

and saw the stunned and bewildered look on Callie's face. "Ma'am, I think it is awful foolish of you to figure you can ride that horse all the way out to Circle T. You are only going to end up gettin' bad hurt."

Callie tested her arms and her legs, and discovered that all she had really bruised was her already badly battered pride. But she had reached the full limit of her endurance, and tears filled her golden brown eyes when she looked down at her dirt-covered skirts and the dangling threads that once held a now-missing button from her jacket.

"Help me up," she said in a quivering voice, and raised her hand.

While David helped her back to her feet, she became aware that Wade Barlow was headed across the street, directly towards them—no doubt to gloat over her foolishness. She hurried in the opposite direction, hoping to be inside the livery and out of his sight before he reached her. She'd had more than enough of his spiteful arrogance for one day.

Wade's voice reached her before she could step safely into the shadows within the livery.

"All right, I'll take you," he stated simply and abruptly. His voice sounded as hard as the tightened muscles in his cheeks. "Get your things and come on. Before you manage to hurt yourself."

Then just as abruptly as he had come, Wade Barlow turned and marched back toward the freight office—slowly shaking his head and running a hand over his tired face as he went.

Women! What exasperating creatures they were!

37

Chapter Three

"Get on in," Wade ordered, his voice abrupt while he shoved two large wooden barrels closer together, then quickly tucked the two battered valises into the little space he made near the rear of the wagon. Lacking any other space, he then placed the small wooden box inside one of the baking compartments inside the stove.

Callie frowned. After having become accustomed to gentlemen constantly and eagerly assisting her throughout her trip, she had at first thought Wade would offer to help her up onto the high-springed wagon seat. But when he turned away from her to circle the rear of the wagon on his way to the opposite side, she quickly realized she was not going to be assisted at all.

"Get in," he repeated. He did not even look at her while he tugged on the harnesses to be sure they were securely fastened. "I'm ready to be on my way."

Pressing her lips together with determination, Callie did what she could to keep control of her anger, but the resentment continued to grow even as she grabbed a hold of her skirts to do exactly what he had commanded. When she tried, her handbag caught on a jutting nail and pulled out of her hand, yet she found her way up onto the wooden bench seat and situated herself, and her skirts, with relative grace.

When she reached down to try to free her snagged handbag from the rusted nail, she heard the material tear.

Upon examination, she discovered the lace trim badly torn. Gritting her teeth, she tried to keep in mind that at least she had a ride out to the Circle T. A very reluctant ride, granted, but it was a ride nonetheless. She would not have to stay the night in Pine Fork. Nor would she have to wait overnight or longer before finally meeting her fiancé. And she would soon see if her future home was truly as grand as Matthew had claimed in his letters.

Not having to wait any longer made all the mishaps she had suffered in the past two hours bearable.

After handing the valises and the box to Wade Barlow, David Gordy had stepped well out of the way and watched with a worried frown while Wade climbed lithely onto the seat next to Callie without saying anything further to either of them. Then, with no warning, Wade slapped the reins down hard to get the two horses and the heavily ladened wagon into motion. David was not as worried about the horses as he was about the young lady at Wade's side. Noticing the way Callie stared straight ahead, her shoulders rigid, and the way Wade did the same, David shook his head with curious concern. Slowly the wagon moved down the street, and eventually out of sight.

Even after they left town, Wade continued to sit stiffly on the wooden, bench-style seat. His only noticeable movements were in direct response to the continued jolting of the wagon itself as they made their way along the rutted gravel road.

His decision to take Callie Thomas to the Circle T had been a reluctant one. And he was even *more* reluctant to start any sort of conversation with the pretty young woman beside him — a woman whose strange combination of stubborn determination and childlike vulnerability had somehow caused him to go completely against his better judgment. And that was something not often done.

When it came to dangerous situations, Wade did not normally behave so impulsively. It worried him. He had not been his usually cautious self in making his decision. Why had he let it bother him that this woman could have

39

been putting herself in danger by riding off alone the way she had obviously planned? Why had he cared at *all* what happened to her? He didn't even know her.

Angry, though mostly with himself for having given in so readily when his always reliable common sense had warned him against it, Wade kept his eyes set on the narrow ruts of the road ahead, and his mind on the trouble he might face the moment he turned the wagon onto Tucker land. He reached down to touch his revolver more than once. Next he moved the heel of his boot back several inches to make certain the rifle he'd placed under the seat was also still within easy grasp. If there was to be trouble ahead, he wanted to be ready.

Callie noticed the attention he kept giving his handgun, and suddenly George Wilkins's voice echoed its fatherly warning to her. "Be careful about who you hire to see you to that ranch. There's a bad lot out there. Don't mistake them for good." Callie felt her skin prickle when she wondered if Wade was the sort of man George had tried to warn her against.

"I want to thank you for agreeing to take me out to the Circle T," Callie found the courage to say as she pushed her other thoughts aside for fear of what she might discover if she examined the situation too closely. Her voice broke the monotonous clomping sound of the horses' hooves and the constant creaking of the wagon with startling clarity.

Wade did not respond. Instead his pale blue eyes continued to study the winding road ahead, his thoughts trained on the man he had been warned all his life to avoid.

"Mr. Barlow!" she said in a much louder voice, perturbed by the stubborn manner in which he continued to ignore her. He could at least be civil towards her!

Wade appeared startled when he turned his head to face her. "What? What is it?"

Callie's golden brown eyes darkened with anger, but she kept her voice as calm and controlled as was possible. "I was gracious enough to thank you for this ride to the

Circle T. You might at least be gracious enough to acknowledge my words in some way."

"You're welcome."

His expression was solemn, his jaw like granite, while he quietly studied her for a long moment, as if trying to form a personal opinion of her. Then he abruptly took his gaze away and stared once again at the road ahead.

Callie sighed. The man was clearly not a conversationalist. It was going to be a *long* and painfully silent trip. She then wondered just how long. Well, there was only one way to find out, though she already knew he did not respond well to being asked a lot of questions.

"How far is it to the Circle T?" she finally asked.

He looked at her again, one dark eyebrow slightly raised. "Don't you know?"

"Not really. All Matthew mentioned in his letters was that his place was west of town somewhere, but close enough for him or his foreman to make a trip into town at least twice a week to pick up the mail and whatever supplies they need."

"Who are you?" he asked bluntly. "I know you said you name is Callie Thomas, but who are you in relation to Tucker? You his niece or something?"

Callie found herself oddly reluctant to answer that question, for some unknown reason. "I'm Matthew's finacée."

Wade's eyebrows shot straight up until they nearly met with the thick tufts of curling brown hair that ducked down out of his hat. "You're his what?"

"His finacée. Matthew Tucker advertised for a wife in a large newspaper back East, in New York, and I answered the ad. We then corresponded for a while. He told me what he was looking for in a wife and how he felt I was just what he wanted, and I decided to take him up on his offer. He seems like a very nice man."

"A nice man?" Wade asked incredulously, his blue eyes stretched wide. "Tucker?"

Callie felt a cold tingling of apprehension along the

sensitive skin at the back of her neck. Her stomach tightened in response to the sudden doubts Wade had caused. Had Matthew Tucker fooled her with false letters? Had he made promises to her he could not possibly keep? She tried not to consider such a thing when she answered, "Yes, Mr. Barlow. In his letters Matthew Tucker was *very* nice."

"The man must have a real talent for writing fiction," Wade muttered, shaking his head with disbelief. "You sure must be a gullible little thing to be willing to agree to marry a man sight unseen. Either that or desperate for a husband. You might find it interesting to know that Matthew Tucker is old enough to be your father."

"I know that," she stated with a defiant toss of her head. "But for your information, the age difference didn't matter to me." The moment she realized she had used the past tense, which sounded all wrong for a woman who was supposed to have already made up her mind to marry, she immediately corrected it by adding, "No, sir. Age *doesn't* matter in the least, nor should it."

"You sure must be hard up then," he stated matter-of-factly, then eyed her suspiciously. "You in some kind of trouble?"

"Why would you ask that?"

"Why else would such a pretty young lady like you be willing to travel all the way out here from New York to marry a man she never even met — a man who is probably twice her age?"

"There are plenty of reasons," she answered with a stubborn thrust of her chin. Suddenly, she was reminded of her awful past. A chill swept through her. "Plenty of reasons a man like you wouldn't understand. But, to answer your question, *no,* I am not in any trouble. I just want. . . ." she started to explain, but then decided this man deserved no explanation. "Really, it isn't any of your business why I've decided to marry Mr. Matthew Tucker."

"You're mighty right about that," he said, pressing his lips together into a fine, white line and turning to stare at

42

the road once more. He did not bother to speak to her again.

Callie was on the verge of tears, and did not know if that was because of the intense anger she felt for having her motives so blatantly questioned—when the man had absolutely no right to question her at all—or because of the sudden fear that now weighed so heavily inside her. Had she been too impulsive? Had she allowed her desperate need to get away from her cruel step-aunt and her selfish cousins to cloud her better judgment?

What if Matthew was not at all the way he had portrayed himself in his letters? What if he had deliberately given her a false impression of himself and of his home just to lure her out here? Callie's stomach twisted into a tight knot when she realized she might have been duped. Was it possible she had left the squalor of New York and the miserable, almost slavelike existence she'd lived there, only to find herself in a similar situation now that she was in Texas?

What if all Matthew Tucker wanted was someone to cook and clean and mend for him, as well as take care of his two daughters? And what if he did not plan to uphold his promise not to make her succumb to her "wifely duties" unless she wished? What if he had misrepresented all that he would do for her and what little he expected in return? But then again, they were not officially married yet. If he really was not the man he had seemed to be in his letters, and if he did not live in a place as nice as he had claimed he did, with housekeepers to take care of the sort of work she had been forced to do for her Aunt Cynthia, and if it was not a place where she would have a large bedroom all to herself, she could simply refuse to marry him. She would then find some way to pay him back the money he had lent her for the trip and go her own way with a clear conscience. There would be no obligation to marry him if he'd misled her with a lot of lies and false promises.

But then again, what did she know of Wade Barlow?

Maybe he was just out to cause trouble. The bartender in town had told her how the Tuckers and the Barlows did *not* get along—never had. Putting such serious doubts into her head might be his way of getting back at Matthew.

Callie decided to keep her mind open until she met Matthew and judged the man for herself. True, he was supposed to be much older than she, but that had not mattered before. Why should it matter now?

Nor had it mattered that she was not in love with him. Callie did not believe in love anyway. Love was a fanciful notion that led only to heartache and a life filled with disappointments. Look at her Uncle Robert. He loved his new wife, had told Callie so more than once, but that had not prevented him from being miserable. Nor had it kept her own mother from being unhappy more times than not, having been forced to live such a poor existence. No, love had not been an important consideration when making the decision to marry Matthew. All Callie sought was a chance for happiness. A chance to live a more normal life. Was that really so much to ask?

Sighing inwardly, Callie refused to worry anymore about Matthew, and quickly turned her attention to the scenery ahead. The vast beauty surrounding her had a calming effect on her fluttering heart and the nervous churning of her stomach. She was very pleased to discover that not only was there indeed civilization in this part of Texas, there was plenty of plant life which she had not expected to find.

Tall, sturdy trees loomed high overhead, forming a thick canopy which shaded large areas of the road and offered cool respite from the blazing hot afternoon sun. There were oaks, elms, sweet gums, walnuts, pecans, persimmons, and many other wide, broadleaf trees she did not recognize mingled in among the more prominent pine trees. Beyond those trees, lining the roadway, lay wide pastures cast in different shades of green, pastures blanketed with thick grass and spotted with pretty yellow and coral-colored wildflowers.

Beyond the rolling fields rose large, rounded hills dappled with dark shades of brilliant green, where still more trees grew in thick abundance. The earth was a deep, rich reddish-brown, and though the road was dry and dusty, the area did not even closely resemble the near-desert or the wide, open plains she had expected to find. Although rain clearly had not fallen recently, the land was fertile.

Apparently, she was surrounded by richly productive cattle country. Fences appeared often along the roadside during their travel, but none of them were made of wood planks like those Callie had seen in New York. Most of the fences here seemed to be made of brand-new, roughly hewed posts set a few yards distant and joined by several strands of wire which seemed spaced about a foot apart. Beyond these fences were all manner of cattle grazing idly in the bright summer sunshine.

"How much further?" Callie endeavored to ask after they had ridden for nearly an hour in total silence. Although she understood they were traveling at a slower rate than normal because of their extremely heavy load, she was more eager than ever to arrive at Circle T, as much to be out of this man's disturbing company as to meet Matthew.

"Not far," he answered without bothering to look at her.

"But *how* far? Is that so difficult a question to answer? You really do try a person's patience, Mr. Barlow. All I want to know is how much longer it will be until we finally get there."

"*Too* long," he muttered beneath his breath, yet loud enough for her to hear the comment. He never took his gaze off the road ahead.

Callie leaned heavily against the hard wooden plank which served as a back for the wagon seat and stared at Wade Barlow with renewed anger.

She understood why he was not exactly happy with her. After all, he had not wanted to have her along in the first place. He had made it perfectly clear; he did not want to go onto Matthew's land for any reason. But what she did not fully understand was why he was so intentionally rude, when the most she had *personally* done to him was call him a few choice but befitting words back in town. In all honesty, she could have called him far worse than a blackheart and a coward—far worse—and might yet.

After several more minutes of cold silence, she finally asked, "Why did you change your mind about giving me a ride to the Circle T when you are obviously set against it?"

Wade glanced at her briefly, then back out at the road ahead. "I've been asking myself that very same question ever since we left town."

"And have you arrived at any answers?"

"Only one that makes sense. That I must gradually be losing hold of all reasoning."

Callie crossed her arms over her heaving bosom, angrier now than she had been before. Again she tried to focus her attention on her surroundings so she would not have to think about what a horrid creature the man at her side really was. He might be handsome beyond all belief, but she decided he was far too arrogant for his own good.

After passing through another densely wooded area, where nothing could be seen on either side of the narrow road but brush, vines, and trees, they finally emerged into another large clearing, this one fenced with fat, sturdy milled posts and much stouter-looking wire. The pastureland which now surrounded them was greener than much of what they had passed earlier and had a smoother, more cultivated look about it. The grassy fields were immense, broken only by small clusters of shade trees and more fence lines, until the woodlands started again in the far distance along a tall, rugged-looking ridge.

Soon, in among several huge spreading oaks at the top of a small hill, Callie noticed a large, impressive-looking house facing north, toward the road, at a slight angle. Though the house was some distance away, she saw that it was a two-story built of brick, soft buff in color, with dark-rose moldings and shutters around the many windows. It also had dark-rose insets along the summits of the four sets of clustered chimneys which emerged from the high, sloping roof. There was movement near the crest of the roof, and she noticed the small windmills which no doubt afforded the house the luxury of ceiling fans.

The outbuildings, including a barn almost as large as the house itself, were made of lapped wood, painted white with dark-rose colored trim—all but the carriage house, which was made of brick and matched the main house in both color and design.

Glad to have her thoughts taken away from more serious matters, Callie studied the house further, wondering what sort of people lived in such a wonderful house. Next, she noticed off to the east side a pretty terrace-garden, with tall, well-manicured hedges. The garden was easily enjoyed from a large, shaded veranda built along the eastern wall. A wide curving drive circled in front of the house and passed beneath a large carriage porch near the front door. The same drive branched off to the right side and curved around to enter the carriage house. It was truly the nicest house they had passed and Callie knew she would be satisfied if Matthew's house proved to be even half that grand.

While they passed along the roadway directly in front of the house, a tall, thick roadside hedge temporarily obscured her view, and she eagerly awaited the chance to see the house again from the opposite side. But to her amazement, just when they were about to pass the carriage drive that divided the wide hedgerow in half, Wade tugged on the left side of the reins and the wagon slowly turned in the direction of the drive.

"That's Matthew's house?" Callie asked breathlessly after they had passed through the opening and she could once again see the magnificent structure before her. Before Wade bothered to answer, she caught sight of the white fence surrounding the homesite and the tall, ornamental-iron gate which had been left open. Designed into the intricate ironwork of the gate was a large emblem that represented Matthew's ranch—the bold letter T placed within a perfect circle.

Wade brought the wagon to a clattering halt several yards short of the house. For a moment, he sat perfectly still, watching the house warily before he suddenly hopped down and began jerking her things out of the back of the wagon.

While Callie waited to be helped down, Wade strode to the front of the house and dropped her two bags and her small box on the bottom-most porch step, then turned to her expectantly, crossing his arms in front of him. Callie's attention was drawn to the way his rolled-up sleeves left much of his arms to her view. It was clear from the way his muscles moved so smoothly beneath the taut, sun-browned skin of his forearms that Wade Barlow was a man who worked long, hard hours outdoors. She wondered briefly if his back would prove to be as sun-bronzed as his arms, and caught herself blushing at her bold thought. She quickly looked away.

This is your new home, miss. Good luck. You are going to need it." He shifted his weight to one well-muscled leg and stared curiously up at her. The movement brought her gaze back to meet with his.

Suddenly aware Wade had no more intention of helping her down than he had earlier of helping her up, Callie snatched at her skirts and attempted to get down on her own. Just as her boot was about to meet with the ground, she felt a sharp tug on her skirt and discovered her hem had become hung on the same jutting nail that had snagged her handbag earlier. To her mortification, the snared hemline revealed most of her underskirts and even part of her leg to open view, a view Wade did not miss. Blushing profusely she gave the garment a hard desperate yank, ripping the material in the process.

"You could have at least looked away!" she snapped, though not daring to look in Wade's direction when she stepped away from the wagon.

"Didn't want to," he replied simply, then shrugged and circled to the far side of the wagon.

"Indeed!" Quickly Callie plunged her hand deep into her drawstring handbag in search of the money to pay him for his services. Frowning with both frustration and righteous anger, she hurriedly fingered the many items stuffed inside the reticule in search of her change purse. Though she knew Wade had returned to the wagon and climbed up onto the seat, she was startled and further infuriated to realize the wagon had suddenly begun to move.

Standing with her hand still plunged deep into her handbag and her mouth compressed into a thin line, she stared angrily after him while the horses slowly began to pick up their pace and Wade drove away without so much as a word or even a nod goodbye. Never had she had to deal with a man so rude or impertinent in her entire life. What a terribly high opinion he must have of himself!

To her utter dismay, though her anger willed her to try, she was unable to pull her gaze away from his strong, rigid back. She continued to watch helplessly as the wagon neared the wide opening in the hedgerow near the road. While she waited for the wagon to disappear from her sight, he turned to glance back at her over his broad shoulder and offered her a quick salute and a boldly arrogant smile. Appalled by his brashness, she felt her cheeks grow instantly hot. The rogue! As if he had fully expected her to be watching!

Furious with herself for having done exactly what he'd expected of her, she turned and hurried toward the house in a flurry of torn skirts and injured pride. Without taking the time to knock and await a response, although she knew she should, Callie marched directly into the house and closed the door behind her. Her only thought was to get out of Wade Barlow's sight as quickly as possible and show him that he really did not matter to her in the least.

It took several minutes of long, deeply drawn breaths before Callie composed herself and noticed her surroundings and the fact that no one had heard her enter. She considered stepping back outside and knocking the way she should have in the first place, but it bothered her that no one had noticed her yet. Something must be wrong.

"Hello?" she called out cautiously. Surely someone had to be home. The door had been left unlocked.

While awaiting a response, she quickly scanned the room, noting immediately that nothing seemed out of place in the elegantly tiled entrance which surrounded her. She saw no movement in the wide hall that lay beyond the entrance and ran north to south through the center of the house. Nor was there movement at the top of the large, curving staircase that was set off to her right and spiraled gently around a huge chandelier cascading in crystal droplets from the ribbed ceiling high overhead.

Callie was immediately aware of not only the stillness which surrounded her, but also of the grandeur. This was truly the most splendid house she had ever seen—inside or out. If nothing else, at least that part of Matthew's letters had been true. His house was magnificent.

"Hello?" she tried again, louder.

This time she heard a noise upstairs—the heavy thump of footsteps—and within seconds a large, strong-boned Negress appeared at the top of the stairs, her brow drawn low over a scowling face and her arms crossed firmly over an ample bosom. The woman wore a dark green dress with a starched white linen apron. On her head was a yellow and green kerchief. In her hand was a gray feather duster.

"Who are you?" she demanded to know before she started down the stairs towards Callie, wielding the feather duster as if it were a weapon to be reckoned with. "And what are you doin' inside this house uninvited? Don't you got any manners? Just what are you up to anyway?"

The questions came too close together for Callie to answer, and it was not until the woman was halfway down the stairs that she took a breath deep enough to give

Callie her first real opportunity to speak.

"I'm Callie Thomas," she began, and was about to explain her reasons for having entered unannounced when the woman's face lifted into a bright, beaming smile.

"You're Miss Callie Thomas?" she asked while her eyes eagerly dipped to take in the slightly bedraggled appearance of the young lady before her. "But you weren't expected for days yet. Not till next Tuesday." She blew out a sharp, approving breath while she came forward to get a better look at her. "I'm Lucille, Mister Matthew's main housekeeper. My, but I'm glad you decided to come early. Mister Matthew's done took a turn for the worse. He's got the black cough so bad he can hardly get out of that bed. Oh, but wait until he sees how pretty you are. It'll be just the thing to perk him up."

Callie returned her smile with earnest. Finally she was made to feel welcome in Texas by someone. Some of the tension drained out of her tired body, but none of the eager anticipation that caused her heart to continue to hammer wildly inside of her.

"May I change clothes and wash my face and arms before I meet him?" Callie asked, gesturing toward her torn skirt and her badly rumpled jacked with its missing button. "I do want to look my best."

Within minutes Callie was escorted upstairs to her bedroom—a room which far exceeded her expectations for it was as large as, if not larger than, the entire upper floor of her step-aunt's apartment back in New York, and was luxuriously furnished.

At one end of her new bedroom, near the three tall, multi-paned windows which commanded a lovely view of the gardens below, was a five-piece Rococo parlor suite consisting of a sofa, a rocker, and three wing chairs as well as several occasional tables. And at the far end of the room, away from the windows but with a large ceiling fan nearby to keep the area cool and breezy in the summer, was a four-piece bedroom suite of a matching Rococo design. The colors in the room were predominantly pink,

51

with splashes of browns and beiges and contrasting blues. It was a beautiful room, a room befitting a princess, and she realized she felt very much like a princess when she set her handbag aside and ran her hand over the cool softness of her satin bedcover.

Suddenly she wished her mother could be there to see the room. Her mother had always hated being poor and had dreamed of one day living in a house like Matthew's.

"I'll be right back up with a pitcher of cool water and a fresh bar of soap," Lucille said just before she deposited the two battered valises beside the large cheval dresser nearest the bed. "Then once you are washed up and changed, I'll take you right on in to meet Mister Matthew." She fluttered her hand near the general location of her collarbone in response to her excitement. "I can hardly wait for him to see how pretty you are."

Callie could also hardly wait to see what Matthew looked like. It worried her that he was sick. Hurriedly, she removed the heavy woolen garments that felt like a second skin. Eagerly, she peeled out of the rumpled jacket and tossed it side. Cool air struck the thin material of her damp blouse with welcome relief and she wasted no time before discarding the rest of her garments.

When the housekeeper soon returned with water and soap, Callie was dressed in only her pantaloons and camisole, glancing at the torn condition of her traveling suit with a dismal frown. She had hoped to wear the garment when she first met Matthew. It was the only thing of quality she owned. But between her fall from the horse in town and getting the hem caught on the wagon seat, she had ruined the dress, and in less than three hours' time.

While she held the skirt away from her, Callie noticed the largest rip, which was along the hem and up into the skirt. The jagged tear was irreparable — as was the damage she felt had been done to her pride. She blushed with renewed mortification when she remembered how Wade Barlow had seen all her undergarments and a goodly portion of her bared leg before she pulled her hem free of that blasted nail. Yet, for one brief moment, she caught herself wondering if he'd in any way approved of what he saw. But she quickly pushed the shameful thought to the back of her mind. She had plenty to worry about without giving Wade Barlow any further attention.

"How long has Matthew been sick?" Callie asked while she hurriedly ran a damp cloth over her skin. The coolness was such a welcome relief, she wished she could plunge into a large tub filled with cool water, and decided to ask for that luxury before bedtime. She hadn't had a good soaking bath since St. Louis.

"He's been sick off and on for several months," Lucille told her while she went about showing Callie exactly where to put her things, and where to find fresh towels or an extra pillow for her bed. "Just last week, it looked like he was about to get over his sickness at last, but then it came back this week worse than ever."

Callie frowned. If it kept coming back, it must be serious. Why didn't he mention it in his letters? "Does a doctor see him?"

"Regular," Lucille said with a nod. "Prescribes him all sorts of medicine too, but I think you are goin' to be the best medicine yet. He's really been lookin' forward to meetin' you. And because he has, I think while you are busy getting yourself dressed up real pretty, I'll go fetch him a comb and a fresh nightshirt so he can feel like he looks his best when he meets you."

"I don't have anything very pretty to wear," Callie admitted as she gestured to the torn garment she'd discarded. "That was the only truly nice dress I owned."

Lucille frowned a moment, but her smile soon returned. "It won't really matter what you wear. You'd look pretty dressed in a burlap feed sack and a rope. Just put on whatever you'll feel comfortable in. I'll be back in just a few minutes to get you."

"What's he like?" Callie wanted to know before she left.

"Mister Matthew. Why, he's a fine man with a good and gentle heart," Lucille said fondly. "You'll like him. Most everybody does."

"What about his daughters? What are they like?"

Lucille's smile faded for a moment, but did not disappear from her face while she considered how to answer the question. "You'll meet those two soon enough."

Then suddenly she was gone.

Chapter Four

When Lucille returned for her shortly thereafter, Callie found herself suddenly at odds. Two entirely different emotions dominated her heart. Part of her was clearly eager to meet Matthew — finally meet the man she had agreed to marry — yet another part of her dreaded it.

Even though she had already dismissed the doubts Wade Barlow had tried to set in her mind, she now wondered if a man so obviously accustomed to elegance would still find her a suitable choice for his wife. Would he still want to go through with the marriage? Or would he see her for what she really was, a mere nobody who did not belong in such a house? Would he then try to send her back to New York?

How she wished she had not ruined her new outfit. The pink and white dress she eventually chose to wear was definitely one of her nicer dresses, one which highlighted the color of her cheeks and the dark tint of her hair, but even so, the garment seemed grotesquely plain in such grand surroundings.

"It's dark in there," Lucille warned as she placed her hand on the shiny brass door handle to Matthew's bedroom. "But that's how he likes it when he's feeling poorly." Then she swung the door open and allowed Callie to enter first.

Lucille was right. It was dark in Matthew's room. The four sets of drapes along the far wall were drawn, though they parted occasionally to allow a light breeze to push its way through the open windows. If it were not for the two ceiling fans twirling slowly overhead, the room might have been as stifling as it was dark.

Moving further into the room, Callie wished the fans would turn a little faster, but knew they were only as effective as the wind blowing outside, since they were operated by the turning of windmills attached on the roof. As a result, a light breeze outside meant they could expect only a light breeze within.

Because Matthew did indeed prefer the dark whenever he was ill, only one bedside lamp glowed in the entire room. A small island of light fell over the frail man who lay propped up against a huge pile of pillows upon a massive oak bed at the far side of the huge bedroom.

"Mister Matthew, this is her. This is Callie Thomas," Lucille said happily as soon as they were both inside the room and she had closed the door.

"Callie." He spoke the name fondly, almost reverently, and held out a weak, trembling hand to her. Though it was a wide hand, it seemed unnaturally thin.

"Matthew," she responded with a smile, and moved forward taking his hand in both of hers. His touch felt oddly cold in a room so warm. "I know I'm earlier than you expected. I hope it's no inconvenience."

"Not at all," he said with a genuine smile that took years off his face, though it did little to change the fact his thick, dark brown hair had started to go gray at his temples and behind his ears. Nor did it change the gray liberally sprinkled into his thick mustache and his perfectly arched eyebrows.

Callie smiled back at him. Although he looked even older than she had expected, and far less handsome than she had hoped, there was a gentleness about him. A true kindness sparkled in his blue eyes which made her like him immediately. She watched the way his gaze swept over her, but came quickly back to study her face, and she blushed slightly. She could not help remembering another pair of pale blue eyes which had assessed her with much more boldness only an hour earlier, and had chosen far more personal areas to focus on. "I hope I don't disappoint you."

"Not in the least," he said with such sincerity it made Callie's smile deepen. She pushed any worries of her personal inadequacy aside.

Matthew paused a moment, eagerly studying her face. "I just hope I don't disappoint you too much. I know I'm not much to look at these days, but this sickness has taken a lot out of me."

"That's true enough," Lucille put in with a sharp nod. "He's lost a lot of weight and a lot of his color. But once he gets over this sickness, he'll put that weight back on and be as spry as ever."

Matthew looked at her with open gratitude. "Always the optimist," he said and chuckled to himself. "But that's enough about me. I want to hear about Callie. Pull up a chair, dear, and talk with me for a while. How was your trip?"

If Callie had felt any disappointment in Matthew's general appearance when she first saw him, it quickly faded when she got to know him better. He was so full of kindness, sympathy, and sincere compliments — things she had longed for ever since her parents' death nine years ago — that she found herself growing fonder of him by the minute. She wondered how she had ever allowed herself to have doubts about him. He was everything she had thought he would be and more, and that was what really mattered.

While they continued to talk and slowly became better acquainted, the strangest feeling began to come over Callie. It was as if she had seen Matthew somewhere before — had perhaps met him — but she knew that was impossible. He had never been East and she had never before been West. Still, he seemed vaguely to resemble someone she knew, and it bothered her. She was sure it would come to her in time.

"You really should have let me know you were coming early. I would have sent someone to town to meet you," Matthew said, and frowned for the first time since she'd entered the room.

"I would have if I'd had the time. My decision to leave came very suddenly. You see, my step-aunt decided I was to allow a friend of hers to pay call on me on a regular basis, but I wanted no part of it. And I knew when I told her that, she was going to make my life even more miserable than it already was. So I changed my plans and left the first chance I had after that."

"You've had a hard life," Matthew said, his eyes so full of understanding, it made Callie want to cry. "First your parents died when you were only eleven, then just a few years later, your grandparents, leaving you nowhere else to go but your uncle's. And the way that wife of his treated you, I'm amazed you didn't leave them sooner than you did."

"I had nowhere to go . . . until I answered your advertisement." It touched Callie's heart to know he had memorized every detail of her letters.

"And I'm very glad you came." Suddenly, dark shadows appeared in the hollows beneath Matthew's eyes. He reached for a handkerchief and pressed it firmly against his mouth. It was only after he'd seen the spell of hard, body-wracking coughs through to the end that he apologized, then continued with their conversation, though his voice was much weaker. "How'd you manage to get out here from town all by yourself?"

Callie felt the muscles in her chest tighten, not knowing how the answer to that question might affect him. After having witnessed the severity of his coughing spells, she was not sure it would be wise to cause him any unnecessary duress. She decided to redirect the conversation instead. "Matthew, how long have you had this terrible cough?"

"Off and on for several months," he admitted, glancing first at her, then at his folded hands. "I know I should have told you about it, but I was afraid you would delay coming if you knew. Besides, when I got your letter agreeing to marry me, I was feeling much better. But I don't want to talk about me. I want to hear all about you. You never did tell me how you got out here all by yourself."

Still hoping to avoid any unnecessary problems, Callie kept her answer vague. "A man who was headed this way gave me a ride."

"Headed this way? Who was that?"

He seemed truly interested, and Callie did not want to lie to him. "A man named Wade Barlow."

At first, Matthew's thin face registered disbelief, but soon relaxed into a deeply pleased smile, forming long creases in his cheeks. When he smiled like that, Callie decided he looked almost handsome.

"Wade brought you out here? I must remember to thank him in some way."

Callie was relieved to learn Matthew did not display any of the hostility she had expected, and wondered if the differences she'd been told existed between the Tuckers and the Barlows were all one-sided. She decided to test his reactions further. "I understand he and his family live near here."

Suddenly Matthew's smile dropped and his head pressed back against the tall mound of pillows supporting his back. When he answered, he did not look at her. "There's only the two of them left. Wade's place is called Twin Oaks. It's just northwest of here. His father's place is called the Rocking W and is directly west."

So there *were* ill feelings between them. She wondered why he had not shown them sooner. "Then they are your neighbors?"

"They are, but it's best to stay away from them. Especially Wade's father, Walter Barlow."

"Why's that?" She wondered if the father could possibly be any worse than the son—aware that if he was, he must be kin to the devil himself.

"The man and I don't get along," Matthew stated simply. Then he abruptly changed the subject. "So, what do you think of the Circle T?"

"It's beautiful. It's everything you promised it would be and more."

Matthew looked pleased. "Then you'll stay?"

"I'm looking forward to it."

"And you'll still marry me, even though I'm a little under the weather? You'll go through with our agreement?"

Callie felt an odd twisting at her heart which caused her to pause for a moment; but she forced the strange feeling aside because it really made no sense to have second thoughts now. Not after all she had gone through to get there. And not when both Matthew and the Circle T far surpassed her strongest expectations. "It will be an honor to be your wife and take care of your two daughters."

"Have you met them yet?"

"No, not yet. I wanted to meet you first."

Matthew's pale gaze left her in search of Lucille, who stood several feet behind Callie, but quickly returned to study Callie's face. "I think I should warn you, they are not exactly fond of the idea of having a new mother. They see it as an intrusion into their lives. It may take awhile before they decide to open their hearts and accept you. But you seem strong-willed enough to overcome that. You'll do just fine."

Suddenly Matthew bent forward again and erupted into another spasm of coughs so strong the veins in his forehead stood out, rigid beneath his pale skin. This time, when the coughing finally subsided, he was left too weak to continue with their visit, and Lucille quickly escorted Callie out of the bedroom.

"We don't want to tire him out too much with your first visit," she said as a way of explanation. "Besides, you need to start puttin' your things away and makin' yourself to home around here."

"When do I meet Matthew's daughters?"

Lucille hesitated. "I think supper will be plenty soon to meet up with those two."

"And when is supper?"

"Usual time in the summer is seven o'clock. But I can send for you when it is time to sit yourself at the table."

"Don't bother, I'll just come on down a few minutes early."

"No bother. I can send Ruby up to fetch you when it's time."

"Ruby?"

"Mister Matthew's other housekeeper. Newly hired to replace Flossie, who ran off and got herself married a couple months ago. Ruby helps me out in the kitchen and with some of the cleanin'. Or at least she is supposed to, but here lately, her head's been up in the clouds and she ain't been a whole lot of help to nobody." Lucille bent toward Callie as if afraid someone might overhear. "She's got the weak knees for Thomas Rett."

"And Thomas is?" Callie prompted her, feeling she might as well know all about people who were soon to become a part of her life.

Lucille's eyes grew wide with concern. "Thomas works over to Mister Barlow's place."

Callie felt her heart thump. "And which Mister Barlow would that be? The father or the son?"

"The son."

"And does that cause a problem for Thomas and Ruby?"

"It does when Wade Barlow has given Thomas strict orders not to set foot on Circle T."

"And does Ruby have orders from Matthew not to set foot on Wade Barlow's land?"

"No. Just Old Man Barlow's land. But even if Mister Matthew had given her such orders, I don't think she'd be able to stay away. She plum' addle-brained over that Thomas Rett," Lucille said with a shake of her head, but then grinned. "Or maybe she just plain addle-brained period."

"Then it might be wiser if I didn't rely on Ruby to come after me at seven. I'll just come down on my own in a couple of hours."

"Whatever suits you the most. You'll find the dinin' room back off to your left once you've gone back down the stairs."

"Will Matthew be dining with us?"

Lucille looked away. "No, he'd be takin' his meal in his room. Maybe later on in the week, he'll have enough of his strength back to come downstairs. But for tonight, it'll just be you and the girls."

"Do I dress for dinner?" she asked, wondering what she would do if their meals were formal. She would have nothing to wear and would feel terribly out of place.

Lucille glanced back at her and grinned at some private thought that occurred to her; but whatever it was, she chose to keep it to herself. "If you mean do you dress fancy, no. They only dress fancy when special company's comin'. What you got on will do just fine." She then left Callie at her bedroom door and went back downstairs.

Seven o'clock arrived quickly, and when Callie realized the time had come at last to meet Matthew's daughters, she put aside her unpacking and went immediately downstairs. Remembering Lucille's instructions, she turned left at the foot of the stairs and followed the wide secondary hallway toward the back of the house. She was able to hear voices long before she decided which door would lead her into the dining room.

"I don't care. I don't want her here. She's not my mother and I don't want her pretending she is," a high-pitched voice cried out, loud enough to be clearly heard out into the hallway.

"Me either," came an immediate response from an even higher-pitched voice.

"But it's what your father wants," Lucille reminded them, low with warning.

The first voice spoke again. "I don't see why. He doesn't love her. He can't love her. Until today he hadn't even met

62

her. She doesn't belong here. And I wish she would just turn around and go back home."

"Me too," came the echoing response, this time clearly from the younger of the two.

"That's enough of that, Janice Louise," Lucille admonished. "You too, Amy Marie. As it so happens the Circle T is Miss Callie's home now. And you'd best remember that she will be down here any minute and it would be wise for you two to do whatever it takes to get along with her. You don't want to go makin' an enemy of your new mother."

"Don't call her that. Even if Father marries her, she won't be our mother. She'll only be our stepmother. I just hope it doesn't come to that. I hope she never marries our father."

"Me too," came the little echo.

Callie paused just outside the open door and debated whether she should go on inside and face the two who spoke so ill of her, or forget about supper altogether and return to her room for a much-needed night's rest. Though it would clearly be easier for everyone concerned if she did indeed postpone meeting the two resentful little girls, at least for a day, she decided it would be better in the long run to take courage in hand and get it over with. Bravely, she drew in a deep breath and stepped inside.

"Hello, everyone," she said with a strained smile, and quickly glanced around the large, elegantly furnished dining room to take in the scene before her. Two dark-headed little girls were already seated at the huge mahogany dining table, side by side, frowning, while Lucille stood off at one end waving a large serving spoon in her hand. They all three looked up at the same time and the reactions varied.

Lucille's eyes widened immediately with concern, clearly worried Callie might have overheard some of the spiteful conversation which had just occurred, while the two girls' already glum expressions quickly darkened into stubborn

63

scowls. The older of the two narrowed her eyes in an attempt to stare daggers right through Callie, while the younger child divided her attention between her sister's stern expression and trying to match it with a scowl of her own.

"Good evenin', Miss Callie," Lucille said nervously. "I was just startin' to put the food on the table. You are just in time."

"Smells delicious," Callie commented, still smiling when she moved forward to take one of the chairs directly across from the two girls.

"I hope you like roasted beef," Lucille said, then placed the spoon she had been holding into a large steaming bowl of carrots. She had sounded apologetic, though it was not clear if her apologetic tone was because of the selection of meat or because of what had been said just before Callie entered. Lucille continued to survey the food on the table while she babbled on. "Because this is a cattle ranch, I'm afraid we eat a lot of beef around here. But then, we do have chickens, turkeys, and geese. And Mister Matthew's got himself a hog a fattenin' out in the lot, so it's not always beef."

"Roast beef is fine," Callie assured her, glancing from one girl to the other while she settled into her chair. From Matthew's letters, she already knew the older child with the cautious blue-green eyes was Janice. Matthew's pet name for her was Jana, but he had warned Callie that ever since the girl had turned ten she'd preferred to be called Janice.

And it was Janice Callie studied first. The elder of the two girls sat very primly before her in a frilly blue dress of cashmere and silk, her shoulders erect and her dark brown hair pulled back away from her oval face, though allowed to flow freely down her back in soft, shimmering waves. Even with such a severe expression pulling at her brow, Janice was pretty enough to make Callie aware the girl would one day become a very beautiful woman; but she would clearly be a woman to be reckoned with.

Next, Callie turned her attention to the seven-year-old with the cherubic face and huge, worried blue eyes. The younger girl could be none other than Amy. She matched Matthew's description perfectly—a spattering of freckles across an upturned nose, sunbrowned skin, and long brown hair—though the hair was several shades lighter than Janice's dark mane.

Amy's hair was worn in long, tousled braids and, although her yellow gingham dress was spotless, there was a streak of dirt along the side of her neck and another smudge at the back of her ear where she had obviously neglected to wash. Callie suspected Amy preferred the outdoors and was as much a tomboy as Janice pretended to be a lady.

"Hello, I'm Callie Thomas," she ventured to say when it was clear neither girl wanted to be the first to speak and Lucille had not thought to introduce them.

"We know," Janice said abruptly, and leaned forward in an accusing manner. "You are the woman who somehow tricked our father into wanting to get married."

Tricked? Callie found it harder to keep her smile. "I don't know where you got that notion. It happens to have been your father's idea we get married."

"That's what you say. But we don't really believe it," Janice said boldly. "We think you are here because you want to get your hands on some of our father's money. Don't we, Amy?"

Amy opened her mouth to answer, but evidently thought better of it. Instead, she lowered her gaze to her lap where her hands lay folded, and merely nodded her head in order to agree with her sister.

"We think you tricked him with a lot of lies, just so he'd ask you to marry him," Janice went on to say.

"That's simply not true," Callie stated calmly, fighting against the urge to march right around that table and take Matthew's elder daughter over her knee. If ever a young lady deserved a sound spanking, it was Janice. Never had she seen such impertinence in a child, not even in her two step-cousins, who until now had been the worst she'd ever known. "I am here because your father wants me here."

"Well, you may as well know it. We don't want you here. We wish you'd go back to wherever it is you came from. Don't we, Amy?"

Again Amy did not find courage to look up when she nodded her head in agreement.

"I'm sorry to hear that," Callie said in a soft voice, looking from Janice's defiant expression to the top of Amy's bent head. "I'd hoped to have you two pretty little girls for my friends."

Amy glanced up at her quizzically, but looked back at the hands still folded in her lap when Janice spoke again.

"Well, we don't want to be your friends. And we don't want you to be our stepmother."

Lucille decided it was time she stepped in. "That's just about enough out of you, young lady."

"I'm only speaking the truth. We don't want her here. We both wish she would go back home and leave us alone."

"When your pa hears what all you've had to say to Miss Callie, I have a feelin' he's goin' to be very angry with you. So angry, he won't allow you to leave your room for a month, except at mealtimes. He might even decide to take the strap to you. And unless you apologize to her right now, I'm afraid I'll have to go on upstairs right now and tell him about your behavior."

"Go ahead and tell him. See if I care," Janice cried out, narrowing her eyes. "I'd rather be stuck in my room and strapped black and blue than have to put up with the likes of her."

"I really don't think it will be necessary to bother Matthew with this," Callie put in quickly, amazed at how calm and reassuring her voice had sounded. "I can understand how they must feel, having a stranger suddenly thrust upon them, a stranger who they have been told will soon become their future mother."

"Stepmother," Janice quickly corrected as one eyebrow

rose with suspicion, not yet ready to believe Callie was quite so understanding. "A stepmother we don't want. Do we, Amy?"

Amy was too engrossed with rearranging the folds in her skirt to glance up again, and this time she did not bother to respond to her older sister's question with either a headshake of a nod, but Janice did not seem to notice. Her eyes were too carefully trained on Callie to notice what her sister's reaction had been.

Callie turned her attention back to Amy for a moment. She felt certain the younger girl would be the first to give up this stubborn dislike the two had decided upon. Amy did not seem nearly as adamant in her hostility as Janice was, and Callie felt because of that, the younger of Matthew's two daughters would eventually come to understand she did not have to feel everything her older sister felt. Amy would then begin to accept her, though Callie knew it would be awhile yet. Still, it was something she could look forward to, because once she was able to win Amy over to her side, she knew Janice might eventually follow. It was a hope she continued to cling to later while she soaked in a cool tub of water, and later when she got ready for bed.

The following morning Callie awoke feeling both excited and apprehensive about her new start in life. Hurriedly she dressed in an amber and white short-sleeved dress before going back downstairs for breakfast. Though she had planned to use the time to try to get to know the girls a little better, she was nonetheless relived to discover they had already eaten and gone outside. Their absence meant she was able to eat her meal in peace.

During the hours following breakfast, she returned to Matthew's room and they talked at length of their marriage and of what would be expected from her. As she had already been told, her main duties would be to take care of the girls and to help run and keep order in the house — though Callie could tell the house was already in very capable hands with Lucille.

"At first, it might be a little difficult getting any cooperation out of Jana and Amy, but eventually they'll come around," he assured her.

Callie nearly choked over the words "a little difficult," and wondered if he knew just how dead set his two daughters were against having her there, but she chose not to be the one to tell him. "I'll do my best."

"I know you will. And as for the house, about all you'll have to do is decide what meals you want prepared and remind Lucille and Ruby of any work you feel has been neglected. You shouldn't have any problem at all with those two. Lucille is very reliable, and as long as Ruby is so obviously afraid of Lucille, you won't have much problem getting her to do whatever you want either. Just let Lucille be the one to relay any orders you have for Ruby." He chuckled. "Lucille can be very intimidating when she wants to be."

I can well imagine," Callie said, and laughed with him. For the first time since having left the girls the evening before, Callie felt she was not making a grave mistake after all. It might not be easy, but she should be able to do everything Matthew wanted her to do, even cope with his two hostile daughters—given time.

"And in return, you'll more or less have the run of Circle T." Matthew told her. "Whatever your heart desires, just ask. For starters, I'd like for you to have Harry, my foreman, hitch up the buggy and take you into town so you can ask Nadine Leigh to make you up the prettiest wedding gown there is. You'll like Nadine. She's not only a good dressmaker, but she's a longtime friend of mine and will see to it that your gown is the best that can be made. Even though we'll be getting married here and not in a church, I still want to do it up right. While you are there, go ahead and have a couple of everyday dresses made up. And you might want to get yourself one of those split riding skirts. Out here you'll be able to go riding whenever you have a mind to."

Callie blushed at the memory of her one and only

attempt at riding a horse and at the thought of the man who had witnessed her foolishness. Quickly she pushed the handsome image aside. "I'm afraid I haven't had much opportunity to learn to ride a horse."

"Well, then we'll have to ask Harry to show you how it's done. If you're going to live on a ranch, you really should know how to ride a horse because there are some places a carriage just won't go," he told her. Then he returned to his original train of thought. "And while you are in town, I want you to stop off at the mercantile and get ribbons and bows and whatever else you think will dress up this place for the ceremony. I'll write you a letter for credit so all you'll have to do is sign for your purchases. And please, keep in mind that money is no problem. I *want* you to have the prettiest wedding a gal ever had."

Callie smiled at the sincerity in his voice and, though overwhelmed by his generosity, promised not to worry about cost.

"I mean it," he said, still not convinced she would spend his money as freely as he wanted her to. "Since I'm still feeling a mite poorly, I'll have to rely on you to see that the front room is made up proper enough for a Tucker wedding. And I also have a letter I want carried over to Reverend Cross telling him you have indeed arrived and that we intend to get married next weekend."

"Next weekend?" she asked, surprised at the swiftness.

"Sure, why not?" he asked, then grinned. "I don't want to give you the chance to back out. I would ask him to marry us this Saturday, but I know he's already got a wedding to do, so it'll have to be next weekend."

"But will you be well enough by then?"

"I'm sure I will," he stated adamantly, "I'm already feeling much better. In fact, I just might make it downstairs for supper tonight."

Callie smiled, relieved to hear he was already starting to improve, but at the same time hesitant to agree to the proposed wedding date. It seemed too soon. "But what about the girls? Shouldn't we wait until they have had a better chance to accept the idea of our marriage?"

Matthew's smile faded. "It might be months before those two come to fully accept the idea of our marriage. I don't want to wait that long. Besides, once it is done, I think they will realize they have nothing to gain by remaining against it."

Callie still felt reluctant to rush into the marriage as quickly as Matthew wanted, though she had no idea why she should be reluctant at all. She had come to Pine Fork for the sole purpose of marrying Matthew Tucker, and everything was exactly the way she had been promised it would be. So why was she suddenly eager to put off the wedding date? A brief image of an arrogant smile beneath a pair of uncanny blue eyes flashed before her, but she refused to pay any attention to it.

"But Matthew, that's only ten days away. Will the dressmaker have time to finish my dress by then?"

"Nadine? Sure. Just tell her to charge me twice whatever the gown is worth and she'll work day and night on it if she has to." He laughed when he thought about that.

"But what about your daughters? Won't they need new dresses too?"

"They've already got new dresses. Lucille saw to that."

"Well, then, what about the guests? Will ten days be sufficient time to get the invitations out?"

Matthew's smile widened. "There are only to be a few friends and I already have those invitations ready to go. All I have to do is put the time and date on them and then have them delivered."

"My, you certainly are prepared," Callie mused, studying his pleased smile and finding that the sincerity of his smile pleased her too. Unable to make herself disappoint such a kind man who was clearly eager to have their marriage ceremony that next weekend, she finally agreed. *After all,* she reasoned with herself, she fully intended to marry him. She had already given her promise, and did not see how delaying the ceremony would serve any real purpose. "I guess if next weekend is all right with the reverend, then it is all right with me."

"Wonderful. I'll have Harry take you into town tomorrow. And if Reverend Cross agrees to next Saturday afternoon, I'll have the invitations ready to be delivered before I go to sleep tomorrow night."

Callie felt strangely apprehensive. She knew that as soon as those wedding invitations were out, there would be no turning back. But then again, why should she suddenly want to turn back?

Chapter Five

The trip into Pine Fork the following morning went well. Nadine Leigh had just enough satin, silk, and imported lace in stock to assure her the bridal gown could be started immediately and would be ready in plenty of time for the ceremony. And the mercantile Matthew used had a large supply of white silk ribbon and pressed bows for the decorations, as well as everything else Lucille had insisted she and Matthew's foreman, Harry Vicke, purchase before their return.

The reverend's house had been just as easy to locate as Matthew had said it would be, and Reverend Cross seemed sincerely pleased to meet her. After he had a brief word with his wife, he was able to verify that he had no plans for the afternoon in question, and promised to come by a day or two earlier to discuss what sort of ceremony they wanted and exactly when he should plan to arrive.

Everything about the shopping trip went smoothly, and by mid-afternoon, Callie and Harry were on their way back to the Circle T, the buggy full of the purchases she'd made plus a few items he had acquired while they were in town. There was hardly room left for the two of them to sit.

At some point during the day, Callie had managed finally to push her earlier misgivings aside, and had begun to look forward to the wedding. She smiled when she thought of the design Mrs. Leigh had helped her select for her wedding gown. It was going to be the most beautiful

72

dress she'd ever seen.

"You look happy," Harry pointed out, joining her in her pleased smile.

"I guess I am," she said, a little surprised to realize just how happy she did feel. She felt as light as a feather inside. She'd never been on such a shopping spree, never had the opportunity to buy so many truly beautiful things: dresses, silk vested shoes, stockings, frilly undergarments, lace handkerchiefs — anything that struck her fancy.

She had even purchased a pale blue peignoir made of pure pongee silk to wear when lounging about her bedroom, and a porcelain hair-grooming set with a matching mirror to sit upon her dresser — all at the constant encouragement of Harry, who had been told her every whim was to be met. And to think, such a life was hers forever, just for agreeing to marry a kind and generous man like Matthew Tucker. Suddenly all those years of forced servitude at the hands of her step-aunt seemed to fade into non-existence. She *was* happy. Very happy.

"I'm so glad to see such a smile on your pretty face. I was also glad to see the old sparkle back in Matt's eyes. He looked like a love-struck school boy this morning when he called me into his room to tell me everywhere he wanted to be sure you went. And he threatened to have my hide stretched out for the buzzards if I let any harm come to you." Harry chuckled as he reached up and lifted his battered work hat a few inches in order to give his balding head a quick scratch.

Though Harry did not look to be but forty years old, his skin was weathered and sunbrowned, and he had already lost most of his hair as well as two of his side teeth. Still, his smile was sincere enough and his eyes caring enough, he was not all that unpleasant to look at.

"Yessiree, you have sure put the color back in Matt's cheeks," he added just before reaching up to give his head another scratch.

"I'm glad. I'll admit I was a little worried to discover he

73

had become so ill. But he's already getting better. Did you know he came downstairs to have supper with us last night?" Callie's smile broadened. The girls had been so surprised and so pleased at their father's presence they had temporarily forgotten to display their aggressions toward her, and Callie had been able to spend the entire evening meal in relative peace. Only after Matthew had ordered the girls up to bed with plans to be alone with Callie for a while had Janice's grim scowl returned to her pretty face.

"Sure did. I heard all about his trip downstairs. Stretch told me how he and Ed had been asked to help him get down, and then later, back up the stairs. I was pleased to hear it. It's been weeks since he's felt like coming downstairs. Yessiree, you are sure good medicine for old Matt."

Callie leaned back in her seat, still smiling while she looked at Harry. Earlier their conversation had been stilted, centering mainly on the fact that the area had had an abnormally dry spring and how badly rain was needed, which accounted for all the dust; but at some point along the way Harry had begun to feel more comfortable around her and slowly relaxed his guard. He'd begun to talk about things more personal in nature until now, Callie felt she'd made a new friend.

In fact, she'd made several new friends since her arrival two short days ago. Some—like Lucille, Ruby, Stretch, Ed, and Harry—were in Matthew's employ; while others, like Nadine Leigh and Mr. Akard, were proprietors of local businesses. Plus there was young David Gordy, who had come running out of the livery to greet her when he'd noticed their arrival in town. It felt good to have so many new friends. She'd rarely had the opportunity to get out and meet new people in New York, and as a result her friendships had been few.

Callie's heart felt lighter still when she closed her eyes and remembered how pleased Matthew seemed to be with her. She was so delighted with Matthew and his easy acceptance of her, she felt absolutely certain nothing could ever take her smile away—not even another cutting remark from Janice. She was just too happy. But that was before she reopened her eyes and noticed a distant rider approaching from the opposite direction.

Even before she was able to make out the rider's face, she could tell by the cocky angle of his scoop-brimmed hat and by the confident manner he sat in his saddle, expertly blending his own movements against those of the horse's, that the rider had to be Wade Barlow. The width of his shoulders and the shape of his lean, well-muscled legs confirmed her suspicion.

She felt her insides knot apprehensively, and did not miss the way Harry's shoulders slowly stiffened when the two grew closer, as if he wanted to prepare himself for the worst. That's when she noticed how narrow the bridge was they both approached at about equal speeds from opposite sides. Her heart froze when she realized one of them would have to give way to the other. If neither did, they would end up face to face on the bridge, and one of them would then be forced to back up. She felt her hands tightened into fists in the soft folds of her dark blue skirt.

To her surprise, Wade pulled his horse to a stop several yards short of the narrow wooden bridge, and he watched while the buggy slowly bumped across the weatherworn planks. She did not notice she had drawn in her breath and held it until after they had completed their crossing, and he suddenly reached up to push his hat back and salute in much the same manner he had the last time she had seen him.

When she tried to gasp at the arrogant way he then raised one eyebrow and nodded at her, while at the same time allowing his gaze to boldly dip down to take in her most feminine features, she discovered her lungs already too full to accommodate the sharp intake of air—and she nearly choked. Aware he had taken adverse pleasure in her startled reaction, she jerked her gaze away from him and struggled to regain her composure while she stared at the dusty road ahead.

Gritting her teeth, she vowed to ignore him; but when

the buggy had finally passed by him, she could not help but toss a quick glance in his direction, and was infuriated by the way he continued to stare at her, slowly shaking his head, as if condemning her for something.

Furious with herself for having shown so little restraint, she snapped her gaze forward again and stared determinedly off into the distance. Her heart hammered so hard, she felt her blood pounding all the way to her fingertips. Her scalp prickled beneath the same small hat she had worn the day of her arrival, much the way it had the first time she met him.

Long after he had been left behind, she felt his gaze still boring into her. She dared not look back again for fear he might offer her another of his arrogant salutes. She refused to give him the satisfaction of any further notice, and tried her best to push his brazen image out of her mind, but found that as impossible to do as it was to still her pounding heart.

Even after they topped the next hill and were at last well out of sight, she could still clearly visualize him, sitting astride his tall, tan-colored horse, boldly staring at her with a solemn, almost angry expression. She also envisioned the faded blue shirt clinging to the breadth of his chest and shoulders, with the sleeves rolled up and the top two collar buttons left undone. Though she'd caught only a glimpse of him, she was embarrassed to realize she had also noticed the way his trousers, which had looked to be made of dark blue duck, had molded to his taut, sinewy thighs—thighs that pressed against and held the gelding in command. This time he had not worn a handgun, though she had noticed a rifle jutting out of the scabbard attached to his saddle.

Frustrated by the images she could not put aside and appalled by the effect his probing gaze had had on her, she pressed her eyes closed and questioned her reaction. Why did she have to find the man so disturbingly attractive? And why had he looked at her as if she disgusted him? Was she so unattractive?

"I hear he was the one who brought you out to the ranch Tuesday," Harry said, finally breaking into her thoughts.

"Y-yes, he was," she admitted, and wondered why she suddenly felt guilty. She had merely ridden with the man. It was not as if she had committed any crime. Then she realized the guilty feelings stemmed from the way her body had just reacted to him — a man whose behavior she could barely tolerate — and there she was already betrothed to someone else!

"Wade Barlow. I just can't imagine it," Harry said with a peculiar expression, then fell into meditative silence for the rest of the trip.

Because the next several days went by in a whirl of activity while plans were made for the rapidly approaching wedding, Callie had little opportunity to think more about Wade Barlow or why he'd looked at her with such open contempt. There seemed to be too much to get done in too little time, even though Lucille and Ruby were both very eager to help and worked long, hard hours getting everything ready.

As expected, Matthew's daughters refused to participate in the planning, but Callie noticed they did seem to keep a careful ear turned to any conversation concerning the upcoming weekend and a grim eye on the many preparations being made. She could tell Amy dearly wanted to help in some way, but was afraid to go against her sister's wishes just yet. On occasion Callie found the younger girl lingering about in the kitchen watching wistfully while the many foods were prepared and the elaborate decorations made.

As promised, Reverend Cross and his wife rode out to the ranch early Wednesday morning, three days before the wedding and met with both Callie and Matthew in Matthew's bedroom. Though Matthew now felt well enough to sit in a chair much of the day, and had even begun catching up on some of the recently neglected ledger work at the desk in his room, he only ventured downstairs for the evening meals. He told the reverend that was because he wanted to save most of his strength for the big day.

After a brief discussion, it was decided the ceremony would be traditional. In absence of a father, Harry Vicke had gladly agreed to give the bride away; and because Callie really knew of no women even close to her own age and both Janice and Amy had refused to participate, Nadine Leigh was chosen to be Callie's matron of honor. Dr. Lowell Edison, whom Callie had yet to meet but who was due for a visit that very afternoon, was selected to be the best man.

Sixteen invitations had been sent out and, as of Wednesday, there were already twenty-seven confirmed guests planning to attend, few of whom Callie had met but *all* of whom she'd heard about in great detail. There were also to be eighteen workhands present to watch Matthew get married. She felt if odd to discover none of the intended guests would be relatives. Weddings were usually affairs to bring families together, even over great distances. If she'd had any family other than the one she'd just escaped from, she'd have wanted to invite them. She wondered then if Matthew had any other family, and felt the odds must be he did not.

Later that afternoon, Dr. Edison finally arrived and Callie was able to actually meet the man Matthew claimed was his dearest and most trusted friend. Lowell was a fairly tall man, slender in build, with stark white hair and friendly gray-blue eyes. He seemed truly delighted to meet Callie, and praised her for the wondrous change in Matthew's health. She was asked to join them for a while, and she listened with interest to the many stories they had to tell about each other. It was not until the doctor reached for his leather medical bag and announced it was time to give Matthew an examination that she was asked to leave.

When the doctor returned downstairs, he was all smiles and reassured her Matthew was indeed doing much better.

It pleased Callie to hear it, and she thanked him for having come while she walked with him to the front door.

"We look forward to your participation in the wedding Saturday," she said as she opened the front door for him.

The doctor's smile changed from polite to sincere. "And I want you to know how pleased I am to be a part of the wedding. I'll admit, I was a little skeptical of Matthew's plan to advertise for a wife, and I even tried to discourage him, but now that I've met you, all my misgivings have been put aside. He's lucky to have found someone like you. I'm usually a very good judge of character, and I sense there is honest good in you. I have a feeling you won't betray him—for *any* reason."

"Thank you," Callie answered, wondering why that comment made her feel uncomfortable. Did he somehow sense her reluctance, or had Matthew's first wife betrayed him in some way? It was the first time she'd really wondered what Matthew's first wife had been like. She considered asking the doctor about Beth Tucker, but decided against it while she watched him fit his stiff-crowned hat back onto his head, then stroll out to where he'd left his carriage. She waited until he had placed his medical bag on the floor inside before offering him a final goodbye and reclosing the door.

Still feeling oddly uncomfortable over the doctor's parting comments, she glanced through the narrow window beside the door, and was further dismayed to discover his warm, friendly smile suddenly gone. On the doctor's face now was a look of true concern. Was there something he had purposely not told her? Worried that it had something to do with Matthew, she hurried upstairs to his room to see for herself.

When Callie re-entered the bedroom and discovered there was no matching look of concern on Matthew's face, she quickly decided the doctor's worried expression must have been because of another patient, or because of some personal problem. Matthew could not have looked more contented while he sat in his favorite wing-backed chair staring through the open window at the surrounding area bathed in bright sunlight. Matthew loved looking out upon the small empire he had built.

"Has Lowell left?" he asked, turning to look at her for only a moment before returning his gaze to the view beyond.

"Yes," she answered, and came forward to gaze out the window with him. From Matthew's window the barn and several of the other outbuildings could be seen in the foreground, while fenced cattle pastures and narrow patches of parklike woodlands filled up the distance. As far as the eye could see lay a part of Matthew's ranch.

After a moment of silence, Matthew looked at her again. "I'm very proud of the Circle T."

"As well you should be," she agreed. "It's lovely."

"I'm glad you think so. I want you to be happy here. I want you to be as proud of this place as I am. I was very young when I started the Circle T. All I had to start out with was a small two-room house, forty acres of land, and a couple dozen head of cattle. I worked hard to make this place what it is."

"I can imagine how hard you had to work. And I want you to know, I already am happy. I love this place. Also, I feel like I'm already starting to make a little headway with the girls. Janice is becoming less caustic with some of her remarks, and I think Amy wishes she could find some way not to have to agree with everything Janice has to say about me."

"Good. I so want you three to get along. It is very important to me that you do." Suddenly his expression was solemn. "They are good girls. It's just that they feel like I'm trying to replace their mother and it makes them angry, makes them feel threatened in some way. In time they will come to understand. And when they do, they'll grow to fully accept you and they will learn to depend on you as I have."

Callie felt those were wonderful compliments, and that night, while they were at the table together, she tried her best to make the girls begin to like her. But judging by the less than enthusiastic responses from both of them, she knew it would be awhile yet before they started to adjust. Far more time was needed. She would have to continue to be very patient with them both, which would not be easy. But in the end, she knew all the effort she must make in order to eventually win them over would be well worth it.

Callie awoke late on her wedding day. It was after nine o'clock. Because she had again suffered severe doubts the evening before, enough to have kept her awake well into the early hours of the morning, she was still very sleepy when she tossed back her covers and climbed out of bed.

Janice and Amy had been on particularly bad behavior the evening before, making her wonder for the first time if they would *ever* truly come to accept her. Suddenly it seemed there was no progress possible. But that had not been the only thing to cause her sudden flood of doubts. There was something else nagging at her, making her wish she had not promised to marry Matthew so soon after her arrival. But she was unable to put her finger on what it was because she could not find any true reason not to become Matthew's wife.

She had never held any romantic notions of one day falling in love, and it had suited her just fine to agree to marry for other reasons. It had seemed enough that Matthew was so likable and extremely kindhearted. They had known each other barely over a week and had already established a warm and caring friendship. Why should she suffer any last-minute doubts?

Still, the doubts were there, and she discovered she was not quite as eager to slip into her beautiful wedding gown as she had expected to be. But she had already promised Matthew they would indeed be married that day, and the guests were soon to arrive. There would be no going back on her word.

All too soon, Nadine Leigh appeared at her door to help her first with her hair and then into her gown as she had promised she would. By mid-afternoon, they stood side by side at the top of the stairs, nervously awaiting the signal to come down.

Stretch Henderson, who Matthew considered as much a trusted friend as a hardworking ranch hand, stood outside the main salon door waiting to relay the signal when the time came for the ceremony to begin. Glancing nervously inside at all the people, he fidgeted with his collar while keeping a keen eye on the reverend, who was supposed to nod when everything was ready.

When the signal came, Stretch turned to Callie and grinned that slow, easy grin of his. Without making a sound, he mouthed "It's time."

Callie's heart beat erratically while she and Nadine carefully gathered the deep folds of her gown and made their way down the stairs, being careful not to step on the hem or muss the bridal veil in any way. While Nadine quickly arranged the folds of Callie's satin skirts just so, Harry came through the doorway looking almost comical dressed in a stiff hat and an undersized black frock coat. He appeared to have very little room to move about, and stood rigid as a board while he waited to link his arm with hers.

"You look very handsome," Callie said with a reassuring smile just before she turned to face the doorway and allowed him to take her arm and tuck in gently around his. "Very handsome indeed."

Harry seemed pleased to hear it, but had no time to comment before the music suddenly began. He scowled. They had not given the second nod to indicate they were ready.

Callie glanced down at her empty hand just as Nadine hurriedly snatched the bridal bouquet off the small table beside them and thrust it at her. Nadine then quickly took up her own smaller bouquet and started immediately down the narrow aisle formed between the several rows of folding chairs. Nadine cast a quick frown over her shoulder, clearly as frustrated as Harry was with the reverend's wife for having begun the music before they were ready.

Callie had to smile at Nadine's gallant recovery, for the woman walked primly down the aisle and into position, then turned to face them with an expression of blissful serenity. Suddenly the music changed, each note became more prominent. Everyone turned in their chairs to watch Harry, with Callie upon his arm, while the two walked slowly down the aisle.

To Callie it felt as if there were more than the forty-eight sets of eyes upon her when she was handed over to Matthew, who looked very handsome in his three-buttoned cutaway coat. She had never been the center of attention before, and had a hard time concentrating on exactly what it was the reverend had to say. But she managed to speak the words "I do" at the appropriate moment, as did Matthew.

Soon the proper vows had been made and it was time for Matthew to kiss his new bride, which turned out to be but a mild peck on the cheek near the corner of her mouth.

Despite the obvious strain it put on him, Matthew stayed by Callie's side for the next hour while the many guests and workhands clamored around them, extending their congratulations and wishing them well. But then, after most of them had found their way into the dining room for refreshments and the two girls had quickly disappeared upstairs, Matthew suddenly excused himself and retired to the library with one of his friends, an attorney who Callie had just met. She had already forgotten his name.

Callie thought it was a little odd, but did not begin to really worry until the attorney came out in search of Lowell Edison. Then without a word to anyone, the two returned to the library, carefully closing the door behind them. Callie worried that Matthew had overtaxed his strength, which was why he had summoned the doctor.

She wanted to go to him and find out; but she knew, if he'd wanted her to be with him, he'd have sent for her. Yet he had not. It was just like Matthew to want to cast no shadows on her wedding day. Though eager to know if he'd endangered his health, she decided to wait until he either came out or finally sent for her.

It was well over an hour before the three emerged from the library, and Callie noticed then Matthew's color was not good. She quickly worked her way across the crowded room to speak with him. She tried to encourage him to go upstairs and rest, but he would not hear of it. He wanted to be with his friends and his new bride.

That evening, after the last guest finally left, Callie insisted Matthew go straight to bed, and helped Lucille get him upstairs and into his room. He continued to complain that he was not tired and wanted to stay up, but neither woman would listen to him. Finally, he resigned himself to obeying their orders.

"I can see I'll have little authority around here," he muttered good-naturedly as he sat down on his bed, his arms crossed firmly in front of his chest. "Not with the two of you taking sides against me."

"When your health's better, you can have all the authority you want, but for now you'll do what we say," Callie told him with a firm nod of her head.

"What have I gotten myself into?" he asked, smiling weakly while Lucille helped him into his night clothing, carefully keeping her eyes diverted. "I've gone and married myself a tyrant."

Lucille chuckled, but offered no comment.

"Tyrant am I?" Callie placed her hands on her hips, but was unable to sound too severe. "You'll have far worse things to say about me if you don't do what I tell you. Now get into that bed and get some rest!"

"But this is my wedding night. Don't I at least get a good-night kiss?"

Pursing her lips, Callie bent forward and placed a gentle kiss on his forehead. It was then she realized he had started to perspire. She reached out to feel his face with her palm and it felt clammy. He was also breathing a little too rapidly to suit her.

"Did you let the doctor look at you this afternoon?" She asked, suddenly very worried.

"Everyone was looking at me this afternoon. After all, it was *my* wedding."

Callie let out an exasperated breath. "You know what I mean."

"Will you quit worrying about me? I'm fine. Just a little tired is all."

"Well, at least he finally admits it," Lucille said, trying to sound unconcerned when her face was drawn into deep lines. "Maybe if we get on out of here now, he'll have enough sense to get himself some rest."

Callie agreed and left the room with Lucille, but no sooner had they closed the door than they heard him burst into a hard fit of rasping coughs. Worried, Callie turned to go back inside, but Lucille reached out to stop her. "He'd prefer you didn't."

"But why?"

"He's a man. He's got a man's pride. I don't think he'd want you to see him like that. Those coughing spells always leave him very weak and make him feel so help-less."

"But he may need my help," Callie reasoned.

"I'll go help him. Through the years, I've seen him at his worst and he knows it. You go on to bed."

Callie opened her mouth to offer further protest, but Lucille did not stay to hear it. Instead, the woman turned and slipped quietly back into Matthew's room, quickly closing the door behind her. The next sound Callie heard was the gentle click of the lock, clearly meant to keep her out.

Chapter Six

When Callie awoke the next morning, the doctor was already there. Harry had been sent to get him in the early hours before dawn, and now that the doctor was inside, he stood pacing the hallway outside Matthew's room.

"What happened?" Callie demanded to know, hurrying toward him. She could tell by the solemn expression on Harry's unshaven face something was very wrong.

"Matt had another hard night. I guess all the excitement from yesterday was a little too much for him. Lucille got worried and wanted the doc to see him," Harry explained. "I'm just waiting around to see what the doc has to say. He's been in there an awful long time."

Callie felt her heart thump with sudden concern. Matthew was worse. Why hadn't Lucille come to tell her? But she knew the answer to that. Matthew would not have wanted her to. "I'll step inside and see what I can find out."

"Think you should?" Harry asked while he ran his hand over the thin strands of hair that still grew along the top of his head, causing much of it to stand straight out.

"I'm his wife," Callie stated firmly. "I have every right to be in there." Still, she had her doubts. Remembering Lucille's words from the evening before, she knew the woman could be right. Matthew might not want her in there. But if he was that sick, she wanted to be with him. He would have to be made to understand that.

Slowly, she turned the door handle to let herself into his room. Her stomach twisted into a tight, painful coil. Having no way to know just how serious Matthew's illness was, she deeply feared what she might discover once inside. But to her relief, Matthew was sitting up in bed, propped with pillows, and smiled at her when she entered.

"There's my lovely bride now," he said and held out a hand to her. Callie noticed how weak his grip was when he tried to clasp her hand between both of his.

"Harry told me how he had to go into town to get the doctor earlier. Are you all right?" she asked, studying the way part of his hair lay plastered against his forehead in flat curls. His nightshirt clung to him with the dampness of yet more perspiration.

"I am now that you are here," he answered reassuringly.

But Callie had her doubts. He looked as if it was a struggle just to focus on her. "You seem pale."

"I had a rough night," he admitted. "But Lowell's already given me what I need and I'm much better."

Callie turned to look at the doctor, and noticed how his eyes avoided her while he began to put his things away into his medical bag. Something was wrong. Something was very wrong.

"Where's Lucille?"

"Went downstairs to get a fresh pitcher of water," Lowell answered, but without bothering to look up. "She'll be right back."

Callie felt Matthew's already weak grip grow slowly weaker, until her hand remained within his grasp only because she held it there. "Matthew, are you sure you are all right? Is there something I can do for you?"

"No, nothing. I'm tired is all. And you'll be happy to know that the doctor there is in complete agreement with you and Lucille. He says I need rest, so I guess I'll have no choice but to stay in this bed for a few days. But don't let that worry you. I'll be up and around again in no time."

Callie noticed the way Matthew had to break his speech in order to snatch quick breaths of air, and how much of an effort taking those breaths seemed to be. Still, he had no intention of admitting anything was really wrong. Callie then glanced at the doctor again, and wondered if Lowell might somehow be persuaded to tell her the truth. She knew he wouldn't say anything in front of Matthew — but perhaps if she could find a way to be alone with him . . .

Smiling at her husband, she said, "Well, since there's nothing to be concerned about here, I'll leave you to your rest and go downstairs to see what there is for breakfast. Doctor, would you care to join me for breakfast?"

"No," Lowell answered a little too quickly. Then he added, more calmly, "No, thank you. Just as soon as I get all my things put away, I'll have to be on my way. There are other patients I must see."

"But you have to eat," she reminded him.

"I'll have something waiting for me when I get back," he explained. "My housekeeper will have prepared my breakfast and placed it on the stove to keep warm before leaving for church. She always does."

"Maybe next time, then," she said with a polite smile, aware she could not persuade him. Then she turned back to Matthew. "I'll be up later to check on you." Before leaving, she leaned over and pressed a gentle kiss to his forehead. He had a fever.

More determined than ever to have a word with the doctor before he left, Callie did not go to the kitchen to see about breakfast. Instead she waited outside beside his buggy. Soon the door opened, and Lowell stepped outside, his face twisted, deep with worry. But when he glanced up and noticed Callie, he quickly changed his expression to one of curious expectation.

"Lovely morning," he commented while he quickly placed his medical bag into the buggy in preparation to leave. "The sun had not yet come up when I first arrived, but I can see now it will be another beautiful day. But then again, it would be nice if we could have a little rain. It's been several weeks since we've had any to speak of. The farmers are already having to haul water in for their crops. It's starting to effect the ranchers too."

Callie had no intention of discussing the weather or the current plight of the local farmers, and finally had to interrupt his rambling conversation. "Lowell, please, I want to know what is wrong with Matthew and just how serious it is."

"I expected as much," he said, and exhaled sharply while he reached out a hand to gently massage her shoulder as if preparing it for some great weight.

"I'm his wife now," she reminded him needlessly. "I think I have a right to know what is wrong with my husband."

"Matthew should be the one to tell you," Lowell said, and looked away, out across the pastures and beyond.

Callie felt he wanted to tell her, but needed more encouragement. "Matthew doesn't want to worry me. He doesn't understand how I'll worry far more not knowing. And if you don't tell me, what can I do but think the worst?"

Lowell paused, lost in his thoughts for a moment. Slowly his gaze came back to meet hers. "It is the worst."

Callie felt a sharp pain in her chest. "What is the worst?"

When he looked away from her again, his face taut with sudden tension, she knew.

"Is Matthew dying?"

"Callie, I really wish you would have this conversation with Matthew. He has asked me not to tell you what is wrong with him and I'd rather not break that promise."

"But he is dying, isn't he?"

Lowell pressed his eyes closed in an effort to hide his pain and she knew the answer. Suddenly her stomach felt as if it was made of lead.

"How long? How long does he have?"

"Callie, please, let Matthew be the one to tell you."

"But what if he won't? What if he refuses to discuss it with me?"

"He'll tell you — in time. We've already discussed the fact that you will have to know. Just give him the time he needs to get up the courage. I've already said more than I should"

The doctor then climbed into his buggy and drove away. Callie stood with her arms hanging limp at her side, staring after him. Her whole body felt suddenly weak and she prayed that she had misunderstood. Matthew dying? It just couldn't be.

* * *

Later that day, Matthew finally sent for Callie, and when she came to him then, he admitted that in a matter of a very few months, she would be a widow.

Though Callie had had hours to prepare herself for such news, the words still came as quite a shock. She knelt on the floor beside his chair and gazed up at him. Gently, she rested her arms across his knees.

"How long have you known you were dying?" she asked. Bravely, she fought the tears burning at the backs of her eyes and the pain that tore at her heart. It did not seem fair to have finally found someone who actually cared about her, someone who wanted to take care of her, someone she could help take care of in return, only to learn he was going to be taken away in a matter of months. And it did not seem fair that a man like Matthew had to die at the age of forty-seven when so many men with far less to offer the world lived well into their seventies and eighties.

"I've known since February." His voice remained calm, almost too calm for a man discussing his own death. It caused chills to form along Callie's neck and shoulders.

"Since before you advertised in the newspaper for a wife?"

"That's the main reason I placed the advertisement," he admitted. "I want to be honest with you about this. The reason I advertised for a wife is because I wanted to make sure my children would be cared for once I'm gone. My only brother was killed eighteen years ago. He never married. I have no family left. There is no one to take care of my girls. I hated to think they might have to leave here in order to be put into someone else's care, and the land sold in order to pay for their raising. The Circle T is the only home my girls have ever known. I couldn't bear to think they might lose it."

"So you advertised for a wife. Why didn't you just marry one of the local ladies?"

"There are no unmarried women around here that I trust, except for maybe Nadine Leigh, but she's not the right type to leave the Circle T with. And besides, I think she has her cap set for Ed Grant, one of my workmen. And he seems rather fond of her too. No, I wanted to find someone young, someone with a lot of spunk. Enough spunk to come to Texas in order to start a new life. Someone who would fight to keep the Circle T going. Someone like you." His gaze searched hers. "It won't be easy. There are those who would like to get their hands on this place."

"But why didn't you tell me sooner?"

"I know I should have, and there were a couple of times I did come close to admitting the truth to you, but I just couldn't chance it. I wanted you to come here, see the Circle T for yourself. Meet my daughters. I knew you would better understand why I did what I did once you were here. I felt sure, once you saw what a beautiful place this is and once you came to understand why it is so important to me my daughters not lose it all, you would be more willing to be a part of it."

Callie felt numb. "But your daughters have not even accepted me yet."

"It doesn't matter. You have accepted them. I've seen that in the way you've acted toward them, in the patience you've shown them. And for now, that's plenty. I am already having a new will drawn up. In fact Wilson should have it ready for my signature any day. We discussed it at some length right after the wedding. Lowell was present to hear what all I wanted it to say, just in case the document was not made ready in time. In the new will, you are to be the girls' legal guardian, and in return you will reap many benefits. The Circle T will be yours to run for as long as you continue to act as a responsible mother to my children, but the land itself will never really be yours. I hope you can understand why."

He paused a moment, then continued. "You can remarry in time, and it will in no way alter the provisions of the will. As long as you are willing to take care of Jana and Amy, the Circle T will be your home. But upon your death, because the land was never really yours, it cannot be passed on to your husband or even your children. Instead it will fall into the hands of Jana and Amy, unless they are not yet of age, in which case Wilson Burns himself will become their legal guardian. Oh, and you may as well know the place cannot be sold without both his and the girls' signatures."

Matthew's expression became wistfully sad when he lifted his gaze from hers and stared out the window at his land. "The Circle T is all I have to leave my children. And I want to be sure it is not taken away from them." His gaze returned to meet with hers. "Please, Callie, see to it that no one takes it away from them. Please. Promise me you won't turn your back on the Circle T or, more importantly, my daughters after I'm gone. Even if something should go wrong and it becomes in their best interest to sell the place, don't ever turn your back on Jana and Amy. Promise me."

Callie did not hesitate, for in her heart she had already made the commitment. "I promise, Matthew. I promise to take good care of your two daughters, and I will do everything I possibly can to keep this place a home for them."

"And in return, you will have complete authority over the workings of the ranch. I promise you the ranch is solvent. As long as you don't go making foolish business decisions, you will never have to worry about money. Nor will the girls."

"But I don't know anything about running a ranch."

"I know and I had hoped you would have more time to learn about such things before . . . well, before I die. But Lowell has told me not to hope for more than a few months, when before he thought I might still have a year. In fact, if I have another spell like I did last night, I could only have a few weeks left, even less."

Callie gasped at the resulting pain. "Weeks?"

"But I'm going to do all I can to last out the months. And I'll have Harry start teaching you what you'll want to know to be able to take over this place once I'm gone. First, you will need to get started on those riding lessons I mentioned to you once before. And it wouldn't hurt to learn how to shoot both a rifle and a handgun. Harry can show you that too. Start this afternoon. Also, I'll want to go over the ledgers with you and explain how I keep my books."

Callie felt a moment of relief at the mention of Harry's name. She hoped to pass some of that on to Matthew. "As long as Harry is here with me, I think I can manage just fine."

"That's just it. Harry has recently bought a place of his own several miles from here. He had already made plans to leave this spring when I first got sick, but then decided to stick with me until I got better. He doesn't know I'm dying. Only Lucille knows. And of course my lawyer, Wilson Burns—and Lowell."

"Then you think Harry will leave once you . . ." Callie paused, unable to finish her statement.

"Once I'm gone?" Matthew finished it for her. His face softened with compassion. He was taking his death far better than she was, but then he'd had more time to come to terms with it. "I don't know. Harry's been eager to get his own place started, and I hate how he's had to delay doing that as long as he already has. It's always been his dream to have a place of his own. And when I die, he'll discover I've rewarded his willingness to stay on as long as he has with a hundred head of cattle, which might make him that much more eager to get his own spread started. I really do hate to make him put that off any longer, but in a letter with the will, I do ask him to stay on at least a couple of weeks after I'm gone to help you find another foreman, someone you can trust. And knowing Harry, he will comply."

"But what about Stretch? He's been with you for years. Why can't he take over the foreman's job?"

"Stretch is a good workhand, and a loyal friend, but he doesn't handle responsibility well. He'll do what he's told and do it to the best of his ability, but when it comes to making his own decisions, he balks. Always has. And none of the other men have the experience."

Callie drew her lower lip between her teeth and worried with it while she thought about the situation further. "Well, then, since it is clear I'll have to have a new foreman, why don't we go ahead and look for one now? While you are still here to help me."

"I don't want anyone else to know I'm dying," he stated firmly. "And if I suddenly decide to let Harry leave, though he has been quite adamant about staying on until I'm better, someone might think it odd. No,

93

I want things to stay exactly like they are until after my death."

"But won't Harry think it a little odd that I want to learn so much about the working of this ranch?"

"Not if you make it seem like natural curiosity," Matthew suggested. "I've already told him I'd like for you to learn to ride a horse. While he is teaching you that, you can begin to ask other questions. Learn the lay of the land. Learn which of the men does what around here. Meanwhile, I'll teach you about the business end of it at night, after the girls have gone to bed."

Suddenly it became too much for Callie to bear, and the tears which had threatened her eyes spilled hot shimmering trails down her pale cheeks. "But what if I can't do I? What if I don't have what it takes to run this place?"

"Oh, you've got what it takes, all right," he said with a confident smile. Tears had filled his own eyes, and his hand trembled when he gently stroked her hair. "I knew that when you agreed to come to a place you'd never been, to marry a man you didn't even know in order to make a better life for yourself. And it makes dying a whole lot easier just knowing my daughters will have you to look after them once I'm gone."

That was all Callie could take. Her heart could only bear so much pain at one time. Unable to hold back the emotions any longer, she bent her head into his lap and wept bitterly while he continued to gently stroke her hair.

Matthew Tucker died two days later.

Though the rest had seemed to help him and he had appeared to be getting better — so much so he had stayed awake going over the books with Callie until well after midnight the evening before — Matthew passed away in his sleep on June 21, 1870, sometime during the early hours before dawn.

When Callie found him, he lay on his back, a bloodied handkerchief clutched in his hand and a trace of blood across his lips. There was no expression of pain or even inkling of remorse on his face, just peaceful repose, as if he held no regrets for having to die so soon.

Looking at him lying there with his eyes partially closed, his sight distant, as if he was gazing into the great beyond — and at the same time knowing he would never again gaze at her, never again reach out to her and take her hand in his to gently comfort her — Callie found her resulting pain overwhelming. She became a small girl again, unable to cope with what she had found as she sank to the floor beside his bed and wept bitterly.

"Not yet, Matthew. Please not yet." She buried her face into the sheets at his side and wished the sudden surge of pain would go away. It was too much for her to bear.

That was how Lucille found her when she entered the room moments later — kneeling at Matthew's bedside, weeping uncontrollably, clutching at the bedsheets. Lucille considered going to her and putting a supportive arm around her, knowing that would be what Matthew would want her to do; but she found that all she could do was join her in her tears, and slowly knelt down beside her. Callie's hand found Lucille's, and together they wept at Matthew's bedside until they could weep no more.

Matthew Tucker would be sorely missed.

The funeral was held two days later. Many of the same people who had come to see them married just days earlier returned to pay their last respects and offered their sympathies to Callie and Matthew's two daughters.

It was a bleak time for Callie, and for a while she was unable to console herself, much less Matthew's daughters. She mourned her husband's death bitterly for, other than her own father, Matthew had been the only man ever to show her any true compassion. And he had given freely of that compassion even though he knew he was a dying man.

Not until the will was read that following weekend, and Callie heard the encouraging comments Matthew had written to her, was she able to regain the strength and the courage she needed to see them all through the troubled times ahead. It touched her heart to know that, although he had been dying and had every right to be wrapped up in self-pity, he had had the compassion to realize how his death would affect them all. He had worded the letter accompanying his will to encourage them to become a family and work together as a unit, for the good of his dreams — for the good of their own dreams.

In the letter, he asked that they not mourn his death, for that was not what he wanted. He agreed they should miss him, because such was natural, and asked that they remember him fondly, but said he did not want anyone to mourn for him because he was now at peace and finally without pain. He also explained how much he hated having to leave them, and hoped they would try to see his dreams through. He also explained how his death could not be helped. He wanted to be especially certain his daughters understood how his dying had not been by choice, and asked them not to be angry with him for having left them. He then explained his reasons for bringing Callie into the family, and asked that they give her a chance to prove herself.

The will itself was pretty much what he had told Callie it would be. Harry was to get his one hundred head of cattle, and each of his employees was rewarded with generous monetary sums. Even Ruby was not forgotten, though the young girl had not worked for him much more than a month.

It was painfully hard to hear the parting words Matthew had for each person, and when his final statement was to wish them all the best, there was not a dry eye in the room. Even Harry had to turn away and face the wall to hide the tears that streamed down his weathered cheeks.

As expected, Harry agreed to stay on for as long as he was needed, and Callie quickly promised to start looking for a new foreman to replace him right away. Because she had not had the time to learn as much as Matthew had hoped she would before his death, she was at a loss as to how she should go about looking for a new foreman. Harry suggested she put up notices in a few of the neighboring towns, and she got busy preparing those notices.

Callie soon learned that keeping busy helped take the edge off her grief, but never did it dull the pain entirely.

Though she had only known Matthew through his letters a matter of a few months, and had known him personally barely two weeks, she missed him dreadfully. She could well imagine how the girls missed him, and she did everything possible to console them whenever their grief became too much for them.

To her relief, and somewhat to her surprise, Janice's attitude changed drastically after Matthew's letter and will had been read. Though the girl had yet to open up to her entirely, for she had obviously not made up her mind how she felt about Callie, at least she was no longer hostile toward her. She remained cautious, but much of the resentment was gone.

Amy, on the other hand, needed Callie. Her father's death had left her confused and angry, though she had no idea who she was angry with. Callie allowed Amy to talk out her bitter feelings and offered her a shoulder to cry on in order to help her through her grief; and because Amy was willing to cry, willing to express her feelings, Callie felt certain the younger girl would be the first to come to terms with her remorse.

Callie worried about Janice, who tried to be *too* brave, *too* grown up. Except during the funeral itself and the reading of the will, the older daughter had managed to hold in her tears. Callie knew from personal experience, though, that holding in such powerful emotions was not good. She had tried to approach her own parents' death in such a way, tried to hold it all in, be brave, until her emotions practically ate her alive. She did not want Janice to suffer like that, but could not find a way to get the child to release the emotional dam she had built.

Because Matthew had been adamant they not mourn for him, Callie tried to get the girls to continue their lives as before. She encouraged Amy to ride her favorite pony, Starfire, and tried to get Janice interested in her embroidery again. And when Harry resumed Callie's riding lessons on Monday, she tried to get both girls to ride along with her for moral support. It was during those lessons, when they became aware just how green she was, that the girls found reason to laugh again, and the laughter was like a soothing balm to them all. Soon the girls were referring to her by her first name instead of "Mrs. Tucker" or "that woman."

Not long after the will had been read, and Callie's position at the Circle T had been made clear, she planned a trip into town to make her acquaintance with the people she would soon have to do business with. Though Amy had agreed to go with her, and had wanted to ride in on horseback, Callie knew her newly found riding skills were still lacking, and chose to have the carriage made ready instead.

Because Callie was not yet very familiar with the handling of a rig, Harry went with them in order to see they arrived safely. He allowed Callie to drive the carriage, but sat beside her ready to spring into action should she somehow get into trouble. It felt very reassuring to her just knowing he was there.

Callie's first stop was to be the bank, where she wanted to be sure she had easy access to Matthew's money. Knowing how boring a trip to the bank could be, Amy and Harry decided to go on to the mercantile and wait for her there. Callie vowed not to take long before she turned away in one direction, while the other two went off in the opposite. Fighting the butterflies that swarmed her stomach, she tried her best not to appear nervous when she stepped inside and looked around at the people milling about in the lobby, most of whom were men.

"May I help you?" asked one of the older men who stood behind the teller wall, his lily-white hands posed on the counter in front of him.

"Yes," Callie responded when she noticed the man was looking at her. Then remembering the name Harry had told her to ask for, she added, "I'd like to see Mr. Langford, if he is not to busy."

"That's his office over there," the man responded, and lifted his hand to point towards one of the two doors along the wall behind her. "Someone's in there with him right now, but if you'd care to wait in one of those chairs just outside the door, Mr. Langford will be with you shortly."

When Callie turned to look at the door the man had

indicated, she saw the name Clint Langford emblazoned across it in bold, black letters and felt a little foolish for not having noticed it before. "Thank you."

Callie felt several curious gazes on her, but tried to ignore them while she made her way across the room. Casually, she picked up one of the paper fans provided by the bank, and had turned to take the chair nearest the door when she heard the doorknob rattle. She stepped to the side and watched apprehensively while the door slowly began to open. She worried what the banker's reaction was going to be. She knew he might not like the thought of doing business with a woman, especially a woman he'd never met. Would he think her capable of making sound decisions? Would he try to patronize her because she was so young—and a woman? She didn't think she could stand it if he did.

Callie's heart hammered rapidly when she realized the door had swung fully open. The time had come to step forward and show how she was the one in authority at the Circle T. She so wanted to make a strong first impression.

Cautiously, she waited for someone to come out, but when the first one through the door was Wade Barlow of all people, she felt every muscle in her body tense. With her nerves already being what they were, she was not certain she could handle another confrontation with that man, and hoped he would not notice her. She stepped farther away from the door.

But such was not to be, because when he turned to say a final goodbye to whoever stood just inside the office door, his pale blue eyes had quickly scanned the room, stopping abruptly the moment he caught sight of her. His brows rose instantly.

Chapter Seven

"Well, if it isn't the poor, grieving Widow Tucker," Wade commented with a clearly sarcastic lilt before he slowly began toward her, a dark blue coat hooked by his thumb and slung casually over one shoulder. "I guess you just couldn't wait any longer to get your hands on some of Tucker's money, could you?"

Angered by such a remark, Callie considered turning her back to the insolent blackguard. But whether because of distrust or sheer unaccountable attraction, she found she was able to do little more than watch cautiously while he slowly continued to move closer.

The epitome of strength and masculinity, Wade walked toward her with the natural grace of a cat. The fitted lines of the white linen shirt he wore accentuated the hard-muscled breath of his chest and shoulders, and emphasized the narrow waist which lured her attention in the direction of his lean hips and strong thighs. How different he looked dressed in such a fine suit with his dark hair combed back away from his face and no faded hat plopped down on his head to hide most of its rich thickness from view.

It occurred to her that at the moment he appeared almost civilized, though there was still something undeniably rugged and extremely cunning about him. Today, he wore no handgun, yet there was still an aura of powerful masculinity about the man which made her insides tighten in response. She realized it had been the man himself and not the gun he had worn that both she and the men from the saloon had feared. There was something in his manner that let one know he was a man to be reckoned with.

Callie's heartbeat increased when he suddenly stopped, barely two feet in front of her. Narrowing his eyes to reveal the depth of his disgust, he looked down at her wary expression. An icy shiver cascaded down her spinal cord like a wintry waterfall that quickly scattered to affect all parts of her. Though she continued to be aware of the whole of him, her attention became temporarily drawn to his lips when he slowly opened his mouth to speak again.

"The man has been in the ground barely a week, dead only nine days, and already you have come to see about his money. But then I guess it was quite a strain for a woman like you to wait even that long."

Although Callie had not hoped for any gentle words of sympathy from Wade Barlow, she had not expected such insulting comments either. Unable to believe he had actually said any of what she just heard, she found herself at a continued loss for words while she stared helplessly at his handsome face.

Wade saw the opportunity to continue and took it. "It's a good thing you rushed that wedding along, isn't it? Another week and all your plans would have fallen through." While he spoke, he continued to look down at her with such deep loathing, it made Callie want to step back; but she refused to cower beneath his hateful glare.

"Sir, you don't know what you are talking about," she said, with clear warning in her voice. Her heart hammered wildly beneath her breast, yet she was able to force a smile onto her face for the benefit of those watching, glad no one else was near enough to overhear any of what was being said. "Matthew was the one who set the wedding date, not me. In fact, he was the one who planned *everything*."

"I'm sure that's exactly what you want everyone to believe," he shot back, arching an eyebrow to display his skepticism. "But I'm afraid I'm not that gullible. I happen to see you for the crafty little fortune hunter that you really are." His gaze dipped boldly to assess her womanly figure so adequately displayed in the pleated and tucked white lawn dress she had chosen to wear. "Too bad Tucker couldn't have lived longer, to enjoy some of the spoils due him. Or is that what finally killed him?"

"How dare you!" she seethed. Her eyes suddenly lit with anger. All desire to appear she was having a pleasant conversation left her. She no longer cared what anyone else thought, or even what they overheard. "If Matthew was still alive, he'd cut your tongue out for saying such things to me."

"Oh, come off it. You came to Pine Fork with only one thing in mind, to marry a dying man so you could inherent all his money and all that land. And the way I hear it, you found a way to get him to change that will of his just in time. In fact, I heard the will was nearly left unsigned. The lawyer did not make it out with the new documents until the very evening Tucker died. That sure was cutting it close, wasn't it? It would have been hard to convince everyone it was what he wanted without his signature at the bottom." He shifted his weight to one well-muscled thigh.

"I don't know where you came up with such a ridiculous notion. I had nothing to do with the changing of his will. That was all his idea. I didn't even know Matthew was dying until after we were married." She lifted her chin in an unconscious gesture of both defiance and indignation as she glared up at him angrily.

Wade fell silent while he regarded her for a moment. The contempt he felt for her was still clearly evident on his face. "Oh, you knew all right. That's why you were so eager to be out there as quick as possible. No wonder you were willing to risk riding that horse in order to get on out to his place. You were afraid he might die before you had a chance to get him to marry you and legally change his will. Actually, I really should be congratulating you for a job well done."

The words stung so deeply that Callie could not bear to hear more. Without truly knowing her own intentions, she suddenly raised her hand high and delivered a resounding blow against his cheek. To the shock of not only herself but everyone who looked on, she then ordered him straight to hell.

Wade's face turned to granite while he stared down at her. His blue eyes blazed with a sudden fury that he fought to contain. Then, while everyone waited to see what would happen next, he spoke in a deep, resonant voice, but low enough, only she was able to make out his words. "That was a mistake you shouldn't have made."

Without another word, he turned and calmly walked out of the bank, his coat still slung casually over his shoulder.

Callie was a quivering mass of uncertainty and disbelief while she watched him stroll out the door and turn to his right. She could not believe she had actually slapped him. She, who had never before raised her hand against another human being in her entire life, had just publicly struck a man—a man who clearly deserved to be slapped but was certain to seek retaliation in some way. Men like Wade Barlow did not accept public humiliation well—they did not accept it at all. Fear climbed her throat at the thought of what he might try to do to her in order to even the score. The constriction caused her voice to come out high and strained when she turned to the banker and calmly introduced herself, hoping to make it seem as if nothing out of the ordinary had just occurred.

If Clint Langford was opposed to doing business with her for any reason, he did not show it when he stepped back and politely asked her to enter his office. With eyes still wide from what he had just witnessed, he offered her a seat facing his desk and got right to the business at hand. Though Callie had a hard time pushing the image of Wade Barlow's angry expression from her mind, she was able to put on a very businesslike front, and soon learned everything she needed to know about Matthew's assets, which were impressive, and was assured she would have no problem making deposits or withdrawals in the Circle T account.

Callie could not have been more pleased with the banker's treatment of her, and felt much more at ease when, fifteen minutes later, she prepared to leave. The banker obviously did not believe her to be the fortune hunter Wade did, for he had shown her nothing but respect. She knew Matthew would be pleased. What would not have pleased him was the way Wade Barlow had spoken to her.

When she stepped back outside on her way to the mercantile, her thoughts were once again fully focused on the one man she had wanted not to think about at all—Wade Barlow. It worried her he might still be in town, waiting for her, watching her at that very moment, eager to seek retaliation for what she had done. Callie's stomach knotted as she hurried along the boardwalk, afraid that at any moment he might step out into her path, ready to confront her, eager to make more of his scandalous remarks about her. She wondered how many other people he had told those horrible lies to and if anyone had actually believed him. Knowing the nature of gossip, she was certain he had found those eager to listen.

As soon as she was safely inside the mercantile and discovered Wade nowhere to be found, she relaxed somewhat. But she hurried with the business she had there, then decided to put off all the other stops she had wanted to make until another time, when there was less chance of running into Wade Barlow again and any gossip he might have started about her could have had a chance to die down. Though she did not truly expect to find him inside a dress shop, she even chose to delay visiting her friend Nadine Leigh. She would be too distracted to hold an intelligent conversation anyway.

Amy seemed disappointed to learn they were not going to stop by the hotel restaurant for orangeades as they had planned, but to Callie's relief, the girl did not argue against their early return. Nor did she question Callie's sullen mood during the ride home. She understood that Callie needed to be left alone to her thoughts.

That same afternoon, shortly after Lucille had helped Callie and Amy put away the things they had purchased in town, she asked to speak with Callie alone, then carefully brought up the subject of what to do with Matthew's clothing and his personal belongings. It was something Callie had not wanted to think about and had hoped to put off indefinitely. Yet once it had been mentioned, she knew it was up to her to go through the things and decide what should be kept and what could possibly be donated to those less fortunate. But because she understood what a strain it would be on the girls, knowing their father's things were being sorted through, she waited until after both girls had gone to bed before beginning the dreaded task.

Things that Callie knew Janice and Amy would want to keep because of possible sentimental value, she set aside for the moment. Items that would be of no use to any of them, but could be sent to Reverend Cross for distribution to those not quite as fortunate, were bound into large bundles and carried downstairs to the storage room behind the kitchen. Lucille had insisted on helping and stayed with Callie until nearly two o'clock that following morning, when Callie decided they had done enough for the time being and could finish the job another night after the girls were again in bed. Because the girls rarely visited Matthew's bedroom and the door had remained closed since his death, there was little likelihood either of his daughters would come into the room and see all the disarray in the meantime.

Tired and emotionally drained, Lucille nodded her agreement while she gathered up two of the large bundles of clothing she had just bound together. "You're right. We both need some rest. Besides, it ain't possible to get finished with this by mornin' anyway. I'll just carry these two on downstairs, then be headin' on off to bed."

Callie remained behind to straighten some of the disarray, just in case one of the girls might enter the room later expecting to see it the way their father had left it. Quietly, she put some of the things away and closed any drawers left open. Then weary from having had to do something so emotionally strenuous when her nerves were already drawn taut due to her earlier run-in with Wade Barlow, Callie sank into the nearest chair—Matthew's desk chair—and leaned her cheek against the cool surface of his desk. She had held her tears back mostly for Lucille's sake, but now that she was alone with so many of Matthew's private things, she saw no reason to be brave any longer and wept openly, purging herself of the anger and sorrow that had been building inside her all evening.

When the tears finally stopped, and she found the strength to lift her head from atop the desk, she noticed the wet area she had created on the polished wood surface. Not wanting to leave a stain, she opened the desk drawer to see if there was something inside with which she might wipe away the tears. Though she found nothing to blot away the wetness, she discovered an unfamiliar leather-bound book that looked like it might be a ledger of some sort.

Though the book was not as tall as the ledgers Matthew had used to teach her about the ranch, it proved twice as thick and looked very worn around the edges. Curiously, she untied the leather strap that bound it, then after wiping the tears from the desk with her sleeve, she placed the book in front of her and carefully opened it. She wondered why he had not bothered to show her this ledger while they were going over the ranch bookkeeping the night before he died.

Inside, Callie discovered the yellowed pages of the book filled with Matthew's handwriting, but oddly enough, there were no columns of figures. The only numbers were in the dates, which interrupted the text periodically. Intrigued, she read a few paragraphs, and realized she had discovered Matthew's personal journal, his diary.

Quickly, she closed the book when it occurred to her she was reading Matthew's private thoughts. But the curiosity to know more about the man who had given her so much made her slowly open the book again and read a little more of what had been written inside.

The more she read, the closer she felt to the man she had known for such a short time, and the more she came to understand him. She read the final entries first. His words brought the instant return of her tears. The love, devotion, and gratitude he felt toward his family and toward his friends poured across those last pages. Though Matthew had erected a bold front, he had suffered greatly knowing his death was imminent. Callie's heart went out to him, and she wished there was some way to comfort him, though he was beyond comfort now.

And the more she read, the more adamant she was to win

his children's love and bring them all together as a real family—for herself as much as for Matthew. It was what he had wanted most in those final days, to know that his daughters would still be loved and well taken care of. Matthew had even worried about *her,* worried he might have done the wrong thing by not telling her the truth about his illness right from the beginning.

Callie carried the journal with her to her room and read more, this time starting at the beginning. Through the passages she found there, she learned not only his innermost dreams, but also the bitter heartache he had lived with. She was saddened by the terrible secrets and the hopelessness he had been forced to harbor all those years, by the dreams he had never seen fulfilled. It broke her heart to learn the many incidents that made up the man's painful past, and somehow it made her own past seem not nearly as horrible as it once had.

By the time she had read the diary through, it was morning. The sunlight that streamed into her bedroom windows seemed to be at odds with her sullen mood.

With eyes reddened from the tears Matthew's words had wrought, Callie carefully closed the book, fastening it again with the leather strap, and vowed to keep the secrets she had found inside.

And because she could not bring herself to actually destroy the book in order to keep those secrets from ever being discovered by anyone else, she decided to hide the book, not wanting it to be easily found. Carefully, she placed it at the very bottom of one of her own drawers, and covered it with several layers of her folded undergarments.

When she closed the drawer, she wondered if someday the girls should be allowed to read their father's diary, but decided it would only hurt them to know how terribly their father had suffered throughout his life. And it occurred to her Matthew might not want them to know.

So tired Callie felt almost numb, she then lay down on her bed to rest, but discovered she was unable to sleep. She eventually bathed, dressed, and went downstairs, just missing breakfast with the girls and having to eat alone.

Later that morning, because she had so much she needed to think about, she asked Harry to saddle her horse. She desperately wanted to go for a ride. For some strange reason, probably because it had been Matthew who had encouraged her to learn to ride in the first place, she felt closer to him when she was on her horse, riding proudly across his land, surveying that which he himself had surveyed many times.

"You want me to go with you?" Harry asked while he tightened the cinch, making it snug but not uncomfortable for the horse. "I know you have taken to horse-riding real good, nearly as good as you took to shooting that rifle, but still, you have only had six riding lessons in all."

"No, you have plenty to do without taking time out to ride with me. Besides, I want to be alone. But to be on the safe side and so you won't worry, I'll keep her at a walk."

It was after Harry led the horse outside to the mounting block that he thought to ask Callie if she'd had anyone apply for the foreman's position yet.

"No, not yet." She shrugged, for they had both thought she would have had several applicants by now.

"I can't understand it," Harry said with a grim shake of his head. "It's as if they are afraid of having to work for a woman, but that's ridiculous."

"Maybe not. I think you may have hit upon the very problem," Callie said, gazing thoughtfully at Harry. "It just might be the men around here *don't* like the idea of working for a woman. Could be the men *don't* like the thought of taking their orders from anyone but another man, not even for what I am willing to pay."

"Well, I'll stay on until you do finally find someone," Harry told her, though it was clear by his disheartened expression, he hoped that would not be long.

"No, Matthew didn't want you to remain tied down to this place. He wanted you to take that one hundred head of cattle he left you and get your own place started." Callie felt fresh tears forming. By not having found someone to replace Harry, she felt as if she was failing Matthew in some way. "We will put up new notices, offering higher pay, and if that doesn't bring in a new foreman within the next week, I will just have to take my chances running this place on my own for a while.

"You've learned a lot these past several days, but you aren't anywhere near ready to take on the running of a place like this," Harry said, stating the obvious. "There's just too many problems that could go wrong that you wouldn't know how to solve. I'll stay until you find someone."

"No, Harrison Nathanial Vicke, you will not," she said with far more bravado than she actually felt, knowing that by using his full name he'd at least understand she was serious. "If I don't find someone within the week, you are to leave anyway. That's final."

Harry decided not to argue about it. But then neither did he intend to leave before she had a new foreman. "We'll see how it works out. Who knows, higher pay may be just what it takes to bring 'em in here."

During her short ride, Callie's worried thoughts centered mostly on somehow finding a foreman with enough experience to replace Harry. She could not expect Harry to stay on forever, and Matthew would have wanted him gone by now.

Grimly, she wondered how much she would have to raise the pay in order to get someone interested enough in the job to be willing to take orders from a woman. She also wondered if Matthew had understood how difficult a task that might prove to be, but could not imagine the man purposely leaving her with the task if it was so impossible. Still, it worried her she might never find anyone to take Harry's place and that, as a result, she might indeed find herself having to oversee the ranch all alone. And then she would run into the problem of getting the other workhands to take their orders directly from her. It seemed a hopeless situation.

When Callie returned the horse to the barn and was on her way back to the house, eager to get the new notice ready, she spied a trailing puff of dust near the roadway hedge, then saw that a carriage was coming up the drive toward the house. Rather than go inside and wait for whoever it was to get out and knock at her door, which was probably the proper thing to do, she turned and headed toward the front of the house to greet the visitor.

By the time the hooded carriage had come to a full stop, she was close enough to call out.

"Hello there. May I help you?"

"Yes," came the immediate response from the gentleman as he climbed down from the back seat of the vehicle and handed a newspaper he'd been reading to his burly driver. "I believe you are just the person to help me."

"And how is that?" she asked, continuing in his direction, curious now to see just how she could possibly help this man.

"First, let me introduce myself," he said, and turned his full attention on her. Dressed in a lightweight calling suit, the man appeared to be about forty-seven years old. His reddish blond hair was cropped short, and his wide hazel-colored eyes sat in a rounded face, surrounded by short stubby blond lashes. The overall effect was not unattractive, but the man was not particularly handsome either. "My name is Walter Barlow. I'm from the Rocking W, a neighboring ranch. And I gather you're the young lady Tucker married just before his unfortunate death. If that's so, then I am here to discuss a few matters of business with you. That is, if you are up to it just yet."

Callie gazed warily at the man, having instantly realized he was Wade's father—and from having read Matthew's diary, she knew he was the very man who had caused Matthew such misery throughout his life. Walter Barlow had not only turned a few of their neighbors against Matthew by spreading lies and hatred about him, he was also the man Matthew had felt was responsible for his first wife's death. "And what sort of business would that be?"

"Why don't we go inside where it's cooler and I'll tell you all about it," he said, indicating the way to the front door with a slight wave of his hand.

Callie was not sure she wanted that man in her house—in Matthew's house—but saw no polite way of refusing his

110

suggestion. "All right, but I only have a moment."

"A moment might be all I need," he said with a reassuring smile. He didn't speak again until they were inside and seated. "I have come here to talk with you because I would like to buy the Circle T from you."

"You what?" she asked, unable to believe he would dare suggest such a thing. Even if she and the girls had any inclination to sell the place, he would be the last person they would ever consider.

"I would like to buy the Circle T, and for a far more than reasonable price. You see, I have a large spread due west of here and have been eager to expand my operations for quite some time, but there has been no land in this area for sale."

"And what makes you think the Circle T would be for sale?"

"Oh, come now. The way I hear it, you know absolutely nothing about running a ranch. You are a city girl. Surely you don't plan to stay on here when you have this chance to sell the place for more than you will need to purchase a fine house in the city of your choice, and still have money to live on for years and years to come."

"Even if I did want to sell, why would I want to sell to you?"

"Because I can pay cash," he said with a cocky shake of his head that let her know just how important he thought himself. "And I probably am the only man around here that can."

Suddenly all the hatred Matthew had felt for the man surfaced inside of her. "I'm sorry, but it appears you have made the trip over here for nothing. I don't have any intention of selling this place, and even if I did, I certainly would not consider selling any of it to you. I happen to know who you are and I would never do such a thing to Matthew."

"Matthew's dead," he pointed out, his face suddenly grim.

"*There* you are wrong. Matthew lives on—in here," she told him as she gently pressed her hand against her heart. "And in the hearts of his two daughters. As long as we are

111

alive, Matthew lives. And I will see to it that all his hopes and dreams are realized. The Circle T will remain our home."

"Such loyalty. I hear Matthew's foreman is leaving soon, which will leave you to run this ranch alone, and you don't know the first thing about running a ranch like this," he stated bluntly.

"I can learn. And until I do learn how to run this place on my own, I can and will hire another foreman to help me."

"I don't think so. The way I understand it, no one wants to work for some foolish city woman who doesn't even know enough about ranching to tell a male horse from a female. Everyone in town has heard by now how you can't even sit a horse."

"That may well have been true when I first arrived, but I assure you I now know the difference between a male and female horse and I can indeed ride with no problem whatever. In fact, had you arrived a few minutes earlier, you would have seen for yourself just how well I can ride." She knew she exaggerated, but was unable to stop herself.

Walter glanced at the divided skirt she wore. "Just the same, you are going to be hard pressed to find a foreman who can handle a spread the size of this one. The Circle T is huge. In fact, it is the largest ranch around these parts. And a place like this takes a man with a keen wit and lots of cunning. Someone special, who knows the workings of a large ranch inside and out, and someone who can be trusted. Major decisions have to be made on a moment's notice, important decisions. Sometimes the decisions are life and death. And it takes a man who knows what he's doing to make the right decisions and then give the orders to back them. It would be wiser for you to simply sell the place now and move back to the city along with Matthew's daughters, while the place is still worth the money to buy you a nice city house and afford you a long and pleasant life."

"I don't think Matthew's daughters would like the city," she responded quickly, tossing her head back and glaring at him. "No, I plan to make their home right here, at the Circle T. It is what Matthew wanted. And it is what I want."

"Don't be a fool," Walter said, his face reddening with the anger that consumed him while his voice rose a notch. His thick brows drew together. "A city woman and two young girls can't possibly run a ranch. You need a foreman, and a damned good one at that. There just isn't anyone like that around here who isn't already tied up working elsewhere."

"Please, sir, don't be too concerned about us. I'm sure I'll find someone," she stated with a firm nod of her head. Suddenly she knew exactly who she wanted. A man whose personality was so strong, and his determination so set, that an entire room full of men had refused to cause him any trouble. Smiling at the sheer thought of it, she added, "Now, if you would excuse me, I have work to do."

Though he rose when she did, she did not bother to see him to the door. Instead she went in the opposite direction, leaving him to find his own way out.

Chapter Eight

Determined to do what was best for the Circle T, and knowing it was what Matthew would have wanted, Callie bravely swallowed her pride the following morning and had her horse made ready. With her heart wedged firmly in her throat, she rode toward the northwest, carefully following Harry's instructions so she would not get lost.

Callie's stomach churned violently. Already aware the task at hand would not be easy, she dreaded it more with each step the horse took. But it was the most sensible answer to her problem. At least she had to try.

When she arrived at Twin Oaks only twenty minutes later, she noticed most of the activity stirred in the area closest to the barn, where two large wagons filled with huge wooden barrels stood side by side. Noticing that the man she had come to see was one of the four standing next to the wagons, Callie rode her horse toward him.

When Wade glanced up, his eyebrows rose at the unexpected sight before him.

"What in the . . ." he said just before he moved away from the others to meet her halfway. His eyes were wide with curiosity when he approached her.

"I need to talk with you," she said, deciding to get directly to the reason she had come.

"I thought you couldn't ride," he stated, dropping one eyebrow to show his immediate suspicion while he took in the overall sight of the woman, dressed in a pale brown divided skirt, sitting regally atop her horse with her dark hair pulled back away from her face, yet allowed to flow freely down her back in shimmering brown waves. "But that was just another one of your little tricks, wasn't it? It was your way of getting me to take you out to the Circle T, wasn't it? It was a way to play on my sympathies. And I fell for it."

"No. At that time, I couldn't ride. But Matthew's foreman, Harry Vicke, has been teaching me. Matthew felt I should know how to ride a horse if I was to get around the ranch with any ease at all. There are places along that north ridge that a carriage can't reach but cattle can if they break fence. And there are times when the weather won't permit a carriage to travel across the pastures at all. Though I understand that hasn't happened in quite some time."

"I see," he said. His eyes narrowed while he considered what she had just said. "So what is it you want to talk to me about?"

Aware the other men had stopped working in order to watch, she nodded toward the house. "May we speak in private?"

Wade studied her businesslike expression for a moment, then glanced back at the men behind him, who at that moment appeared to be all eyes and ears.

"Okay, we can talk on the veranda," he said. "I'll meet you there in just a few minutes. I need to finish giving the men their orders. Then I'll be right with you."

Callie rode back toward the house and dismounted. Carefully, she tied the horse's reins to one of the posts out front before climbing the planked steps and turning to wait for Wade to join her. While she waited, she carefully smoothed out her divided skirt and brushed any dust from her blue linen blouse, then studied her surroundings with interest. Though not as fancy as the Circle T by any means, it was a busy place with almost as many outbuildings scattered about, if not more. But the house itself was only half as large as Matthew's lovely home, and was made of lapped boards instead of brick.

115

Though Callie had expected Wade to make her wait for quite a while out of sheer spite for what she had done to him in town, within minutes, while she still studied her surroundings, he was already headed in her direction. Her heart pounded with a violent force while she watched him slowly move toward her with his usual animal grace. She decided the strange reaction was because of how deeply she dreaded the ordeal ahead, knowing her chances for success were slim. Self-consciously, she brushed a curling strand of hair from her shoulder with an easy flick of her hand.

"And to what do I owe this visit?" he asked. His expression remained cautious while he climbed the steps, then came to stand directly in front of her, shadowing her with his height.

"I need help and I honestly think you are the best man for the job," she began, not wanting to struggle with any pointless conversation about how lovely his home was or how hot the weather.

"You have come here to ask help from me?" he asked, astounded by her audacity. "After what you did to me in town?"

"You deserved that," she stated evenly, tossing her head back to show she felt no remorse for her brash actions in town. When she looked at him again, part of her dark hair whipped forward over her shoulder in a most appealing manner. "You said some terrible things to me."

"Sometimes the truth hurts."

Callie felt her muscles tighten, and curled her fingers to form tight fists at her sides in an effort to keep her angry emotions under control. Suddenly, she wondered if coming had been such a good idea, but still she felt she must try, for the girls' sake, for Matthew's sake. "The reason I have come here is to ask you to help me run the Circle T until I can find a qualified foreman to take Harry's place."

"You what?" he responded, eyes wide, unable to believe her gall. "You have come here to ask me to help you run the Circle T? Didn't it occur to you that I might not care that you need help? That I might even be a little busy running my own place?"

"Yes, it did," she said with a firm nod. "But I still had hopes you could find it in your heart to spare a little of your time to come over and help me keep my place going. You see, Harry is leaving soon and I have been unable to replace him. I need someone who knows all about the ranching business to come over and help out until I can find someone else."

"But why me?" he wanted to know, staring down at her and noticing the attractive way her almond-shaped eyes slanted downward toward a perfectly formed nose. He wondered then if Tucker had known what a beauty she was when he'd first invited her to come to Pine Fork.

"Because you are exactly the type man I need. You know the workings of a ranch and know what it takes to keep one going. You have both the skill and the knowledge to do the job right."

"That may be true, but I'm afraid I'm not interested in running the Circle T. I've got too much to do around here to keep my own place going." He pulled his gaze off her before he became too entranced with her beauty, and stared off toward where the men had just climbed onto the two wagons, preparing to distribute the rest of the water to his cattle and his horses.

"I'll pay you twice what the job is worth," she put in, hoping to make him change his mind, not yet ready to give up.

"And how do you know what the job is worth?"

"I'll pay you twice what Harry is now making, and I'll only ask that you put in half a day's work. Six hours a day. That's all I'd ask of you. And if you think about it, that should actually make the pay *four* times what the job is worth."

"Forget it. I'm still not interested. Not only am I not too sure I could tolerate bending to a lady boss—especially when the lady is as manipulative and conniving as you are—I also don't particularly care for the idea of going against my father like that. Pop and I may rarely see eye to

117

eye on anything, and I may have chosen to go my own separate way years ago, but I still have to respect the fact that we are family. And my father would be furious with me if I went to work over there, helping you keep Tucker's place going. Especially when he has always wanted to own that land himself. Maybe I should be trying to convince you to sell the place instead. Then maybe I could get back on his good side."

"Won't work. He's already been over trying to convince me to sell the place to him. And I already explained to him how I have no intention of selling the Circle T to anyone. So he can't possibly blame you for any decision I have made to hold on to it. I told him then how the Circle T had been far too important to Matthew for me to ever consider selling it." Her eyes studied his expression while she spoke. "Please, I need your help if I'm to keep it going."

Wade fell silent for a moment while her words sank in, and for a moment, Callie thought he might be changing his mind. But when he spoke again, it was with a regretful shake of his head, which led Callie to believe that for the first time Wade was actually starting to believe her—and may also have begun to sympathize with her plight. Even so, he had not seen any way of helping her.

"I'm sorry. But I've got too much to do around here. Especially since it hasn't rained in nearly seven weeks. The only source of water I had for my cattle was Creel Creek, and it dried up almost two weeks ago. I'm now having to haul water in for my cattle from Rutledge Crossing twice a day, and that is an expensive and time-consuming choice. And once the lake over there plays out, I'll have to go all the way to Sobey Mills, which is eight miles from here." He glanced across his yard at the large patches of heat-weary grass that were slowly dying from lack of moisture.

Callie frowned, feeling defeated, but then remembered the two spring-fed streams which ran across her land, one only a few hundred yards from Wade's fence line. Her wells were also still full of water.

"There's still plenty of water on the Circle T," she told

118

him, her eyes alive again with hope. "Why don't you tear down a portion of your fence and let your cattle run on part of my land until the drought is over and your creek and ponds are full again . . . in exchange of course for helping me run the Circle T." She could tell by the way Wade's eyes rose to meet hers that he was sorely tempted. She had found his weak spot — his ranch. She hurried to add even more temptation. "Then your men would be able to get some of their regular work done and wouldn't have to spend as much time hauling water in to your cattle."

Wade pressed his lips together, a movement that caused Callie to focus temporarily on the sensuous curve of his mouth. She wondered absently how many women had been allowed to sample the sweetness of that mouth, but did not stay with that thought for long.

"Please, Wade. I can't do it alone and I do so want to keep Matthew's dream alive. I want to keep the Circle T going so his daughters can continue to live there and eventually make their own homes there."

"I'm not too sure Tucker would want a Barlow working on the Circle T," he commented, while he continued to look at the proposition from all sides.

"It's your father Matthew held no regard for, not you. Matthew would not be upset in the least if you decided to help me. In fact, he would be grateful. The Circle T meant so very much to him."

"Even if I didn't have to worry about hauling water in twice a day, I don't know if I could spare six full hours each day," he added, but without the same tone of conviction he had used earlier.

Certain he was very close to agreeing, she quickly responded, "Whatever you can spare. If on some days it can't be a full six hours, I'll understand. I realize your own place would always have to come first with you."

Wade tilted his head to one side, stared at her a long moment, then shrugged his shoulders. He was out of arguments. "I'll get my men started on taking down a couple of sections of fence after lunch. Tomorrow's Sun-

119

day, and I imagine most of your hands will have the day off, so there wouldn't be much point my showing up then. And the next day is the Fourth of July. So, I guess, I'll try to get over there the day after—Tuesday sometime before noon. I'll want Harry to show me where everything is and explain to me which of your men is best at doing what before he goes."

Callie's heart soared to lofty heights. Because she had convinced herself she had asked Wade to be her foreman purely for Matthew's sake, she felt far more delighted than she had expected. The thought of seeing Wade on a daily basis and the two of them working side by side made her insides flutter. "Thank you, Wade. I appreciate this. I know we somehow got off on the wrong foot. I'm just glad I was able to change your mind about me."

"Wait a minute, I want it made clear that the only reason I'm doing this is so my cattle can get good, fresh water. The health of my stock is important to me. I haven't changed my mind about *anything*." He wanted to make that clear.

Just as instantly as her heart had taken wing, it fell back into darkness. Keeping her head held high and her shoulders erect, she tried to hide her disappointment. "Oh, I see. Well, at least we will both get what we want out of this. You will have your water and I will get the help I need until I can find a qualified foreman." Then, as she turned to leave, she realized that, in a way, Matthew would also be getting what he'd always wanted, though far too late for him to enjoy it.

Wade appeared at Callie's back door at eleven o'clock Tuesday morning. His blue shirt was already stained with the sweat he'd produced getting as much of his own work out of the way as possible before taking off for the Circle T. When Callie met him at the door, she was dressed in a lovely pale yellow cotton dress with puffed short sleeves edged with white lace. Since she had devoted the morning to book work, she had not seen the need to put on her riding skirt, which was quickly becoming her usual outfit for daytime, so much so that she had asked Nadine to prepare at least three more.

Wade waited outside, trying not to notice how beautiful she was in the modestly low-cut dress that clung provocatively to all the right curves. When she finally stepped out onto the veranda, he forced his gaze away from her and quickly suggested she introduce him to Harry, which she did immediately.

Harry had been surprised to learn who Callie had found to replace him, at least temporarily, but had seen no real reason to protest, especially when it meant he would finally be able to take off for his own spread later that same week. He knew enough about Wade Barlow's reputation to be aware that about all the young man would need from him was a little general orientation. By the end of the week, there should be no questions left unanswered, and Harry was certain he would be free to leave at last.

"Harry, come over here," Callie had called out the moment she and Wade had entered the barn and found the man busy tightening a loose hinge on one of the stall gates. "I want you to meet Wade Barlow, the man who has agreed to help me until I can find a more permanent man to replace you."

Harry approached cautiously while he slipped his weathered hands out of his leather work gloves.

"Wade, this is Harry Vicke, Matthew's longtime friend and trusted foreman," Callie continued. "Harry will be able to tell you anything you think you might need to know."

"I've seen him many times, and I've heard a lot about him; but never had the pleasure of meeting him," Wade said with a genuine smile as he gently wiped his right hand on his pants leg in preparation of a handshake. "I hear he's not only a good cattle man, I hear he's also quite good at breaking in new horse stock."

Reluctantly, Harry thrust out his hand and shook with

Wade. It was as if he did not trust the complimentary remarks Wade had just made—as if he still was unable to believe a Barlow actually intended to help a Tucker manage the Circle T.

"Well, I'll leave you two to get better acquainted," Callie said, hoping they might attempt to get along better after she left. Once she was gone, they would not feel it necessary to put on an arrogant front, the way men sometimes did in the presence of a woman. "I have book work to do."

Wade watched while she lifted her skirts several inches and stepped carefully toward the barn door then disappeared.

"Quite a lady," Harry said with sincere admiration while he too watched her leave.

Frowning, Wade chose not to comment, and immediately turned his attention to his surroundings. "Well, let's get started. I have a lot of questions I'll need to ask if I'm to know what I'm doing." He refused to think again of the pretty young woman who had gone to all the trouble to manipulate Tucker into marrying her, charming the poor man into changing his will so she could get her hands on his ranch and all his money—but then, surprisingly, had decided not to sell it right away. Instead, she actually wanted to try running the ranch herself. It didn't make perfect sense, but then nothing about that woman made perfect sense.

That afternoon, after Callie had long since grown tired of bending over ledgers, she decided to take a short break and see how Harry and Wade were getting along. She found them inside the tool shed going over the vast inventory of tools and hardware stored there.

"And as you can see, on that wall is where the garden-type tools are kept. Since Manuel is the gardener and groundskeeper, he is pretty much responsible for their upkeep. And I'd advise you to let him know if you plan to take a garden spade or a rake out of here. Manuel is real sensitive about his tools," Harry was explaining to Wade when Callie entered.

122

"And he's also very sensitive to any suggestion of possible changes in the way the yard looks," Callie supplied, smiling as she joined them in the center of the wooden shed. Wade was aware that her smile seemed to brighten their otherwise dull surroundings, and again wondered if Tucker had known what a beauty she was when he'd sent for her.

Unaware of Wade's close scrutiny, Callie continued. "Manuel doesn't seem particularly fond of the idea of planting petunias."

Harry laughed, knowing how insulated Manuel had become over just such a suggestion. "No, he's definitely not one who appreciates a petunia. Mighty fond of roses, though."

"Any particular color?" Wade asked, though he really did not care. But for some reason, he did not want to feel left out of the conversation.

"Red!" Harry and Callie answered in unison.

"I couldn't even convince him that they come in yellows and pinks too," Callie explained. "Too bad, because I adore pink roses."

Wade was not sure why, but decided to remember that fact. "And do you plan to order some in so he can see that other colors do exist?"

Callie paused to consider that. "I might. I just might." Her smile broadened at the thought of what Manuel's expression would be when suddenly some of his rose bushes began to sprout pink and yellow roses.

Wade frowned. It bothered him that her smile affected him at all, but there was no denying the woman had a very beguiling smile, shaping a most attractive little dimple at the right corner of her mouth.

"So, have you two made a lot of progress?" she asked, aware now of how Wade made a study of her every movement. Suddenly, she felt uncomfortable.

"Pretty much," Harry answered. "He knows where everything is in the barn, in the carriage house, in the blacksmith shed, and in the bunkhouse. At lunch, he saw where most of us eat during the summer and met a few of the hands that came in around that time. And I was just about to show him where we chow down in the winter once it gets a little too cold to be eating outside under the trees. Then I plan to show him the smokehouse, the manure shed, the chicken coop, the preservatory, and where everyone goes to wash up after work—out behind the water cistern, near the well. By then, the rest of the men should be trailing in and I can introduce him to anyone he hasn't already met."

"You two have been very busy," she said to them both. She then turned her attention to Wade. "Do you think you will be able to find everything once Harry's gone?"

"Shouldn't be too hard. Most everything is organized about like you'd expect. But I do think you and I need to talk more about my cattle having the run of your northwest pasture. My men will need to go in and check on them from time to time. I'd like to be certain I have your permission for them to do just that."

"Of course, I expected as much," Callie told him. "I don't see any problem there."

"And since your cattle will have access to my land while that fence is down, your men on occasion will need to go into my southeast pasture to tend to any of yours that stray," Wade added.

"I hope that poses no problem," she said, drawing her brow, waiting to hear whether or not it would.

"Not really. It's just that I wanted to get that clear between us before some problem arose," he stated. "Also, if something comes up at my place that needs my immediate attention, one of my men will have to come over here to get me. I've got a good foreman, but there are times when he'll want me to make the decisions. And like I've already told you, my place will have to have top priority with me."

"Of course," she responded, beginning to wonder why he wanted to talk about such minor little details.

"It's just that for years now, my men have not been allowed onto Circle T land. I only want to make sure that's all changed now, and that your men are made aware of the change."

"As I understand it, it was your father and his men who were ordered to keep out, not you," she stated, noticing how Harry's brow rose with curious interest. Aware she had come by that information only through Matthew's diary, she quickly added, "Matthew explained to me how he and Walter Barlow did not get along, hadn't in years. But that was between the two of them."

Wade looked at her skeptical. "Are you sure? It was my understanding that he meant me and my men too."

"I'm certain he didn't. The statement was made to your father to stay off the Circle T and also to keep his men off. Matthew never intended that order to apply to you." In fact, if she remembered the diary entry correctly, Wade had not even been around the day that decree was issued. Wade's father must have told him about it, after deciding Matthew had meant all Barlow workmen were to stay off his land. "Your men were never barred from the Circle T."

Wade still was not sure he believed that, but saw no reason to argue about it. "As long as it's okay for my men to come over now. Like you yourself said, my place has to come first with me. And I need to be able to keep an eye on the cattle that come over here, as well as have a man able to keep me informed of any emergencies."

Callie frowned thoughtfully. "I'll make sure my men understand that the no-trespassing rules does not apply to you or any of your men." Then, she turned to Harry. "You can see to that, can't you? Explain to them how Wade and his men are more than welcome on the Circle T."

"Will do," Harry said with a nod, while his attention went from her concerned expression to Wade's, then back.

"I'd appreciate it," Wade told Harry, though he never took his gaze off of Callie.

Callie felt suddenly awkward at the way he continued to stare at her and quickly excused herself, claiming she was eager to get back to her book work. All she was really eager to do was get away from such close scrutiny from a man who set her insides to spinning like a child's top.

Later, just before it came time for Wade to leave for the day, he stopped by the house to tell Callie he was leaving and explain he would try to return the following morning around eleven. Because he was adamant about not coming inside the house as dirty as he was, Callie stepped outside onto the veranda in order to apologize for not having had any time to be with him that day. But she quickly assured him she should have more time to spend with him the next day—though she was not sure her fluttering heart could stand a whole day in his intimidating presence.

"What for?" he wanted to know, his brow drawn with sudden suspicion as he pushed his hat back on his head and looked down at her.

"So I can help you." Callie's insides tightened with anticipation of yet another disagreement.

"I don't need your help," he stated bluntly. "I can do just fine without you. Probably a lot better."

Angered by his cocky attitude, she responded, "Just the same, I want to be a part of the running of this ranch. And because I do want that, I'll be spending a lot of my time helping you, learning as much as I can from you, so that when you are not able to be here, I can eventually start to make sound decisions of my own."

Wade tilted his head and let his gaze sweep over her in a very condescending manner. "I think you'd better leave that sort of thing to us men. Although I won't be getting here until around eleven every day because of my responsibilities at my own place, I will have already given your men their morning work orders the afternoon before. That way, even when I'm not here, the men will already know what I want them to do. I'd really appreciate it if you wouldn't try to butt in at all."

Callie felt the blood climb to her cheeks as her anger grew. "I didn't think my helping would be considered butting in. And I have every intention of doing what I can to learn as much as I can about what it takes to run this place. You may as well know that now."

126

Wade leveled his gaze at her, wanting to tell her to forget the whole deal. He was not about to have any woman tagging along behind him all day watching his every move and telling him what to do. But at the same moment, he remembered how much of the neglected work his men had been able to get done over at his own place since they had taken that fence down and no longer had to spend ten hours a day hauling in water. Nor did he have to pay outrageous prices for water that smelled more and more like dead fish the closer Rutledge's lake came to being emptied. He must remember that the whole reason he had agreed to come over and help was because of Twin Oaks, and that the situation there had not changed one bit.

Wade continued to stare down into her defiant face while his jaw muscles flexed back and forth. She had him over a barrel all right — a water barrel. And she knew it! Finally, when he did speak again, it was through tightly clenched teeth. "You're the boss, ma'am. Whatever you say."

Then, while continuing to hold his temper as best he could, he politely touched the brim of his hat and quickly turned to leave.

"See that you remember that," Callie called out, angered by his cocky response. And when he showed no indication of having heard her, she became even angrier and quickly decided the man was far too arrogant for his own good. Watching while he rode away, his head held high and his shoulders a little too erect, she silently vowed to do whatever she could to bring him down a notch or two, until he came to understand he was actually no better or worse than she was.

Chapter Nine

Wade soon discovered that Callie was serious about learning both the business and working ends of ranching. Not only did she seek his advice often, becoming an endless fountain of questions, he noticed he was rarely bothered with explaining the same thing over and over again the way he had expected. Most of what he told her, she quickly absorbed and put to use. Though he would be hard pressed to admit it, he was actually impressed and a little puzzled over her fortitude—at how eager she was to learn and *do* more, even after she had discovered what hard work ranching really was.

By Friday afternoon, he had started to become rather used to having her tag along behind him, observing everything he did and offering to help with what she felt she could handle. At first, it had bothered him to have her take on any of the work, but soon he began to enjoy watching her master different skills. At times he was certain he could almost see her mind at work while she solved some of the problems on her own.

When he rode for home that afternoon, a little later than he had expected, Wade's thoughts were on how she had given no second thought to picking up a hammer and nail in order to repair a loose support in the corral. She'd seen the need, and instead of asking someone else to do the work, she'd done it herself. That had impressed him more than he cared to be impressed by her, and he found it harder and harder to think of her as the slick, scheming little opportunist who had somehow manipulated herself into a small fortune. It was also becoming harder for him to keep his emotions as completely unaffected as he would like them to be.

It was while his mood wandered from being oddly pleased by her spunk to being strongly bothered by her determination to do things she should leave for the men to do that he noticed his father's carriage sitting in his yard. As he turned in and rode along the short dirt drive which led from the main road to his house, the skin along the back of his neck prickled with apprehension. No doubt by now his father had learned about the unusual amount of time he was spending at the Circle T. Sometimes, like today, he spent as many as eight hours over there, far longer than he was actually required to stay.

"Hello, Father," he called out when he spotted him sitting in the tall, winged-back wicker chair that was Wade's own personal favorite. "I wasn't aware you would be paying me a visit. Can you stay for supper?"

Walter Barlow's eyes narrowed while he watched his son bring his horse to a halt only a few feet away from where he'd left his carriage. His nostrils flared. "This is not exactly a social call."

Wade could tell by his father's angry tone exactly what sort of call this would be, even before he climbed down from his horse and tied the reins to the nearest post. The muscles around his stomach hardened. "I'm sorry to hear that. But if you change your mind, the offer stands. I'm not sure what we are having, but whatever Sam puts on the table, you can bet it will be good—especially since I bought him that brand new cookstove."

"I'm not here to eat," Walter reiterated. He never bothered to rise from his seat. Instead, he sat there in the tall chair, staring down at his son like an angry king on his throne. "I'm here to see if the rumors I've been hearing are true."

"And what rumors are those?" Wade asked, removing

his hat and wiping the sweat from his brow with the rolled-up portion of his shirt sleeve while he slowly climbed the planked steps. Though his father's angry expression caused a sickening hollow feeling in the pit of his stomach, he met the man's gaze straight on when he set his hat atop the bannister, then came to stand before the man.

"Rumor has it you've been helping Tucker's widow keep that place going. That you have been acting as her bloody foreman. Is that true?"

"Yes," Wade answered simply.

"Why?" Walter thundered, coming out of his chair at last.

"Because my cattle need water. My creek is dry as dust, has been for weeks, and Callie promised to give my cattle the run of her northwest pasture in exchange for a few hours of my help each day," he answered, though he was no longer as certain the water was the *only* reason he had decided to help out over there.

"Callie? You are on a first-name basis with the woman?" Walter's thick eyebrows rose high into his forehead.

"I guess so. I really hadn't noticed," he answered with a curious raise of his own brows. He wondered when he had quit referring to her as the Widow Tucker and had begun to use her Christian name.

"How could you? How could you do this to me?"

"I'm not doing anything to you, Father. I'm merely looking out for my own interests," he said, meaning his cattle. But his father quickly took it the wrong way.

"And you are interested in *that* little trollop? Is that why you were so quick to turn your back on your own father? You're looking to warm her bed?"

"No," came Wade's quick response, though he was not completely against the idea. In fact, the thought of bedding a woman like Callie Tucker intrigued him far more than it should.

"Then why? If you needed water that bad, why didn't

you come to me? My water's low, but I've still got enough for us to last out this drought—both of us."

"You can't be sure of that. Besides, I quit going to you for help a long time ago. And with damn good reason." Now it was Wade's turn to glare at his father. "I won't be made to feel like I'm begging for your favors—and that's exactly what you always try to make me feel every time I come to you for help. I've told you before, I can make it on my own without you or your help."

"Wade, you've gone too far this time. I've turned my back on some of the things you have done and said in the past. I've even forgiven you for walking out on me when I needed you most. I fully understand a man's needs to make it on his own—to be his own man. But I can't forgive this. You've turned completely against me this time, and for a scheming woman like that."

Walter was so angry now, the veins in his neck and forehead stood out and he clutched at his chest with a doubled-up fist as if he couldn't get quite enough breath to expel his wrath. "I won't let her get her greedy claws into you. I won't. I forbid you to go back over there. I forbid you to continue to help that woman in any way."

"And how do you plan to back that up?" Wade asked, curling his own hands into fists, but keeping them at his sides.

"If you dare go back over there and help that woman again, I'll—I'll rewrite my will so you'll get nothing from me. Do you hear me? Absolutely nothing!"

"I thought I was already cut out of your will," Wade stated evenly.

"Not completely, but if you defy me this time, you will be. I swear it!"

Wade stared at him a long moment, trying to keep his temper from raging any further out of control. It was true, his father had one of the nicest spreads around. Maybe not quite as grand or as prosperous as the Circle T, but clearly it was one of the nicest in East Texas. And he had to admit it was far nicer than his own. But then

131

Twin Oaks was coming along at a respectable pace, and would one day be as prosperous as, or possibly even more prosperous than, the Rocking W. That he would see to. Even so, he could not deny how, at the moment, the Rocking W was indeed one of the better ranches in the area.

Still, it was not so much that it could buy back Wade's loyalty and adoration. That was the sort of thing that must be earned.

"Father, I will not be manipulated like that," he said, his voice so low and so restrained, it came out almost a growl. "You just keep that inheritance of yours, with my blessing. In fact, why don't you leave it *all* to that bastard son of yours, because I assure you, it's not that important to me. It never has been. What is important to me is my own place."

"Big talk from the sort of man who can easily turn his back on his family. Maybe I *should* rewrite my will so that I leave *everything* to Evan. At least *he* would appreciate it."

Fighting the disgust that gnawed at his gut, Wade felt certain Evan would appreciate it. Evan had been groveling at his father's feet for practically as long as he could remember. "Do whatever you feel is necessary, because I've already promised Callie I'd help her and I don't intend to go back on that promise. I happen to believe in keeping my word, no matter the cost."

"Wade, don't do this. You will be sorry," Walter warned. He reached out to grasp his son by the shoulder in an effort to shake some sense into him.

"I don't think I will," Wade responded, quickly twisting himself from his father's grip and stepping away. "I'm really rather proud of myself for what I'm doing."

"Wade, I'm warning you."

"You've been warning me since I was a little boy. Well, I'm no longer that little boy, and I've had about enough."

"Don't go back over there," he said with finality. "I want that woman out of there so I can eventually take

132

over her land. You know how important owning the Circle T is to me. Without your help, she's certain to fail. With your help, she'll find a way to keep that place going indefinitely."

"I'm not too sure the place would fail even if I did quit going over there to help. Callie happens to have a damn good head on her shoulders, and more determination than sometimes I think is good for a woman."

"A damned good head on her shoulders?" Walter responded doubtfully. "Damned pretty maybe, but without your help, I guarantee she'd have that place in a shambles within the year."

"I'd almost agree to stay away just to prove you wrong, but I've given my word and I'm not going back on it."

"You'll be sorry you went against me like this. You both will," Walter said, his voice suddenly calm and strangely controlled while he continued to stare daggers through his son.

Weary from being at odds with his father, Wade dropped his shoulders and pressed his eyes closed for a moment. "I'm sorry you see it the way you do. I didn't do it as an act of rebellion against you. But I'm not going against a promise I made just because it does not quite suit your needs."

"After all I've done for you," Walter muttered before suddenly spinning up on his heel and making for his carriage.

No, after all you've done to *me,* Wade thought, fighting a sudden wave of anguish as he slowly turned to go inside.

Evan Samuels could not have been more pleased than when he learned of the heated argument which had occurred between Walter and Wade Barlow. He had always been jealous of Wade for being allowed to proudly bear the Barlow name when he was not. Evan enjoyed hearing his father rant and rave about his fool-hearted, traitorous son, and was especially happy to learn that Walter had decided to have his will redone yet again, leaving everything to him this time—and leaving absolutely nothing to Wade.

It was what he had hoped for from the day he learned who his real father was. It was why he had been willing to stay on as Walter's foreman no matter how many insulting remarks the old man hurled at him—and despite the fact he had never been allowed to openly claim that the man was his father. Still, Evan had always hoped that sticking with the old man no matter what his treatment would eventually pay off, and it looked like it was about to do just that.

"I can't believe Wade could go against you like that," Evan said, narrowing his hazel eyes in a show of deep concern. He hoped to worsen the gap between father and son by encouraging Walter's anger. "What sort of gratitude is that? Where is his loyalty?"

"To himself." Walter muttered his response while he jerked the glass stopper from the decanter Evan kept filled for him and poured himself a tall glass of whiskey. "I don't know where I went wrong with that boy."

"I don't think it is your fault," Evan said soothingly. "Wade was just determined to turn out bad."

"Oh, I can't say that he's bad exactly," Walter responded just before he turned toward his favorite chair with his glass in hand. He groaned aloud when he sank into the leather softness and leaned his head wearily against the back of it, unhappy over what had happened but at the same time glad to be home. "It's just that he is so damned independent."

Evan's shoulders drew back at Walter's sudden defense of Wade. Determined to keep his father and his stepbrother at odds, he quickly commented, "To the point that he has lost all regard for his own family."

"Maybe it's partially my fault. After all, I'm the one who raised him. Maybe I did something wrong," Walter said just before he lifted his glass to his lips and drained half the contents in one large gulp. He winced at the effect the liquor had on him, then glanced over at the son who looked so much like himself, though born out of wedlock and under another man's name. "Maybe I've been too hard on him in the past."

"No harder than you have been on me. And I never saw the need to turn my back on you the way he has."

"That's true. And I appreciate it, Evan. I really do," he said before raising the glass and quickly draining the rest of the whiskey in two more easy swallows. "That's why I am serious about changing my will so you get everything. I'll speak with the lawyer about changing my will right away. You have shown far more appreciation than Wade ever did. And if I find a way to get the Circle T away from Tucker's widow, I plan to see that you end up with it." He smiled when he realized how giving the place to Evan would make Tucker want to turn over in his grave.

"Let me have the Circle T? I'd sure like that," Evan said, smiling as he picked up the whiskey bottle and carried it across the room to refill Walter's glass. "I'd like that an awful lot."

Because Sunday was normally considered a day of rest and most of Callie's workhands had the day off—which was usually spent in town or in the bunkhouse with a hangover—Wade decided to wash up, change into a clean pair of denim trousers and one of his newer workshirts, and then rode over to the Circle T about mid-afternoon to make certain no problems had arisen which might need his attention.

Though he wouldn't mind finding some minor problem to help her with, there was one possible major problem he hoped neither he nor Callie would have to face anytime soon. Still, he felt it was inevitable they eventually would have to deal with it.

It was something he had worried about ever since his father's visit Friday afternoon. And despite the fact he

135

felt Callie should be able to handle the situation well enough on her own if it did indeed arise — even though she was a woman — he wanted to be around just in case she did need someone to intervene.

When he arrived, he was relieved to discover Callie, Janice, and Amy sitting outside among the lawn furniture, alone, enjoying the gentle afternoon breeze that drifted through the vast shaded area beneath the tall, stately oaks which shaded the southern portion of the yard just beyond the gardens. What a pretty picture the three made, sitting idly together, wasting away their afternoon — three lovely females without a care. It pleased him that nothing seemed amiss when he stopped his horse near the gardens and tethered the animal beneath the shade of another nearby oak.

"Hello," Callie immediately called to him when he dismounted and began walking across the garden in their direction. Delighted to see him, and curious to find out why he had come, she rose from her lounge chair and hurried to meet him halfway. Though her walk was actually a short one, it left her feeling a little giddy and short of breath; but she tried not to show it for fear he would see it as some sort of womanly weakness after she had strived so hard to prove herself just as able-bodied as any man. "We were about to ask Lucille to bring out a pitcher of lemonade. Would you care to join us?"

Wade also felt a little short of breath while he took in the way Callie looked in the cap-sleeved yellow and white dress she had chosen to wear that afternoon, and the way her thick brown hair was held in place at the sides with tiny silver combs but allowed to cascade freely down her back to her waist. The style accentuated the delicate oval shape of her face and the high arch of her shoulders.

That was when Wade noticed how very different she looked compared to the past few days, when she had usually dressed in a divided skirt and a loose-fitting blouse that closely resembled a man's shirt, with her hair always pulled back into a tight knot. And to make her

136

daily dress seem even more ludicrous, she had covered that glorious mane of hair with an oversized man's hat, which she'd insisted on wearing for fear the sun would darken that spattering of freckles starting to appear across her nose. Wade did not fully understand the concern about her freckles because he thought they were kind of cute, but knew better than to try to convince her of that.

In contrast to the odd costume which had become her everyday working attire of late—and which in all honestly had kind of a floppishness about it—what she had on now was alarmingly feminine.

Though the scooped neckline was modest by most standards, it revealed just enough of her tempting curves to catch his interest and set his imagination immediately to work.

"I didn't really come for refreshments," he started to explain, but then decided he would appreciate a reason to linger for a while, if for no other reason than to see her dressed more like a woman again. "But if it wouldn't be putting anyone to too much trouble, a cool glass of lemonade would be nice about now."

"Why *did* you come?" she asked while she turned to escort him to where Janice and Amy were still seated— Janice with her needlepoint, and Amy studying a glass jar in which she'd just trapped half a dozen bumblebees.

"I just wanted to be sure everything was all right over here. With most of the men away and the rest asleep, I was afraid something might come up that you might not be able to handle too well and you wouldn't have anyone around who could really help you." What worried him most about her being alone was that his father would probably pick that sort of moment to pay her a rather domineering visit to try again to convince her to sell the Circle T. He was certain his father would not pretend to be as friendly toward her during the second visit, and knew from experience just *how* intimidating his father could be. "I decided it would be better to find out about any problems today than wait until tomorrow, when they might be harder to solve."

Callie found it hard to believe he was suddenly so considerate, and studied his expression for any sign of his usual sarcasm, but when she found none, she smiled. Her heart fluttered. Maybe there was hope for the man yet. "I appreciate your concern, but nothing has gone wrong today. In fact, it has been a very pleasant day."

"I'm glad to hear it," he said, glancing only temporarily into her wide, almond-shaped eyes before looking away again. There was something very disturbing about the way she looked at him, as if seeing him for the first time. He swallowed to clear his throat, then reached up to run a hand over the dark hair at his nape, which suddenly felt as if it was sticking straight out. "It's just that when Harry left out of here Friday, I promised him I'd look after you, and I'd hate to think I'd failed to do that."

The statement struck Callie the wrong way. "And why did Harry think I needed such looking after?"

"Because you are a woman," he answered simply, as if that should be reason enough.

"And a woman can't possibly take care of herself," Callie surmised, tossing her head back to show the offense she had taken. Her golden-brown eyes sparkled with angry defiance.

"It's not that she *can't*," he quickly amended, not wanting to start yet another argument, especially over something he already knew she felt so strongly about. "It's just that she *shouldn't* have to."

That appeared to satisfy Callie for her smile quickly returned. "You know, Mr. Barlow, I do think we are starting to understand each other."

"Mr. Barlow? I thought you had started to call me Wade," he commented with a smile of his own, glad the sudden tension between them was gone. Suddenly, he was again aware how beautiful she was when she smiled and felt his body react accordingly.

Callie thought about Wade's comment, realized she had

indeed called him by his first name on several past occasions, and decided that was probably because whenever the men referred to him, it was always by his first name. "You're right. I have started to call you Wade. And since you don't mind, Wade it will be from now on."

Wade's smile grew dimple deep. He was pleased they were getting along that well, but wondered how long it could possibly last. It just did not seem natural for them to be so openly pleasant with each other. Maybe they actually *were* starting to understand each other. He and this headstrong, fiercely determined woman who stubbornly refused to see herself as just a woman. *Understand each other?*

He shuddered at the thought.

When they finally reached the area where the two girls sat watching them, it was easy to see that Janice did not approve of his arrival in the least. And when Callie then invited him to sit with them, Janice's eyes widened with righteous indignation as she quickly rose from her chair and took her leave, pausing long enough to toss an angry look of deep disdain at Wade before she went.

"What's her problem?" Wade asked, not yet having taken the seat offered him, watching while the young lady flounced her way across the yard and into the house.

"Janice has not yet adjusted to the fact I asked you to help out around here," Callie tried to explain as tactfully as possible. But children being what they are, Amy was quick to provide what Callie had hoped to leave out.

"My sister doesn't like you because you are a Barlow," she stated simply, cocking her head to one side while she looked at him in a very judgmental fashion. "She thinks the only reason you are pretending to be nice is because you want to trick us out of our home. That way, you and your father could live here instead."

"That's ridiculous," Wade tried to reassure her. "I already have a home that I'm very pleased with."

"Then why are you so interested in our place? You've come over every day since Tuesday. Why do you spend so

139

much of your time over here?" Amy wanted to know, indicating by her tone that she did not trust the man any more than Janice did.

"To help your stepmother."

"That's what she says too. But why?"

"Because I promised her I would in exchange for letting my cattle have access to the water in the northwest pasture. You see, the creek which runs across my land and fills all my ponds has dried up. I barely have enough water in my well to take care of the household needs."

"Then you are after our land for the water," Amy said, coming to what appeared to her a logical conclusion. Then lifting her chin she added, "But you aren't going to get it. No matter how nice you are to our stepmother, it won't do you any good. Callie can't sell the land without our signatures, and we are not about to sign." Then she too rose from her seat and flounced into the house, her dark braids bobbing while she went.

With his mouth agape, Wade watched, stunned not only by the girl's reaction but by the fact that Callie did not have complete and outright ownership of the Circle T as he had thought. She had not manipulated Tucker into giving her sole possession of the place after all. He wondered then if that was because she had never wanted sole possession or if old Tucker had seen through her game and had made certain provisions to keep her from ever having complete control. Slowly, he turned his gaze to Callie's unfathomable expression. "Is that what you also believe? That I'm after the Circle T?"

"Are you?" she asked, for the thought had crossed her mind more than once. It was certainly possible that out of some sort of family loyalty, he just might want to help Walter Barlow get his hands on the land the man so dearly wanted—though she truly did not want to believe it, and she wasn't sure how Wade could hope to accomplish such by helping her. And she had to admit he had indeed been very helpful since he'd taken on the responsibilities of Circle T foreman.

140

Angry she had even considered such a thing, Wade lashed out at her. "Look, just because you tried to get your hands on the place and couldn't, don't think that everyone else is out to do the same."

"Do you still believe I came here with the sole intention of tricking some poor dying man out of everything he owned?" She thought he understood by now just how wrong that assumption had been.

"What's a fellow to think when a woman comes to a place she's never been to marry a man she's never even met, even though that man is twice her age and all he really has to offer her is money?" he asked, his eyes narrowing until they were two slits of angry blue.

"There were certain circumstances which you know nothing about that brought me here," she told him. "And they had nothing to do with any aspirations to trick a dying man out of everything he owned. I already told you, I didn't even know Matthew was dying until after we were married. And he made the decision to change his will to include me, all on his own."

"Sure, you can say what you want and who is to dispute your word? A dead man? Can you prove you came here as innocent of Tucker's illness as you claim? Am I to believe you came here out of undying love for a man you never even met?"

Callie was so angry, every muscle in her tightened and her heart began to pound rapidly against her chest. "I don't really care what you believe. I don't have to prove anything to you."

"No, you don't. And I don't have to prove anything to you. And if you believe the main reason I've been helping out over here is because I'm out to find a way to get my hands on the Circle T, you can just forget our agreement," he shouted angrily, then turned and stalked back the way he had just come.

"Can you forget that your cattle need my water?" she called out to him before he had gone twenty feet, having suddenly remembered the clear advantage she still had.

Wade stopped dead in his tracks but did not turn around. She stared at his broad shoulders and rigid back and knew she had his full attention. "No, I think not. Our agreement still stands, Mr. Barlow. And you will see to your part of the bargain."

Wade glanced up at the sky visible between the spreading branches of the oak trees, praying he would discover a rain cloud visible somewhere overhead, but finding only a few feathery splashes of white streaked across an azure blue background. Feeling defeated, knowing she was absolutely right—his cattle did need her water—he turned back to face her, his eyes glowing with barely controlled anger.

"Have you nothing to say?" she goaded him, finding perverse pleasure in the fact he looked just as angry as, if not angrier, than she was.

Wade's hands were drawn into useless fists at his sides while his jaw muscles flexed rapidly in and out. He looked as if he considered stepping forward and breaking her in two.

"Well?" she prodded, crossing her arms defiantly over her rounded bosom. She hoped she did not display any of the fear she felt while she waited for his reply.

Throwing up his arms and dropping his shoulders as if aware he would gain nothing by any further display of anger, he drew his lips against his white teeth and muttered, barely loud enough for her to hear, "God, how I wish it would rain."

He then turned back around and continued on his way through the garden toward his horse, wondering where he'd ever gotten the idea that females were a helpless lot—and if the benefits he would gain by working there were truly worth such total aggravation.

"See you tomorrow then, Mr. Barlow," Callie called out to him in a singsong voice, feeling deeply elated and a little weak-kneed over the fact he had not chosen to quit.

Chapter Ten

Barely half an hour after Wade had ridden away, still clearly angry, Walter Barlow's tall, black carriage came to a jangling halt in front of Callie's house.

Callie had gotten over her own burst of anger shortly after Wade left, but had remained outside to think about all the things that had been said during Wade's short visit, trying to decide why the two of them were always at such odds with each other.

Not having thought the situation through quite as fully as she wanted, she was in no mood for company, and was especially in no mood to face Walter Barlow again. She did not bother to rise from her lawn chair. Nor did she offer any form of greeting. Instead, she pretended she had not noticed his arrival at all, and turned her attention to a small herd of cattle grazing in the distance.

Having already noticed her seated out on the lawn, Walter headed in her direction the moment he stepped down from the carriage and had dusted his clothing with the brush his driver handed him. By the time he had finished with that and had crossed the yard, he'd worked up a light sweat beneath the high collar of his white starched shirt and stretched his neck to relieve some of the discomfort while he reached into his coat pocket for his handkerchief.

Once he had placed himself directly in front of her, Callie had no choice but to look up at him and acknowledge his presence.

"Another hot day," he commented while he quickly mopped his face and neck, glancing around at their immediate surroundings. "Mind if I join you out here beneath the shade?"

Watching him warily, Callie shrugged and motioned to the vacant chair beside her.

Angered that she had yet bothered to speak to him, he stiffened. "Are you having some sort of difficulty with your tongue? Or are you always this rude to your guests?"

"Only to uninvited guests who visit at a time when I'd really prefer to be left alone," she said, raising a delicate eyebrow in a most meaningful manner, determined to remain calm, though she didn't mind the thought of irritating *him* to the fullest. Well remembering how angry she'd been after his last visit, she found great pleasure in the way his nostrils flared at such an insulting remark, and wished Matthew could be there to see the man that flustered.

"Well, then, I won't stay long," he said, making a great effort to seem unaffected by her brash comment. "I just came by to see if you were ready to talk a little business yet. You've had a chance now to see that ranch life is not quite as glamorous as you might have thought. Even with a fancy house and servants to wait on you hand and foot, it is nothing like what I am sure you were accustomed to in the city."

"No, it isn't," she readily agreed, grateful that it wasn't. She considered telling him all about the *glamorous* life she'd led back in New York, down on her hands and knees scrubbing and polishing floors until they gleamed, or bending over a hot tub of dirty laundry for hours on end, but decided it was really none of his business what her life had been like before. Self-consciously she pressed her hands into the folds of her wide yellow skirt to hide their rough, work-worn appearance, which had come from years and years of hard, manual work.

Unaware, Walter went on with his little well-rehearsed speech. "And I'm sure you've discovered what hard work

144

running a ranch can be, even with my son helping you what little he can each day. But then you can't hope that will go on forever, because just as soon as the drought is over, he'll have no need for your water anymore and you'll be on your own."

Callie felt her stomach knot in reaction to his words, but refused to let her concern show on her face. She did not want the man to know how she actually dreaded the day she could no longer expect Wade's help—or how she hoped it would not rain for months yet, though she knew it was a terribly irresponsible thing to wish for. "I know Wade's cooperation can't go on forever, but maybe by the time this drought is over, and Wade's ponds are again full, I will have found a reliable foreman to replace Harry, someone just as skilled at ranching as Wade is."

"Not around here," he told her. "The reliable men in these parts already have good jobs and aren't about to be persuaded to quit them in order to go to work for a city woman who doesn't even know the first thing about ranching. I thought I'd already explained all that to you."

"Well, then maybe I'll have to start advertising a little farther away," Callie suggested, finding it harder and harder not to display the anger she felt.

"But why go to all that trouble when I'm willing to pay you the going price for your land and all the improvements right now?" Walter dabbed at his face with his handkerchief again, clearly unaccustomed to wearing a full suit in the heat of the afternoon.

"Because, as I thought *I'd* already explained to *you,* neither I nor the girls have any desire to sell," she said, crossing her arms in front of her to emphasize the fact she still meant every word.

"Don't be so stubborn. Just because you have been lucky this far and haven't had any real trouble to contend with, don't think that's always the case. Ranching is a hard business and times get tough—*mighty* tough."

Callie did not like the way he had emphasized his words, as if he thought he might frighten her into selling just by what he had to say. It seemed ludicrous that he felt she could not handle tough times, when she had suffered through some of the toughest.

"And you'll find that I'm pretty tough myself," she told him, smiling sweetly and batting her eyelashes at him in a most feminine manner, knowing how that might irritate him further.

"Tough indeed. You may think that now, but I have a feeling you won't feel the same way for long. I guess you'll just have to learn the hard way that ranching is not the business a lady like yourself should be in. I'll be back in a week or two, after you've had more time to realize the hardships you are putting on yourself and on those two little girls who have been left in your care. My offer will no doubt sound a little better to you then." He stared at her a long moment as if he hoped she would suddenly see the foolishness of her ways and decide to sell to him right then.

"Is that all?" she asked after he had remained silent for several minutes. She had not cared for the way his words had come out sounding almost like a threat and was ready to be rid of him.

"Yes, for now, I guess it is."

"Then I really wish you would take your leave, sir, because if you don't get out of here right now and leave me alone, I believe you are going to find out that I'm not quite the lady you seem to think I am."

Walter's eyes widened while he studied her for a long moment.

"I'll be back." he said, biting out his warning. Then he abruptly stood and marched back to his carriage, mopping at his face and neck as he went.

As soon as Walter's carriage was out of sight, Callie tried to push all thought of his visit from her mind, but found it impossible to do. Later that evening, after most of the men had returned and were already in bed, Callie's thoughts were still in such a mass of tumbling confusion, she discovered she was incapable of sleep and decided to take a stroll through the garden to help soothe the restlessness she felt.

Aware one of the men could be about, even though the hour was late, she slipped her dress back on before padding out into the garden barefoot, enjoying the feel of the cool earth beneath her feet and the gentle night breeze against her skin.

Though visions of Walter's angry face continued to intrude on her thoughts, the person she most wanted to think about at the moment was Wade. She had not really wanted to alienate him any more than she already had, and considered the possibility of apologizing to the man for having questioned his integrity when he had given her no real reason to.

She wondered if, in turn, he would then apologize to her for some of the awful things he had said. Then, once they were again on good terms, perhaps they might find their way back to the pleasant relationship which had started to surface just moments before they had allowed their tongues to once again overpower their common sense. And maybe, if they found a way to become better friends, when the time came that he *could* leave her and no longer worry about water for his cattle, he wouldn't be as eager to go.

The thought of running the place without Wade's help made her so utterly miserable, she felt a strong physical pain somewhere in the vicinity of her stomach and had to sit down. Choosing the very chair she had offered Wade earlier, she leaned back and gazed longingly at the patches of star-filled sky visible through the overhanging branches of the huge oak tree.

As she stared at the twinkling lights above her, she wondered if Wade was asleep or if he too might be outside, enjoying the same view. Or did men find pleasure in such things? Did men enjoy the beauty of nature, the gentle night sounds of the crickets and frogs, joined by the occasional bellow of a cow wondering where her calf had wandered, or the high-pitched whinny of a horse eager for a

147

little night play. She closed her eyes to listen to the sounds of horses galloping about in the pastures and owls questioning the wisdom of such activity so late at night and with a moon of so little consequence.

It was then she noticed the faint smell of smoke. It wasn't quite like wood burning in a fireplace, but almost.

Turning her nose toward the scent, expecting to find that one of the men had stepped out into the yard to enjoy a late-night smoke, she immediately glimpsed a dull orangish glow coming from the one window near the back of the barn.

"Fire! In the tack room!" she cried out, stricken with panic. She hurried as fast as her bared feet would let her toward the bunkhouse to alert the men. But before she was able to cross the yard, the men had already begun to pour out the front door in various stages of undress, some looking to her for direction, others searching out the true seriousness of the situation themselves.

"Bucket brigade!" Stretch called out, buttoning his trousers while he ran toward the nearest pump, which was attached directly to the main well, closer to the house than to the barn.

"Bucket brigade!" echoed several other men as they quickly fell into line while two others hurried to open the barn's front door in an effort to get the animals out, then save what they could of the equipment inside. Clearly, the men had dealt with such emergencies before. Callie appeared to be the only one at a loss over what to do, and watched with stunned confusion, her heart thudding violently against her chest.

Andy and Tony Rutlege, brothers barely a year apart, hurried to save as much of the equipment and supplies as possible. Smoke rolled out the opened barn doors in huge, billowing clouds. The pungent odor of burning leather washed over the area, reaching Callie with a sickening force.

Finally Callie realized she was doing nothing to help, and rushed to join the brigade. She immediately began to

148

pass the heavy water buckets from Lucille, who had come running out of the house the moment she'd heard the commotion, to Manuel, who had materialized out of the bunkhouse with the rest of the men. Frantically, she handled the heavy buckets again and again, until her arms ached from the strain. Unable to see the fire itself from her position off to the side of the barn, she could only hope the men who were eventually receiving the buckets inside the barn had the fire under control by now. She dared not leave her position to find out. Everyone was needed.

But the fire was not yet under control because only moments later, the flames bit through the roof in a loud burst of red sparks, which were promptly whisked away on a gentle night breeze. The men who had gone inside scurried back out seconds later and began battling the blaze from the outside—some shoveling dirt as fast as their strength allowed, while others tossed the water from the buckets again and again. Andy and Tony had stopped hauling things outside and tossing them haphazardly into the yard, and had joined in the fight to put the blaze out.

"The whole back side of that thing is on fire," she heard someone call out. She thought it might have been Andy, but because everyone's backs were to her, she could not be sure who was talking. "What could have started it?"

"Damned if I know," came the response.

"We'll all be damned if those sparks catch the pastures on fire. As dry as it is out there, we won't have a chance," someone else shouted. "The whole county will go up in flames."

"Keep the water coming," came the next cry.

Callie did her best to comply, taking hold of the buckets as soon as they were presented to her, passing them as quickly as her aching arms would let her. Her skirt was soaked from the water that splashed over the rim and her toes sank into the small patch of mud she had created.

Suddenly she heard Amy's shrill voice cry out her horse's name, and when she glanced back, she saw the child was already running toward the barn as hard as she could. Callie had no choice but to leave the line to try to catch the child before she entered the burning building, which she felt certain the child would do. Amy's pony meant the world to her.

"Amy, come back here! Your pony is safe. The men have turned all the animals loose."

But Amy could not hear her over the constant shouts of the men and the loud popping of the fire still eating its way through the barn. The child's white night dress billowed behind her as she hurried forward, toward the smoke-filled door, desperately calling her horse by name.

"Amy, come back here," Callie called out again, and ran as quickly as she could, fearing for the child's life. She ignored the pain that shot through her ankle and leg when she carelessly stepped on a sharp rock and stumbled as a result. Her wet skirts weighted her down, slapping sharply against her ankles, fighting her efforts, but never fully stopping her.

Lucille and Manuel closed the gap Callie had left in the bucket line, never pausing in their effort to keep the brigade going. Each movement they made was to either hand off another full bucket or send back one of the empties. Tears streamed down Lucille's plump, sweat-soaked cheeks while she helplessly watched Callie chase after little Amy, slowly gaining on the child, but clearly not about to reach her in time. Fear froze the woman's heart, but the rest of her kept moving, kept passing the heavy buckets, hand over hand, while she prayed for the child's safety — and for Callie's safety as well.

"Amy!" Callie screamed out, her voice shrill with panic when she saw the girl disappear into the barn, aware that large portions of the burning roof might start falling at any moment. She was able to feel the heat from inside burning against her skin as she passed the men so engrossed with battling the blaze, they had not seen the child run past them nor heard her cries over their own frantic shouts.

"Callie," don't!" she heard just before she was about ⸗ follow Amy inside, and glanced back in time to see Wade and several of his men riding up into the yard, their horses in a dead run, many of the men with shovels or blankets in hand.

"Amy's in there!" she cried out, trying to be heard over the angry roar of the fire. She turned back to face the inferno before her, lifting her heavy skirts again, ready to pursue.

"I'll get her," Wade called out as he jumped from his horse, not bothering to tether the animal in any way. "You stay back."

Callie watched with stunned horror while Wade grabbed a bucket from one of the men before it could be pitched empty and doused his clothing with water. Then with no further hesitation, he disappeared into the orange glow inside the barn in search of Amy. She was able to hear his voice calling out the child's name, but had to look away when she felt a sharp tug on her sleeve. Janice now stood at her side, pulling on Callie's sleeve with one hand and clutching her night dress with the other, her dark hair tousled from sleep.

"Amy's in there?" Janice asked, her blue-green eyes wide with fear.

Unable to speak, Callie could only nod, then took the girl into her arms and held her close. Together they turned to watch the orange glare in the opening before them, unable to see where either Amy or Wade had gone. All they could do was pray Wade would find Amy in time and get out safely. Before the barn started to collapse.

Suddenly Callie's worst fears came true. There was a deep groan from high overhead, then a large section of burning roof crashed to the floor inside the barn. But from where they stood, it was impossible to tell if any of it had landed on either Amy or Wade. Her heart leapt to her throat, screaming out its message of pure panic.

"No!" she cried out frantically, pushing Janice away just before she snatched up her skirts to go inside, oblivi-

151

the flames dancing across the floor of the barn the collapsed section of roof had landed. The new n of fire was not ten yards from the doorway.

"Callie, come back," she heard Janice cry out. "Please, Callie, come back."

But Callie was desperate to see if Wade and Amy were all right and did not pause until she was inside the barn, and then only to search her surroundings for sight of the other two.

The heat against her skin was almost unbearable, but not nearly as unbearable as the pain in her heart when she called out to both Amy and Wade by name. The only response she received from her cries was the angry roar of the blaze, warning her to go back. Fearfully, she squinted against the heated glare while she tried to make out the shapes that remained in the small section of the barn still unaffected by flame, hoping against hope to find them both there, still safe—still alive.

"Callie, get out," she heard Wade call out. "I have Amy."

Weak with the most profound relief she had ever known, Callie gathered up her skirts and impulsively ran in the direction the voice had come from. Her eyes were bright with tears when she finally was able to see Wade's dark shape through the huge flames and the black smoke. He had Amy in his arms. Clearly frightened, Amy clutched at him, her face buried deep into his neck.

"Callie, I said get out!" he shouted again when he saw that instead of returning to the outside, the crazed woman had come farther into the burning structure. "More roof could fall at any moment."

As if his voice had given a command which the roof felt it should obey, another large section of burning wood collapsed between them, barely missing her as it obliterated Wade and Amy from her view.

"Wade! Are you all right?" Callie screamed, trying to peer through the fresh wall of flames that had risen from the newly fallen debris. The temperature inside the barn

152

rose another five degrees. Each breath Callie drew roasted her lungs. The rancid stench of scorched leather and burned wood railed at her stomach. Smoke now hovered only inches above her head, causing her to cough spasmodically. "Wade! Answer me!"

"Get out!" His angry response was barely heard above the renewed fury of the fire that billowed between them.

"Damnit woman, for the first time in your life do what I tell you!" He also began to cough—short, rasping coughs that reached inside him and twisted his lungs. Soon, Amy began to cough too. The smoke hovered ever closer to the ground.

With tears spilling from her eyes, Callie looked for a way to get to them, but found no clear passageway left. Fear clung to her like a black shroud. Fire was everywhere. Then, upon hearing a splintering crack above her, she turned and ran out the door just before a large flaming beam crashed to the floor, right where she had stood.

She heard the curses of the men who continued to battle the blaze, and saw the horror frozen on Janice's smoke-streaked face when the older child hurried forward to fling herself once again into Callie's arms. Holding desperately to each other, they turned to watch with stunned disbelief while the fire continued to rage out of control, eating away at the roof and walls, with Wade and Amy still trapped inside.

The next few minutes were fraught with unbearable suspense while Callie and Janice watched the door, hoping to see Wade and Amy dash their way safely through the flames at any moment. Another thundering crash. This time part of a side wall caved in, crumbling to the ground with inane slowness. Callie stifled a cry of anguish when she realized all hope was gone. The entire barn was in flames now.

The pain she felt was unbearable. Wade and Amy. Both dead. Horrible deaths. Amy. Her dear precious Amy. So young. So very young. And Wade. Her strong, handsome Wade. So full of life. So full of spirit. Wanting to save

153

Amy. Wanting desperately to save Amy. But he couldn't. He didn't. Now they were dead. Both dead.

Callie did not think she could bear it.

"Look, Callie. There!" she heard Janice cry, and obediently glanced in the direction the child pointed, but saw nothing in the corral but the flickering shadows created by the fire. The shadows soon blended into one, blurred by her tears. She closed her eyes to the pain that continued to grow inside of her.

"Didn't you see?" Janice sobbed. "Didn't you see?"

Callie looked again toward the corral, where Janice still pointed. A cough came out of the darkness, out of the shadows, just beyond the orange glow of the fire. Then another. Her pulse bounded at an incredible rate, then froze into nothing. Someone was out there. It looked like Wade, still carrying his precious cargo, running and stumbling like a madman across the far side of the corral toward the open gate, not daring to slow down until he was well away from the fire. Not daring to look back long enough to watch yet another section of barn tumble effortlessly to the ground.

Once the man was safely through the gate, he turned his face toward them. It *was* Wade. Crying out with astonished relief, Callie flew across the yard, with her arms flung wide. When she neared, Wade deposited Amy into her arms.

Callie saw tears in his eyes. From the smoke? Still not believing he was really there, she stared at him. He was one sooted mass of gray and black except for the two rims around his eyes, which stood out stark white around two glimmering pools of blue. He reached out to touch her, as if unable to believe they had all managed to get out of there alive, but he said nothing.

"Thank God you are both still alive," she sobbed brokenly while she pressed Amy against her, hysterical from her relief. "I thought you were both dead." Callie looked up into Wade's blackened face, her eyes brimming with the gratitude she felt. "How'd you ever get out of there?"

"No time to explain that now," he insisted, bent forward to press a kiss against her forehead, then hurried to join the other men in their continued fight against the blaze.

The kiss had come so naturally, that Callie had not thought it odd. It was as if such a show of affection was a common part of their relationship. But there was no time to really think about it then. Wade was right, there was still a fire to fight. Pausing long enough to make sure the two girls were safe and well away from the fire, Callie too quickly returned to help battle the blaze in any way possible.

By dawn, the danger had completely passed. There was nothing left of the barn but a smoldering black heap, but at least it offered no further threat to the other buildings or the pastures beyond.

One by one the men laid down their shovels and buckets, proud that although the barn was a total loss, they had been able to keep the fire from spreading to the other buildings and had put out all three of the grass fires ignited by stray sparks long before they were able to do much damage.

While several of the men began to round up the animals which had been turned loose and had strayed from the yard, Wade and Stretch Henderson began to pick their way through the rubble to see if they could find any useful remains, but discovered very little. The heat had been so intense, it had melted and disfigured even items made of sturdy metal. Everything inside the tack room was a loss. Everything inside the entire barn had been reduced to ash and cinder.

Though she was exhausted, Callie stood at the edge of the black smoking mass, watching dismally while the two continued to poke at the debris with long sticks, until she could bear to watch no longer. Turning back toward the house, she headed for the veranda, where Lucille busily tended to the men who had received minor injuries while fighting the blaze. She felt she should try to help, though she didn't know the first thing about treating burns.

Sadly, she crossed the yard littered with the items Andy and Tony had somehow rescued from the fire—so tired that every muscle in her body felt numb. Barely halfway to the house, she overheard the men again question how such a fire had gotten started. She paused near where they sat in a group and listened to their conversation.

"It sure spread fast. Almost as if it had had a little help."

"I think it did. I think that fire was deliberately set."

"But who would do such a thing?"

"Hell, if I know. It's just that when Tony and I went in there to get those animals out, it seemed to me the flames were on the outside eating their way in."

"That right?"

Suddenly the group got to their feet to go investigate. Callie followed at a distance as the lot of them converged on where the back of the barn had once stood and began prodding the ruin with the tips of their boots, then with broken boards and sticks.

"What's going on?" Wade asked, quickly joining them.

"We think the fire was deliberately set and wanted to see if there might be any proof of it lying around," Tony answered, eyeing the blackened mass speculatively.

Wade and Stretch exchanged glances and quickly started to help them look for anything that might reveal the fire had indeed resulted from arson. It was the next day before they discovered an empty metal container lying out in the pasture not too far from the house—a container that still smelled of kerosene.

With the proof finally found, speculation quickly began about who would have wanted to do such a thing. Some thought it was the prank of some rowdy just passing through, while others wondered aloud what sort of enemies Tucker's widow might have they didn't know about. They wondered who could be so angry with her that he would want to burn down her barn and at the same time risk the whole county going up in flames. Dry as the area was, they were lucky they had managed the fire as well as they had. And they were lucky no one had suffered any worse injuries than the minor cuts and burns Lucille had doctored the following morning.

Once it was evident the fire was indeed the result of arson, Wade became furious. After having gone through such a terrifying ordeal, one that had threatened their very lives, he was a jumble of tangled emotions ready to burst out in any way possible. They eventually burst out in anger that at first was targeted at everyone around him; but eventually he turned his anger on himself.

Callie too felt angry and frustrated, and she was also very confused. After such a terrifying experience, she and Wade both had been forced to view things a little differently—forced to analyze the strong feelings they had for one another and see just how important they had become to each other. The possibility of losing one another had been very real during those awful moments before Wade escaped the barn with Amy. And the resulting fear had lingered long after any real danger was gone.

Callie especially had been forced to examine her deepest, most secret emotions. She now understood just how important both Wade and the two girls were in her life. At first she tried to convince herself the strong emotional reaction she had felt after the fire was the result of the danger Amy had been in. After all, she had pledged to be responsible for the girl. But she knew it was much more than a feeling of having failed in her responsibility. Amy had come to mean more to her than she realized. And so had Wade.

It was startling to discover exactly how strongly she had come to care for the man in such a short time. In fact, when he and Amy had been temporarily trapped by the fire, before Wade had literally kicked his way through the side wall and escaped to safety, it had felt to Callie as if her own life was in danger—that if he died, or if Amy died, she would surely perish too.

The depth of her fear at that moment had amazed her. She had never thought it was possible to feel that strongly

157

about anyone. And the fact she did was not only surprising, but downright frightening. Especially when she realized she felt just as strongly about Wade as she did about Amy. The thought of forever losing him had somehow opened her heart to him. And once it was opened, she discovered emotions linked to Wade Barlow she had never known existed, and though she was not sure exactly what these new emotions were, she did understand that they were important. Later, when she went inside to take a much-needed bath, and had glimpsed herself in the mirror, she had seen where his mouth had left a streaked imprint on her forehead and remembered how easily he had kissed her. The memory of it warmed her. She wondered then if he might actually feel something for her, and also wondered how she might discover if he did.

When Wade later suggested they find someplace where they could be alone to privately discuss who might have started that fire, Callie hoped it was actually an excuse to be alone so he could finally tell her how he now felt. Her pulsebeat sped erratically when she followed him into Matthew's study, then became even more noticeable when she watched him slowly close the door behind them, putting the rest of the world outside the room.

Although Wade was indeed experiencing new emotions where Callie was concerned, he had no intention of telling her, at least not yet. He was the sort to keep such feelings to himself until he was more sure of them.

Even so, his first thought once they were indeed alone in Matthew's study was how easy it would be to take her into his arms and kiss her, see if she would want to pull away from him or if she would return the kiss with the passion he hoped for. But he knew that was not why they had sought a place to be alone. He knew they needed to discuss who might have set that blaze. Someone must have had a reason for doing such a thing. And whatever the reason turned out to be, that person needed to be prevented from doing anything like that again.

Wade's next thought was of how angry Janice had been

158

the afternoon before. He had never seen a child display such open hostility, but then he was not often around children.

"I know it is a little farfetched, but do you think Janice could possibly have had something to do with the fire?" he asked as soon as he had taken the chair beside her and turned to face her, trying not to concentrate on how beautiful she looked in the pale blue summer dress she had chosen. He needed to keep his mind on the business at hand. "Could Janice have slipped out of the house without you noticing, in order to set fire to the barn? Maybe as a way of protest—unaware of just how much damage she would cause?"

Callie understood the seriousness of the situation, and did not take offense at such a suggestion. Instead, she answered his question in a straightforward manner. "It wasn't Janice. I looked in on the girls just before I went outside. They were both asleep in their rooms."

"That's right. You were outside when the fire broke out," he remembered. "Didn't you hear anything? Didn't whoever was out there make any noise at all?"

Callie thought back, pressing her hands against her temples as if that might help. "I heard horses running, but I thought that was just our own horses prancing around in the pasture the way they sometimes do at night."

"Horses?" Wade asked, leaning forward in his chair and locking his fingers together. Looking at her from this new angle, he asked, "How many? Which direction did it sound like they were headed?"

"As I recall, there was more than one," Callie answered, closing her eyes in an attempt to remember more clearly. "Two, maybe three. But I don't know which direction they went. I wasn't really paying attention. My mind was preoccupied with other things."

"Like what?"

"Like the argument we'd had earlier. I felt terrible about that." She looked at him then, hoping he would view her words as a form of apology. "And the argument I later had with your father."

"My father? My father was here?" Wade felt suddenly ill

"Yes, still hoping to convince me to sell him the Circle T," she admitted with a heavy sigh. The thought of his father's visit no longer evoked anger, just a tired sort of reservation.

"And you refused?"

"Of course. You know my feeling about that."

Wade paused, afraid to ask his next question. "Did he leave angry?"

Callie smiled sheepishly, and glanced down at the deep folds of the skirt she had chosen to wear merely because of its color. She was now certain blue was one of Wade's favorite colors because of how often he chose to wear it himself—even now. She then glanced at his azure blue work shirt and the dark blue trousers that clung to the lithe muscles of his tall, lean body in such a way it made her even more aware of his extreme masculinity. "After a few of the things I said to him, I have no doubt he was *very* angry when he left." Then her eyes widened with sudden realization. "You don't think your father could have had something to do with that fire, do you?"

"I hope not," Wade responded morosely, leaning back in his chair again. Absently he ran a hand through the brown thickness of his hair as he stared momentarily at the ceiling. "I'd hate to think he could stoop that low." He then looked at her again, his blue eyes searching hers. "Callie, I-I—"

Whatever he was about to say was interrupted by a sharp knock at the door. Feeling oddly relieved Wade did not have to speak whatever painful words he had obviously planned to say, Callie hurried to open it. Her thoughts were still on the fact Wade's father might have been responsible for the fire when she pulled the door back and found Ed Grant, one of the stockmen Matthew had recently hired, standing in the hallway, his battered work hat in hand.

"What is it?" she asked, looking curiously at how repentant the man looked, his head bent and his shoulders drawn. And though Ed was usually meticulous about shaving, his chin sported at least two days' growth of beard. Had *he* started the fire? Was he now here to admit his crime?

"I-I came here to tell you I might know the reason someone set fire to the barn." Ed stared down at the powder-blue carpet that covered the study floor while he slowly took a single step into the room.

Wade was on his feet in an instant. "What? What do you know?"

"That fire might have had something to do with the fight me and a few of the other men got ourselves involved in Saturday night," he said, lifting his eyes briefly, but looking immediately back down before he was really able to see either one of them. "We didn't start the fight or nothing like that. But we bloodied a few noses and split a few lips before it was over, and maybe even broke one man's jaw."

"And?" Wade prodded when Ed suddenly fell silent.

"And, well, we've been talking it over, and think maybe those other men decided the fight wasn't yet over and came out here to set fire to the barn."

"Who were they?" Callie wanted to know.

"Don't rightly know. They hadn't been in town a week. Came in for the big Fourth of July doings. But it seems one of them took a fancy to Jim's girl and had started hounding her, trying to pay call on her even though she didn't want him to. That one's name was Alvin, but none of us can recollect his last name. Nor the names of any of the others. Just that they talked like they came from over in Louisiana. Cajuns." Again, he fell silent.

"And?" Wade prodded again when Ed had remained silent far too long.

"And when we found out about it, we all sort of took it upon ourselves to see that fellow, Alvin, didn't go bothering her no more and made ourselves to home in her front yard."

"And they took offense to that," Wade surmised, a grin twitching the outer corners of his mouth for Ed was clearly adamant that they had not done *anything* to provoke the fight.

"Sure did," Ed said, looking bewildered that such a thing had happened. "They threw that first punch, and next thing I know'd the sheriff was there pulling us all apart."

"Who got the worst of it?" Wade asked. He glanced at Ed's face and forearms and saw no signs of bruises, just a bad burn he'd received while fighting the fire.

"And what difference could that possibly make?" Callie asked, looking at the two with disbelief. "What we need to know is who these men are. And if they did have anything to do with that fire, I want them arrested."

"Last I know'd, all seven of them was being hauled off by the sheriff," Ed then supplied. "After all, *they* started the fight. They threw the first punch. They did. Jeanne herself can attest to that."

"Jeanne?"

"Jim's girl," Wade commented, already having figured that much out. Then turning back to Ed, he asked, "Do you think you'd recognize the men if you saw them again?"

"Sure, they'd be the ones with all the new bruises and cuts on their faces." Ed grinned. "One probably has a bandage around his jaw by now. I did that one myself."

"Well, let's go," Wade said, laughing and reaching for his hat, which he had laid on the table beside the door. When he turned back to Callie, there was a look of eager anticipation on his handsome face, and she wondered if it was because there was another fight on the make, this time one he could be involved with, or because he was relieved the suspicion had shifted from his father to someone else.

"I'll need to take a few of the men with me in case there's trouble," he said offhandedly. "While I'm in town,

162

I'll go ahead and order some of the lumber and supplies we'll need to build the new barn."

Though Callie felt a little offended he had not offered to let her go with them, when it was *her* barn that had burned, she caught herself smiling and slowly shaking her head while she watched Wade and Ed hurry determinedly down the hall, in long, steady strides toward the back door.

Men! How they did love a cause.

Chapter Eleven

Callie watched from the the top step of the back veranda while Wade and Ed hurriedly called to the men who had until then been hard at work, shoveling the blackened remains of the barn onto wagons, then dumping the ruin into a large gully near the high ridge that jutted out along the northside of the Circle T. The men had chosen the ridge for their dumpsite because it was so rarely traveled. The area was too dangerous to both man and beast to be put to any real use, and because it was, it seemed the perfect place for them to dump the ash.

Though the men had been gradually slowing down in their work, affected mostly by the high afternoon heat, they suddenly came alive at the suggestion they head into town to confront the other men again. Jim especially was excited. He had worried the ruffians might try to take a little of their anger out on Jeanne, and wanted to make sure they had not bothered her again.

Moments later, the men rode out toward Pine Fork, double file — like the calvary heading off to the rescue, with Wade and Jim in the lead. Eventually, Callie forced herself to turn back to the house. Somehow, she pushed aside the nagging fear Wade was headed for some unseen danger, and noticed Lucille was somewhere inside calling out Ruby's name at the top of her voice.

"What's the matter?" Callie asked when she entered

the kitchen from the outside just as Lucille entered from the dining room.

"I'm tryin' to find out where that Ruby's gotten herself off to now," Lucille muttered, her brow lowered and her lips puckered with obvious suspicion. "This is the second time since Saturday she's plumb disappeared on me. She's supposed to be upstairs dustin', but when I went to check, she wasn't up there. And I guess you noticed she wasn't around while we were busy fightin' that fire the other night. I think she's still slippin' off and seein' that no-good Thomas Rett from Twin Oaks! And when there's so much work to be done around here! With half of Mister Wade's men over here helping clear off that mess outside, I've got nearly twice as much supper to get cooked. I could sure use some help peelin' those taters and she knows it. When I do find that girl, I swear, I'm going to wring her fool neck."

Callie had not really thought about who had been at the fire and who had not. But now that Lucille mentioned it, she did not remember seeing Ruby at any time that night. In fact, she did not remember seeing Ruby until breakfast was being served to all the men shortly after dawn.

Briefly, Callie wondered if Ruby might have had something to do with the fire. Had the two lovers had a clandestine meeting inside the barn and accidentally knocked over a lantern while in the throes of passion? Had Ruby run away out of fear after realizing the fire had gotten out of hand? But then she recalled the container they'd found, and remembered the fire had been no accident. Still, she wondered where Ruby had been.

"I'll have a talk with her," Callie offered, hoping to calm Lucille before the veins popped right out of her neck.

"No, you won't, I will," Lucille retorted. "That is if I

can ever find her useless hide so that I *can* talk with her." Then suddenly, Lucille stormed on passed Callie, outside, still shouting out Ruby's name with all the force in her lungs.

Callie shook her head, very glad she was not Ruby, while she returned to the study to see if it was possible to get some work done. She needed to project what the new barn was going to cost, using the estimated figures Wade and Stretch had given her earlier. But mostly, she wanted to get her mind off what was soon to happen in town, after Wade and the men found the group they suspected had started the fire. She worried that this time those seven men would be armed and ready.

She hoped Wade would show the good sense to stop by and see the sheriff first, and wished she had thought to suggest just that before they rode out. She also hoped that if another fight did break out, or if it came down to gunplay, Wade would come out of it unharmed. Though she worried for all the men, the thought of someone bloodying Wade's handsome face or putting a bullet into that strong, virile body made her hurt inside. Almost enough to go out and try to saddle a horse herself so she could ride into town and see if there was something she might do to prevent such a thing.

But then she remembered how her saddle had been one of the ones to burn in the fire. Except for the men's personal saddles, which they always kept in the bunkhouse for what now seemed obvious reasons, *all* the saddles had burned. And Callie knew nothing about riding bareback.

Since she was unable to do anything but wait, the next several hours crept by at a snail's pace. She tried to concentrate on her work, but found her thoughts unwilling to stay with the tall columns of figures on the desk in front of her. When a soft knock sounded at the door shortly after five, she was so lost to her worries that the gentle noise startled her far more than it should have. Her hand flew to her throat.

"May I come in?" she heard Janice call softly through the closed door.

Eager for the intrusion, Callie hurried to the door to let the girl in.

"What is it? Is supper ready?" she asked, and quickly glanced back at the clock, wondering if she'd lost track of so much time.

"No, I just wanted to come in and see if you needed anything," Janice told her, looking up at her briefly, then back down at the small clasped hands in front of her. "I thought maybe you were thirsty or something."

Callie's heart went out to the child. Though Janice had stopped being openly hostile to her weeks ago, the girl had yet to offer any outward show of friendliness. Since her father's death, Janice had not once indicated whether she would be willing to accept Callie as part of her life or not. There had been only a cautious politeness between the two. But now, the girl had obviously come to a decision about Callie, and to Callie's relief, it was to finally accept her. Callie's patience and quiet understanding had won out at last. Janice had come to offer her first real sign of friendship, and Callie felt the resulting tears of joy rush to her eyes. Her first urge was to hug the child to her, but decided that might frighten her. No, Callie knew it would be wiser to let Janice set the pace for their budding friendship.

"Why, you must be able to read my thoughts. I was just now sitting there wondering if I dared stop long enough to go to the kitchen and get a cool glass of apple cider," Callie said with a generous smile, then knelt beside the girl. She reached out and touched Janice's hair, and noticed how the girl bit nervously into her lower lip. Callie slowly pulled her hand away. This was something so new for both of them that she did not

167

want to make any mistakes. "I wonder if I could persuade you to bring me a tall glass of apple cider. Maybe you could get one for yourself too and we could enjoy it together."

"Sure I can," Janice responded, smiling timidly at Callie. "I'd like that."

Callie's heart soared while she watched the girl leave the room.

Though Janice was gone only a few minutes, it gave Callie enough time to reflect on the reasons the girl had finally decided to accept her. She knew Matthew's parting letter had something to do with it, because it was right after that Janice had stopped being as hateful, but what had finally made her decide to accept her?

The fire must have affected even her. Not only had the horrible event altered the way she herself felt about the girls, and about Wade, it had altered the way Janice felt about her. Callie was certain of it. Suddenly, all the damage and all the inconvenience of not having a barn seemed worthwhile. Very worthwhile. She wished Matthew could be there to be a part of it. Suddenly she missed him. Almost as much as she used to miss her own parents. Maybe even more.

As Callie had hoped, Janice stayed to join her in a glass of cider, then sat and watched while Callie worked on her cost figures, even venturing to ask questions about how long it would take to rebuild the barn. All too soon, though, Amy came in looking for her older sister, and the two left together to see what they could do about Amy's shoe, which was well lodged in one of the trees in the back yard.

For a while after the girls had left, Callie drifted into a deep feeling of euphoria, having seen the first signs of acceptance from Janice at last. Finally she was being allowed to feel like a true part of the family, and it was a good feeling. A feeling she wished would last forever.

But all too soon, her thoughts returned to Wade and, once again, she found herself lost to despair, desperately worried for his safety.

Glancing at the clock for what had to be the hundredth time, she realized the men had been gone an awfully long time—too long. She tried not to think about what prevented their return, and at the same time, was unable to think of anything else. In the back of her mind, she could hear Walter Barlow's angry warning about the hardships that lay ahead for her. The man's deep voice echoed again and again, warning her there would be even more hardships ahead—until she thought she could no longer bear it.

For the first time since Matthew's death, she wondered if she would indeed be able to handle all the problems that went with running a ranch. She felt more grateful than ever to Wade for the help he had given her, and was still giving her. Even to the point of neglecting his own ranch.

The time continued to creep slowly by, but Callie did her best not to notice. She tried to return her attention to her work. For a while she was able to do just that, until she thought she heard the sounds of approaching horses. She paused to listen. Instantly, she knew the sounds were real. The men had finally returned. *Wade* had finally returned. With an aching heart, she tossed down her pencil and hurried outside to see if they were all right.

The moment she stepped through the door, Callie felt deeply relieved to see that although the men were sweaty and covered with road dust, it appeared none of them had been in a fight of any sort. Obviously, they had handled the situation without having to resort to any form of violence after all. Happily, she hurried down the back steps to greet them out in the yard, wishing she had the courage to fling her arms around Wade and hug him close in order to show him just how truly relieved she was to see him back unharmed.

"What happened?" she asked as soon as Wade had dismounted and walked over to speak with her. She looked up at him with eager anticipation.

"Couldn't find them. Sheriff said he let them out of jail early Sunday morning and, at his request, they left town shortly after that. He hasn't seen them since. No one has." He looked apologetic, as if he had failed her in some way.

"Then there's no way to know if those men had anything to do with the fire or not," Callie realized aloud, frowning.

"Or if they are still around hoping to repeat their little performance," Wade pointed out. "The sheriff told me what troublemakers they were. The type that might not let it go with just the one fire. And because of that, we will need to post a few extra men outside tonight. In fact, for the next *several* nights, with orders to keep their eyes peeled for trouble."

Callie thrilled at the way he had said "we" when the problem was actually hers. He was starting to feel like a real part of the place. "How many men should we consider sending out?"

"At least four, maybe five, at a time. We'll keep them out there in four-hour shifts starting just before it turns dark. That way everyone will also get a chance at some sleep. I'll stay and take one or two of the watches myself."

"But what about your own place?"

"What about it? It's not my men they are angry with," he pointed out, not giving a second thought to the neglect he was suddenly so willing to give Twin Oaks. "No, the danger is here. I'll just stay out in the bunkhouse with the other men and take my turn just like all the rest."

"But," Callie said, thinking to offer him the hospitality of the house, but not sure that would be appropriate or how he might interpret such an invitation.

"But what?" he asked when she did not finish her thought. He bent forward a little in order to better look into her face.

Callie felt suddenly awkward. "I'd feel safer if someone would stay in the house in case those men try to do something to one of us."

Wade nodded. "That's a good idea. Someone really should be in the house to protect you women. I should have thought of that myself."

He continued to nod while he considered it further. "Yes, there definitely needs to be at least one man in the house all night. Armed and ready for any sort of trouble," he said, then turned back to talk with the men about their evening duties ahead. He even mentioned Callie's suggestion that there be a man posted inside the house.

Having stayed to listen to the discussion, Callie felt disappointed when he did not mention whether or not he planned to be that man, and wondered if she should suggest it herself. She really did think she would feel safer with Wade right there in the house with her. But she was afraid he would make too much of her suggestion that he be their personal guard, and decided it would be wiser to remain quiet. Still, she hoped he would think of it himself.

She was further disappointed when darkness neared and Wade ordered Stretch to go inside and guard the house while he himself mounted a horse, his rifle jutting ominously out of his scabbard, and rode off to station himself where he would be able to see the entire homesite from a distance.

Jim Jones, who normally would have pulled night duty that night, and Hank McKenzie, who had been one of the first to volunteer because he was eager to get even for a broken tooth he'd suffered during the fight in town, also mounted horses and rode off in different directions. Meanwhile, Ed Grant made himself comfortable on the veranda along the east side of the house where he had a chance to view most of the outbuildings yet still remain protected by the shadows.

The rest of the men, three of whom Callie did not recognize but knew worked for Wade, went on into the bunkhouse to catch some sleep and await their turns at watch.

Callie was glad the girls had gone on to bed before Stretch let himself in, then carefully locked the doors behind him. She did not want to have to explain his presence in the house to them. Thus far, she had managed to keep the possibility of more danger from both of them by remaining calm throughout dinner and by reading a story to help put them to sleep the way she usually did.

After the girls were asleep, Callie stayed in the room with them until she was sure they would not waken again, then quietly slipped off to her own bedroom. She was weary from all the worry she had put herself through and desperately hoped to get some sleep. But, because the tormenting thoughts would not let go of her, she found herself up again, staring out the window into the eerie darkness beyond more times than not. She wondered just where Wade was and if he was safe. Vividly, her imagination portrayed all manner of danger, and at times she found herself nearly in tears. It was several long, fear-filled hours before she was finally able to find the sleep she so desperately needed, and when she awoke again, the sky outside her window was turning a soft ash gray, indicating morning was already on its way.

Surprised she had fallen asleep at all, Callie quickly

slipped out of bed. Blinking with sleep-muddled confusion, Callie paused to listen to the eerie silence that surrounded her. Because she usually slept until the sun had already turned the sky a pale blue and the sounds of waking animals virtually filled the morning air, she was unaware pre-dawn nearly always crept into dawn without as much as a whisper. The silence terrified her. She worried something had gone wrong and she had somehow slept right through it.

Hurriedly, she began to get dressed and, not bothering to do more than brush her hair back away from her face, she rushed downstairs with her long, dark mane flying loose behind her. She had barely taken time to put on her slippers and was still buttoning her blouse when she scurried down the stairs. She planned to return to her room to exchange her slippers for boots and put her hair up into its usual twist as soon as she had assured herself Wade was safe, but for now she had no time for that.

Because she was in far too much of a hurry to take the time to light a lamp, it was still very dark inside the house when she finally had the back door in sight. The only light to guide her rapid footsteps was the faint grayness radiating through the outdoor windows. But Callie hurried despite the darkness and never noticed the lumpy black form which lay on the floor just a few feet from the back entrance.

A startled scream pushed past her lips as she tumbled face forward over the dark lump, landing squarely on top of it with a loud "ooaf." Suddenly the huge thing beneath her started to move. She tried to scream again, but discovered the breath had been knocked right out of her as a result of the fall. She did not have enough air in her lungs to squeak, much less emit the scream that swelled in her throat. She began to panic.

"What the . . ." she heard Wade say even before her

eyes became accustomed enough to the darkness to see his surprised expression. Though she finally managed to gasp a much-needed breath, she was too stunned by what had happened to attempt to stand and continued to lie across him in an awkward manner, her breasts pressed hard into his stomach, her startled face only inches away from one of his muscular, cotton-clad shoulders. She noticed the gentle fragrance of pine and tobacco on his clothing and found it to be quite masculine—disturbingly so.

"Wade!" she cried out at last. Her voice was sharp, but more from embarrassment than anger. "What are you doing stretched out in the middle of the floor?"

"I needed to get some sleep and thought if I bunked down on the floor, right behind the door here, that if someone tried to . . ." he began to explain, but when he realized their situation more fully, he was unable to finish the statement. All intelligent thought left him as he stared at her still lying on top of him, her long brown hair cascading wildly about her face like a glorious waterfall, first flowing past her shoulders, then falling across his chest in a pool of shimmering darkness.

He blinked with disbelief, trying to pull a rational thought from his head, but all he was able to concentrate on at that particular moment was the fact Callie actually lay there—on top of him.

Curiously, he reached out a hand and felt the hair tumbling softly to his chest, then reached further up to caress her cheek. She was there all right—lying on top of him—her blouse half unbuttoned and much of her creamy flesh exposed to his view. His next thought was how good it felt to have her there.

Reacting strictly on impulse, and before any form of reason or self-restraint could intervene, he reached down, grasped beneath her arms, and pulled her higher

174

to put her mouth much closer to his. Then without warning, he cupped the back of her head with his hand and pulled that magnificent mouth down to meet his. It just seemed the natural thing to do.

Though the kiss started out to be a tender sampling of her sweetness, a gentle exploring of a woman who had slowly but surely been driving him insane with her bold beauty and her fiery temper, it quickly exploded into something far more demanding. With the passion of a man who had far too long denied himself something he had not even been fully aware he wanted until now, he rolled until he was the one on top. Hungrily, he continued to devour her with deeply demanding kisses, pressing his body firmly against hers.

Callie's eyes flew open with surprise at such a quick, unexpected change in their positions, but before she could react with protest, her eyelids slowly began to drift closed again. A strange tide of delightful sensations moved slowly through her body, leaving her with a warm, languid feeling, a feeling of overwhelming contentment. For the moment, her mind was unable to concentrate on anything but the sudden wonder of his mouth on hers. No thought of protest entered her mind.

Even when his hand slipped beneath her head and brought her mouth to a better angle to be kissed, she did not consider a protest—though deep down she knew she should. She was too caught up in the spinning vortex of pleasure Wade had created inside her. She was unable to believe the intensity of the emotions which had so suddenly sprung to life, unable to cope with their volatile strength. Instead of protest or a valiant struggle to free herself, she brought her arms up to encircle his strong neck and allowed her fingers to slip into the soft thickness of his curling brown hair.

When he felt certain she was not going to try and stop him, Wade began to tease the sensitive curve of her

175

lips with his tongue until she parted them further, enabling him to enter at last. Eagerly, hungrily, he darted the tip of his tongue into her mouth and sampled the honeyed sweetness. But a sampling was not enough. Never had he wanted to possess a woman more than he wanted to possess Callie. His kiss became even more demanding.

Callie gasped. Suddenly the room did not seem to have enough air. She began to breathe in short rapid breaths. The feel of his lips fiercely caressing hers along with the gentle teasing of his tongue inside her mouth drove her to a fine point of madness. Wave after fiery wave of pure liquid desire poured into her bloodstream, possessing her quickly. That coupled with the feel of her breasts pressed intimately against his hard, muscular chest made Callie cry aloud with a pleasurable need she had never known existed. Suddenly she wanted to show him just how wondrously he affected her, and pressed her mouth harder against his, hoping that by doing so she could share with him some of the passion she felt.

Never had Callie felt such a startlingly strong response to anything or anyone in her life. It was as if a strange sort of fire now raged uncontrolled inside of her, a fire just as threatening and just as all-consuming as the blaze which had taken the barn. The intensity of it was as frightening as it was thrilling—so frightening, Callie clearly sensed the danger and wanted to pull away before it was too late, but somehow was unable to find the strength needed to actually do so. It was as if Wade suddenly had some sort of power over her, a power that made her body refuse her own commands. She felt helpless, but at the same time wondrously alive. Soon the feeling of danger began to lessen as she was lured into a higher state of madness.

It was not until Wade shifted his weight to one side so he could slip his hand into the partial opening of her blouse and gently cup one of her breasts through the thin fabric of her camisole—while his mouth continued to claim hers with deep, hungry kisses—that the odd sense of danger finally grew to overpower the first awakenings of Callie's passion.

"Wade, don't," she gasped, making her first attempt to resist, but the words came out muffled, lost in the warm depths of his mouth while he continued to work his strange magic over her. A magic she was becoming more and more lost to despite her sudden fear.

Slowly, the desire to stop him, stop him before it was too late, grew gradually weaker until she had no resolve left at all. She allowed him to slip his hand beneath the thin fabric of her camisole and claim the breast at last. She trembled from the effect his touch had on her naked skin, and found herself clutching weakly against him by the time his fingers reached for and found the sensitive peak.

Had there not been a knock on the door at that precise moment, Callie was not sure what might have happened. Though she had been kissed before, she had never experienced anything like what she had just experienced with Wade.

Her senses were still reeling, making her very light-headed, and her heart still pounded hard against her chest when he slowly rolled away from her and forced himself to his feet. Though the spell between them was broken, sanity was slow to return. Unable to move, Callie lay there breathless and bewildered, until a second persistent knock brought her more fully to her senses.

"Who is it?" Callie called out in a voice which sounded foreign when she finally stood and quickly finished buttoning her blouse. She was still able to feel his touch beneath the layers of fabric when she swallowed against the painful swelling in her throat and called out again. "Who is it?"

"It's me. Stretch," came the response. "Is that you Mrs. Tucker?"

"Yes."

"Doesn't sound like you. Is Wade still in there?"

"Yes, Yes, he is. He's right here," she answered just before she reached first for the security bolt, then the doorknob in order to let him in. She hoped Wade could not see how her hands trembled when she tried to perform such simple tasks. She felt it a wonder she had managed the last of her buttons.

When the door finally opened, Stretch had a puzzled expression on his thin face, as if he wondered why Callie and Wade both happened to be standing just inside the door, but didn't say anything about it. Instead, he quickly turned his attention to Wade. "Sun's about to come up. Want me to bring in that last group of men and let them get some rest now? You said yourself it was unlikely those men would try anything in the daytime. Too cowardly for that. So there's really no sense keeping anyone out there for very much longer."

"Go ahead. Call them in," Wade said as he bent over and snatched up the blanket and the chair cushion he had used to make his bed. "I'll be right out."

Stretch passed another look from Wade to Callie, then to the blanket draped over Wade's arm, before he turned to leave, making Callie wonder how much he suspected. Suddenly afraid to be alone with Wade again, she stood with one hand still on the doorknob and the other pressed to her throat while she watched Stretch leave. Even after the older man had tromped back down the steps and out into the yard, Callie hesitated to close the door again.

"Callie, I didn't . . . ." Wade started to say, but his words died on his tongue. Knowing the reason she had yet to close the door was because she was afraid to, afraid to be alone with him again, he stared at the deep indentations his fingers made in the cushion's softness and tried to think of some way to put her at ease. Slowly, he looked up to face her, his blue eyes glimmering with concern. "Callie, I didn't mean for that to happen. I don't think I was really awake. I know I wasn't thinking straight. I'm sorry."

Callie didn't know what to say either, but did finally close the door while she considered what her response should be. She wasn't sure she *wanted* him to be sorry for what he'd done, but didn't dare tell him that. What would he think of her? To her relief, she did not have to say anything. Lucille's heavy footsteps were coming down the stairs behind them, and soon the soft glow of the lamp she carried reached out into the hallway where they stood.

"I thought I heard voices down here," Lucille said, unaccustomed to finding any of the household up and dressed before her, especially since just before Matthew took ill.

"Yes, I wanted to find Wade to see if anything happened last night," Callie quickly explained, lowering her hand from her throat and letting it hang limply at her side.

"And *did* anything happen?" Lucille wanted to know when she came forward to join them. The lamp she carried cast eerie shadows across their faces.

"Nothing important," Wade assured her as he tossed the cushion aside and began to fold his blanket in a haphazard manner.

For some reason, Wade's response bothered Callie. *Nothing important.* Was he secretly referring to the kiss? Was that his way of letting her know the kiss had meant nothing to him? Was that why he wished it hadn't happened?

"Good," Lucille responded to Wade with a pleased nod. "Maybe those men have done all the damage they

179

intend to do and have already moved on." Then she turned her attention to Callie. "You planning on an early breakfast?"

"No, you go ahead and feed the men first like you always do. Now that I've found out nothing *important* has happened, I should return upstairs to change into my boots and do something with my hair," she answered, an unexplainable edge to her voice. She hurriedly took several steps in the direction Lucille had just come from. She was eager to get away from both of them. She needed time to think.

"Yes'm, I'd say that hair could use a good brushin'," Lucille commented aloud, tilting her head and tapping her slippered foot lightly while she watched Callie hurry toward the stairs. "And that dress of yours could use a good brushin' too. It looks almost like you've been wallerin' in the floor. In fact, maybe you should change dresses entirely and bring that one down to be washed." Then she cut an examining eye to Wade's rumpled clothing. "You look like you could use a fresh change of clothes yourself."

Wade shifted uncomfortably beneath Lucille's knowing gaze as he tucked his folded blanket under his arm. "That'll have to wait. I didn't think to send anyone for an extra set of clothes and I'm not quite ready to leave here just yet. Not until I've heard a full report from everyone who took a watch last night."

But that was not the real reason he did not want to leave just yet, and he knew it. He needed to find another chance to be alone with Callie, to better apologize for what he'd just done. He'd had no right to take advantage of her like that. It was just that she had looked so beautiful, and had *felt* so *good* lying there on top of him the way she was, he had been unable to stop himself.

He was glad Stretch had interrupted them when he

180

had because he was certain he would have tried to take his newfound passion for Callie too far, and she never would have forgiven him for that. As he turned to go outside, he vowed to be far more careful of his emotions in the future, because if he wasn't, he knew there was a good chance he might actually fall in love with the woman, and he was not at all ready to complicate his life any more than it already was.

Restlessly, Callie stood at her bedroom window gazing out at the activity in the yard until after she heard Wade leave the house, then she began to pace about her room at a frantic rate, wondering how she had ever allowed him to kiss her like that. It had been wrong. It had been all wrong, and she knew it. What had caused her to respond to him the way she had, like some wanton fool, starved for affection?

Maybe that was it. Maybe she *was* so starved for affection that she was willing to go to any lengths to find it. But wasn't she confusing affection with a man's innate passions? And what of her own passions? What had caused her to respond to his kiss with such hunger, with such open abandon?

Gingerly, she reached up and touched her lips where he had just thoroughly kissed her, then she gently touched her stomach. A languid warmth lingered where once there had been fire, causing her heart to speed up again as she recalled the kiss more fully. Then the words *nothing important* echoed in the back regions of her mind and the warmth was suddenly gone. In its place was an ache, a painful hollowness that bore down into the very core of her, and she wondered what it would take to make it go away. She supposed only time held the cure.

Because Callie was not eager to face Wade again,

though she knew she would never be able to avoid him forever, she decided to return to Matthew's study to finish working on the cost estimate for the new barn instead of going outside to join the men in their regular duties of the day.

Normally, after breakfast, she spent a little time with the girls, then went outside to be at Wade's side, helping in any way possible and asking questions about the things which did not quite make sense to her. She wanted to learn as much about ranching as she could, in preparation for the day Wade no longer had a reason to work for her. She needed to become as self-sufficient as possible.

But today, she did not want to be by his side. She was too embarrassed over what she had allowed to happen, and did not want to see the condemning expression she knew would have returned to Wade's face—the same look of disgust he'd displayed back when he thought she'd married Matthew for his money.

By now, he'd had plenty of time to think about what had happened between them, and would have decided once again that she was a woman of very questionable morals—which obviously she was, or else she never would have succumbed as willingly to the powerful passions his kiss and his touch had aroused in her. He had already had such a poor opinion of her. It hurt to consider what he must think of her now.

Sadly, she wondered how she would ever convince him she was not the sort of woman she had seemed. How could she possibly convince him she did not normally allow a man to be that bold with her—when she had not even tried to free herself from his embrace, but instead had accepted both his kisses and his touch eagerly? The situation was hopeless.

Though hours slowly passed, Callie was still too lost to her overwhelming misery to notice the footsteps when they first sounded in the hallway outside the study door. It was the gentle rapping at her door that startled her out of her dark reverie enough for her to notice someone wanted her.

"Who is it?" She hoped it would be Janice. Or Amy, wondering why she had missed both lunch and their afternoon tea.

"It's me. Wade."

Callie's heart froze in mid-beat, just from having heard the deep sound of his voice. She was not ready to face him again. Not yet. She decided it would be better to send him away for now. "I'm busy. What is it you want?"

"We've got trouble again," Wade told her. She knew by his tone of voice he was very upset.

"Serious trouble?" she called out as she rose from her desk and hurried to the door, her previous concern suddenly forgotten.

Wade waited until she had opened the door before he answered. His expression was grim, barely containing the anger he felt. "Yes, it's serious. Very serious!"

Chapter Twelve

Wade waited until Callie had stepped back away from the door before he entered the room made of dark hardwoods and pale, dusty blues. How he hated being the harbinger of yet more bad news. "Someone's cut the north fence in several different locations, each about a half a mile a part. As a result, a lot of our cattle from the northwest pasture and some of your cattle from the northeast pastures have wandered up onto the ridge. Several have already fallen over the cliffs on the far side and have died."

Wade's words struck her hard. Stepping back, she leaned heavily against the desk, and did not look at him when she asked, "Who discovered the downed fence line?" Her skin prickled with a combination of anger and fear while she awaited the answer.

"Not downed. Cut. Stretch noticed it this afternoon while he and Ed were out riding boundary. No telling how long it's been that way. They signaled for help, and while Andy and Tony rode over to find out why the emergency shots were fired, Stretch and Ed went on up onto the ridge to see if they could determine how many of our cattle might have taken advantage of the open fence to get to the greener grass up along the slopes there."

Aware she had turned pale from the sudden news, he reached out a hand and placed it on her shoulder, to steady her. It was a caring gesture that sent a flicker of warmth and reassurance through her when she needed it most. At least, she would not have to face the dilemma alone. She felt deeply grateful to him for always being there when she needed him most—grateful, and something more. Something so strong, so all-powerful, she could not identify it—just knew that it existed.

"How many cattle did they see?"

"They told Andy it was hard to tell with all the trees and the brush up near the top, but that clearly more than a dozen had already fallen to their death. Stretch, Tony, and Ed immediately began running what cattle they were able to find on out of there while Andy came back for more help. Problem is, it will be dark in a few hours. And because of the rocky terrain, it's not only going to be hard to find most of those animals once it's dark, but it will also be very dangerous."

His expression hardened, yet the touch at her shoulder remained gentle when he continued to explain. "But we've got to try to get them out of there, because more and more cattle are stumbling to their deaths all the time. The men are getting ready to conduct a night search now. Meanwhile I've already sent some of the men out to mend the fence so no more of the cattle can get through, and I sent a couple of your men up onto the ridge to try to keep as many as they can from approaching the cliffs at all. I also sent Andy on over to my place to get some more of my own men over here to help guard the house while the rest of us work to save what cattle we can."

"Guard the house? Then you do think it is the same men who burned the barn," she realized aloud, though she already suspected the same thing.

"Who else could it be?" Wade asked. As his frustration grew, he let go of her shoulder in order to rake the hand through his dark hair. "We were so busy keeping

185

an eye on the house and the other buildings, thinking that was where they'd cause trouble, we neglected the back fence line. Made it real easy for them to just ride up to that fence and cut it."

"But there's a law against carrying wire cutters in your saddlebags," Callie said, just as frustrated as he was. A coldness quickly settled where his hand had just lain. She wished he'd put the hand back.

"There's laws against burning down a person's barn, but that didn't stop them either."

"What can I do?"

"When my men get here, tell them I want them to spread out and watch for trouble. I'm heading on out to the ridge to see if we can't get a few head rounded on up before it gets too dark."

Wade then turned to leave the room, but Callie called him back. She could not let him go without telling him at least some of what was in her heart. "Wade. I want you to know how sorry I am you had to get caught up in all this."

Wade looked back at her, smiling just enough to produce a dimple in his right cheek. "It's not your fault, kitten."

Callie returned his smile. That was the first time he had ever called her that. It felt good to be called something as sweet and endearing as a kitten, even though it meant he must see her as a vulnerable, almost helpless little creature. Then again, at the moment she felt very vulnerable. After twice being made the victim of some horrible game in which she had not chosen to play, she felt very vulnerable indeed. Very much like a poor defenseless little kitten.

She shook at the thought.

"But I feel guilty just the same. If it wasn't for me, your cattle wouldn't have been in that northwest pasture and would not be in such danger. Nor would you.

Please believe me when I say that I hope all the dead cattle turn out to be mine." Then she shuddered when she thought of the cruel deaths the animals had suffered, and knew that still more would suffer before the night was over. Suddenly tears filled her eyes. "Should we send for the sheriff?"

"I already have. McKenzie's to bring him and whatever deputies he can get hold of straight on out to the ridge." Wade started to leave again. "Meanwhile, I'd better get going."

"Wade?"

He glanced back once more.

Though a part of her ached to tell him how much he meant to her—how very, *very* much—and how truly grateful she felt toward him, another part of her warned her not to be that open with her feelings. By revealing everything she felt toward him, she would just end up making herself even more vulnerable than she already was. When she finally did speak again, all she could say was, "Be careful."

In response, he smiled one of his cocky smiles, which he usually used to irritate her. But this time was clearly meant to cheer her, and before he left, he saluted her with a fingertip to his forehead. "Always am."

Still Callie worried frantically while she waited for word of what was happening at the ridge. In her mind, she visualized those other men hiding away, waiting for Wade and any of the rest of her men from behind large rocks and thick bushes with their guns ready. Even while being careful, Wade could easily be caught unaware and badly hurt—or even killed. She tried desperately not to let such fears get the better of her, but soon discovered she was defenseless to stop them.

As expected, Wade's men appeared at the house barely an hour after he had ridden off toward the ridge, just as darkness descended. After a brief round of introductions

187

in which Callie barely caught their first names, the men were off, ready to follow the instructions Wade had left for them without question or complaint. Callie was amazed at their loyalty, at their obvious devotion to their boss. Then she realized Wade had amassed that same sort of loyalty from her own men. Or was their willingness to work so hard more a result of the loyalty they still felt toward Matthew, wanting as much as she did to keep his dream alive? Or was it merely guilt for having started this whole ruckus in the first place? Whatever the reason, she knew they were all working extra hard to see her over these sudden hardships.

Suddenly, Walter Barlow's harsh warning shot through her mind. He'd hinted there might be hardships ahead, and had mentioned something about learning the hard way how ranching was no business for her—and she could not imagine lessons any harder learned than those which had been thrust at her that week. It was as if he had prophesied the incidents. For a brief moment, she wondered again if he'd had anything to do with the many problems she'd suffered since his last visit, but then remembered the obvious culprits, and decided she was overreacting to the stress of having to suffer through yet another horrifying ordeal.

She tried instead to focus on the confidence Matthew had shown in her. She tried to remember the reassuring words he'd spoken just days before his death. He had believed in her. He'd believed she had the ability to see any problem through. It was up to her to remain strong and do just that. Whatever the problems to come her way, she had to see them through to the end, had to come out on top. For Matthew's sake. And for the girls' sakes.

Desperately, Callie tried to hold on to her renewed determination. Occasionally, while sitting out on the veranda waiting for someone to return, she heard gunshots. Carefully she watched the darkness for sign of a rider, anyone who might explain to her what was happening. Yet she did what she could not to worry.

But as the hours passed with no word to offer her encouragement, her determination gradually weakened, until she began to jump whenever there was another sound of gunfire. With each new gunblast, her apprehension grew. She wondered if her earlier visions concerning the danger Wade might be facing out there had somehow come true. Had the men been hiding in the dark, waiting, and were they now out there picking everyone off one at a time? She had no way of knowing.

Eventually, the waiting became too much to bear, and Callie went inside to try to reassure the girls everything was all right and get some much-needed rest, futile though it seemed.

It was after midnight before Ed and Tony made the ride back to get more lanterns. At last, Callie would be able to get some sort of a report on what was happening up on the ridge.

Having been able to actually fall asleep, she was awake and still dressed, and she hurried outside. She met the two men just as they emerged from the toolshed with their arms weighted down with the supplies they were sent to get.

While they worked to strap the lanterns securely to their saddles, they explained the fence had finally been repaired, and how the men who had been working on those repairs now wanted to help the others search the vast, wooded area along the upper ridge for more of the strays. That meant they not only needed more lanterns, but more rope to be able to lasso the cattle they did find and haul them to safety.

After he finished attaching all he had brought out of the toolshed, Ed made a second trip into the toolshed for more rope while Tony went on to explain how they were having to bring the cattle out one at a time through the only gate as soon as they were found, and how dangerous that was with such insufficient lighting.

"We already had one horse stumble pretty bad, and they thought they were going to have to shoot it, but it turned out the leg was not broken. Eventually, the horse got up and walked," he told her as he reached out to lovingly stroke the neck of his own horse. "We were all glad to see it."

Aware the two were about to remount and ride on back out to the ridge. Callie remembered the gunshots she'd heard and asked about them. She also asked if either of them knew how many animals had been lost.

"The gunshots are because they've been having to kill the poor animals that fell over the cliffs, but were not fortunate enough to die right away and lay writhing in pain at the bottom of the ravine." Ed told her.

As for the number of cattle already dead, neither man could even guess. But Tony understood her need to know *something*.

"I hear there was probably twenty or more down at the bottom of that ravine when it first started getting dark," he told her, grimacing at the thought of it. "But since then, there's been several more fall to their deaths. It's heartbreaking. We were helping to repair the fence, so we weren't really up on the ridge. But still, every now and then we would hear some poor steer bellow out as he fell to his death."

Callie closed her eyes and tried not to imagine it. "Did the sheriff come?"

"Oh, sure. But there's not much he can do until daybreak, when he can finally send out telegrams to the neighboring towns and then start making the usual sort of rounds—questioning all your neighbors about having seen anything suspicious-looking. Right now, though, he's out there helping the men round up some of the strays. And we'd better get on back there too. The sooner we get there with these lanterns and this rope, the sooner we can all get out and help find those poor strays. It's heartbreaking. It really is."

"Be careful," Callie called out to them instinctively as they again rode away, each carrying a lantern high over his head.

"Yes, ma'am," she heard Tony call back to her. Then he reached forward with the hand that held the reins between his thumb and forefinger and patted his rifle stock reassuringly. "We definitely plan to be that."

Again, all Callie could do was wait, and keep a wary eye for any unusual movement in the various shades of darkness that surrounded the house. Though she knew Wade's men were out there somewhere, watching for any real signs of trouble, she felt so personally responsible for the girls' safety that she found herself at her bedroom window carefully searching the shadows more times than not.

Anxiously, she kept her vigil the entire night, and continued to watch and wait through the excruciatingly slow breaking of dawn, wishing someone would return to tell her what was happening out on the ridge.

Shortly after sunrise, Wade's men returned from having kept a close watch on the area, learned Wade was still out at the ridge rounding up the strays, and headed immediately in that direction, declining Lucille's offer to prepare breakfast for them before they went. Only Manuel remained at the house, with orders to fire three shots into the air should anyone who looked even remotely suspicious try to approach.

Callie saw no one else until after one o'clock, when Stretch and one of Wade's men rode in, dust flying. Fearing the worst, she rushed outside to discover what made them hurry so.

"The men are starving," Stretch explained just before he pulled his horse to an abrupt halt in the yard, only a few feet from where Callie had stood holding her breath.

At the same moment Callie sighed out her relief, Lucille stepped out onto the back veranda, wiping her hands on the lower corner of her apron.

Neither woman looked as if she had slept.

Neither had.

"Lucille, can you round up a little chow for the men?" Stretch called out the moment he noticed her.

"Which you want? Breakfast or lunch? I got both already cooked," Lucille asked. She watched while the two hurriedly dismounted, then tied their horses to the nearest posts.

"Bless your scrawny old heart," Stretch shouted back. A tired, but grateful smile spread across his narrow, unshaven face. "I'll take both. Whatever you've got. Box it all up while Rebel and I get a wagon hitched."

"There's no need," Callie explained, wiping a loose strand of hair away from her temple with the back of her damp hand. "Wagon's already hitched. Since you men had already missed three entire meals, Lucille and I were just about to take the food out there ourselves."

"Who hitched her up?" Stretch wanted to know, remembering Manuel didn't know the first thing about a wagon harness. In fact, the only real thing Manuel seemed to know about horses was that manure had proven good for helping his plants grow.

"I hitched the wagon myself," Callie told him proudly.

Stretch's eyebrows rose with immediate surprise as he turned and headed for the carriage house, where most of the wagons were being stored now that there was no barn. He wanted to see for himself. Only moments later, he drove the wagon she'd hitched out the doors, shaking his head with true amazement.

"You did a good job. How'd you ever know how to rig her up like that?" he asked while he slowly drove passed her.

"I've been watching you," she explained, as if anyone who watched the process should be able to duplicate it — though even she'd had her doubts when she had finally decided to give it a try.

"Well, since we don't have to waste any time hitching up the wagon, maybe we'd better go on in the house and help Lucille pack up that food. The sooner we get something out there, the sooner those men can eat and quit complaining about their empty stomachs."

Lucille grinned at the men's surprised expressions when they turned toward the house and discovered she had already come back outside and was on the back veranda, casually seated beside a half-dozen boxes filled with food. "You two about ready to get these boxes loaded?"

Stretch laughed, but made no comment as he continued toward her. While the four of them hurriedly put the boxes and a huge stoneware jug of cooled milk into the back of the wagon, the men told Callie about the progress being made. "Looks like we are about to find the last of them. We've pretty well combed that area over, first in the dark and again once it got light."

"Then why didn't some of the men come on back here for lunch? Surely they need rest. Aren't they ready to collapse by now?"

"Oh, but there's still work to do," Stretch told her. "I know it pains you to hear it, but there's probably forty or fifty head of dead cattle at the bottom of that ravine. Can't let them lay there and rot in the sun. Wolves and cats might eat the rancid meat and then spread disease to the rest of the animals. Gotta cover them up."

Callie's eyes widened at the thought of having to dig such a grave. "But you don't even have shovels."

193

"Yeah we do. Got several. Wade sent over to his place for them since it's just about as close. Some of the men have already gotten started with that. Then once the dead animals are covered, Wade plans to dump the rest of the ashes from the barn over the area to help discourage wild animals from digging up any of the remains."

"How long do you think all that will take?"

"Should be finished before dark," he assured her as he climbed up onto the wagon seat. "Unless we run into trouble."

After a brief glance to see that Wade's foreman, Rebel Morey, had already mounted his horse, Stretch looked at Callie again. "See to my horse, would you? There's shade over there right now, but later, he might find himself stuck out in the sun. Old Dander hates standing around in the sun."

Callie promised to see that Old Dander was made comfortable under the shade of several nearby oaks, in the small makeshift pen the men had put together near the carriage house after the fire had damaged the main corral beyond use.

Only moments after Stretch and Rebel were gone from her sight, she decided against bothering Manuel, and went about unsaddling the horse herself.

It was late afternoon before Callie saw anyone else, and then it was only the four men who came in to start loading ash into the wagon, but at least they were able to assure her everything was still all right. Then just before nightfall, everyone finally returned. Most of the men were near exhaustion, a few too tired to even eat supper. Still, Wade was able to get four volunteers to take the first watch, and by dark the guards were in place and the rest of the men were in their bunks sound asleep.

Callie too was finally able to fall asleep, far too weary

to lie awake and wonder what might happen next, far too exhausted to worry anymore about what Wade thought of her after her wanton show of passion earlier. She was deep into a dream in which she and Wade worked together, side by side, rebuilding a new barn, when the sound of gunfire penetrated the night. Three shots in rapid succession indicated someone was in trouble. Callie's heart hammered with renewed fear. When would it all end?

Hurriedly, she got out of bed, but did not take the time to do more than don her wrapper, and this time light a small oil lamp, before heading downstairs to see what might have happened. A quick glance at the clock let her know it was only a few minutes past three in the morning.

When she finally moved the two metal door bolts back out of her way and stepped out onto the veranda, still holding the lamp, she noticed six men already on their horses, armed with both handguns and rifles. Others still worked to adjust their saddles and gunbelts, before also mounting their horses.

Wade was one of the men already in his saddle, holding up a bright lantern for the others, waiting impatiently for them to climb into their saddles.

Callie felt a warm wave of relief when she saw him. She had worried he might be the man in trouble. But then she realized he was about to go out with the rest of the men to face whatever the trouble was. Her stomach coiled into a painful knot. He might not be in danger at the moment, but Callie knew he soon would be. Her heart ached with renewed fear while she stared at him, so handsome and so terribly proud. How she wished he would stay and let the others take care of whatever was the matter, but she knew that would never happen. He had already begun to issue his orders.

"Ed, you and Rebel stay here, keep your eyes peeled

for trouble. Manuel, you stay here too. The rest of you break up into three groups. The shots came from the west, which must mean it's McKenzie who's in trouble. We'll go in on him from three different directions," he called out rapidly while he held his horse with a tight rein. He divided his attention between the men's quick preparations and the surrounding darkness until he caught sight of Callie standing on the veranda steps clutching her wrapper together with one hand, holding the lamp out at her side with the other—like a beautiful specter in the night. "You get back in the house and lock the doors. If you have a gun, get it, and make sure it's loaded."

Callie hurried to do just that. Shortly after the men had left, she found both Matthew's pistol and his favorite rifle, loaded them both, and then set them on the kitchen table where she could easily get to them. With her pulse pounding rapidly, she spread back the curtains on the tiny window at the top of the kitchen door so she would be able to see out into the yard, then opened the hallway door so she could also keep an eye on the only other back entrance. With Ed guarding the east door and Manuel and Rebel the outbuildings, that left only the front door unmanned, but carefully locked.

Glad the commotion had not waken Lucille, Ruby, or the girls—for she was not sure she could deal with anyone else's panic at the moment—she turned out the lamp, then settled into a ladder-backed wooden chair and waited for whatever was to happen next. Both guns were well within her reach.

Callie did not have to wait long. Just moments after the clock chimed the half hour, she heard Ed call out, "Rebel? Is that you? Manuel?"

She could tell by the direction of his voice that he was still situated somewhere along the east veranda, and by the tone of his voice that he was frightened. She wondered what had frightened him.

"Reb? Manuel?" he called out again. "Who's out there?"

Callie took the pistol in her hand and cocked it, wishing she'd had more than the one shooting lesson before Harry left. Quietly, she tiptoed through the house toward the parlor, knowing it opened out onto the east veranda.

Dark shadows danced across the double doors, which Callie knew would not offer much protection since they were made mostly of glass. Were they human shadows? Or were they caused by the many trees out in the yard? She thought she remembered a gentle breeze tugging at her clothes when she was outside, and hoped the wind was what caused the dark movement across the doors.

Her heart slowly edged its way into her throat while she quietly moved through the eerie shadows that filled the room, toward the multi-paned doors. Her gun poised. Ready.

"I said, who's out there?" Ed shouted again. This time he sounded more angry than frightened.

Callie was halfway across the large room and could see him now, pressed hard against the north veranda wall, which helped form a dark corner just large enough for him to hide. He held a pistol in one hand, pointed at an upward angle, prepared to lower and fire in an instant. He had a rifle in the other, pointed downward, but ready to back him should the pistol fail. She edged her way farther into the room. She wondered why Rebel and Manuel did not answer. Were they hurt? Or worse?

She fought the fear that gripped her soul. What would Matthew do? What would Wade do?

"Well, whoever you are, I think you should know I'm armed and ready to shoot the next person I see," Ed shouted. "And so are the two men inside the house."

Though Callie knew there was no one in the house

with her other than Lucille, Ruby, and the girls — and they were all asleep — she looked around as if she halfway expected to find someone there. But clearly Ed was making a bluff. She decided to help him. Ever so slowly so as not to be detected from the outside, she sank to her knees, then crawled over to one of the windows at the opposite end of the veranda from where Ed stood. Quietly, she eased it open, but only wide enough to stick the barrel of her pistol outside.

When Ed then added, "And one of those men is just itching to shoot someone," she took advantage of the situation and fired once into the air.

Ed nearly jumped out of his skin. Then realizing either Lucille or Callie had heard the commotion and come to his aid, he shouted out, "Not yet, Joe. Wait until you have a clear bead on one of them. Don't waste your bullets."

Despite the seriousness of the situation, Callie had to grin at how quickly Ed had recovered from his fright and played his part to the hilt.

"Now, I'll ask again. Who's out there? And if I don't get an answer this time, me and my buddies are going to have to come out there, beat those hedges until we find out who you are. And I warn you, we'll come prepared to shoot."

Still there was no response. Again Callie worried about Wade's foreman and her groundskeeper. Why didn't Rebel and Manuel let their presence be known too? Wouldn't it be better to let whoever was out there know there were yet *more* men to be reckoned with? Or had they already been reckoned with? She shuddered at the thought.

Bending close to the slight opening she'd left in the window, she whispered so only Ed would be able to hear her. "Do you want me to unlock the door and let you inside?"

Ed paused to consider that option before he answered, "Not yet."

"Tell me when," she responded quickly, then pulled back away from the window. She replaced the bullet she had used from the extras she had slipped into the large utility pocket sewn into the side of her wrapper.

An eerie silence awaited them. All Callie could hear while she knelt beside the window was the heavy pounding of her own heart, which seemed to match up with the gentle ticking of the clock just the other side of the hallway door. The only thing she smelled was the unpleasant odor of her own burnt gunpowder. Nervously she glanced around the room, praying that the movement around her was nothing more than shadows from outside. She listened carefully for sounds that didn't belong, and once thought she noticed a board creak from somewhere inside the house, but could not be sure.

Suddenly she heard something outside. When she glanced back through the window, she realized Ed was no longer pressed against the wall where she could see him. Thinking he might be edging his way toward the door, she lowered herself to her hands and knees and crawled just below the level of the windows toward the two glass doors. She hoped the movement would not be noticed from outside. But when she finally reached the edge of the doors, where she was able to peer outside again, she did not see Ed anywhere. He was gone. He had disappeared into the dark shapes of the garden beyond.

She froze. Still down on her hands and knees in the dark room. Listening. Waiting. Wondering if Wade was in danger too. Then she heard a scream. A woman's scream. It came from somewhere behind the house. Perhaps from the carriage house or the smokehouse. Callie couldn't tell. But where did a woman fit into any of this? Then she thought of Jeanne. Jim's girl. Had they forced Jeanne to come with them?

Again she heard a scream so horrifying it raised the hair on the back of her neck. *Someone* definitely needed help—and that someone was a woman.

Scampering on her hands and knees across the floor, Callie waited until she was well away from the glass doors before she stood and ran back toward the kitchen for the rifle. If she was going outside to help, she wanted to have both weapons with her.

When she stepped out into the darkened hallway, her mind was so set on getting to that rifle, she did not notice that someone stood waiting, only several yards away.

"Who's that?" a voice suddenly sounded from the darkness.

Callie screamed in response, before she recognized the voice. Lucille.

"Miss Callie, it's me. What's goin' on down here?"

"Lucille. Thank Heavens! I thought—" she started to say, but was interrupted by the sudden sound of shattering glass in the parlor behind her, followed almost immediately by a loud thud. Then for the first time, she detected the collective sounds of footsteps just outside, possibly on the veranda.

Quickly, Callie spun around and aimed the gun at the parlor door, waiting for whoever had just broken into the house to come through to the hallway and praying the others would not soon follow. It amazed her how, although her heart virtually trembled with fear, her hands remained steady and her legs and arms strong.

When no one came immediately through the dark opening, she pressed herself against the hallway wall and began to inch her way toward the door, wanting to take a look inside but not wanting to make herself an easy target. It was then she heard the gentle sobs of a woman.

200

"Who's in there?" she called out, unable to see into the room yet.

"M-Me," came the broken response.

"Who's me?"

But before the woman had a chance to answer, Lucille burst past Callie, bounding quickly into the darkened room, heedless of any danger. "Ruby! Land sakes, child. What happened to you?"

Callie immediately followed, her pistol still raised and ready to shoot. Her gaze darted around the room in search of more than Ruby and Lucille's dark forms.

"I'm bleedin'," Ruby cried. "They cut me with a knife to hush me up. Then the carried me to the house and threw me through the window. I got cuts all over me."

"Who? Who cut you with a knife?" Callie wanted to know.

"I don't know. I didn't get a look at them."

Suddenly they heard more noises outside the broken window. Someone was still outside, either in the garden or in the backyard—or possibly even on the veranda itself.

"We need to get you out of here," Lucille announced in a low voice, and helped Ruby to her feet. She didn't speak again until they were deeper into the house.

"What were you doin' out there anyway?" she wanted to know after they were safely away from the parlor. Still she kept her voice at a whisper. "What do you have to do with all this?"

"Nothing," Ruby sobbed. Then she admitted, "I-I was on my way back from havin' gone to meet Thomas. I heard someone m-moving about outside when I got near the house, so I hid out in the carriage house hoping they wouldn't see me. I figured you'd get mad at me for slipping off again if you was to find out. But somebody followed me inside and grabbed me."

"What about the night of the fire? Where was you

201

then?" Lucille wanted to know.

"With Thomas," Ruby confessed, hanging her head in shame. "Here lately, I've been with Thomas most every night. He meets me just the other side of Mister Barlow's fence."

There was another noise. This time it sounded like someone walking on chards of broken glass. It sounded as if it came from *inside* the parlor. Someone else had entered the house.

"Did you see Ed?" Callie asked, her voice barely above a breath.

"I didn't see nobody. They got me from behind and pulled my blouse up over my head to where I couldn't see nothin'. Then they hand-carried me and th'owed me through that window." Ruby answered softly, her voice choked with fear, her wide eyes clearly visible in the darkness that surrounded them.

Callie bit the inside of her lip. The intruder wasn't Ed. If Ed had been anywhere near the veranda, he would have tried to stop those men from tossing Ruby into the window. But where was Ed? Callie's blood ran cold, chilling her to the bone. She had to do something. She could not let whoever it was get to the children.

"Hide." The command came out a whisper, but was clearly heard.

Quickly Lucille and Ruby did as told. Lucille squatted down in the shadows near the bottom of the staircase and Ruby crawled under a small, ornate table near the entrance hall. Their dark skin and dark clothes helped hide them. Callie moved to where she could get a better view of the parlor door and still remain in a shadow, though her white skin and her pale blue wrapper seemed to catch a non-existent light and reflected in the darkness.

Again they heard the crunching sound of glass. Callie raised the heavy pistol, aiming at the vacant area beyond the door. She wondered if she should call out to see who was in there, but was afraid of letting her exact location be known. Besides, if it was Ed, Rebel, or Manuel, she felt certain they would have spoken out. Her heart felt like it was about to explode while she waited for a shadow to appear in the doorway.

Unexpectedly, there was a gunshot. Outside. In the distance.

Panic-stricken, Callie bit back the sudden impulse to scream.

Chapter Thirteen

Another gunshot sounded. Then another. Soon there was a whole volley of gunshots in the distance. Whoever had been inside the parlor made a hasty retreat. Heavy footsteps hurried out of the room, across the veranda, then out into the garden.

The gunfire came closer to the house. Each blast sounded a little louder than the last. Then Callie heard a jumble of horses, all running. But she could not tell if those horses were leaving or arriving. Or both. She held her breath. Eventually the shooting stopped.

"Ed? What the hell happened?" she heard someone call out. *Wade*. Wade was back. Relief washed over her, leaving her momentarily weak, but eager to see him.

Shoving her pistol into the wide pocket sewn into the side of her night wrapper, Callie flew to the rear door and jerked back the bolts to go outside. But once she had the door open, she found herself suddenly too afraid to actually step outside for fear someone might still be out there hiding. Instead, she watched cautiously from just inside the open doorway. Her hand fingered the shape of the heavy pistol pulling at her skirt.

Wade and several men walked as a group across the yard toward someone trying to get up off the ground who kept stumbling back to his knees. Callie realized it was Ed. Her hand flew to her throat.

"We heard the gunshot and hurried back," Wade told

him. "Who was it? Where's Callie? Is she safe? Are the girls safe?"

Callie could not quite make out Ed's reply while McKenzie helped pull him to his feet, but heard Wade's sharp response. "Was it Callie?"

Then before Ed had time to answer, Wade bolted toward the house in a dead run. Just as he reached the steps, Callie forgot her caution and stepped outside. Without a moment's hesitation, he took her into his arms and pressed her hard against him. "Thank God you are alive."

Callie could not help it. Now that the terrible ordeal was over and she was safe in Wade's arms, she began to cry large, rasping sobs. Her whole body felt weak, making her lean against him for enough strength to continue standing.

"But if it wasn't you, who was it Ed saw the three men carrying across the yard?"

It took Callie a moment to sniff back her tears and regain the composure she needed to answer. "Ruby," she finally told him when she could. "She was outside and they found her."

"What the hell was she doing outside at this time of morning?" he demanded to know, leaning back to look down into her tear-streaked face, but not yet letting go of her.

Callie sniffed back the sob still lodged in her throat, then tried to explain. "She went to see one of your men on the sly. It's not the first time either. She's been slipping off regularly at all hours to meet with him. But when she came back tonight, hoping to slip back into the house unnoticed, she heard someone outside and decided to hide in the carriage house, where they found her."

"Fool girl!" Wade growled out in anger. His gaze left Callie's face to stare into the darkness of the house behind her. Callie felt his muscles flex with unreleased tension, and for a moment thought he might storm into the house and do physical harm to the girl; but before he had time to do anything, Stretch's voice interrupted him.

"Wade, do we take out after them now or wait until daylight?"

As if he'd forgotten all about the men gathered in the yard with lanterns raised high above their heads, Wade slowly turned back with a puzzled look on his face.

"What do we do?" Tony wanted to know.

"Where's Rebel and Manuel?" he asked, just now remembering the other two.

Quickly the group disbanded and began a search for the missing two. Wade held Callie close for only a few seconds more, then he too went to help search.

Over and over, the men called out the two names, opening doors to the various buildings and parting the shrubbery to see if either of them might be there.

Lucille joined Callie out on the veranda to tell her Ruby's cuts weren't too bad, and watched for a moment while the men continued their search. Though there was no chill in the air that night, Callie rubbed her thinly clad arms self-consciously while she waited for the two to be found.

"Lord, Lord, let them still be alive," Lucille muttered under her breath, pressing her hand flat against her breastbone.

"Here's Manuel," someone called out. "He's hurt." Moments later, most of the men converged on the wood-shed to see how serious Manuel's injuries were.

"Help me take him to the house," said the same person who had found him.

Lucille immediately disappeared inside.

Callie watched, horrified, while several men carried Manuel's limp form toward her. Then light fell through the doorway behind her and she knew Lucille was getting things ready for him. Next she heard someone cry out that Rebel had been found.

"How bad's he hurt?" Wade wanted to know as he turned away from the men who carried Manuel and headed in the direction of the other voice.

There was a mumbling sound, then Rebel's own voice called out, sounding more disgruntled than in pain. "I'm fine. I just got hit over the head with something." Then he stumbled out into the yard from shadows near the side of the house, tenderly rubbing the back of his head. The two men who had discovered him followed.

"Sorry, boss," Rebel said, frowning. "But they caught me completely by surprise. I didn't even hear them come up behind me." He then glanced over to see Callie still standing on the veranda, and a look of pure relief washed over him. Wade's eyes followed where Rebel's gaze had gone, and he too looked relieved all over again.

Callie's heart fluttered at the realization that they both had cared about her welfare. It was especially comforting to see Wade so concerned. Despite her wanton behavior of before, and despite the fact she had gotten him caught up in all this trouble in the first place, he still cared about her. She smiled when she remembered how easily he had taken her into his arms only moments earlier and how wonderful it felt to be held firmly against his body. She still felt a lingering warmth.

"I really blew it this time," Rebel said with a regrettable shake of his head, then reached up to tenderly touch the injured area at the back of his head. He was unable to look Wade in the eye.

Callie knew more had been hurt than Rebel's head. His male pride had suffered just as severe a blow. Watching while the young man slowly turned away, his shoulders drooping, she felt extremely sorry for him, and a little guilty. If she had not manipulated Wade into working for her the way she had, his foreman would not have been there in the first place and never would have gotten hurt. She felt she should go to Rebel and apologize—apologize to them both—but knew she was not dressed to walk out into the yard. She really shouldn't even be out on the veranda. She would have to wait.

She watched while Wade followed Rebel away from the house. He continued to glance back at her while he listened to Rebel's explanation about how they had gotten the jump on him. When he first noticed she was still watching him, he smiled briefly, which caused Rebel to look around in bewilderment, not knowing of a single thing worth smiling about in light of what had happened.

By then, the men carrying Manuel were inside and Lucille was heard directing them to one of the upstairs bedrooms. Callie felt torn between going back inside to see if she could help in some way or running headlong into Wade's arms again and begging him to hold her close. But because there were so many men still standing around, waiting to see what Wade wanted them to do, she refrained from running out to him and stood patiently watching—waiting for him to come back to the house.

Finally Wade had to turn his back to her in order to give the matters at hand his full attention. First he examined Rebel's injury by lantern light, then ordered him to go lie down in the bunkhouse until they were able to get the doctor out there. He then ordered six of the men to go back out to make sure no one tried to slip back and do more harm. The rest of the men he told to get some sleep—all but Andy and Tony, who he chose to ride into town and bring back the doctor and the sheriff.

"Where's Ed?" he wanted to know as he looked

around for him. "I want to see how badly he's been hurt."

"I'm here," Ed answered, standing now just behind Callie.

Still skittish, Callie jumped at the sound of his voice coming from so close by. She had been unaware that Ed had joined her in the dark shadows along the veranda. When she turned to look at him, her heart hammered violently inside of her.

Wade headed towards them, his concerned gaze falling on Ed. "Are you all right?"

"Yeah, I'm fine. Just a little fuzzy headed. But I need to talk with you and Mrs. Tucker in private about something." His deep voice sounded foreboding.

Curious to know what Ed had to say to the two of them, Callie quickly led the way to the study. She wondered if he had somehow gotten a good look at the men. Did he know something about them the rest didn't?

"What is it?" Wade asked just as soon as Callie had one of the table lamps well lit and he had carefully closed the door behind them.

Ed blinked hard, grimaced, then leaned heavily against the desk, bracing himself with both arms. Aware he was in pain, Callie rushed to his side, and gasped when she noticed the trail of blood down his neck which had started to form a large, dark red patch on the back of his green shirt. But when she reached up to examine the injury, he pushed her hands away.

"Don't fool with it. It hurts."

"I imagine it does," Callie agreed, then reached up to try again to examine it, only to have her hands pushed aside a second time.

Ed moved away from her with a determined frown bearing into his face.

"Do you want to hear what I got to say or not?" he

209

asked. His eyes narrowed as if to say, "Keep that up and I won't tell you anything."

"What is it?" Wade asked, stepping closer and resting a hand on Callie's shoulder, encouraging her to leave Ed alone.

"Those men gave me a message for Mrs. Tucker, but I thought maybe you should hear it too."

"A message? What sort of message?" Wade asked. Callie felt his grip tighten on her shoulder.

"Right after they caught me trying to slip around to the side of the carriage house, they grabbed me and began to pistol-whip me. While they took turns hitting me, they told me to be sure and tell Tucker's widow that the worst is yet to come. That if she had any sense, she'd pack up her things and go back to where she belongs, and take the two girls with her." Ed looked apologetic. "They said something about her kind not wanted around here."

Wade's expression darkened, and he suddenly drew his hands back to his sides. Every muscle inside him was rigid. "Are you sure you heard them right?"

"Oh, I heard them right. I don't know who they were because the three of them had flour sacks pulled down over their heads with holes only big enough to see and breathe through. I could tell all three of them were white men, but I don't think they were any of that group we had the fight with in town. Those men in town had talked like they were from down south Louisiana, but these men talked like they were probably from around here or maybe from up Red River way. Though I can't prove it one way or the other, I really don't think it was those same men we had that fight with. No, I think it was probably someone else. Someone who wants Cal—I mean, Mrs. Tucker—out of here. Someone with a big grudge against her. That's what I figure." He then glanced in her direction, but took his gaze quickly away.

Callie realized he was trying not to look at her because she was still in her night clothes, with her hair spilling across her shoulders and down her back like some sort of wild creature. As serious as Ed had sounded when he had asked to see them alone, she had not wanted to take the time to run upstairs and change into her regular clothes or take a brush to her hair. And she had no intention of leaving the room now, not until she knew far more than she did.

"But who would want to run me out of here?"

Suddenly her eyes were drawn to Wade's. They both knew the answer to that, yet neither spoke the name aloud. Wade quickly looked away, as if ashamed. Callie's heart went out to him. Hurriedly, she tried to think of someone else. Someone other than Walter Barlow.

"What about that man from town?" she asked. "The one who tried to force his attentions on me the first day I came here."

"Gordon Jones?" Wade asked.

"That was his name. Gordon. What about him?" She knew she was grasping at straws, but she hated to see Wade hurt, and could tell how it hurt him deeply to think his father might have had something to do with the attack on the house—and probably with the damaged fence, and the barn fire too. No. Surely it had to be someone else. She had to try to think of *all* the other possibilities before Walter's name was mentioned. "Do you think maybe Gordon holds a grudge for that little episode in the saloon?"

Ed could not help himself. He looked at her then, his eyes wide. "In the saloon?"

"It's a long story," Wade told him. "She went in to look for me and had a run-in with Gordon Jones."

"Well, he's certainly the type to get a few of his drinking friends together for something like this," Ed said, nodding. "He has been known to seek revenge on people he thinks wronged him."

"Yes, I guess it is a possibility," Wade agreed, remembering how Gordon had succeeded in running off the best schoolteacher Pine Fork had ever had just a few months earlier, all because the teacher refused to show any favoritism to his son. And as rumor had it, when Gordon had shown an interest in her, she had staunchly refused to let him pay call on her. "When the sheriff gets here, I'll mention Gordon to him so he can check him out."

"And too, it still might be those men we had that fight with," Ed went on to say. "It could be one or two of them never talked enough for me to be able to recognize their voices if I did hear them again. Though most of them were definitely from south Louisiana, talking that funny Frenchie talk, one or two of them could have been from around here. They may have said that about Mrs. Tucker and the girls just to throw the suspicion off of themselves. So don't let the sheriff completely forget about those men just yet."

Callie frowned as she tried to come up with still more possibilities. "Or maybe it's the result of a few of the ladies in town having taken my going into that saloon all wrong. Those men did say they didn't want 'my kind' around here."

"Those warn't ladies who took their pistol butts to me," Ed said, and for the first time he clutched at his ribs. "Besides, women would probably find less obvious ways to let you know you weren't wanted. Like having some big social doings and not inviting you."

"Or by sending Reverend Cross out here to try to save your misguided soul." Wade grinned at the thought, but quickly sobered when he remembered the seriousness of the situation.

"Well, whoever it was, maybe they left some sort of clue outside," Ed said. "Let's get some lanterns and go see what we can find."

"You aren't going anywhere but upstairs to bed to wait for that doctor," Callie told him with a firm shake of her head. "If you won't let me have a look at that head injury, then you'll just have to lie down until the doctor gets here."

Ed's lips curled down into a boyish pout as he looked from Callie to Wade, then back to Callie. "Okay, have a look at it, but be careful."

Callie was indeed very careful while she examined the injury, and was appalled by what she saw. Though the bleeding had almost stopped, the wound at the back of Ed's head, only inches behind his right ear, was very deep, and in definite need of stitches. "You are still going upstairs to wait for the doctor. He will want to shave that area and stitch it closed."

Ed's eyes widened as he reached up to cover the hair on top of his head. "Shave my head? Stitch it closed? With a needle and thread? Whatever for? Besides, I can't go letting nobody shave my head for *no* reason. I ain't hardly got enough hair up there as it is. What do you mean *shave* my head?"

Though Ed's voice had risen degree by degree, Callie remained calm when she explained, "Doctors sometimes stitch a wound to make it stay shut. That way, it won't keep bursting open and start bleeding all over again. And he'll have to shave part of your head so he can get to the wound easier, and also so the hair you do have won't become matted in it after he's through."

"Not my hair. He can stitch the thing shut if he has a mind to, but he's not shaving a single hair off my head." Ed was adamant.

Wade had to turn his back to keep Ed from seeing the huge grin playing on his face. Though he himself had a thick head of hair, he understood how sensitive those men who didn't could be. He decided to change the subject before Callie made an issue of it. "We'll just have to let the doctor decide what is best. For now, though, let's go look around for any clues. Just be careful not to let that wound of yours start bleeding again. You've already lost a lot of blood."

Against Callie's protests, Ed went outside with Wade to look around. The rest of the men, except Stretch, who was unable to sleep and had come back outside, were either in the bunkhouse or posted at strategic locations around the area. Callie eventually returned upstairs to check on the girls, relieved to discover they had obviously slept through the entire ruckus. Assured of their well-being, she went on to her room to dress, and put aside her pistol for now. Afterwards, she looked in on Manuel, and stayed to keep an eye on him while Lucille went downstairs to start breakfast.

By the time the doctor and the sheriff arrived, the sky had already begun to turn a glorious shade of pink off toward the east; but in all the time that had passed, no real clues had been found. The best thing Wade, Ed, and Stretch had come up with was a series of partial bootprints in the parlor.

After having stepped in a small patch of Ruby's blood, whoever had entered the house had left a fading trail across the floor, up until he had reached the carpet in the center of the room, where the blood had been promptly wiped from the boot. But the bootprint was like any other, and could have come from anyone's boot. About all it really told them was that the man who had entered the house had shorter feet than most men. And if Callie had not already mentioned how very heavy the footsteps had sounded, they might have thought one of the culprits was a woman.

It was after Ed had left the group to go upstairs and allow Dr. Edison to examine his head wound, and the sheriff had followed Wade and Stretch into the parlor to look at the bloody bootprints they'd found, that the sheriff first mentioned having finally heard from someone who had seen the men they were looking for.

"Got word, all right." As he carefully stepped over the broken glass to get a better look at the darkest prints, he explained further. "Seems they rode into Willow Springs yesterday afternoon. All seven of them. I got the wire about it shortly after five o'clock. So, if the same group of men who did this is the same group who burned down the barn, you can just about cross those seven men off your list. That's a good nine hours' ride from here, even at top speed on good horses. I'll check back with Sheriff Butler there first thing when I get back to town, to see if the men were seen in town again at any time last night, but even if they weren't, it would have been an awfully hard ride to get back in the time they would have had to reach here."

Wade had to agree. It was not logical to think they would have ridden all the way to Willow Springs only to turn around and ride right back. He was starting to believe Ed was right. It was someone from around there. But still he hated to consider his father a possible suspect, or more likely, some of his father's men working under his father's strict orders—*if* his father had had anything at all to do with Callie's troubles.

Though he knew the man to be cold and unfeeling at times, he truly hated to believe his father could stoop that low—no matter how much the man wanted the Circle T. Maybe Callie was right, maybe the main troublemaker was Gordon Jones. He wondered what size foot Gordon had. He decided to tell the sheriff about the incident in town.

"Might be old Gordon," the sheriff agreed, slowly nodding as he took his hat off and ran the wide hem of his shirt sleeve over the dampness that clung to his weathered face. Though the sheriff was a thin man, he seemed to sweat more than anyone else Wade knew. "Yep, Gordon and his drinking buddies are just the type to want to sneak around and harass a poor widow woman like that. Especially after you ordered him away from her the way you did. We all know what he did to poor Miss Hays, though nobody could really prove it. While I'm poking my nose around, I'll also check into his whereabouts last night."

"I'd appreciate it," Wade told him. "I'd like to get whoever's been doing all these things behind bars where they belong so Cal—Mrs. Tucker and the girls can rest a little easier at night. But until you do catch them, I guess I'll have to continue to stay over here and help keep an eye on things—even at night." Though he tried to make it sound like a sacrifice on his part, mostly for appearance's sake, he fully realized it was what he wanted to do. He preferred being near them. He like the feeling of protecting them. And as long as he kept his priorities straight, he felt little harm would come from his staying there and focusing on her problem for the time being.

"Might be the best thing, all right," the sheriff agreed just before he replaced his hat. "And you say McKenzie didn't get a look at whoever was slinking around in the dark out there?"

"Nothing but shadows," Wade answered, clearly frustrated.

"Well, I'll go on back to town and see what I can find out there. Then I'll ask your neighbors what they might have seen or heard. I'll send word to you if I find out anything important."

"I'd appreciate that," Wade told him while they walked back outside together to where the sheriff had left his horse. He stayed beside the sheriff until he had swung up into his saddle and gathered the reins into his hands.

"Explain to Doc why I wasn't able to stay and ride back with him," the sheriff said just before he pressed his heels into his horse's side and sent the large animal off in a brisk canter. Once he was out onto the main road, he flicked his reins and increased the animal's speed to a fast gallop.

One by one, the men awoke and came outside to ask how Ed and Manuel were. Knowing Lucille would not want the lot of them tracking up the house, Wade agreed to stop boarding up the broken window long enough to check on the two men's condition, aware it would also give him a chance to see Callie again.

The men waited outside while he hurried upstairs to see what he could find out. As he topped the stairs, Callie came out of one of the nearby bedrooms, quietly shifting a white porcelain pitcher from her right hand to her left just before she reached behind her to pull the door gently closed. When she looked up and smiled at him, he felt his heart take a tiny jump. She had one of the most endearing smiles he'd ever seen on a woman. His blood stirred when he remembered the kiss he'd stolen from those very lips only two mornings ago. Yet suddenly it seemed a lifetime ago.

"How are they?" he asked, eager to speak with her.

"Like a couple of spoiled children," Callie told him, laughing softly.

The gentle sound of her laughter brought Wade's heartbeat to a faster pace. Everything about her seemed to be doing that. He fought a very real urge to reach out and touch her, knowing it might remind her of his earlier behavior.

"Manuel complained half the time in English and the rest of the time in Spanish, right up to the moment he finally passed out from all the whiskey Lowell made him drink," she explained further. "As for Ed, Lowell was just getting started on him when he asked me to get a fresh pitcher of water and more clean cloths. But Ed was already starting to complain when I left. I'd better

217

hurry."

Wade watched while she moved away from him, aware just how beautiful she looked dressed in pink with her long, dark hair held back away from her face with nothing more than a rose-colored head scarf. He knew that to remove the head scarf would send the thick mass of hair tumbling down over her shoulders.

Smiling to himself, he wondered how she managed to look that beautiful when she'd had so little sleep over the past few days. He then wondered what he must look like, not having had any more sleep than she had, nor the chance to shave or change clothes for two mornings in a row. He vowed then to find the time to at least borrow a razor and scrape the whiskers off his face just as soon as he was finished boarding up the broken window. When she saw him next, he wanted to look far more presentable.

Though Wade reached immediately for the doorknob to the room Callie had just left, he did not actually turn it and enter until Callie was well out of his sight. When he did, he discovered the doctor standing on the far side of the bed, bending over Ed's motionless form. Manuel lay next to them, neatly bandaged across his forehead and along his shoulder, sleeping peacefully, with a half-empty whiskey bottle on the table beside him—well within reach.

Ed too had a partially empty whiskey bottle on the small table nearest him; but he lay motionless on his side fully awake, staring wide-eyed at Wade while the doctor worked to stitch the wound at the back of his head.

Remembering Callie's remarks about what the doctor might have to do, Wade stepped closer to see if a razor lay among the instruments on the table beside the doc. He was glad, at least for Ed's sake, that none was in sight. When he moved again and was finally able to peer around the doctor's bent head, he saw Lowell had braided the hair near the wound to keep it out of his way. Wade grinned, wondering what Ed would say when he learned he might have to wear part of what hair he had left in tiny little braids for a few days. He wondered what the rest of the men would have to say.

"So how do the patients look, Doc?" Wade asked, noticing how Ed's eyes flinched but never fully closed whenever the doctor touched a particularly sensitive spot.

"Manuel is going to be fine. He'll probably be up and about in a few days. But old Ed here is another story. Not only does he have this bad wound here and those huge lumps on both sides of his head, I suspect he has several broken ribs. I'll bandage him so he won't have as much pain, but he'll be in bed for at least two weeks."

"The hell I will," Ed grumbled, his brows coming down hard while the rest of him remained perfectly still.

"The hell you *will*," Lowell responded. And whether he meant to in order to stress his point, or whether it was an accident, he jabbed the needle into a very sensitive area of the wound without warning.

Ed jerked his head in response. "Ouwch! Damnation, Doc. Be careful."

"I'm nearly through. You be still," he ordered Ed just before he took his last stitch, then tied it off. After he cut the special thread in two, he glanced up at Wade, his expression serious. "Though he can be moved out to the bunkhouse if he wants, I do want you to see to it that he does not go back to work for at least two weeks. And then he is not to lift anything heavy for another three or four weeks."

"Not lift anything heavy?" Ed cried out. "We got that hay to cut and bundle next week. I'll have to help load the wagon and haul it in and find somewhere to stack it until the barn gets built back. And as soon as that shipment of lumber is ready, I'll be needed to help build the new barn. I *have* to get back to work." He then turned his head to glance up at the doctor, wincing at the pain which resulted from the sudden movement. Stubbornly, he reached for the bottle still sitting on the nearby table, bent his head, and took a quick swig, but never once took his eyes off the doctor's determined face.

"Not for two weeks," Wade said, agreeing with the doctor. He watched while Ed followed the short swig with a longer swig, then haphazardly set the bottle back into place. Clearly, Ed would soon be just as soundly inebriated as Manuel and, for now at least, there would be no problem keeping him in bed. "And after those two weeks are up, I'll have to find ways for you to help that won't put any strain on your ribs."

"Woman's work. That's what I'll get," Ed complained, scowling at the thought of it. "McKenzie will never let me hear the last of it. Neither will the other men. It's bad enough I let myself get hurt, but to end up doing woman's work!"

Ed was still grumbling about their decision to give him the lesser jobs, and about the way the doctor was bandaging his ribs way too tight, when Wade left the room to go back downstairs and tell everyone all he just learned, and caution McKenzie against teasing Ed too much—at least until he was well enough to take a punch, in case the argument should come to blows the way it often did between the two best friends. Also, he wanted to be sure Rebel went upstairs and let the doctor have a good look at him before he left.

Lucille and Ruby were already serving the men a hardy breakfast when he returned outside. He spoke to the group while he too accepted a plateful of ham, eggs, biscuits, and gravy—explaining Ed was the more seriously injured of the two. He wished Ed could somehow

220

overhear the concern they all showed upon hearing he had broken several of his ribs, especially McKenzie. He knew by the time Ed was well enough to talk with them, they would have put that deep concern back inside them somewhere where he could not see it. It was a shame, but that's the way men were. Wade knew he was no different. A slap on the back for a job well done was one thing, but to show true and gentle concern was a horse of an entirely different color, a horse no man around these parts would be caught dead riding.

After the men had all eaten their fill, they looked and behaved more like their old selves and were ready to get back to work. Several chores had been neglected because of the time lost rounding up the cattle that had strayed up onto the ridge and then burying those killed, so there was plenty to keep them busy for quite a while.

But because things were finally getting back to normal, Wade sent all but a few of his own men back to Twin Oaks to help those who had remained there to catch up on the chores they surely had neglected while being so shorthanded.

By nine o'clock, the girls were up, eager to learn all the details about what had happened, information Callie proved very selective in giving for fear of frightening them. She then put them to work straighting up their rooms in order to get their minds off the latest incident and keep them, especially Amy, out of everyone's way. Ever since her pony saddle had burned in the fire, which meant she could no longer ride Starfire when she wanted, she had been at a loss over what to do with herself in the mornings, and was found more and more often getting in the men's way, hoping to finagle a short ride with one of them.

Once things were more the way they should be, Wade was able to concentrate on less serious matters, like what to do about Ruby. At first, he had considered a severe reprimand for the girl, for having slipped out into the night the way she had. But after seeing how sullen and repentant the girl had seemed while serving breakfast, then again when cleaning up afterward, he felt she had already suffered enough and decided to let it go.

When he approached her later that morning, it was merely to ask if he could get some warm water to shave with, and to find out exactly how the girl had intended on getting back into the house with all the doors locked and the lower windows latched. He was amazed to learn she had actually planned to scale one of the trees that grew near the house, drop lightly to the roof, then lower herself into her own bedroom window, which was left open like all the rest to allow a cool breeze to flow into the room.

"Weren't you afraid of falling and getting hurt?" he wanted to know.

Ruby looked confused. "No. Why would I fall? I've been climbing trees since I was a little girl."

"Still, there's always the chance you might slip and fall. Instead of chancing such injury, why don't you just have Thomas pay call on you in a more conventional manner—and at a far more decent hour."

"You mean have Thomas come to the door and ask for me?" Ruby wondered aloud, as if amazed by such an innovative idea. Her huge eyes blinked rapidly at the mere thought of it.

"Then Callie and Lucille could know where you are and that you are safe," he told her.

A wide, toothy grin stretched across Ruby's thin face while she considered it further. "You mean be called on proper? Yessir, I think I'd like that."

It was settled. Starting that very night, Thomas Rett would be informed of the new procedure. He was to start coming to the door and asking for Ruby by name. Wade sent word with Andy later that afternoon, after he had asked him to ride over to Twin Oaks to bring him several changes of clothes.

Though the new rules did not set well with Thomas at first, because it meant having to go all the way to the Tucker house to get her, and also because it meant everyone was aware they were together, the young man appeared at the back door that very evening with his hair properly combed, carrying a handful of wildflowers and politely asking to see Miss Ruby Faye.

Chapter Fourteen

Later that same night, after the men had eaten and gone to bed, except for the four who had taken the first watch, Wade strolled across the yard toward the house. He wanted to be certain he had boarded that broken window properly. He also wanted to make sure all the doors were securely locked and the other windows latched. He had neglected to grab up his hat on the way out, and a warm breeze ruffled his hair, blowing it gently forward into his face.

It was still five hours before he was due to go out on watch, but he knew it would be pointless to go back inside the bunkhouse and try to get any sleep. He was far too restless, especially after hearing what the sheriff had had to tell him when he came by earlier.

Wade was disappointed to learn that the seven men had indeed been seen at Willow Creek as late as ten o'clock the previous night. It would have been impossible for them to have returned to the Circle T in time to set up a subterfuge by tossing rocks at McKinsey, then attack the house after most of the men had left to help the man supposedly in trouble. Wade knew it was impossible to have covered that much ground in only five hours. There was no longer even a remote chance the men they had originally suspected were actually involved.

He was also disappointed to find out Gordon Jones

had an alibi for the entire night in question. It seemed he'd spent that night and most of the following morning with Nita Denty, one of the women who worked at the Blackbird Saloon. And though the sheriff admitted Nita's word was sometimes questionable, too many people had seen him in the saloon earlier, drinking until he was barely able to stand up, much less ride a horse all the way out to the Circle T.

No, the sheriff was pretty certain Gordon had indeed passed out in Nita's room only an hour or so after he had left the saloon, just as Nita claimed, and as he had been known to do in the past. The sheriff had also noted that Gordon had a huge foot and couldn't possibly have made the bootprints they had seen. He'd also checked out the bootsizes of Gordon's favorite drinking buddies, who were gathered around him at the time the sheriff questioned him. All of them had respectable-sized feet.

Which led Wade to wonder again about his own father. Still, he did not want to believe it possible. He knew his father could be a vengeful, unforgiving man — but never to the point of such madness.

True, his father and Matthew Tucker had feuded constantly, and never had they had a kind word to say about one another, but not once to his knowledge had his father actually brought harm to the man. Not physical harm anyway. Oh, there had been rumors that Walter had had something to do with Matthew's wife's death, but that's all those had been — rumors. No, Wade did not believe his father was behind this sudden rash of violence. Yet still, he *was* the only other person they could think of who had a motive.

Wade was so lost to the disturbing thoughts concerning his father and the rash of trouble Callie had suffered over the past few days that he did not notice her at first, not until she called out to him. When he finally

225

realized she was there, it surprised him to see her outside, standing only a few feet away.

He was startled at having been caught off guard like that when he should have been extremely cautious of any sounds or movement, and his heart jumped, then began to throb rapidly against his chest.

"I thought I told you to go on up to bed and get some sleep," he said, trying to sound stern when actually he was very pleased to see her. Very pleased indeed.

"I was unable to sleep," she said with a shrug. "My body says it's tired, but my brain refuses to stop worrying about all that has happened lately. I thought maybe a short walk in the fresh air might help." What she did not tell him was that one of the reasons she had not been able to sleep was because she wanted to see him. Be with him. If only for a few minutes. It was why she had chosen to come back downstairs in one of her prettiest pale-blue dresses with her long brown hair brushed and shaped until it fell soft and shimmering across her shoulders and down her back.

"You plan to take a walk outside at night without a lantern? Don't you know it could be dangerous out here?" he asked, his gaze sweeping over her, noticing how both her hair and her dress caught the glimmering moonlight. His next thought was to order her back inside, but somehow the words would not form on his lips. He liked the thought of being all alone with her, outside—with nothing but warm darkness and the soft sounds of crickets and cicadas surrounding them.

A pleased smile formed deep dimples in his lean cheeks, letting her know he was not truly annoyed with her. Her blood raced warm, tingling trails through her body.

"You don't have a lantern either," she pointed out, helpless to do anything but smile back at him. "Besides, when I glanced out just now, I noticed that you were already out here. I knew I'd be safe. But if you are really that concerned, why don't you walk along with me?" Her heart beat recklessly while she waited to hear his response.

"Where to?"

"Just across the yard and into the garden," she told him, and began to move toward the shoulder-high hedgerow that surrounded the small area of paradise Manuel had managed to keep green and beautiful despite the rising July temperatures and the ongoing drought. Her heart held perfectly still while she waited to see if he'd follow her. "I may have my faults but I do know better than to go *very* far from the house."

"Even with me for your protector?" he teased, then did indeed fall quickly into step beside her.

"Especially with you as my protector," she shot back, delighted at the way her remark made him turn and look at her. Suddenly, she felt all giddy inside.

"I guess after the way I behaved the other morning, you have every right to think you needed a protector from *me,"* he said. His smile faded as he prepared to apologize again for his unforgivable behavior. He paused to find just the right words.

Callie felt a bold streak run through her and came to a stop within the shadows of the trees in order to gaze up at him. "I'm not too sure I *want* to be protected from you."

When he looked at her then, he saw the timid smile on her lips, letting him know he had indeed understood her correctly. It was all the encouragement he needed. Despite his earlier resolve to keep better control over his emotions and not lose sight of what his main priorities should be, he reached out and drew her quickly into his arms, crushing her soft body hard against his. Aware she had already closed her eyes in anticipation of his kiss, he wasted no time in claiming her lips, branding her with a passion he felt for no other woman.

Callie was overwhelmed by both the intensity of the kiss and the hot bolt of desire that shot randomly through her when he pressed her body even more firmly against his. Her senses reeled until she began to feel dizzy. She had to lean against him to keep her bearings. Never had she felt such a need coursing through her, a need so strong and so basic it startled her; but no longer did it frighten her. Instead, she welcomed the strange new feelings he aroused in her, found herself eager to explore each and every one of them to the fullest.

Slowly, she eased her arms upward to encircle his strong neck in an effort to draw herself even closer to him, if that was at all possible. When she was then able to press her breasts harder against his firm chest, hot shafts of sensual delight circulated wildly through her body with such fiery ferocity it left her weak. The powerful sensations quickly moved and entered every fiber of her being until they had consumed all of her, relentless in their onslaught.

Somewhere in the back of her fog-filled brain, an alarm sounded, trying to warn her to pull away before it was too late, before she again made a wanton fool of herself. But she was unable to obey the silent command. She had become lost in a swirling sea of emotions so strong, so turbulent, that it made it hard for her to think. It made her not want to think at all.

Wade's strong demanding hands pressed into the small of her back, helping pull her as close as possible, then slowly began to move up and down the curve of her back—bringing her yet more undeniable pleasure while at the same time continuing to mold her tightly against him.

Callie trembled with an aching weakness when one of his hands began to stray from its course along her back

228

and slowly edged its way across her ribcage, then slowly upward to gently cup the underside of her breast. Despite the clothing between them, she could feel his touch burning her delicate skin, and once more the silent alarm sounded, warning her she was allowing him to go too far—but again she chose to ignore it.

Instead of pulling away and chastising him for his boldness, she responded to the sensations he had created inside her by timidly sliding one of her own hands across the hard contours of his back in what began as shy exploration. Marveling in the feel of the strong muscular back and the firm powerful shoulders which lay just beneath the thin fabric of his shirt, she pressed harder.

Wade responded immediately to her intimate touch, and the kiss deepened. Starved for the taste of her, he slipped the tip of his tongue through the slight opening of her lips and gently urged them further apart. Hungrily, he glided over the velvety curves and contours of her mouth, sampling more and more of her.

To his delight, she responded in kind, though timidly at first. He could not remember ever having known such sweetness nor having craved a woman so deeply. Desire for her pounded through him, and he realized he would need to be extremely careful or chance losing his heart to her. And that would never do.

But it was too late, and he knew it. Despite his firm resolve not to, he had already lost his heart to her. He wanted her. And not just for one night, or even just a few. He wanted her for all time. The thought of it stunned him. Frightened him.

Although Callie had anticipated being the one to pull away from the kiss, she had been unable to. It was not because he had overpowered her or restrained her in any physical manner. She simply had not wanted to. She had fallen prey to the lunacy of passion and wanted more of

229

whatever pleasures he had to offer her. Her common sense had completely abandoned her, and her womanly desires, now fully awakened, had quickly taken over.

It was Wade who finally broke the kiss.

"It's getting late," he said in a gruff tone. He was having as difficult a time catching his breath as she was hers. His chest heaved laboriously with his every attempt to draw more air. "We both need to get some sleep."

Callie had never felt more confused in her life than when he spun around and hurried away from her. Barely moments later, he was inside the bunkhouse and she was standing in the darkness alone, wondering what she had done wrong. Then, with an aching heart, she realized what she had done wrong. *She* should have been the one to pull away, not him. She should have shown more restraint.

Glumly, she turned toward the house, wondering how she would ever face him now. It had been hard enough before, but after the way she had just behaved in his arms yet a second time, it would now be impossible. He had even more reason than before to believe the very worst of her.

Her misery was overwhelming. She knew she needed to somehow get better control of her emotions where Wade was concerned. And if she found she couldn't, she should stay away from him. Far away from him. Before things got too far out of hand.

Wade sat crossed-legged on the small iron-framed bed, leaning back against the wall. Absently, he watched the other men sleep while he relived the incident outside again and again in the back of his mind—though at first he tried not to. He was not ready for the powerful feelings Callie had aroused in him.

It had been more than the natural urge a man got

when he was attracted to a beautiful women. It far surpassed that; otherwise, he never would have pulled away from her like he had. He would have let nature take its course. But the intensity and the importance of what he felt had been too great. And what worried him the most was that he was dangerously close to falling in love with her, if he hadn't already. He had not expected that, nor did he want it.

Marriage, or even falling in love with Callie—with anybody—simply did not fit into his future plans at all. Not now. He could not remain dedicated to making Twin Oaks just as prosperous and just as productive as his father's ranch and be equally dedicated to caring for a woman—or the two little girls who had been entrusted to her care. But what was he to do about it? What he felt was already a part of him. There was no way to change that.

Still, if he allowed his emotions their full rein, he would find himself spending less and less time overseeing his ranch. But then, if he was to be honest with himself, he had already allowed that to happen. All his previous convictions were falling slowly to the wayside. All the things he had thought important no longer seemed as important. He could not let that happen. He refused to let his heart get in the way of his personal goals.

Yet, if he didn't at least explore what he felt for Callie, he would always be thinking of her, wondering what might have been—never able to get anything done. It was quite a predicament. One he should have never allowed himself to become involved in. Not at this time anyway. If only he had not met Callie until after his ranch was on firmer footing, after he had proven that he could indeed make it on his own and be just as prosperous as, if not *more* prosperous than, his father was.

His very manhood was at stake—or was it? He must

keep his priorities straight. But what were his priorities? Rubbing his stubbled chin as he tilted his head back and stared up at the dark ceiling, he was no longer certain. Was there any way to find a balance between the two? Between his need to prove himself to his father and his love for Callie? He doubted it. Ever since he'd started helping Callie with the Circle T, he'd begun to spend more and more time away from Twin Oaks, until he was hardly ever there anymore. He had practically left the running of his entire ranch to his men.

And why? Because of what he felt for Callie, and even what he felt for Janice and little Amy, who were finally starting to accept him. He'd come to dread the thought of ever leaving the three of them, dreading the day when he would no longer be a real part of their lives. Even if the danger they had found themselves in did eventually pass, and his own ponds again held the water needed to supply his cattle, he still did not like the thought of leaving them to fend for themselves.

When his dearest wish had once been for there to be rain so he would no longer have to work for Callie Tucker, no longer have to be constantly at her beck and call, now he hoped it never rained enough to fill his ponds again, only enough to keep the grass alive. What was happening to him?

When the pointed hands of the huge mantle clock eventually edged their way around to four o'clock, Wade found himself no closer to a solution to his newly discovered problems than he had been when he had first began to probe for answers. He had yet to come to any clear understanding about what he really felt or what he should do about those feelings—only that the feelings did exist and were starting to rule not only his heart but his head as well.

Finally the time had come to wake the men who were to ride out with him for the final watch, and as he slid out of the bed, he knew that whatever he decided to do about Callie, he'd better decide quickly—and then get on with his life.

"You know, you really would have been proud of her," Ed said while he jabbed a fork into the plateful of food Wade had just brought him. Though it was completely against his nature to sit idly by while others worked, Ed had little choice, and had stayed in his bunk for nearly three days now—as ordered. The loneliness was unbearable, and he made up for it whenever someone came to visit with him by talking his visitor's ear off. "She never once let her fear get the best of her. Even when it was clear somebody was out there, she remained calm and level-headed. Not at all like most women."

Wade was in no mood to hear any more praise concerning Callie. For the past two days, ever since their late-night encounter in the yard, he'd done his level best not to think about her at all. And as if by mutual agreement, she'd done nothing to force him to.

Saturday, she'd closed herself in Matthew's study and tended to her books for most of the day. Then on Sunday, she and the girls had stayed inside and played cards all afternoon. He'd had no real occasion to see her at all until Andy and Tony had returned from town earlier on Monday, just before noon, with news the lumber they had ordered to rebuild the barn was ready to be picked up at the sawmill just outside of town. Even then he had barely talked with her long enough to agree to send several wagons on over to the mill to get the lumber and haul it back.

"I understand you remained pretty calm yourself," Wade said, hoping to shift the focus of the conversation from Callie to Ed.

"Not really. I was scared to death," Ed admitted with

233

a sharp expelling of air. "I'm just glad nothing else has happened since then. Maybe whoever was pulling all that meanness around here has finally given up."

"Maybe so," Wade responded, though he doubted it. He had a horrible feeling whoever was responsible for the earlier incidents was just laying low for a while — waiting for him and the men to let down their guard. Frowning, he walked over to one of the open windows and glanced outside to where several of the men had already finished their lunch and gotten back to work with huge spools of string and pointed stakes, marking the exact spot where the next barn was to be rebuilt. A light breeze gusted suddenly through the window and tugged gently at his hat, making him aware he had forgotten to take it off when he came inside.

"Looks like it's clouding up out there," Ed commented just before he shoved a large bite of ham into his mouth. It was clear to everyone that his injuries had not affected his appetite. "Do you think we are finally going to get some rain? Sure could use it. It's been at least three months since our last really good rain. In fact, I can't remember there ever being a drought to last as long as this one has."

Wade glanced up into the darkening sky, and felt a strange mixture of hope and melancholy. Though there had been a few afternoon showers in the past several weeks, Ed was right, there had not been a good, ground-drenching rain since the end of April. A long, steady rain was needed, but then again, if it rained too hard and for too long, he would lose his reason for being a part of the Circle T. "Can't tell if we are in for rain or not. They look like rain clouds, but you can never really tell."

"Good thing the men didn't go out to try and cut that hay today after all. A good rain would mean a far better grade of hay." He paused long enough to take another

234

bite. "Hmmm, this is good. Have you eaten yet?"

Wade was only halfway listening to Ed. Because of the suddenly darkening sky, Callie had stepped outside to glance up, evidently wondering like everyone else if they were in for rain. His heart quickened at the mere sight of her. It was not until he noticed the way her skirts whipped against her slender leges that he realized the breeze had started to pick up until it had become a strong, steady wind. Frowning, he glanced back at the churning clouds. There were still clear patches of sky to be seen off to the east, but to the west, there was nothing but a dark blanket of rolling clouds.

The men who had been busy staking off the area for the barn also stopped what they were doing to stare up into the dark sky overhead. The brisk wind whipped McKinsey's hat off his balding head, and he had to go chasing across the yard after it. No sooner had he bent over to recapture it than the first large drops of rain began to pelt the sun-baked earth, sending up tiny puffs of dust and steam wherever they landed, followed only seconds later by an instant downpour.

Sudden whoops of joy rose from the men as they began to dance around like children, beating their hats against their thighs and turning their faces skyward to catch the fat drops of rain in their open mouths. Lucille appeared at Callie's side, grinning up at the clouds and letting the water drench her. Janice and Amy soon followed, laughing and clapping, and splashing in the rapidly forming puddles at their feet, not caring that they were splattering mud on their slippers and their dresses. Ruby came next from the direction of the chicken coop, holding out her soggy skirts and twirling about in the rain, laughing right along with the girls.

Callie seemed to be the only one not affected by the rain. She merely stood motionless while she watched the clouds move in wide circular motions across the sky, her hair and clothing already soaked. Wade noticed the way the clinging garments displayed her womanly shape, and felt that same longing for her he'd felt the other night. He tried to shake the feeling, but was unable. His desire for her was too strong.

"That's some rain," Ed said, staring up at the ceiling with wide-eyed fascination while listening to the steady rhythm of rain as it slapped against the roof. "Wonder how long it'll keep up."

Wade did not answer. Instead he walked over to the door and stepped outside. By the time he reached Callie's side, water poured from the brim of his hat in a steady stream and his own clothing was soaked—his shirt plastered against his tall, muscular frame like a second skin.

Callie glanced at him only briefly, then returned her attention to the sky. Her voice was sharp and her words clipped when she spoke. "Well, there's your rain, Mr. Barlow."

Her words stung and confused him. "My rain?"

"Yes. Look at it. The clouds go on forever. This is no quick summer shower. It looks like it could rain all day," she said, accusingly. Then she turned to glare at him, blinking reflexively as the rain struck her sharply in the face. "It's just what you've been praying for, isn't it? And if it continues like this for very long, your ponds are sure to fill back up and you won't have to worry about being dependent on my water anymore."

All the emotions she had kept bottled up inside, since the night he'd so abruptly walked away from her—leaving her weak and wanting—now rose to the surface and she found herself unaccountably angry with him. "And since there have been no more attacks, no more trouble of any kind, you can go back to Twin Oaks with an easy conscience, can't you?" A loud peal of thunder caused her to jump, but she bit back the startled scream that swelled deep inside of her. Suddenly, though, her lips began to tremble. "Well, then. Rejoice. Round up your cattle, Mr. Barlow. Rebuild your fence. And—and forget I ever existed."

"Callie, I . . ." Whatever he'd been about to say died on his tongue when she suddenly lifted her wet skirts and fled into the house. He heard the sob that tore from her throat even over the heavy downpour and the trailing rumble of distant thunder. He looked at Lucille, whose eyes were wide, clearly just as surprised as he had been by Callie's sudden outburst.

"Don't ask me," she said with a heavy shrug of her well-rounded shoulders. "She's been actin' mighty peculiar for the last several days. I don't know what's got into her."

Janice and Amy looked surprised too as they all four turned to stare curiously at the place where Callie had just stood.

To Callie's dismay and everyone else's obvious delight, the rain continued the rest of the day and well on into the night. Though she was not consulted on the matter, she noticed that just before it turned dark, Wade sent four men draped with rain ponchos out on night watch, just as he had in recent days.

Because she seemed so oddly drawn to her bedroom window, she had also noticed how often Wade came out of the bunkhouse to peer up into the sky. The more it rained, the more she had to try to accept the fact she was about to lose Wade Barlow as her foreman. Though she had started to realize Ed Grant might make a good foreman and could probably replace Wade when the time did come that Wade left her, she was not at all ready for that to happen. And with his ribs still bandaged and sore, neither was Ed.

When Callie dressed and went downstairs the following morning, the sun was out again and only a few lingering clouds remained; but as far as she was concerned, the damage had been done. Wade would check his ponds—if he hadn't already—and find they held water. He would then happily announce the fact he no longer needed her or her water. Callie wanted to cry. She knew he would then leave her, just as she had always known he would.

It was only minutes after ten o'clock when Wade knocked at the back door and asked to see her. And, as expected, the first thing he had to say after he had entered the house was that he'd just ridden over to his place to see how much good the rain had done. She could tell by the way he was smiling that his ponds must be full again. He was about to leave her.

"You can't believe the difference that rain has made," he told her while he followed her into the parlor, with its one window still boarded shut—a grim reminder of what had almost happened. "Everything looks so green. The grass, which I thought was practically dead, is green again. The bushes are green. Even the trees look greener. It's like someone took a paintbrush to everything. It's beautiful. I wish the new saddles were ready so you and the girls could ride out and see it all. Maybe after the ground dries a little, you should take a short carriage ride just so you can see how beautiful it is."

"I suppose you'll be rounding up your cattle and sending them back on to your own place now," she said as she sat down in one of her favorite chairs, preparing herself for the worst.

"Can't do that just yet," he said, and his smile faded while he studied her grim expression. "Though my grass is green again and is sure to start growing again, it seems there was hardly any water runoff. I guess the ground was so dry and the grass and trees so thirsty that

238

they soaked it right up, almost as fast as it fell. There was hardly any water at all in my ponds. And if it doesn't rain again soon, what water I do have will be gone within a few days. I still need to keep my cattle over in your northwest pasture. That is if you don't mind."

Mind? Callie was overwhelmed with relief. "Of course not. My water is your water for as long as you need it."

"Good. For a moment there, you had me worried. I thought maybe you were having second thoughts about our arrangement." His smile returned, causing his dimples to form at the outer curves of his mouth.

Callie's heart skipped with random little beats. He had such a handsome smile.

Unaware of the direction her thoughts had taken, Wade went on. "I know we've not been on the best of terms ever since we . . . encountered each other in the yard the other night. I was afraid you had decided to show your anger by refusing to allow my cattle any further use of your land."

"No, what happened the other night has nothing to do with our business relationship. It was just something we should never have allowed to happen. It's best forgotten."

"I'm willing to try if you are," Wade told her, though he knew it would be asking the impossible of himself when it was really all he thought about now.

Even now, his pulses hammered uncontrollably inside him, from simply being in the same room with her. But eager to continue the conversation in the direction it had taken, he sat down in the chair beside her so he could more easily study her expression. "Shall we start over? As friends?"

Callie smiled and reached out to touch the dimple pressed into his freshly shaven cheek. How smooth his skin felt. "I'd like that. How will I ever learn all there is to know about running this place if I can't get out there and help?"

Wade no longer argued against her desire to help. Instead, he felt delighted to hear she still wanted to. "We are about to get started on that barn. Do you want to come out and help me get things underway?"

Callie was instantly on her feet. "Of course I do. Let's go."

When Wade offered her his arm and she took it, a warm feeling passed through her. She realized it was going to be impossible to push her feelings for him fully aside, but at the same time she knew it would be even harder to try to stay away from him altogether. These past few days of trying to keep her distance had been a living nightmare.

No, even though Callie knew she would suffer dearly whenever she was at his side, aware they were destined never to share more than a friendly business relationship, she felt certain it was better than no relationship at all. And at this point, she would gladly take whatever she could get.

Chapter Fifteen

The sun was perched high in a brilliant blue morning sky when Wade and Stretch left for town to get yet another keg of nails and the other materials they needed to hang the heavy doors which had already been built along the front, back, and east sides of the new barn.

Barely half an hour later, a large carriage turned in off the main road. Though only four days had passed since the heavy downpour that had soaked the area—the same rain that had officially broken the drought at long last—the ground was already starting to dry out again and a faint trailing of dust welled up around the carriage as it came to an abrupt halt near the front of the house.

Amazed at how adept the men were at building the new barn when all they had was Wade's simple sketch to go by, Callie was already outside, watching with keen interest while the men raised yet another heavy plank into place and quickly began to hammer it at both ends.

Having heard the clattering noise of the carriage, she glanced over just as Walter Barlow climbed down from the back seat and headed in her direction.

She frowned as a cold prickling of anticipation slowly shrouded her. Reluctantly, she turned away from the progress being made on the new building and began to walk toward him. She dreaded yet another confrontation with the man, but at the same time was eager to get it

241

out of the way so she could get back to watching the men work on the barn. As she stepped closer to him, she became oddly aware that although her heart now beat at an amazing rate, the rhythmical hammering behind her had suddenly ceased. She knew if she was to turn around at that moment, she would find everyone's curious gaze turned in their direction.

"Hello," Walter called out with a cheerful wave of his hand, as if there had never been a cross word between them. She noticed he had not bothered with a calling suit today. Instead he wore a stark white cotton shirt and a pair of dark gray duct trousers with wide gray-striped suspenders. Having chosen to remain hatless, he looked far more comfortable and far more pleased with himself than he had during his past visits. "I see you are already hard at work getting your barn replaced."

Walter did not seem very curious about the reason she was having to rebuild, which must mean he already knew about the fire. Callie's pale brown eyes narrowed when she looked at him. She wondered if his knowledge came firsthand. Was there any evidence of guilt on his smiling face? None that she could detect, but then Walter Barlow seemed like the type of man who was used to hiding his emotions whenever he deemed it absolutely necessary—which he obviously did now.

"We can't go without a barn for too long," she told him, and paused in the side yard long enough to allow him to walk over where she stood. Then she wondered what she should do with him. She did not want to invite him inside. Nor did she want him snooping around her back yard. In the end, she remained right where she was, though the hot July sun bore down on them uncomfortably.

"I heard about the unfortunate events you've suffered as of late," he said when he came to a stop. He shook his head with feigned sympathy while he glanced at the

242

structure across the yard made of fresh, yellow lumber. "First your barn, then your fence, then an attack on the house itself."

My, but he was well informed. "Yes, I've had quite a run of bad luck recently."

"I'd say you have had more than a run of bad luck. I'd say someone was looking to run you off. That's why I decided to come back by here and see if you might be ready to sell this place yet. Now that Wade is no longer helping you and you have had a taste of running this place on your own, and what with all the terrible things which have happened here lately, I imagine you have begun to seriously reconsider my previous offer." His hazel eyes sparkled with hopeful expectation.

"What makes you think Wade is no longer helping me?" she asked, bewildered by such a statement.

"Oh, come now. After that heavy rain we had? I know for a fact my ponds are now very full. They were even overflowing there for a while. That was a veritable flood we had. And with so much water, there's no reason for Wade to still be helping you. No, I'm sure he is hard at work getting his own place back in shape after all the neglect he has had to show it here recently."

"I'm afraid you are wrong," she said, feeling a certain satisfaction in being able to inform him of that fact. "There was not enough runoff on Wade's land to help his ponds very much. He is still having to keep his cattle on my land, and as a result, he is still helping me run this place. In fact, at this very moment he and one of my men have gone into town to get more nails and larger hinges for the doors. And, as you may recognize, he even has two of his own men here helping build. That way, we can get finished sooner."

"That's impossible. We had nearly eighteen hours of solid rain. His ponds had to catch some of that. Why, one of the creeks that runs through my land is the same one that crosses over his, and I know for a fact *it* has plenty of water now." Walter's eyes glinted with anger as he lowered his stubby red lashes. "Just what are you trying to pull?"

"I'm not trying to pull anything. Wade told me that he himself went out to inspect his ponds and found they had hardly benefited at all from the rain."

Walter fell silent for a moment, and when he spoke again, his nostrils flared with the anger which had quickly consumed him. "Has it ever occurred to you that Wade might be lying to you?"

"And why would he lie about a thing like that?"

"It could be he's not ready to give up whatever he has gained here. Consider those recent incidents you've suffered. Hasn't it occurred to you that he might be the one behind them? Hasn't it occurred to you that he wanted to find a way to make you feel grateful to him? So grateful that when the time came for you to sell this place, you would sell it to *him* and not me?" Walter's eyes widened as if he suddenly realized something. "That boy will go to any length to see to it I don't get my hands on this place. He's still damned determined to do all he can to try to prove he's better than me."

Callie's stomach tightened painfully when his words struck her full force. Suddenly it felt as if someone had spilled burning acid into her bloodstream. "Wade wouldn't do anything like that."

"And how well do you think you have come to know him in the six and a half weeks you have been here? Not nearly as well as I do. That boy would do anything to keep me from getting the Circle T. He knows how much I want it, always have. And he's just conniving enough to do whatever it takes to gain your confidence in him. I'm surprised he hasn't tried to seduce you into his bed so that you would have to marry him. Then he could have it all, couldn't he."

Callie had had enough. "I think you'd better leave now, Mr. Barlow. I've heard just about all I want to hear from you."

"Not yet. Not until you hear my offer. I want this place. I want the springs that feed it water even in a drought. I want the rich bottomlands in your north pastures. I want that ridge where you can survey the entire area in one sweeping glance. I want it all. Whatever Wade eventually offers you for your land, I'll pay a thousand dollars more. In fact, I'll offer you twenty dollars an acre for it right now. As is. With only that shell for a barn. That's almost twice the going rate. And because I know what prime stock you have, I'll pay you six dollars a head for your cattle. Even the calves. That's more than fair." And it was far more than he'd ever intended to pay, but that was before he had learned he still had Wade to contend with. He certainly did not want Wade to end up with the Circle T.

"I've told you before. I don't have any intention of selling this place," she stated in a barely controlled voice. "Good day to you, Mr. Barlow."

"You don't believe me about the water, do you? Then why don't you take a ride over there and see for yourself? His place may not have quite the water capacity mine does, having less bottomland, but I'm positive you'll see that I'm right about those ponds he does have. They're full of water. I'm sure of it. Go look for yourself. Then you'll see my son for what he really is."

"Good day, Mr. Barlow," she repeated, then without further comment, she whirled around and headed for the back of the house, her hands curled into tight, determined fists.

"You'll be sorry. I know Wade. He's like me. He's not about to give up until one of us has gotten his hands on this place. There'll be more trouble ahead. Just you wait and see."

Callie never glanced back, nor did she acknowledge Walter Barlow's angry statements in any way. Instead she continued up the steps and into the house. When she stepped inside, she found Lucille standing at a nearby window, scowling while she continued to keep a keen eye on the man outside, as if she fully expected him to sprout horns and come charging at the house. Callie was torn between a sudden urge to chuckle at Lucille's frowning expression and the sudden need to scream out with rage. The man had put doubts in her mind she did not want to admit possible. But still, as she continued on up the stairs, she began to wonder if there was any validity in what the man had said about Wade.

While she bathed her heated face with a cool, wet cloth, she realized Wade *could* have been the one to set fire to her barn. He and his men had certainly appeared on the scene quickly enough to help put out the blaze, but not quite so quickly that they had been able to save the barn. And the fence had been cut in the early afternoon while everyone was off attending to their regular duties. Wade could have easily slipped away unnoticed for that. But then, some of the cattle to die as a result of the cut fence had been his. Would he have been willing to risk the death of some of his own stock in order to create a situation in which he would then be able to lead the others in a valiant rescue? She didn't want to believe it.

And what of the attack at the house? He had been right there in the bunkhouse when McKenzie fired his emergency shots. And Wade had been with the men when they rode off to help. He couldn't have been involved with the attack itself. But he could have hired someone else first to cause McKenzie to fire those three shots and then, while he himself led most of the men away from the house, to attack those who were left behind. He had definitely been the one to come hurry-

246

ing to the rescue yet again and had saved her from further harm. And she had to admit, she'd never felt more grateful to him than she had that night.

As for seducing her into his bed, he had certainly planted the seeds of passion within her. But if he was that eager to bed her, why had he pulled away as he had? Why had he appeared so eager to establish a strictly business-type relationship with her?

No, she did not believe Walter Barlow. Wade was not conniving enough to do all those things just to make her feel grateful toward him. And too, Wade was aware she did not have full authority to sell the place even if she wanted. But then again, he also had the girls feeling grateful towards him—grateful for having saved Amy's life. Was there any way he could have known Amy would run into the barn the way she did? No, he could not have planned such a thing. Walter Barlow was simply trying to deflect suspicion away from himself.

Still, the tiniest seed of doubt had been planted, and she decided to confront him with Walter's accusations as soon as he returned.

It was a few minutes after two o'clock before Wade and Stretch got back from town. Finally, she would have an opportunity to speak with him. Only moments after she heard the wagon pull into the drive, then glanced out a window to make sure it was them, she hurried to the area where she knew he would bring the conveyance to a stop and waited for him.

"Wade, I want to talk to you," she said calmly as soon as he had climbed down from the wagon and had turned to help Stretch unload their purchases.

"Sure, just as soon as we get these things unloaded," he said with a quick smile.

"He can get someone else to help him. I would like to speak with you *now.*"

Her tone of voice was so firm, so serious, that Wade's

smile faded into an immediate expression of concern. Quickly, he turned to oblige. "Sure, what is it?"

"Inside. I want to talk with you inside."

He knew by her tense expression that something terrible had happened while he was gone. Filled with sudden apprehension, he followed her toward the house. "Are the girls all right?"

"They're fine. They are both upstairs playing with Amy's doll house." Her eyes narrowed as she looked back at him. "They are delighted with the new furniture you and Ed have made for it."

Wade felt as if she was accusing him of something, though he couldn't fathom what it was. "All I've done is paint the things. Ed does all the real work. It gives him something to do while he's tied down to that bed. It makes him feel more useful. And he gets a real kick out of seeing the smile on Amy's face whenever he presents her with a new piece. He even has McKenzie helping him with the project. McKenzie has started keeping an eye out for the better wood scraps from the barn and keeps Ed's whittling knife sharpened for him."

"I see," was all she had to say on the matter. She then fell silent during the rest of the walk to Matthew's study.

Once they were inside the large room, behind carefully closed doors, Callie turned to face him with her arms crossed, more as a way to steady her churning stomach than out of any feeling of defiance. She sought the right words to begin her inquest.

Wade could stand the silence no longer. "Have I done something wrong?"

"I don't know. You tell me." Though she continued to keep a stern voice, her earlier suspicions had already started to dissolved inside of her. When she looked up into his handsome face, so full of confusion, worry, and honest concern, she found she could in no way believe he was the sort of person Walter had portrayed him to be. No, Walter must have been the one lying about everything. Not Wade. "I had a visitor while you were gone."

"Father," Wade quickly concluded. He heaved a sharp, disgruntled sigh when she nodded yes. "What did he want this time? Though I can pretty well guess."

"He wanted to make yet another offer to buy the Circle T. A very generous offer."

"You aren't seriously considering it, are you?"

"No. I've already told you I don't plan to sell this place to anyone. I promised Matthew and I promised the girls. I don't intend to sell even a small part of this place for any amount — *to anyone*. I would be unable to even if I wanted. As you probably will recall, the girls' signatures also have to be on any agreement to sell and they are just as adamant about staying as I am."

"I know. Now that Janice no longer sees me as some sort of evil villian, I've had a chance to talk with both of them about it. And I agree. This is their home. They should be allowed to stay here — as a family."

Callie frowned. Although that was what she had hoped he would say, she was not completely sure she believed it. There was still the tiniest bit of doubt nagging at her — a doubt she was eager to have cleared away. "Wade, he also told me that your ponds had to be full. He said the creek which runs across your place also runs across his and that it definitely has water in it now, which in turn would mean your ponds should also have water. Is that true?"

Wade reached out and grasped her gently by the shoulders, as if to steady her for the answer to come. "Yes, it's true. My ponds have plenty of water. Though they've receded some in the days since the rain, there is still plenty of water. Enough to supply my cattle for quite some time."

"Then why did you lie to me?" she asked, looking up

at him with wide, luminous eyes.

Callie looked so hurt and so vulnerable, Wade could not stand it. He took her into his arms and held her close, pressing her soft cheek against his chest. "I lied because I was not ready to leave here just yet. I was especially not ready to leave you, kitten. Not when I honestly feel you might still be in very real danger."

"Is that the reason? Is that really the reason?" she asked, turning her face toward his so that her chin rested gently on his chest. Her pale brown eyes glimmered with childlike hope.

"Yes," he answered simply, then smiled. "That's the truth. I couldn't bring myself to leave you. Not yet."

Callie believed him. Relief washed over her, making her feel a little weak. Tears stung her eyes. "Then it is not some sort of game you are playing just to be able to get your hands on the Circle T?"

Wade stiffened. "So, we are back to *that,* are we?"

"No, not really," she answered quickly. "It's just that your father had hoped to make me believe you were trying your best to get on my better side so, when the time came for me to sell, I'd sell to you instead of him."

"He what!" Wade thundered, instantly angry.

"He seemed to think you were out to get the place before he could," she answered honestly. "He made it sound like you had made some sort of contest out of seeing who could claim this place first. Only, he felt you were using an entirely different approach than any he was able to take."

"The man is insane. I'm beginning to believe he is actually insane." Wade's nostrils flared with a combination of hurt and anger as his jawline turned granite hard.

"How insane?" Callie asked. "Insane enough to have anything to do with all the horrible mishaps that have been happening around here lately? Insane enough to hire men to attack the house?"

Wade's arms tightened around her. "I don't know. I just don't know anything anymore. I've tried so hard to please that man, to somehow make him believe in me, yet he continues to look for only the worst in me. I don't understand why that is. But no matter *who* is behind your trouble, I honestly don't think they are through with you yet, and I'm not leaving here until I am absolutely certain you and the girls are completely out of danger—if I have to stay over here forever."

"Thank you," she whispered, and wrapped her arms around his waist in response. Gently, she pressed her cheek against his chest again and listened to the steady rhythm of his heartbeat. How reassuring the sound seemed, never once faltering.

They stood like that for a long moment, clutched in each other's arms, thinking their separate thoughts, though linked by a common thread, until Wade finally found the courage to speak again. "I want you to know that I care about you, Callie. Very much. And because I do care, there is no way I'd do anything to hurt you. I want you to believe that."

Callie snuggled closer to him, breathed deeply the now familiar scent of him, and felt wonderfully protected. "I need you, Wade. I couldn't make this place go without your help."

"Yes, you could," he told her, and he truly believed it—that is, if they ever caught the troublemakers who continued to plague her and finally got them out of her way. She might be a woman, and she might seem terribly vulnerable at times, but she was a survivor. She'd make it whether he stayed or not. "Matthew Tucker knew what he was doing when he entrusted this place and his two daughters into your care. He was a wise man—a very wise man."

Callie felt a sudden surge of tears burning her eyes.

251

Her throat tightened until she could barely swallow. If only Matthew had lived to hear such wonderful praise coming from Wade Barlow's own lips. "I wish you could have known him. Matthew *was* a wise man. And he was a good man. You would have liked him. I know you would."

Wade lifted her chin with the tips of his fingers until she was looking at him again. "I never had anything against the man. He was my father's enemy. Not mine."

Callie closed her eyes to hide the glimmering tears that had continued to fill her eyes. If only Matthew could have known that was the way Wade felt. If only Matthew had been aware he had only *one* true enemy — and that was Walter Barlow.

Wade stared at her, at the long, damp lashes lying softly against the high curve of her cheek, at the perfect shape of her upturned nose, then at the delicate pink lips that suddenly seemed very inviting. He could not help himself. No matter the consequences, he had to kiss her.

Before Callie quite knew what was happening, Wade lowered his lips to hers and, though the kiss began a truly gentle one, it ignited into a veritable powder keg of emotion, setting off an explosion of pure desire in both of them.

Pressing closer, Callie responded with the hunger of a woman half-starved. Eager to again sample the pleasure only Wade could offer her, she strained almost feverishly upward, entwining her arms about his neck. Her lips parted beneath the gentle pressure of his while he quickly worked to loosen her luxuriant mane of hair from its many pins, until it finally tumbled in a wild disarray about her face and shoulders. Quickly, he lost his fingers in its softness and moaned aloud his approval.

Though Wade was not sure *when* he had actually

decided he wanted her to become a true and lasting part of his life, it was clear to him now. He wanted Callie—wanted her desperately—for now and forever. His independence be damned. His ranch be damned. This time, there would be no turning back. This time he would show her how very much he had come to care for her—to love her as he had loved no other woman. He would make her his. He would brand her with a passion so strong, so powerful, she would never turn away from him. He wanted her to understand they were meant for each other.

At that moment, turning away was the furthest thing from Callie's heart. She too had come to realize how important Wade was in her life. Though she was not too sure it was actually love she felt for him—never having had much experience in that area—she did know she wanted him, wanted to please him, wanted to be pleased by him. Overpowered with need, she pressed her mouth harder against his, molded her soft curves against the hard planes of his body. Suddenly, it felt as if she belonged there, belonged in Wade's strong arms, belonged to his rapturous kiss.

While she tried to keep her sanity long enough to consider such a stunning revelation, Wade's hands began to roam up and down along the gentle curve of her spine. His fingers again became lost in the dark softness of her long, silky hair. Deliciously warm and starkly tantalizing sensations rippled through her, delighting every inch of her, making her delirious with need. Boldly, she pressed her fingertips into the back of his neck, urging him on, while she continued to mold her body hungrily against his.

Wade needed no further encouragement, and slowly moved his fingertips to the center of her back, then began to undo the many pearl-shaped buttons that ran along the back of her dress, all the while continuing to work his wondrous magic with one devouring kiss after another.

Consumed with her desire, Callie trembled with expectation when he gently slipped the garment off her shoulders. She found the room suddenly without air when he began to gently work the material past her hips until it fell to the floor in a soft puddle of aqua blue. She closed her eyes as she fought for each breath, reveling in the sensations now flaming brilliantly inside her.

Slowly Wade moved his hand between them, gently cupping one of her rounded breasts through the thin fabric of her camisole. Lightly his fingertips played with the tip until he felt it grow rigid with a strong desire for more. But he waited to undo the tiny sashes that would remove the flimsy undergarment and would finally allow him to actually touch her delicate skin. Instead, he continued to let his hand prowl about along the outside of the thin wisp of clothing that still separated them — seeking, searching, but never quite finding.

Callie was lost in a deep swirling torrent of emotions. Heated desire coursed through her veins, and her ever-growing arousal quickly possesed every vacant crevice of her being. She was wondrously alive, eager to know more.

Every part of her yearned for his hand to hurry and claim its prize. She moaned aloud from the exquisite pleasure that shot through her when his hand finally did return to cup her eager breast yet again.

Filled with longing, Wade pulled away from her and gazed down into her drowsy expression. He knew by the way she strained her breast against his palm that the passions inside her were now fully ignited, burning deep within her. He knew he could take her then and she would let him, but he chose to move very slowly. He wanted this to be as much for her as it was for him. Gently, he reached for the satin sashes of her camisole and tugged on the tiny bows until they easily gave way. Callie trembled when he allowed the thin fabric to drop first from one shoulder, then the other, giving himself full view of her thrusting breasts.

He then turned his attention to the ruffled underskirt and the pantaloons that hid the rest of her exquisite body from his view. Soon, the flimsy garments joined the rumpled dress at her feet and, except for a pair of silken slippers, she was gloriously naked before him.

For a brief moment, he stood and stared longingly at her, then bent down and gently gathered her into his arms. Lifting her out of the pool of tangled clothing, he quickly carried her across the room and placed her on the large velvetine couch, which could easily pass for a small bed. His eyes were dark with desire when he looked down at her then. Slowly, he bent down to trail tiny kisses along her cheek and jaw, which she bent her head back and accepted willingly.

Unable to resist the slender column of her neck, he trailed the tiny kisses ever downward, across the pulsating hollow of her throat, until he reached one of her ripened breasts. When his mouth finally claimed the hardened peak, Callie's fingers curled compulsively, digging into the firm muscles of his back. When his tongue began to pull at the sensitive tip, Callie moaned aloud in response to the searing heat that shot through her. The exquisite pain was unbearable.

He left her then only long enough to remove his own clothing, and found her just as willing to accept him naked as she had been to accept him with his clothing on. She offered no protest when he lightly lowered his weight on top of her.

Rolling partially to one side to give him easier access to her splendid body, he quickly brought his lips down on hers yet again while he began to run his hand freely over her. His fingertips gently teased and taunted as they

255

came ever closer to the sensitive peaks of her breasts in light circular motions.

Callie arched her back to accommodate his touch, wishing his hands would hurry and reach their destination. Eagerly, her own hands began to roam over his body, exploring the firm muscles along his back and down his arms. His body's warmth seemed to intensify the already sensitive tips of her fingers when she felt first of the curved planes of his shoulders, then of the gentle contours along his back. She strained her arms to be able to feel the taut, lean muscles that were a part of his hips and upper thighs. His lightly haired skin felt good to her touch. She marveled at the many differences in his body when compared to hers.

While his lips continued to sample the sweetness of her mouth, Wade allowed himself the pleasure of exploring every feminine curve of her body with a warm, gentle hand. Then, slowly, he let his lips leave hers to again trail tiny kisses downward until he once again reached one of her straining breasts. Deftly, his tongue teased the tip with short tantalizing strokes until she arched herself ever higher, eagerly seeking more. Slowly he moved to take in the neglected breast, pulling and playing with it until she began to come up off the couch with her newly awakened passion.

Such sweet ecstasy. Callie was not certain how long she could bear this tender torment, and began to clutch at his shoulders as the wild sensations continued to assault every inch of her body. Her head tossed restlessly while a deeply demanding ache filled her. She wanted him to stop before the sensations became too much to endure, but found herself arching ever upward in an effort to give him easier access to whatever pleased him. She shuddered from the delectable sensations building inside her, higher and higher, degree by degree, until she was sure she would burst.

A strange throbbing pain had centered itself some-where low inside her, and had reached such an intensity she could no longer bear it. Her body craved release from the sensual anguish burning within her, but she did not yet understand what might bring her that relief.

"Wade, please," she moaned aloud, so lost to the sensual haze that surrounded her she was unaware she had spoken at all.

Drawing on first one breast, then the other one last time, Wade finally moved to fulfill her, gently, until the barrier inside her was broken, then with far more force, until he brought their wildest longings, their deepest desires to an ultimate height. When release came for Callie, only moments before it came for Wade, it was both wondrous and shattering. She had to bite into the soft flesh of her lip to keep from crying aloud her pleasure. Her fingers dug deep into his flesh as she rose to meet him time and time again. Suddenly, she knew what it meant to be a woman. Never had she felt so fulfilled. So deeply satisfied. So gloriously alive.

Wade remained on top of her for a long moment afterward, until they both had their erratic breathing back under control. Then he again moved to one side. All that remained on top of her was one long, muscular leg.

"What a splendid lover you are," he murmured, bend-ing forward to kiss away a strand of dark hair clinging to her cheek.

Callie tensed. "Is that all I am to you? A lover?"

"For now, yes," he said as he began to stroke the sensitive skin along her collarbone then down closer to her breasts. Tiny bumps of sensation rose beneath her ivory skin. "But one day—after I am absolutely certain you don't think I'm marrying you just so I can find a way to get my hands on the Circle T, and after whoever it is that keeps tormenting you is finally caught and behind bars where he can't ruin what should be a truly special time for us—you are going to make a damned good wife."

Callie's eyes widened when full implication of what he had just said sank into her still passion-clouded thoughts. "Wife? You'd marry me?"

"After today, I'd be a fool not to," he said, grinning. There was a devilish glimmer in his eyes as he glanced down at the perfection that was her body. "Kitten, you are not only beautiful, you turn into one wild hellcat in bed."

Chapter Sixteen

The prospect of their getting married was not mentioned again while they quickly redressed, nor while Callie tried to find all the hairpins that had fallen to the floor in order to make the needed repairs to her hair. Even so, it was all she could think about. Even after Wade had left, having been the first to make himself presentable, her thoughts remained centered on what had happened between them just moments earlier, and the fact he had actually mentioned marriage.

Never having really considered getting married again, she was stunned at how eagerly she now looked forward to such a thing. It would be wonderful to share the rest of her life with Wade. Her blood heated again at the mere thought of it. But what would Janice and Amy say to such a thing? Although the girls had become much, much friendlier toward him since his daring rescue of Amy from the fire, they still might not accept him as their stepfather. They might not care for the thought of his living there with them. And she would want to have their full acceptance before she agreed to make such drastic changes in their lives.

Knowing what a good father Wade would be for them, Callie hoped the girls would eventually come to see how good it would be to have him around on such a permanent basis. *She* certainly liked the idea. Her entire body tingled when she considered what it would be like to be married to Wade Barlow. Such pleasures, like those they had just shared in each other's arms, would be hers forever. And better still, she knew Matthew would approve. He would want her to be happy as long as his girls were happy too.

But even so, Callie was aware she could not force the idea of Wade becoming such an important part of the girls' lives too suddenly. Something like that needed to be brought to their attention gently. She decided to start getting them used to the thought of Wade having a more personal part in their lives by inviting him to eat dinner with them instead of eating outside with the rest of the men as he usually did.

To her surprise, both girls took readily to the idea of Wade joining them for dinner. Each had quickly expressed a desire to have the honor of sitting at this side. Wade too appeared pleased at the invitation, and took special care with his appearance before knocking at the back door. Rather than donning one of his regular workshirts and denim pants, he had gone home to dress in a pale blue dinner shirt, which he wore with a pair of dark blue, narrow-ribbed trousers and dark blue cross-back suspenders, which accentuated the width of his shoulders and the narrowness of his waist.

Callie and the girls had also gone to extra care to look their very best. The three met him at the door dressed in their Sunday finest and escorted him directly into the dining room, where tiny bowls of tomato soup already awaited them. Even Amy had gone to the trouble to take her thick brown hair out of her usual braids, and had had Lucille arrange it into a demure twist at the top of her head. Very ladylike indeed.

Flanked by the two admiring young women, Wade found he had little room to move during dinner, and had to keep his elbows pressed into his sides when it came time to cut his steak — or chance jabbing one of the two girls in the chin. Each seemed extremely eager to pass him whatever he asked for and keep his water glass full to the rim, while an amused Callie watched from across the table. When it came time for the four of them to retire to the veranda, he found himself surrounded yet again by two eager, upturned young faces.

"I do believe you have two very devoted admirers," Callie told him as soon as the two girls had finally gone off to bed and there was room enough on the bench seat beside him for her to join him.

"Quite a difference from the first day I met them," Wade said, grinning at the obvious change in the girls' attitudes.

"But that was before you made your daring rescue. Amy now feels she owes you her life, which in a way she does, and Janice sees you as the ultimate hero. Like the ones in her storybooks."

"And how do you see me?" he asked, reaching out to take her hand in his. Though the evening darkness had started to settle in, he could see her clearly, and watched to discover just what her reaction would be to his sudden decision to touch her.

"I see you as the devil himself," she answered, smiling playfully. "Oh, yes. As the very devil himself."

"I wish I could show you just how much of the devil I have in me," he said. One dark eyebrow shot up to let her know in what direction his thoughts had gone. "But I promised to take first watch tonight and it's about time for the four of us to get on out there."

Callie felt a sudden boldness. "Well, then, perhaps another time."

"Another time indeed. If your bedroom wasn't so darned close to the girls' bedrooms, I'd find a way to slip into the house tonight to join you once I've come in off watch around midnight."

He was hinting, and she knew it, but she was still in awe of what had happened between them that afternoon, and a little frightened of the intensity of it all. "You are right. I'd hate for the girls to wake in the middle of the night and come into my room only to discover you there with me. And what if Lucille or Ruby came down from their rooms on the upper floor to get a glass of milk or something and encountered you on the stairs?"

Wade frowned, obviously not too pleased that she had so readily agreed with him. "Could I at least convince you to take another late-night stroll in the garden?"

"Perhaps," she answered as if undecided on the matter, when in truth she was already planning what she would wear. If he'd considered her a beautiful little hellcat before, wait until he saw her wearing her silky peignoir with only her skimpiest of summer nightgowns underneath. Her blood ran hot paths through her when she considered what his reaction would be. Though they would not be able to culminate their passion as they had dared to do that afternoon, at least he would have had another reminder of what lay in store for him once they were married.

"If I don't fall asleep first, I'll meet you out on the garden veranda just after midnight," she teased.

"I'll be waiting," Wade promised, then glanced around to see who might be watching. When he saw no one, he quickly stole a brief kiss from her willing lips before hurrying away to get ready to stand watch.

To Callie's relief, both girls were sound asleep when she slipped in to check on them just before midnight, and Lizzie and Ruby had both decided to go on up to bed early—certain also to be fast asleep by now. There would be no witnesses to the fact she was slipping downstairs to meet Wade at the side of the house while dressed in so suggestive an outfit, with her hair brushed

262

until it gleamed, then shaped to fall softly across her shoulders and down her back.

Her heart hammered wildly as she hurried down the stairs, knowing she looked very alluring in the long, flowing silken robe. In the end she had wickedly decided to wear nothing underneath. She hoped Wade would notice the creamy flesh revealed by the deep parting of the garment at the neckline, and then wonder if she was actually willing to be just as daring as he was in such matters. She hoped it would encourage him to discuss the possibility of their marriage in more depth, for she was sure she would not feel comfortable bringing up the subject herself. If for some reason he'd changed his mind on the matter, she did not want him to think she was trying to trap him. If they were to be married, she wanted it to be because he truly wanted her for his wife and for no other reason.

Because she had not bothered with a lamp, she was forced to slow her steps, but not her heartbeat, while she made her way through the hallway and into the parlor. Due to the silvery moonlight that bathed the garden beyond, she saw Wade's darkened silhouette already standing on the veranda, waiting impatiently while she hurried toward the two glass doors.

Sweeping them open wide, she smiled warmly at him and spoke in a deep, sultry voice. "Hello."

"Hel-lo," Wade said, his eyes growing wide and reflecting a glimmer of something more than mere moonlight. "Do I know you?"

Though Callie wanted to pretend to be innocent of his sudden awareness of her, she could not help but smile at his obvious approval. Her pulse raced wildly. "Yes, I think you've made my acquaintance at least once before."

"Ah, yes, I remember now. You are that woman I met earlier in the study," Wade said as he moved forward to envelope her in his arms. "*You* are that woman who proved to be such a fiery hellcat of passion. So much so, I immediately decided to make her my wife."

Though Callie had expected to join him outside in the night shadows that shrouded the veranda, she found herself quickly swept back inside into the dark privacy of the parlor. His mouth found hers instantly and she fell weakly against him, eager to know his passion again. Though she had come downstairs thinking they might be able to share a stolen moment alone on the veranda, maybe even a tantalizing kiss or two, Wade had different expectations. As his ravenous mouth parted hers, she knew exactly where they were headed. To that same pinnacle they had shared earlier that afternoon. She moaned softly at the realization.

Wade wasted no time in undoing the sash and the two buttons holding her only garment in place. He moaned upon discovering no further barriers underneath, and quickly slipped his hands inside to seek the treasures he knew he would find there. As he cupped both breasts at the same time, while his lips hungrily ravaged hers, Callie began to tremble with renewed desire. Only this time, she knew what lay in store for her, and she reached for it eagerly.

As the robe slid quietly to the floor, Wade bent to replace one of his hands with his hungry mouth, bringing Callie more and more of his exquisite pleasure. Tossing her head back, her hair streaming riotously to her hips, she leaned into him, giving him easier access to the breast he so greedily suckled.

While he continued to devour her breast, Wade quickly worked to rid himself of his own clothing. She was driving him wild with his need for her. He could not wait to know the fulfillment she could offer him. With clothes flung in every direction, he recaptured her in his arms, pressing their naked bodies close, reclaiming her mouth with his, tasting her sweetness again and again.

This time Wade took no time for teasing or taunting, and Callie found she did not want him to. This time there was an urgency that had to be met. By gently pulling at her shoulders, Wade brought her down to lay beside him on the thick carpet that covered much of the parlor floor, finding her eager to meet his needs with the strong needs of her own.

The passion he'd released inside her was almost frightening as she tossed her head restlessly from side to side, moaning softly the deep feeling of ecstasy she had so rapidly become lost to as he quickly and adeptly brought them both ever closer to the extreme pleasure they sought. Again she rose to meet him, and when she did, found the rewards to be almost unbearable. It was unfathomable to imagine such ecstasy could be hers for the rest of her life. That this man, who brought her such wondrous pleasure, wanted to be her husband seemed in that moment too good to be true. Yet she knew it was.

Her happiness grew, as did her desire, until she was filled with an indescribable joy, a joy so intense, so pure, it made her ache all over. Made her realize the depth of her love. Made her hope he felt the same.

Barely moments later, release came in a glorious explosion for both of them. For Callie it was just as mysterious as it had been before, but also just as rewarding and fulfilling. For Wade, it had been no less than astounding. Never had he known a woman with such a passionate nature. Having had a second taste of the pleasures she could offer him, he was more determined than ever to make her his wife. Just as soon as they had the men who continuously tried to terrorize her in jail, and just as soon as he was certain she believed he was marrying her out of love and not out of some

265

strange need to control the Circle T, he would see that she married him.

Quietly, the two of them lay there, on the thick carpet, languishing in each other's embrace for nearly an hour afterward, listening to the gentle sounds of nature through the still-open doors. No words were spoken. None needed to be. What they felt for one another was obvious. And each needed to think about how those feelings were to affect their futures. Finally, Wade noticed the hour, and forced himself to get up and leave her.

When Callie went back upstairs to bed, she was dazed by the aura of giddiness that filled her. She felt lighter than a cloud adrift on a summer breeze. It was then she came to suspect she was truly in love—in love with a man who actually wanted to marry her.

The next morning, she awoke nearly bursting with joy. She now knew what it meant to be a woman. And it was a wondrous revelation. She could hardly wait until the girls became comfortable enough with Wade to accept him as part of the family. She eagerly anticipated the morning when she would awaken to find Wade at her side. No longer would it be necessary for him to leave her in the middle of the night. No longer would they have to plan clandestine meetings at midnight.

Suddenly she understood why Ruby had been willing to steal away at all hours in order to be with Thomas Rett. If Ruby loved her Thomas with half the intensity that she herself had come to love Wade Barlow, she fully understood why the girl had eagerly risked her supervisor's anger as well as her own safety in order to be with him. Callie knew she would run the same sort of risks if it meant having another chance to be alone with Wade. She would risk anything short of the girls' happiness for any opportunity to share another stolen moment in his arms.

Hurriedly, she got dressed. Because the saddles they had ordered to replace those lost in the fire were not ready yet, she knew she would have no need of a divided skirt, and chose a lovely pale yellow and white billowy dress with short, puffed sleeves and a low, rounded neckline. And instead of pulling her dark hair back into a tight knot at the base of her head, she chose to collect it higher, nearer the top of her head, and shaped it into a thick, elaborate twist with trailing curls that touched her neck.

She was well aware she had taken such special care with her appearance to impress Wade further, and really did not care if anyone else suspected the same. She knew everyone would become aware of her feelings for him soon anyway. Unless they were blind, they would have to. Her newly discovered emotions had to be evident in her face. There had to be a special glow that said she was in love at last.

As she had expected, even though it was Sunday, she found Wade outside helping with the barn, when she and the girls stepped out onto the back veranda after breakfast to see what progress was being made. Most of the men were hard at work, helping to hang the heavy doors or hammering away at the boards quickly being fitted into place. Two of the men had already begun to put the first coat of white paint on the side already completed. As had become customary since they had begun to build the new structure early Tuesday, only two men had been sent out to ride boundary and check the herds. Everyone else was hard at work doing something constructive toward getting the barn ready for use — all except Ed, who was forced to sit and watch from the small porch in front of the bunkhouse.

And because it *was* Sunday, Callie and the girls stayed outside only long enough to see what all was going on, then went back inside to read several passages from the

Bible. Reading aloud from the Bible on Sunday morning was a tradition at the Circle T that Callie knew had begun shortly after Matthew's marriage to the girls' mother. And it was a tradition she herself had not been allowed to join in on until the Sunday after Matthew's will had been read, and he had expressed his deep desire that they all strive to get along.

It was while Callie, Janice, and Amy sat in the parlor, taking turns reading while Lucille and Ruby worked at getting lunch ready in the kitchen, that all the noise outside came to an abrupt stop. Curiously, Callie rose from her chair and went over to the glass-filled doors to find out what had suddenly caused everyone to stop working.

"Continue reading," she told Janice while she opened one of the doors and stepped out onto the veranda. Though she was still able to hear Janice's voice artfully present the words of the Scripture passage she had chosen, her attention was drawn to the men gathered around Andy and Tony, who still sat atop their horses, their eyes wide with concern. Quietly, she moved away from the door, hoping to catch part of what was being said.

Several men began to walk back toward the barn and quickly put their tools away, while McKenzie hurried over to tell Ed something. Wade then turned to head for the house, and when he spotted Callie standing at the edge of the east veranda, her hand pressed to her throat, he hurried in her direction.

"Trouble again?" she asked as soon as he was close enough to hear her without having to shout so loud she would alert the girls. Her heart felt heavy with dread while she awaited his answer.

"Evidently, some of the cattle have fallen sick out in the northeast pasture. Andy said we've got half a dozen or more already down. I don't want to worry you needlessly, and I won't go into the gruesome details, but judging from Tony's description, the animals have probably been poisoned."

"Poisoned?" Callie's eyes widened.

"Until I've been out there to see for myself, I can only guess at that. But because there is that possibility, and because there could be trouble waiting for us out there, I'm taking about half of the men with me and leaving the rest here. Though they will continue to work on the barn, they will be armed and ready to fight."

Callie's hand flew from her throat to her mouth while she watched the men hurrying to get ready. She noticed McKenzie return to Ed's side to hand him a shotgun, then turn to double-check his own rifle to be sure it was loaded. Her heart pounded rapidly.

"I want you and the girls to stay inside. I'd tell you to get that pistol Matthew left you and keep it at your side, but I don't want the girls to become frightened. It's possible those cattle really are just sick. But considering some of the events in the past, I'm not about to take any unnecessary chances. And I don't want any of the men to either. So try to keep the girls inside as best you can. If they suddenly see all those guns, they will start to ask questions you don't want to answer."

"I understand," she said through the splayed fingertips still pressed against her lips. And though it was starting to seem like a habit with her, she closed her eyes briefly, then told him in a deeply emotional voice, "Do be careful. Be very, very careful. I could not bear to lose you now."

Wade smiled that cocky smile of his. "Don't worry. I can take care of myself. I'm a big boy now." Then he turned and strode away as if he was headed for nothing more frightening than a Sunday picnic.

Though Callie wanted to stay and watch until Wade and the eight men who planned to ride out with him were ready to go, she knew she needed to return to the parlor, or risk the girls becoming suspicious of this new possibility of danger. Smiling as pleasantly as she could, she stepped quietly back inside and returned to her chair. From then on unable to concentrate on what was being read, she merely nodded and praised the girls for their reading whenever she felt it was appropriate to do so. All the while her thoughts were with Wade and her ear attuned to the sound of gunfire, which thankfully never came.

A little over an hour later, after the girls had gone upstairs to play for a while before lunch, Wade and the group of men who had ridden out with him returned. There was an uneasy expression on his face when he climbed down from his horse and met her in the yard to tell her the bad new.

"It's poison, all right," he said grimly. "Someone has poisoned both the ponds in that pasture. I'm afraid about forty head of your cattle are already down. Most of them will probably die. We've moved the cattle that seem unaffected over into the southeast pasture, and I've sent McKenzie on into town to get the veterinarian. There's probably not much Doc Studdard can do for them, but I do want him to have a look at them. Just in case."

Having truly hoped the trouble was over with, Callie felt certain she was about to cry. Not wanting anyone to witness such a moment of weakness, she turned immediately away from him, and from the other men, and began to walk toward the house, her head held high and her shoulders erect. As she expected, Wade followed and she did not try to stop him. When she felt she was able to speak again, she asked, "Did you check the ponds in the other pastures?"

"Yes, and they haven't been tampered with. But that doesn't mean they can't be tampered with in the future.

That's why, I want to post a man in each of the other pastures from now on. *Day* and night. I'll be willing to use some of my own men for that since part of the cattle in the northwest pasture are mine anyway, but I really think you need to hire a few extra men for a while. And I think when you hire them, one of the things you should find out is if they are good with a gun."

Pausing on the bottommost step, she pressed her lips together in order to steady them and nodded. Then, glancing at him with tear-filled eyes, she asked, "How many men should I hire?"

"Four or five, at least. I have a feeling things are just starting to get bad around here."

"I'll start working on the posters to put up in town this afternoon," she promised, and went on into the house to do just that. She wanted those posters up on display the first thing the following morning.

During the next three weeks, the Circle T hired five more men, all of whom met first with Wade's approval, then with Callie's. Although they were plagued with only a few small incidents after that, Wade continued to keep at least one man posted in each of the outer pastures, and two somewhere near the house at all times. He was not about to let down his guard again. Because he'd been so eager to get the barn rebuilt, he'd become lax during the daylight hours while all the work was being done, sending only two men out at a time to keep an eye on things—and Callie had paid a very high price for that neglect. In the end fifty-three head of her cattle had died from the poisoning of those two ponds.

Since then, they'd had a few cattle shot ambush-style, and they'd had another fire started in the same pasture as the poisoning, which was the only one not being guarded at the time, since there were no longer any cattle in it. Luckily, the smoke had been spotted in time to put the flames out before much damage had been done.

There had also been another attempt at poisoning when someone tampered with the main creek itself further upstream, probably where it crossed the main road; but Wade had anticipated that and had built a temporary dam to prevent any new water from flowing into the good ponds. They had chosen to rely solely on the water which came from the two springs that originated on her land and from the wells scattered across the ranch.

The affected water was diverted to another branch of the creek which eventually ran into the two ponds already contaminated. And though they hoped to contain the poisoned water there, they sent word downstream for the other farmers and ranchers to beware. If they had another heavy rain before they found a way to empty out those ponds, the poison could very well spill out.

But other than those few incidents, there had been very little damage done. Yet it was like sitting on a powder keg. The danger was still there—and it was still very real.

Because of the necessity of adding extra surveilance, both in the pastures and in the yard, Wade and Callie had found it nearly impossible to be alone together for any real length of time, and had had to satisfy themselves with a few occasional stolen moments in Matthew's study under the pretense of having to discuss business.

Even with their own relationship hampered the way it was, progress was constantly being made with the girls, and it had quickly become customary for Wade to have his evening meal and Sunday lunch in the house with them. Even the men had quit raising eyebrows over the fact that Wade had become close enough to the family to be included in their family dinners, and also to have his laundry done by Lucille each wash day. Though every man had access to the laundry room, each had been made to wash his own clothes, all except Wade.

But such had come to be accepted as simply being a part of the way things were around there, and most suspected it was because he had saved the youngest daughter's life. Yet, no matter the reason, it had become quickly understood that Wade was more than the acting foreman of the Circle T. He was now a very close friend of the family—and a man who could be relied upon to keep a level head in the event of another emergency.

It was the third week into August before anything else really major happened. And to Wade's growing frustration, it happened without anyone seeing who was responsible. A steer with no brand mysteriously appeared among the cattle in the southeast pasture. And though Wade first thought the animal had broken the fence and wandered over from either Howard Oakley's ranch or Virginia French's small farm, no break was found. There was no damage to the fence line anywhere.

Wade was baffled, and he ordered the steer to be singled out and placed in the northeast pasture until he could figure out exactly where the animal had come from. Because the ponds still held traces of the poison dumped there weeks earlier, Wade ordered a temporary rope corral built and a water trough provided for the animal.

While the men worked to build a small holding pen out of sturdy hemp rope, using a small stand of trees for support posts near the furthermost corner of the pasture, he noticed a portion of the fence there had been cut. The steer had obviously been brought through the northeast pasture and taken into the southeast pasture by way of the gate, which is why there had been no downed fence in the southeast area at all.

Suspecting the animal was diseased, though it looked healthy enough, he immediately sent for Doc Studdard. Later that afternoon, he learned he was right. The steer had anthrax, a deadly and highly contagious disease—and every animal in the southeast pasture had been exposed. They had no way of knowing how long the steer had gone undetected, or if it had come into contact with the other animals or their drinking water, but if even one of them developed the symptoms, all of the cattle in that pasture would have to be destroyed. Every single one.

Chapter Seventeen

Four days later over one hundred head of cattle had to be destroyed, their bodies piled into a huge pit and burned. Though the disease rarely affected humans, the men took baths in tubs of diluted carbolic acid as a measure of precaution. Their clothing was also immediately burned to prevent any further spreading of the fatal disease.

No one had yet to discover just who had slipped the infected steer onto the Circle T, but the men were quickly developing their suspicions. Some went as far as to suspect their coworkers, or men who had worked there before but had left under unhappy circumstances. Lone Wolf, one of the newly hired hands who was part Indian, thought it was the work of Matthew's own spirit, angry about having to die so young when he still had very much to live for.

Soon, everyone had an expressed opinion, and began to keep a suspicious eye on everyone else. Wade, though, felt certain it was the work of an as yet unnamed outsider.

Even though he continued to be remotely suspicious of his father, he still did not want to believe the man would be willing to see that many strong, healthy cattle die just to better his chances of running Callie and the girls off their ranch. Wade had always believed his father had too much respect for animals to allow such a thing; but then again, who else had a reason to cause Callie such heartache?

Yet, despite his efforts to dispel the nagging thoughts, the consideration that his own father might be involved continued to plague him with more and more frequency. Walter Barlow not only had motive, but also as much opportunity as anyone else, and plenty of manpower. Wade began to wonder just what sort of man his father really was—deep down. Was his father's character as strong as he'd always believed?

Years ago, Wade had managed to keep an open view about Beth Tucker's death. He had not wanted to believe the ugly rumors which had sprung up in the days immediately following—rumors that claimed his father had deliberately led her to suicide as a way of getting at Matthew. Wade had no more wanted to believe any of that nonsense than he wanted to believe the man could be the one behind any of Callie's troubles now. There had to be someone else. Someone yet to be considered. The hatred his father had always felt for Matthew could not be reason enough for what had happened. Or could it?

Even though Wade never fully understood the deep hatred between his father and Matthew Tucker, he was well aware that bitter feelings had indeed existed between the two men. Long before he was ever born they'd existed.

His father had tried several times to make him hate Matthew too. But Wade had been unable to hate a man for no real reason, and had never been given a reason worth believing in. True Matthew had been ambitious, and he had amassed incredible wealth, sometimes as the result of someone else's misfortune. But if the truth were to be known, Wade had actually respected Matthew Tucker for all he accomplished in his lifetime, against sometimes hostile neighbors and a town which had been slow to accept him. And Wade was now very pleased to have a hand in keeping Matthew's small cattle dynasty going so one day it could be handed over to his two girls.

Wade just wished he could find a way stop the terrible rash of trouble before the Circle T suffered any more unnecessary losses. Nearly a fifth of Callie's herd was gone, and that had to be a terrible setback emotionally as well as financially. If only he could come across some good, strong evidence that would finally link the culprit to his crime. He had to have a lot more than his suspicions to go on. Even if the troublemaker did turn out to be his own father, at least he would finally be able to do something about the situation. He could confront the man with the evidence and demand he stop.

But until he found out exactly who he was up against, there was not much he could do, other than continue what he was already doing. Which at the moment seemed damned little.

Callie also wished they could find a way to stop all the trouble. Though she had a strong suspicion concerning who might be behind the terrible incidents—she kept it to herself, for Wade's sake. But because it made little sense for the culprit to be anyone other than Walter Barlow, she felt almost certain he was the man behind everything that had happened to her in the past two months—since Matthew's death. The terrible mistakes from Matthew's past had risen up to haunt her—through Walter's own driven need to destroy her. But until she could prove such a thing without any doubt, she would continue to keep that opinion to herself. She would suffer her losses in silence.

But despite the many tragic losses, and despite the fact that on the day the cattle had to be destroyed she broke down emotionally and wept several times, wondering if she could possibly endure anymore such hardships—Callie refused to give up.

In fact, instead of finally giving in to her frustration and bitter misery, instead of packing her things in the hope of leaving the many troubles behind, she grew more determined than ever to stay. So much so, she wanted to go into town the following week to attend the monthly fourth-Saturday cattle auction.

"I want to replace some of the cattle I've lost," she explained, when she presented the idea to Wade. "Will you go with me?"

"Callie, that's really not a good idea," he quickly pointed out. "If you bought more cattle right now, you'd just be putting them into senseless jeopardy. No, my advice is to forget about the auction. Wait until we can catch whoever is causing all your trouble before starting to rebuild your herds."

Reluctantly, Callie agreed to stay home. But on the day of the auction, Wade and Stretch did go into town, to pick up the saddles, which were finally ready, and get the money for the biweekly payroll due that afternoon. Because Amy was extremely eager to see her new saddle, she went with them. Callie saw it as an opportunity for Wade and Amy to establish an even stronger relationship, and chose to stay home.

It was while the three were gone that a man rode up into the yard of the Circle T and handed one of Callie's more recently hired men an envelope.

"Give this to the Widow Tucker," he stated simply. Then as soon as he'd handed the letter over, he rode quickly away.

Inside the envelope Callie found a letter from Walter Barlow, increasing his offer a dollar an acre and urging her to sell before any more senseless harm could befall her. He awaited a response that very afternoon.

Callie became instantly furious, but because the elder Barlow had not felt it necessary to face her with his latest proposal, she could not let him know just how furious she was. And because she had no intention of acknowledging such a letter, at least not until she had spoken with Wade, she was forced to stew in her own juices—waiting anxiously for his return. She was eager to show him the letter and see what his reaction might be.

Only hours later that same afternoon, Ed came in from the northwest pasture with another envelope he'd found nailed to a tree a few feet from a section of recently repaired fence line which separated that particular pasture from the wooded ridge. The envelope was a dull spotted-yellow, and looked like it had been out in the weather for several days. "Mrs. Matthew Tucker" had been scrawled across it in bold letters, but the ink had faded to the extent that it was hardly detectable. Inside, though, the ink had fared better, and she was able to clearly read the threatening message, warning her to go back to where she'd come from before more than just her cattle were found dead. It was the last paragraph in particular that made her anger reach a stage where she visibly began to tremble.

"If you value your life, and the lives of Matthew's two daughters, you will sell out and move away before it is too late," the neatly penned message read. "We don't want your kind around here. You do not belong here anymore than Matthew did. Go back to where you came from."

Callie quickly compared the threatening note with the letter she'd received from Walter. The handwriting was decidedly different, and the envelope was different in both size and quality of paper, but the textured writing paper itself was the same—exactly the same. But whether or not it was a common sort of paper around East Texas, she had no way of knowing. She waited for Wade to return, eager to get his opinion on the matter.

Because Amy had convinced Wade and Stretch to first go by Nadine Leigh's dress shop for two new ribbons for her hair, then convinced them to stop off at the hotel for orangeades and mint cookies, Wade was much later in returning than Callie had expected. When he did finally arrive, she wasted no time in summoning him into Matthew's study. But because Wade had not yet sensed her anger or her growing frustration, he thought it was just a ploy to get them alone for a few minutes, and quickly moved to take her into his arms.

Needing comfort far more than she had realized, Callie allowed him to kiss her long and hard before pulling away to show him the two letters she'd gotten that day. She noticed that after he finished reading them both, he too felt the quality of the writing paper, obviously trying to decide if it might be the same for each letter.

"We need to double up on the men we send out to keep watch on the ranch," he commented when he handed the letters back to Callie.

"Because of the threatening note Ed found nailed to that tree?" she asked. "Then you believe whoever wrote it was serious and will try to harm one of us?"

"Yes," Wade answered, though he knew it was giving her only part of the truth. The real reason he had decided they should double their precaution was because he had slowly come to realize the worst incidents always seemed to happen shortly after Callie refused another of his father's offers to buy the Circle T—coincidence or not. So it was actually the letter requesting yet again the opportunity to purchase the place that had made him suddenly very nervous, because he knew Callie fully intended to refuse his father's offer once again.

"And I think it is time the girls be warned of the danger, if they aren't already aware of it," he added. "They need to be told enough to know to protect themselves at the first sign of anything suspicious. And I think you should start keeping your pistol close by at all times—and if Lucille knows how to shoot, she should keep a gun of some sort near her too."

Callie's blood turned ice cold. Deep down inside she felt she and Wade should discuss the possibility both of the letters had come from his father, but just could not bring herself to say anything. Knowing Wade was not a stupid man, she felt certain he was already very aware of the possibility. And she did not want to make him uncomfortable by forcing him to express any doubts he may have come to have about Walter Barlow—so again she chose to keep her opinion on the matter to herself.

Moments later, Wade returned outside to tell the men of the threatening letter Callie had received and to request that they double their precautions in every way.

"I know it is too late this afternoon, but first thing in the morning, I want to round up all the cattle from the more distant pastures and bring them into the two pastures nearest the house. That way, we can keep a closer eye on them. Then I want to place you men where every single animal can be watched. And I don't want anyone out there alone," he told them. "You men are to go out in pairs from now on, each covering the other's back at all times. This is a serious situation. All other work will have to be put aside for now. And if any of you feel your job is not worth risking your life for—and I'm afraid that might be what you will be doing from here on in—I'll understand. I've got the money for today's payroll and will gladly pay you now and let you be on your way. No hard feelings."

The men who had gathered around Wade in a wide half-circle looked at each other curiously, but no one made a move to leave.

"We can't leave now," Ed said, speaking for the group. "We can't let whoever keeps hounding Mrs. Tucker get away with any more of their troublemaking. If there's danger involved, so be it." He paused to touch his still slightly tender ribs. "I for one well remember what sort of men they are, and intend to stay and fight those bastards to the death if necessary."

281

Callie stepped outside in time to hear a low murmur of agreement spread through the gathering of men. As she realized the implication of what they were saying, tears began to sting her eyes, but she kept them at bay. Slowly she made her way across the yard to speak with the group herself.

"I want you to know how grateful I am for this display of loyalty," she said, her voice displaying only a trace of the trembling emotions she felt. "Matthew would be proud of you. All of you. And I want you to know I do plan to reward your noble willingness to stay and help despite the obvious danger. I plan to reward each of you generously."

"You don't have to do that," Ed quickly responded with a slow shake of his balding head. "We're doing it because we want to."

"That's right," McKenzie was prompt to agree, and he reached over to pat Ed on the back for having made such a statement. His beard parted with a wide smile that revealed his chipped tooth. "We want to do it."

"Because it's the right thing to do," Andy quickly inserted, shaking a determined fist in the air.

"We don't want no reward," his brother, Tony, assured her.

"Just the same, the reward will be yours," she told them. "And it's not just for your willingness to see me through this latest threat. It's also for your recent willingness to work so extra hard, even on your days off. Not only did you get the barn finished in an amazingly short time, you have kept a continuous night watch over the place since those first signs of trouble. You men deserve a bonus and I'm going to see that you get it. Matthew would have wanted you to have it."

She then shrugged. "That's all there is to it. There will be a bonus in your pay money this very afternoon. And another bonus in you next pay as well. In fact, I will continue to give you men bonuses until the danger is finally over."

Worried some of the men might decide to see to it the danger was never fully over, so they might continue to collect their bonuses, Wade quickly inserted, "And there will be a generous reward for whoever finally helps us catch the people behind all these terrible acts against Cal—against Mrs. Tucker."

"Yes, we should have thought of that sooner," Callie said, reinforcing what Wade had just stated with a firm nod of her head. "There will be a very generous reward for whoever helps us finally catch the people behind all these recent incidents. In fact, I would gladly pay each man involved in capturing them five hundred dollars apiece."

As if challenged to a contest of some sort, the men glanced at each other eagerly. Then those Wade had appointed to take the next watch hurried to get ready, each one discussing what he would do if he suddenly had five hundred dollars.

Shortly after the first watch had left—twelve men instead of the usual four—the others went into the bunkhouse to get a little rest before they had to go out for their own turn on watch. To enable the men to have a better opportunity to get full rest between their shifts as lookouts, Wade changed the time each man was to be out from four to eight hours. It meant longer hours at watch, but it also meant longer hours off watch and longer periods to get rest in order to stay alert.

As soon as everything had settled down, Wade went inside the house to be sure Callie and Lucille had armed themselves and that the girls understood they were to stay inside. Then, after he was certain they were all as prepared for trouble as they could be, he went back outside. Without telling anyone where he was headed, he immediately swung up on to his horse and rode away.

Callie assumed he wanted to check on the men and see that they were positioned in the best and safest places, and did nothing to try to stop him. Watching as he rode away, she prayed he would return to her quickly and unharmed.

But Wade had other things on his mind. After having seen the paper on which both letters had been written, he was more suspicious than ever about his father's involvement. Not only was the paper the same for each letter, he was almost certain where it had come from. He was aware his father bought the expensive ivory-colored stationery from a little print shop in Shreveport, Louisiana, whenever he was over there on business, as much because of the pretty girl who sold it as for the quality of the paper itself. Wade felt it was very unlikely anyone else in the area shopped for stationery at that same little shop well over ninety miles away. And he doubted anyone around East Texas carried the exact same grade of paper.

The time had come to confront the man with what little evidence he had. For Callie's sake.

When he eventually rode into the dooryard in front of his father's sprawling two-story house, he noticed how wary everyone seemed of him. Feeling as if he'd ridden right into the very middle of a hungry lion's den, Wade slowly and cautiously climbed down from his horse and loosely tethered the animal to a nearby post for a quick escape if necessary. Slowly, he made his way across the well-kept lawn to the wide planked steps which led to the veranda that surrounded the house on three sides. As he approached the house, he glanced back, and noticed how several men had gathered just outside the barn, all watching him carefully. Suddenly, he was very glad he had thought to wear his handgun.

Never pausing, he continued toward the front door, and was not too surprised, though a little annoyed, when Evan came outside just as he topped the front steps and stepped into the cooling shade of the veranda. It was easy for Wade to guess that Evan hoped to have a first word with him.

"I'm here to see my father," Wade said sternly while he continued to move toward the front door, waiting to see if Evan would have the good sense to step out of his way. Though he and his half-brother had never truly come to blows before, he would not be opposed to smashing a fist into his arrogant young face. He only needed half a reason.

"He's not feeling too well," Evan told him, and crossed his arms while he braced his legs by spreading them slightly apart in an obvious effort to block the doorway. Evan was shorter than Wade, and younger, though only by eight days, but he was no less sturdy in build and had clearly decided to stand his ground.

"He was feeling well enough to write a letter and have it sent over to Tucker's widow a few hours ago."

Evan's hazel eyes widened—eyes that were even more like Walter's than Wade's were—much more. "What letter?"

"The letter in which he made yet another offer to purchase the Circle T from the woman."

"And is she seriously considering this new offer?" Evan wanted to know. His thick eyebrows rose with true interest, as he temporarily forgot his antagonism and waited to hear if Wade had brought good news.

"Not in the least. That's what I've come to tell him. He might as well give up and be satisfied with what he already has. He won't be adding the Circle T to his little empire."

Evan's expression fell as he snorted and cocked his head to one side. "Our father does not give up that easy. Not when he wants something as much as he wants that ranch. You should know that by now."

"Evan, move out of the way. I'm here to speak with Father on the matter, not you." Wade took another step toward him.

Evan thought better of his decision to defy Wade and

finally moved aside to let him pass, though he continued to stand with his arms crossed defiantly in front of him. Again it occurred to Wade how much more like their father Evan looked than *he* did, and how he himself had taken on more of his mother's traits. Which was where he had gotten his willowy height, his pale blue eyes, his thick brown hair—and his temperament.

"Go ahead. Talk to him," Evan told him with an arrogant lift of his rounded chin. "But I can tell you now, it is not about to do you any good. Our father has already made up his mind to have that land, and have it he will."

Wade chose to ignore Evan's comments, and when he then entered the house, he discovered his father coming down the stairs, dressed in his usual duct trousers, cotton shirt, and gray-striped suspenders. If his father was feeling at all ill, as Evan had just tried to make him believe, the man certainly did not show it.

"Wade," Walter exclaimed when he glanced up and noticed he was not alone in the house. He spoke the name with neither endearment nor anger, it was merely a statement of surprise. His round, hazel eyes then flickered a glance passed him to where his other son stood watching the two of them closely and frowning with deep displeasure. He chose to make no comment to Evan.

"Father, I want to talk with you," Wade said as he moved toward the man with long, determined strides. His boots clicked heavily across the highly polished wooden floor. Then, after motioning to his father's study with a slight wave of his hand, he glanced at Evan briefly. "And I would prefer to talk with you alone."

"Fine. Let's talk," Walter said calmly. His expression was void of any emotion, good or bad, when he turned and headed toward the room Wade had just indicated. "Evan was just on his way outside to make sure Pablo remembered to soak Golden Boy's injured fetlock in the solution Doc Studdard made up for him."

Evan was aware he was being dismissed, and his sharp intake of air was easily heard the full length of the hallway. Still, he did not openly protest his father's decision, and turned as if he had planned to head right back outside anyway.

As soon as Wade and his father were both inside the large, masculinely furnished room, and Wade was certain Evan was not just outside the door listening to them—which was a very annoying habit his half-brother seemed to have—Wade began his well-rehearsed speech. "Callie received your letter this afternoon."

"Would you care for a drink?" Walter asked as he headed for the partially filled decanter which sat on an elaborately ornate liquor cabinet. His usual glass stood right beside it, waiting. Other glasses not quite as large rested on a shelf nearby. "My throat is dry as a desert rock."

"Father, this is not a social call. I'm here to tell you to back off Callie. I want you to quit pressuring her."

"Why? To better your own chances of getting the Circle T?" Walter asked, turning to glare at his son with the decanter still clutched in his burly hand.

"You know that's not true. I have no real need for the Circle T. I'm doing just fine without it."

"Oh? But after that drought we had, I'm sure you are much more aware how very limited your water resources on Twin Oaks really are. And being able to get your hands on Tucker's land would mean never having to worry about anything like that again. Why else would you still be there helping that woman the way you are when your ponds are now so aptly full of water?"

Wade did not want to argue, nor did he care to explain to his father how deeply he had come to care for the woman. "I'm here to warn you that I'm on to you. And I don't intend to let you get away with any more of your terrorizing. You need to be aware that I've given

Callie's men orders to shoot to kill if they even halfway suspect they are in any sort of danger."

Walter's bushy brows rose as his expression turned indignant, almost righteously so. "You suspect me, your own father, of foul play?"

Wade was not about to allow himself to be intimidated. "Yes, Father, that's exactly what I suspect you of. Foul play. Very foul play. And if you keep it up, I will be forced to do something to stop you — something drastic."

"You came here to threaten your own father?" Walter demanded to know. His face rapidly turned red while his jaw worked furiously to contain a sudden burst of anger.

"I'd prefer to think of it as a simple warning, but if you want to call it a threat, then yes, that's exactly why I've come. I want it stopped. Callie has suffered enough."

"I don't know why you think I have had anything to do with the rash of incidents I hear have occurred over there, but I can assure you I am innocent. I have not set foot on Circle T land, except for the three occasions when I paid personal calls on Tucker's widow in hopes of convincing her to sell out."

"That's because you have sent your men to do your dirty work. I'm not stupid. And I want it stopped! I don't want the terrorizing to go any further. You'd better stop before the trouble suddenly doubles back on you."

"And you, son, can go straight to hell!" Walter shouted, throwing the whisky decanter across the room, shattering it against the far wall. He then reached up to clutch his chest as if suddenly he could not get enough air to vent his furor. "How dare you come into my own home and say such things to me! How dare you take sides against me like this!"

The vein in the side of his neck bulged as he ordered

Wade out of his house. "You are no longer welcome here. Get out! And stay out!"

"Gladly," Wade said, more convinced now than ever that his father had had something to do with the incidents at the Circle T. "But before I go, I want to make it absolutely clear to you that if I do happen to catch you or any of your men on the Circle T, I won't hesitate to shoot. And neither will any of Callie's men."

As Wade turned to leave his father's house, he wondered if it would indeed be for the last time. He felt a sudden heaviness inside his chest, an ache that began in the vicinity of his heart, but quickly spread to consume every part of him. There had almost always been a sort of barrier between the two of them, a barrier which had grown worse since his mother's death, but now he knew the barrier was permanent. They would never again be close, and he was a fool for ever hoping that one day they might. He was a fool to hope that one day he would somehow regain his father's respect, instead of his ridicule, and they would finally be able to establish a more solid relationship. No, he and his father had grown to be, and always would be, worlds apart.

Never once looking back, Wade marched down the long hall toward the front door. Hurting from far more than the mere anger eating away at his gut, Wade hurried outside, eager to comply with his father's demand that he leave. He was a little startled, but not totally surprised, to find Evan standing in the yard beside his horse, reins in hand. Evan's weight shifted insolently to one leg while he waited for him.

"Leaving so soon?" Evan asked. A knowing smile stretched across his face. It was obvious he had somehow eavesdropped on the entire conversation, but then considering the way his father had begun to shout there at the end, it would have been hard not to overhear at least that part of it.

"Not soon enough," Wade answered just before he

snatched the reins from Evan's hands.

"Just don't forget that you are no longer welcome here," Evan stated coolly. His smile grew taut across his face.

"It's not something I'd easily forget," Wade assured him as he lithely swung himself up into the saddle. "Just see that *he* doesn't somehow forget that he's not wanted over on Circle T property. See that he stays away."

Evan's smile broadened. "Our father will do whatever he damn well pleases."

Throwing Evan a final look of deeply felt disgust, he turned his horse toward the main road and pressed his heels sharply into the animal's sides. Never had he been in such a hurry to leave the Rocking W than he was at that particular moment.

Chapter Eighteen

Wade was too disturbed over what had happened to eat. Instead of joining Callie and the girls at the house for supper, he went first to warn his own men there might be trouble, even at Twin Oaks, then rode out to check on Callie's men.

Because they could not possibly move the cattle from the outer pastures to the two closer pastures until morning, the men were forced to station themselves much further apart than Wade would have liked. But in order to keep the men paired off in twos, the distances between the pairs of men was temporarily unavoidable. They were doing the best they could with the situation they had.

In an effort to protect as much of the area as possible, a pair of men had been posted near each outlying corner of the nearly rectangular region of land. Two men had also been placed closer to the center, where the outer pastures interlinked with the main pasture, which ran along the back and east side of the house, as well as linking with a smaller pasture that skirted around the vegetable garden off to the west. The other two men, also a part of the first watch, had been told to keep only a short distance away from the house itself, and had hidden themselves accordingly.

Because they had all clearly understood the seriousness of the situation, each pair had ridden out heavily armed and wary of any peculiar sounds or any movement seeming even the least bit unusual.

Despite the approach of darkness, Ed had spotted Wade riding across the northwest pasture, and waved his rifle once into the air so his boss could see where he and McKenzie had hidden themselves in among a tall tangle of bushes growing near the largest pond on the ranch. Rather than chance giving the men's hiding spot away to anyone who might be watching from just the other side of the boundary fence, Wade stopped nearby and pretended to let his horse get a drink of water while he spoke with Ed in a low voice.

"Any sign of trouble?" he wanted to know, glancing off into the distance, as if scanning the darkening countryside with casual interest. Slowly he swung his leg over his saddle and dropped agilely to the ground, knelt at the water's edge, and pretended to wash his neck and hands.

"Nothing yet," Ed's voice assured him from just inside the bushes. "Something spooked a few of the cattle awhile ago, and that sure set our hearts to pumping. But I guess it was just a rabbit or something, because we never did see what caused it. That was probably about an hour back."

"But nothing since then?"

"Except for an occasional cow nagging at her calf, it's been as quiet around here as a saloon on Sunday."

"Good. Maybe it will stay that way. But don't let all this quiet lull you into a false sense of security. I fully expect there to be trouble. If not tonight, then tomorrow."

It was an uneasy feeling he'd had ever since he'd left his father's ranch. Something would happen, all right. His father would want to show him exactly who the boss was in their family. It was something that could be counted on ever since the first time Wade had dared to question the man's keen sense of authority. Whenever Wade rebelled, his father retaliated. Only this time, Wade feared the retaliation would be not only against him, but against Callie too. Despite the warnings he'd given the man, or perhaps even because of them, he had a strong feeling his father would do something to display his anger, something drastic. And soon.

He had already started to wish he had shown more restraint by not having gone over there at all. Because he had armed himself with nothing more than his own suspicions, he had accomplished nothing—and might have stirred up a hornet nest which should best been left alone. The simple fact was, he had not expected his father to actually deny the major part he'd played in Callie's troubles. He'd always considered his father a fairly honest man.

"Just continue to keep your eyes and ears open. I'll check back in a few hours," he told Ed, without once glancing in the direction of the bushes. Looking off toward the ridge, he added, "Around midnight or a little after, someone will come to replace you both. Then you can go get yourselves some sleep."

"Good. I know I sure could use some rest," Ed replied, then snorted a soft laugh. "I guess I was starting to get used to the easy life. I really haven't done anything today, but I'm already bone tired. Besides, sittin' out here in the dark with nobody but McKenzie for company isn't exactly how I like spending my Saturday nights."

McKenzie responded in a low, gruff voice, "Let me assure you, you aren't the only one who feels that way. I'd much rather be in town sittin' in a saloon with a tall glass of whiskey in one hand, five good poker cards in the other, and some pretty gal on my lap than sittin' out here in the bushes with you! I guarantee, I'd much rather be slappin' at some well-rounded bottom than at these confounded mosquitoes all night."

Wade chuckled softly. Though it had gotten a little too dark to see much more than black shapes against gray shapes, in his mind's eye, he visualized the disgruntled expression on McKenzie's bearded face. "Maybe by next Saturday night, all this will be over and you'll have that pretty gal on your lap, Mac. Just remember to keep those

293

eyes and ears open like I told you."

"Right," Ed responded, still laughing lightly. "McKenzie and I just might go ahead and capture those bastards for you tonight. Then we wouldn't even have to come out here tomorrow night, much less next Saturday. I for one could certainly use that five-hundred-dollar reward."

"Oh, sure," McKenzie muttered. "You'd just go into town and throw it away on that gal who runs the dress shop—despite the fact Miss Leigh rarely ever pays you any notice at all. Now me, I'd use that money to get me some sweet, pretty young thing about half my age interested in me."

"She'd also have to have about half your brains before she'd have anything to do with an ugly old scoundrel like you," Ed commented, still chuckling softly as he baited McKenzie into another argument.

The bushes began to tremble.

"Ugly? Old? *Me* old?" McKenzie muttered, almost strangling in his efforts to keep his voice low, yet still be clearly heard. "What about you? You are a good two years older than me."

Wade glanced up into the rapidly darkening sky, trying not to laugh out loud at the two men's antics. He truly believed that if the two were not such good friends, they surely would have killed each other by now.

"I think I'd better go before the two of you come to blows again," he commented just before he returned to the side of his horse and prepared to mount. Then, after he swung himself into the saddle, the smile that had been on his face slowly faded as he again remembered the seriousness of their situation. "If I was you two, I'd save this argument for later, when there's nothing better to do and plenty of witnesses to keep you two from killing each other. For now, I think I'd work a little harder to keep my mouth shut and my eyes open. There really could be trouble before the night is over."

There was no reply other than a low grunt, followed by

one last brief chuckle as Wade rode off, back the way he had come. Then all was silent again.

Because Wade knew Callie would be worried and would want to know he had already checked with all twelve men and had discovered nothing out of the ordinary yet, he decided to stop back by the house to talk with her and see if he might get a quick cup of coffee from Lucille.

With the girls now aware of the danger, Callie had had a much harder time getting them to go upstairs to bed that evening. Even after she had convinced them to go to bed, she had found it necessary to stay in the room until they had both drifted off to sleep. But as soon as she'd been absolutely certain they would not wake up again, she'd returned downstairs to wait for Wade. It worried her that he had yet to return.

Too restless to sleep, she eagerly joined Lucille and Ruby in the kitchen. They had already finished washing the dishes, and the three sat across the small table from one another talking about whatever they could think of in an effort to keep their minds off of the fact trouble might be brewing at that very moment. All three held their breaths when they first noticed the sound of an approaching horse. Callie and Lucille reached for their weapons, and listened carefully for some indication of who it might be.

In unison, the three of them sighed with relief the moment the familiar voice called out, "It's me, Wade."

They hurried to the window to peer out.

"About time you came in for something to eat," Callie reprimanded him when he entered the kitchen only a few moments later and hooked his hat over a small wooden peg near the back door. She frowned when she noticed how tired he looked, and wished she could take him into her arms and comfort him somehow, but was afraid that would somehow embarrass him. "What kept you? Lucille's been keeping your plate warm for hours now."

"I'm not that hungry. All I really want is a good hot cup of coffee," Wade told them. Then, upon seeing Lucille's eyebrows lower into a very determined expression—an incredibly dark expression he knew only too well—he relented. "But I guess I could force something down."

"You'd better," Lucille muttered just before she stepped over to the stove and lifted the yellow linen napkin off a plate which had been left there to keep the food on it as warm as possible. "You have got to keep up your strength just like everybody else. Get on in the dining room and I'll bring this out to you right away."

"I don't have long," he warned them as he sat down at the kitchen table where Lucille and Ruby usually ate instead of heading for the dining room. "I plan to go right back out to check on all twelve men again at least once more before they change watch."

"And when will that be?" Callie asked.

"Half past midnight."

"*Then* are you going to get some sleep?" Callie wanted to know, showing her disapproval while she poured him the cup of coffee he'd mentioned.

"Not tonight. After the letters you got today, I don't think I could sleep if I wanted to." For a moment, he considered telling Callie about the visit he'd had with his father, but for some reason decided against it. He did not want to worry her anymore. Noticing that she did indeed have Matthew's pistol on the table, loaded and ready to shoot, and that there was a shotgun leaning against the wall near the door, he realized she was already worried enough to take the necessary precautions—and that was all that really mattered.

"But you have to sleep," she protested when she handed him the steaming cup and watched him set it gently beside the plate Lucille had just placed before him. Frowning more deeply, she sank into the chair next to him, resting her chin on top of interlaced fingers, while Lucille laid a fork and a sharp knife on the table well within his reach. "How will you ever be able to get all those cattle herded into the main pastures tomorrow if you haven't had any sleep?"

"I've gone without sleep before," he reminded her, then picked up the fork and drove it into a hefty piece of broiled potato. "I'll manage just fine."

"Not without sleep."

"If I thought I could get some sleep, I would. It's just that right now, even if I tried to lay down for a while, all I would do is toss and turn, and worry about what might be happening out there," he told her, nodding toward the nearest window. His own expression grew very grim.

Callie decided he was letting himself worry a little too much. "But that letter looked to be days old. If whoever wrote it had planned to do anything immediately, they would have already done something."

"Not if they have been keeping an eye on that note to see exactly when it disappeared. That way they would know when you actually did receive the message," Wade pointed out just before he shoveled a second forkful of potatoes into his mouth. Now that he'd tasted food, suddenly he was hungry. Very hungry. It took him a moment to clear his mouth enough to speak again. "No, the danger *is* out there. And I plan to do what I can to help those men protect your cattle and themselves."

Callie could tell she was not about to change his mind on the matter, and reached out for the hand that rested on the table beside his plate. Feeling a fluttering of warmth spread through her as she ran her fingertips over the firm muscles of his wide fingers, she smiled. "Just do me a favor and be very—"

"I know, I know. Be very careful," he said, winking as he smiled back at her. "You'll be pleased to know that's exactly what I plan to be. Very careful."

Callie was not easily swayed by his charm this time. She was too concerned for his welfare.

"Why can't you just send for the sheriff and let him and a few of his deputies come out here to help you?" she wanted to know, remembering his earlier decision not to involve the authorities just yet.

"The sheriff has more to do than hang around here waiting for something to eventually happen," he explained as he reached for his knife and quickly cut his steak into manageable pieces. "Especially on Saturday night. I would not feel right asking him to do something like that. It wouldn't be fair to him. And it also would not be fair to the townspeople, who would have a heck of a time keeping all the area ranch hands under control while they enjoy their usual weekend of revelry at the different saloons."

"Still, I wish you would have at least notified him of the possibility of trouble," she told him.

"If it will make you feel better, I'll send someone in tomorrow," he promised as he stuck a large chunk of beef into his mouth. Then, when he finally finished chewing and had swallowed to clear his mouth, he added, "But I don't think there's anything he can do. Until we have something more to go on than one man's bootsize and the fact he or one of his friends can write nasty little letters, there's not a whole lot the sheriff *can* do." Besides, Wade wanted to take care of it himself. He wanted to be the one to catch either his father or his father's men red-handed. Because it was *his* father who was involved, he felt responsible somehow. That was the real reason he wanted to head right back out after he finished eating. He wanted to be there when something happened. He wanted to have a part in stopping them.

Callie sighed heavily while she watched him pick up his coffee cup and quickly drink down the last of its contents. "I guess you are right. It's just that I don't like the thought of you being out there when there's such a strong possibility of danger. I'd rather someone who has had more experience in such matters be the one to stick his neck out."

Wade paused long enough to lick away a tiny droplet of coffee from the corner of his mouth with the tip of his tongue, a movement which attracted Callie's attention to his enticing lips. When she remembered how wonderful those lips felt against hers, Callie's heartbeat jumped into rapid motion. Suddenly, she wished that Lucille and Ruby were in another part of the house so she could lean forward and take a kiss from him. Taste the familiar sweetness of those lips. Feel the reassurance of his embrace.

As if he was able to read her thoughts, he laid down his cup, blotted his mouth with his napkin, then motioned for the back door with a quick jerk of his head. "I've got to get on back. Walk with me outside to my horse."

Well aware of each other's thoughts, they eagerly pushed their chairs away from the table, paused at the door long enough for Wade to retrieve his hat, then left the room together.

Because the back porch was well lighted—in hopes of deterring any notions of breaking in and harming someone in the house on a night in which there was only a sliver of a moon to be found—Wade took Callie's hand and led her out into the back yard, away from the light.

Callie glanced back to see if Lucille was watching, and when she saw no suspicious-looking movements at the kitchen curtains, she allowed Wade to pull her towards the side of the house, where the shadows were the darkest. Though she knew the two men posted somewhere near the house could be close enough to see what was happening between them, she allowed him to draw her into his arms and kiss her long and hard. She fully realized that if Wade was to get badly hurt, that kiss might be their last. She held on with all her might.

"I want you to go on up to bed now," Wade told her. His mouth lingered only inches away from hers while they continued to hold on to each other one more desperate moment, as if he also was well aware this could be the very last time they ever saw each other.

"Why? I can't possibly sleep knowing you are out there. No more than you can knowing the rest of the men are still in danger," she said, savoring the feel of his warm breath across her cheek. She breathed deeply the masculine scent of him. Tears filled her eyes, but she quickly blinked them away. How it would destroy her if he allowed himself to get hurt. What would she ever do without him?

"You have to try. For the girls' sake. They will be even more frightened if, in the morning, you look as if you haven't slept. They don't need that."

Callie smiled briefly, staring up into his concerned face. Though they still stood within the darker shadows beside the house, she saw his expression clearly. How truly handsome he was. "Tell you what. I'll try to get some sleep, if you promise to do the same. If you will promise me that after the men have changed the watch just after midnight, you will come back and indeed try to get at least a few hours of sleep, then I will promise to do the same."

"I promise," he stated, then looked away. He knew it was a promise he would probably be unable to keep. As long as there was the slightest chance of trouble out there, he would be out there too.

Callie stood on tiptoe to place another kiss on his lips. As she savored the moment, her lips lingered several minutes before she gently pulled away. "I will go right up to bed."

Wade took her hand in both of his and stared at her for a long moment before moving away from her.

Reluctantly, Callie returned to the veranda while he walked over to where he had left his horse. She waited just inside the open doorway, watching until he had ridden out of the island of light that surrounded the house. Then, when she could no longer see him, she closed her eyes and listened to the fading sound of his horse's hooves as they rapidly struck the hard ground again and again.

When she no longer heard anything but the cheerless sounds of crickets, and the melancholy call of a lone whippoorwill, she turned to go back inside. Just after she had closed the door, and before she had yet to reach for the bolts that would lock it in place, she heard the first gunshot.

Wade!

For a moment, she froze, unable to move, then instantly, she flung the door back open wide and stepped out onto the veranda. Her heart thumped hard against her breast while she desperately searched the surrounding darkness for sight of something, though she was not sure what.

Barely seconds later, the men poured out of the bunkhouse, dressed and armed. Callie pulled her gaze to them, then beyond. Horses stood in the yard already saddled.

Before even she realized what her intentions were, she was on one of those horses, reins in hand. Though her slippered feet barely reached the stirrups on the horse she had chosen, she was able to get the animal into motion before anyone could stop her. Immediately she headed in the direction she believed the gunshot had come from.

"Mrs. Tucker, come back," she heard Jim call out after her. "You can't go out there. It isn't safe."

Callie did not bother to respond.

"Somebody go get her," she heard Stretch cry out. Then moments later, she heard the sounds of other horses behind her.

Despite the darkness that lay ahead, she kicked the stirrups against the horse's sides as hard as she could to make him go faster. She refused to chance the men catching her. She knew they would make her go back when Wade could be in trouble. If he was hurt, he would need her. She must find him.

301

* * *

Wade reached for the stock of his rifle at the same moment he swung himself out of the saddle. Because of the noise his horse was making as well as the blanket of darkness that surrounded him, he had been unable to tell exactly where the gunshot had originated—or even where the bullet had eventually struck. But he was well aware the sound must have come from very close by.

The sliver of moon offered barely enough light for Wade to make out the jagged shape of the bushes he intended to use for cover. Slapping his horse to keep the animal running even though the saddle was empty, Wade turned and made a dash for the bushes, hoping to reach them before anyone noticed where he had gone. It was his only hope.

As he dove head-first into the foliage, Wade prayed he would not find someone already there. After coming to a rolling stop, he lay on his stomach, perfectly still. Ignoring the pain in his shoulder, he held his breath and waited to see if his whereabouts had been detected.

He closed his eyes and listened carefully, but the blood pounding in his ears drowned out everything else, even the clamor of his horse's hooves as the animal hurried on across the pasture, leaving him far behind. He took several deep breaths in an attempt to steady himself.

Another shot sounded.

Wade quickly brought himself into an upright, kneeling position and raised his rifle in readiness. That time he had been able to detect the direction. The shot had come from the ridge. Aware of the ridge's height, he hoped whoever it was had kept his eye on the dark movement of his horse and had missed the fact he had rolled off when he did.

Squinting in an effort to see better, he kept his gaze trained on the area where the gunshot had sounded. He saw no movement other than those caused by the gentle

302

night breeze. He heard no noises that could not be easily attributed to the cattle which surrounded him. He wondered if Ed and McKenzie had a better view than he did, being much closer to the ridge than he was.

Suddenly, a faint crackling noise caught his attention. He felt certain it had come from the wooded area at the base of the ridge. Then he noticed movement near the fence line. He wondered if it was the same person who had fired the gunshot. Or should he assume there were at least two people out there? One higher on the ridge and one near the base. He decided it would be safer to assume there were indeed two—or more. Again he wondered if Ed and McKenzie could see anything from where they were. He focused for a moment on the bushes where he knew them to be. Though the bushes were only a few hundred yards away, he saw no movement. They were being careful not to give their location away just yet. He returned his gaze to the ridge.

The sudden sound of one of the steers behind him bellowing out an obvious protest to the late-night disturbance seemed startlingly loud, causing Wade to jump and turn in a reflexive reaction. He became immediately angry with himself for having done so, though he honestly did not think he had made enough sound to alert anyone.

Still, there was no way to be sure. His blood ran cold and hard through his body when he slowly turned back to face the ridge again and continued to wait for something to happen. Another sound came from the direction of the fence line. Again he thought he saw movement. It was impossible to tell what the movement might have been, but he felt certain there had been one. He held his breath perfectly still while he studied the area closely.

Though he saw no further movement, he heard a sharp snapping sound, as if someone had just cut a wire. Then he heard another. Aware the fence had just been cut, he prepared himself for an upcoming attack. As he brought the rifle level to his shoulder again, he wished he had better cover than just a few scraggly bushes, but there was no time to try to make it to a better location.

Suddenly there was a loud shout and the black shadow of a horse burst forth, through the fence, not very far from where Ed and McKenzie were supposed to be.

A gunshot quickly followed. This time he felt certain it had been either Ed or Mac who had fired because he had seen a brief spark of amber flare within the bushes. He held his breath, hoping the man on the ridge had not seen the same thing.

At about the same moment Wade was able to tell that the horse bounding toward him was riderless—a decoy obviously meant to draw their fire—there was a volley of gunfire from several locations along the ridge. At least five shots had been fired. Possibly more. Suddenly, he heard Ed cry out. He could tell by the yelp of pain that he had been shot. He wondered how many times.

In that same instant, McKenzie bellowed aloud his anger and charged out of the bushes, headed straight for the ridge, shooting like a madman. A second round of gunshots brought him down.

"McKenzie!" Wade cried out, no longer caring if he gave away his own location. Scurrying out of the bushes on hands and knees, with his rifle tucked precariously up under his arm, he hurried through the thick pasture grass to help him. When he was about halfway there, he was able to see Ed already making his way to McKenzie's side. He was relieved to realize that though Ed might have been hit, he was obviously not badly hurt. He hoped the same could be said for McKenzie as he continued to work his way toward them.

The sounds of horses running swelled across the darkness from somewhere behind him, and once he became fully aware of them, he prayed it would prove to be some of Callie's men coming to the rescue after having heard the gunshots—and not more of the group who had staged this attack. There was another round of gunfire from the ridge, and he heard several of Callie's steers bellow out their outrage just before he heard something heavy hit the ground. His anger grew. They had started to pick off the cattle.

Dropping instantly back onto his stomach, he tried to figure out what to do next. That was when he noticed the two steers already down and close by. Another steer wailed out in pain for several seconds before it finally collapsed and became silent only a dozen yards away. Two more shots were heard and another steer dropped. This one not very far from where Ed and McKenzie were.

Cover. The fools were unwittingly providing them with cover.

Seeing that Ed must have reached the same conclusion and was already trying to drag McKenzie's body toward the closest of the dead animals, Wade pulled himself back up on his hands and knees and hurried to help. The men on the ridge finally spotted him. The next three bullets to bite into the hard earth were only inches away. His only chance now was to stand up and make a run for it.

The sound of the horses behind him grew increasingly louder, and just as he finally reached the spot where Ed still struggled to move McKenzie's heavy body, gunshots came from behind. Though bullets continued to spray the earth around them, some so close he felt the dirt scatter against his skin, Wade managed to help Ed get McKenzie behind the closest dead animal. Then, aware the steer's body could shield only so many, he dove for the protection of another of the dead animals.

A bullet just missed him as he rolled to a stop against the second animal's still-warm body. Though he'd lost his pistol in the fray, he still had his rifle, and quickly swung it into position to fire. About the time he felt he had a bead on where at least one of the men was situated, the shooting suddenly stopped. He paused, waiting for whatever was to happen next. Listening for movement, he was startled to suddenly hear Callie's voice call out.

"Wade? Are you all right?"

Anger shot through him at the realization she had foolishly put herself into such danger. He turned, trying to figure out where her voice had come from. Though he had not yet spotted her anywhere in among the cattle still standing, or among the horses which had been quickly abandoned, he shouted out with rage, "Callie! What the hell are you doing out here?"

"I heard the gunshots like everyone else. I came to help," she said in a clear, determined voice. "Will you answer my question? Are you all right?"

"I'm fine, but McKenzie and Ed have both been shot."

"Where?" Stretch called out, surprisingly close. "Where are they?"

"Over here," Ed shouted, the sound of his voice strained. "Over here behind this dead steer. Over near the pond."

Soon Wade was able to see movement close to the ground as several of the men appeared from behind other dead animals and from behind nearby trees. Slowly, they began to work their way to where Ed and McKenzie lay. But he was more concerned about Callie at the moment, and returned his attention to her. Again he scanned the area for any sight of her. To his further dismay, when he finally spotted her, he saw that she still sat on top of a horse, easy pickings for anyone with a long-barrel rifle.

"Callie, get down!" he shouted, his heart in his throat, expecting at any moment to hear the gunshot ring out that would bring her down. "Get down or get the hell out of here!"

Not understanding what he meant by get down, Callie merely bent forward in the saddle, but in such darkness Wade could not tell what she had done, only that her shape had disappeared from atop the horse.

"I think we *all* need to get the hell out of here," Stretch strongly suggested, then whistled to bring his horse to him. "McKenzie's pretty bad hurt. We need to get him back to the house."

Wade felt a strong surge of relief to hear the man was still alive. When he had helped Ed pull him back out of the way, he had been able to see at least two places where he was bleeding badly. Wade was well aware there could be more. "Then get him out of here. Ed too. And anyone else who is injured. But the rest of you spread back out and wait to see what else develops". Then he remembered Callie.

"Callie, I want you out of here too. Get back on that horse and ride ahead to warn Lucille that injured men are coming. Stretch will be along with them just as soon as we can get them safely onto horses and on their way."

Aware Wade could still be in danger, Callie wanted to stay. She wanted to be nearby in case he should be injured too, but knew there would be hell to pay if she did not mind him. Besides, she realized that if McKenzie really was badly injured, it would be best to have Lucille ready for him and Manuel already on his way into town for the doctor.

And the sheriff.

307

Chapter Nineteen

Barely an hour before sunup, the doctor, the sheriff, and three volunteer deputies finally arrived. Lucille, Callie, and Stretch had managed to carry the semiconscious McKenzie into the house, but had decided not to try to move him on upstairs. Instead, they'd made him a makeshift bed out of a small pillow, linens, and the dining room table, then worked to stop his bleeding.

Because Ed had flatly refused to leave his friend's side, even for the comfort of his own bunk or an upstairs bed, Stretch had brought in a large upholstered chair and covered it with old sheets and towels to avoid bloodstains, then ordered him to sit there until the doctor arrived.

Though reluctant to do so — because he thought his own injury was very minor in comparison to McKenzie's — Ed eventually complied, but positioned the chair where he could keep a close eye on his friend.

Fortunately, the bullet that had struck Ed had gone straight through his shoulder, which meant there would be no need for surgery. But McKenzie had not been as lucky. Out of the four bullets that had struck him, two were still lodged somewhere inside his body. One had severed a small artery.

By the time Dr. Lowell Edison had arrived, McKenzie had already lost a lot of blood, and his pulse was becoming harder and harder to locate. If the doctor had come any later, Ed felt certain McKenzie would have been dead.

Originally, Callie had planned to stay and help Lowell remove those two bullets in any way possible, knowing what an ordeal it would be. But whether because of her near-exhausted state or because of the tension which still gripped her from knowing Wade and the rest of the men were still out there, still risking danger, Callie found herself unable to cope with all the blood and the jagged appearance of McKenzie's many gaping wounds.

With a high-pitched whining in her ears, and prickling fingers of dull heat slowly climbing up her neck until they reached into her paled cheeks, she realized she had to get out of there.

Stretch had already been banished from the room, since he was notorious for fainting at the sight of human blood—and had come close to doing just that twice already. Callie joined him outside on the veranda, and paced right along with him beneath the soft glow of lantern light while they waited to hear whether or not the burly McKenzie would be all right.

"I really should get on back out there," Stretch finally said. His gaze strayed in the direction of the northwest pasture where all the trouble had occurred while he continued to walk aimlessly about the veranda. He reached up to run his boney hand over his stubbled chin again and again, as if that might help calm him, though it never did.

"But the doctor and Lucille may need you to help turn McKenzie over again, or move him to another room," she reminded him. "I know Ed claimed he could handle that sort of thing, but the doctor hasn't even had a chance to look at him yet. His own injury might be worse than he thinks."

She stopped to think about that for a moment before going on. "Besides, we haven't heard any more gunshots since we left. And the sheriff is out there now. Surely, once he announces his presence, whoever attacked will turn and run. You are needed here more."

309

"Maybe so. I just hope that if those varmints do turn tail and run, it's right into the arms of those deputies," Stretch muttered. He paused in his pacing long enough to slam his fist against the top of the wide bannister that encircled a large portion of the veranda. "I just hope the blackhearts were still out there hiding somewhere when the sheriff first got there, and that they ran right into his trap."

So did Callie. Then all the trouble would be over. And once it was over, once all danger was gone, she and Wade could again discuss the possibility of marriage. Finally, they could all get on with their lives without any clouds of fear or uncertainty hanging over them. Though she knew it would hurt Wade to finally discover, without a doubt, that his father was involved, at least the danger and all the turmoil caused by that danger would finally be over. Then they could work to put everything that had happened behind them and face the future with far more certainty. It was the only real hope she had at the moment, and she clung to it desperately.

Unable to do anything else, Callie and Stretch began to pace aimlessly about the veranda again, still aware of each other, but not bothering to speak again for there was really nothing more they could say.

Ever so slowly, the bleak darkness of night gave way to the first delicate rays of morning. As a bright rose hue began to streak across the eastern sky, Callie thought she heard horses coming in at a slow trot. She trained her eyes on the low rise that prevented the two of them from actually seeing the distant pasture and waited with her breath held deep in her throat. Stretch reached for his rifle and held it in readiness.

Soon they saw a group of riders headed for the house. Callie's heart took an amazing leap at the realization some of the men were finally returning. She prayed one of them would be Wade.

Stretch was down the steps first, having taken them two

at a time with his long, gangly legs. Even so, Callie remained only a few feet behind as they hurriedly crossed the yard and waited at the pasture gate for the approaching group of men. To her disappointment, none of the riders sat tall enough in the saddle nor had shoulders quite broad enough to be Wade. Nor did any of them appear to be the sheriff.

"What's going on out there?" Stretch called out to them, too anxious to know something—anything—to wait for them to reach the gate.

"Nothing," came the tired response. It was still too dark to be able to make out faces at such a distance, but that had clearly been Tony's voice.

And where Tony could be found, his brother Andy was usually not far behind, so Callie was not too surprised when Andy's voice sounded next. "Nothing at all. It's just now getting light enough for them to try to do anything anyway."

"Then what are you men doing back here?" Stretch wanted to know.

"Wade told us to come in and get a few hours' rest. He also mentioned how he hoped you had gotten some rest too, because we are all to go back out to help them get that cattle moved later this morning, and then this group is to plan on staying out there to take the next watch sometime this afternoon."

Staying out there to take next watch? Callie's heart sank. That meant no one had been caught after all. The danger was still out there. How she wished she could be out there too, where she would know if Wade was safe or not, but she knew she was needed where she was at the moment. The girls would be waking soon.

"What's the sheriff doing?" Stretch asked. His face had drawn into a deep scowl. Slowly, he opened the gate to let the men into the yard.

Tony responded to Stretch's question first. "Since it looks like whoever did all that shooting at us had already hightailed it off that ridge long before the sheriff and his deputies ever got there, he and Wade, as well as those three deputies who came along with him from town, were just about to take advantage of first daylight and ride up there to see if they could find any clues. Anything that will help them figure out just who it was that opened fire on that pasture last night."

Callie's stomach twisted painfully. "Wade is going up on that ridge with them?"

"Yeah. And then once they are certain it is safe, certain that whoever attacked is indeed long gone and not just lying low, they plan to bury the dead animals, then move the cattle that's still alive closer to the house. And then, all but the next round of lookouts—which I'm afraid is to be us—are going to come on back in for some rest."

Callie did not think she could bear it. Wade was putting himself in needless danger again. He planned to ride up onto that ridge when he knew those men might still be up there, hiding somewhere. Just because he was Walter's son did not mean he was immune to the risks involved.

It frustrated her even more to know it would be hours yet before she might know anything definite—about anything. She wondered if this time their search for clues would be successful. Would they finally find the proof they needed to make any arrests? Her insides ached when she considered the pain Wade would feel if he was the one to come across such evidence and then have to turn it over to the sheriff—that is, if Walter Barlow was indeed the man behind it all. There was still a chance, however slight, that the troublemaker could prove to be someone else. She hoped so.

But rather than dwell on any of that at the moment, Callie decided to see what she might do about getting the men something to eat. Though Lucille had never allowed her to actually help in the kitchen, she had been in there often enough when Lucille was cooking to know where most things were kept. Soon all the experience she'd had having to prepare so many of the family meals for her step-aunt had been put to use, and she had a presentable breakfast prepared and outside on the table for the men. Then, after she washed the dishes and had put them away, she rejoined Stretch on the veranda for yet another round of restless pacing. The rest of the men eventually wandered into the bunkhouse for some greatly needed sleep.

Shortly after nine, after the sun had risen well above the distant treetops into a clear blue sky, Lowell Edison stepped outside, his shirt sleeves rolled up past his elbows and his collar button undone. His silvery white hair was damp from hours of tedious work and his eyes were red-rimmed and watery. He looked exhausted.

"How's Mac?" Stretch wanted to know, stepping forward to learn what he could the moment he noticed the doctor had joined them outside.

"Hard to say. We found the two bullets and got them both out and, thankfully, there were no major organs injured. No bones splintered. But he's lost a lot of blood and is very weak."

Stretch's nostrils constricted and the muscles in his thin face tightened under his unshaven cheeks. For a moment Callie thought he might actually cry, but he kept his emotions in check.

"Is he awake?" Stretch asked, his voice strained.

"No. He hasn't been awake since I arrived. But it was better that he wasn't awake when I had to go looking for those bullets." Lowell took a white handkerchief out of his trousers pocket and wiped the perspiration off of his forehead. "You can go in and see him if you want. But he won't know you are there."

"What about Ed?"

"Upstairs. I had to give him something to make him sleep before I could get him to even let me examine his wound. He was adamant that he was all right. Kept saying Mr. McKenzie was the one who needed my attention—my full attention. I gather those two are very

313

close."

Stretch swallowed hard and nodded. "Best of friends. They've known each other since boyhood."

Callie reached out a hand and rested it on Stretch's thin shoulder, for he was a close friend of theirs too, though he had known the oddly matched pair for only a few years. As she recalled, from some of the passages in Matthew's journal, it had been Stretch who had gotten the other two their jobs in the first place.

"Well, I finally got a chance to look at Ed's wound and cleaned it up for him. And as much medication as I had to give him, he should sleep most of the day. Maybe by then I'll have some good news to tell him about his friend. Right now, though, all we can do is wait. And since there isn't much I can do for either of them at the moment, I'd really like to get a little rest myself." He turned to Callie. "Would you be so kind as to offer me the hospitality of one of your bedrooms?"

"Of course." Callie felt ashamed for not having already done so.

Quickly, she led the doctor upstairs to Matthew's bedroom. Though no one had actually used the room since his death, and she herself had not been in there since she had finished sorting through his things only a few nights after she had discovered that heartbreaking journal, it had the most comfortable bed she had to offer the doctor, and was one of the few rooms with a ceiling fan to help stave off the steadily rising summer heat.

A sad feeling swept over her when she first entered the room again. Although many of Matthew's personal items were now gone, the room seemed virtually unchanged. It was much like it had been when Matthew was still live. Glancing around, she could almost see him seated at his desk, pouring over his ledgers, pausing just long enough to look up and smile at her in that reassuring manner of his. But before the sudden need for tears overwhelmed her, she pushed the melancholy thoughts aside, and hurried to make sure the new sheets Lucille had insisted she be allowed to place on the bed shortly after Matthew's death were still fresh enough. Then she left the room to get Lowell a pitcher of cool water to wash with.

After she returned and gave the doctor a pitcher of fresh water and a new cake of soap, she heard noises down the hall and knew the girls were finally awake. Having been so reluctant to fall asleep the night before, they had slept later than usual, which Callie had considered a godsend. She wanted all the blood to be cleaned away and the dining room made far more presentable before the two had any opportunity to see it. Though Lowell had been adamant that McKenzie not be moved just yet, but instead be allowed to remain on the table, she knew Lucille would do all that was possible to make the room less intimidating, especially for the children.

"Good morning," Callie said cheerfully when she entered Amy's room and found both girls bent over Amy's boot, trying their best to force her chubby little stockinged foot into the thing. Janice was pushing on the heel while Amy tugged at the top. Obviously, Amy's foot had grown considerably since the boot had been purchased, and Callie made a mental note to take the girl into town for new boots just as soon as all the trouble was over. *Whenever that would be.* What a shame the girls had to be prisoners in their own home.

Still trying to push all melancholy thoughts aside and sound cheerful, Callie stepped further into the room and asked, "How'd you two sleep last night?"

"Well, I guess," Janice responded with a smile that quickly dropped the moment she actually turned her head and looked over at Callie. Her eyes widened with sudden alarm. "What happened to you?"

"What do you mean?" Callie asked, glancing down to see what might have caused such a reaction. Her own eyes grew wide at the sight of the large, dried bloodstains on the front of her dress. She should have noticed them

315

earlier. She should have thought to change clothes before allowing the girls to see her. She next wondered what her hair must look like, and reached up to tuck away several loose strands.

"Were you hurt?" In her haste to see about Callie, Janice left Amy to struggle alone with the unyielding boot. "Are you all right?"

Callie knew they would soon know most of the details anyway, and decided to prepare them for the fact McKenzie lay seriously injured on their dining table and Ed also lay injured in a room just down the hall. "I'm not the one who was hurt. There was trouble last night."

"Is Mr. Barlow all right?" Janice then asked, her blue-green eyes round with sudden fear. "Did he ever come back?"

Callie reached out to take the girl into her arms, though careful not to press her against the bloodstain. "As far as I know, Mr. Barlow is just fine. Ed and McKenzie were the only ones who were hurt."

"How?"

"They were shot," she told them honestly, then went on to explain what she knew of all the events that had occurred while the children slept.

"So there *was* trouble," Janice said, nodding as if she had truly expected it. "Do they have any idea who those men might have been or why they would want to shoot at our cows and at our workmen like that?"

Callie shook her head. Earlier, when she had first had to warn them of the impending trouble, she had carefully avoided mentioning any reasons why they may have been threatened, and had no intention of telling them any such frightening details now. "I'm afraid not. At least not yet. But Wade and the sheriff are searching for clues right now."

"I wish I could go out there and help," Amy said, frowning as she gave her boot another hard yank. At last the boot slipped over her heel, right into place. "I bet I

316

would be able to find something."

With a sudden feeling of alarm, bordering on pure panic, Callie turned to face the child so notorious for her impulsive, sometimes thoughtless, actions. Callie's eyes were wide with the cold fear Amy's comment had caused her. When she spoke again, her voice came out harsher than she intended and her hands began to tremble.

"Don't you dare even think of such a thing! You two girls are not to leave this house. You are not to so much as step outside until this is completely over. Do you understand?"

Amy and Janice exchanged startled glances.

"Yes, ma'am," they said in unison, then exchanged glances again.

Callie let out a breath she had not even realized she had been holding. Just the thought of Amy slipping off to help look for clues and falling into danger had left her feeling weak-kneed and gasping for breath.

"Are we going to read our Scriptures this morning?" Janice asked suddenly, as if aware Callie needed something else to think about. Something to help calm her. She remembered how their reading Scriptures aloud had always calmed their mother in times of duress.

"Scriptures?" Callie had forgotten that it was Sunday. "I don't. . . ." She hesitated while she considered it further. "Why yes, yes, of course we are. As soon as you two have had breakfast." It would be just the thing to help keep their minds off any more trouble.

"Have you already eaten?" Janice asked, glancing to the Jeffrey clock that sat on Amy's bedside table to see just how late it had gotten to be.

Callie paused to think. She had cooked breakfast for some of the men hours earlier, but she had failed to eat anything herself. "No, I haven't. So I guess we can read Scriptures after the *three* of us have eaten."

Thinking Lucille would be too busy to bother at the moment, the three went down together to see if they

317

could find anything to make do for their breakfast. But to Callie's amazement, Lucille and Ruby had finished cleaning the dining room, and Lucille was already in the kitchen preparing a hearty breakfast for them while Ruby worked to get the lunch preparations underway.

Since the dining table was otherwise occupied, Amy, Janice, and Callie joined Ruby and Lucille at the small table in the kitchen. The girls decided it was really quite handy to be so close to the stove when the time came to ask for a second serving of johnnycake, and wondered if it might be permissible for them to have breakfast in the kitchen more often. To which Callie promised to give careful consideration — but later, when she had less on her mind, when she did not have to worry so about Wade and the men still out there with him. And when the men who had attacked the Circle T were finally in jail where they could cause no further harm.

By eleven o'clock, Callie thought she would go insane waiting for Wade's return. Though she tried to concentrate on the verses being read alternately by both girls, she found it becoming more and more difficult to do. No one had bothered to return from the northwest pasture since the one small group had returned at daybreak. As a result, there had been no recent reports to let her know what was happening out there. Nothing to reassure her that Wade was still safe.

It was not knowing that was slowly eating away at her, slowly turning her stomach into a painful mass of knots.

Finally, shortly before the girls had finished with their reading, a commotion was heard out in the yard. Several of the men had awakened and returned outside, and Callie distinctly heard one of them shout out so everyone could hear him, "Here they come."

After urging the girls to put their bibles away and return upstairs to play until lunchtime, Callie hurried to the double doors which led from the parlor onto the eastern veranda and stepped outside. To her chagrin, but

318

not at all to her surprise, only moments later both girls stepped out onto the veranda beside her, having chosen to completely ignore her suggestion they go up to their rooms.

Callie considered ordering the two of them upstairs, but decided that would be unfair. They were just as worried as she was. Deciding to let them stay, she prayed that whatever news the men who had just returned had for them would be good news. She slowly descended the stairs and stepped out onto one of the cobblestone walkways that curved through the garden area to wait for whatever was to happen next. The girls immediately followed.

"It's Mister Wade," Amy squealed with delight, clasping her hands together over her heart the moment she recognized him.

Callie was relieved to see that Amy's sharp eyesight had proven right yet again. Wade was among the men who had just passed through the pasture gate into the yard.

The tired smile on Wade's unshaven face had never looked more endearing to her. She was so happy to see him back unharmed that she paused barely long enough to close her eyes and thank God for his mercy before hurrying across the yard to greet him. Despite the fact that all the men were out in the yard awaiting a report, and both Lucille and Ruby had stepped onto the back veranda, Callie rushed headlong into his arms. Eager to feel his strong embrace around her. Eager to embrace him in return.

Wade did not hesitate to oblige, closing his eyes and holding her close while he pressed his cheek firmly into her hair. He also no longer cared who witnessed their display of affection. He needed to hold her. He needed to be reassured she was all right.

"Wade, I'm so glad to see that you were not hurt!" she said in an emotionally strangled voice. Tears brimmed her pale brown eyes, threatening to spill down her flushed

319

cheeks at any moment.

"And I am mad as hell at you for what you did last night," he warned her, though his face bore none of the anger he spoke of when he finally put her away from him minutes later. He took the two waiting girls into his arms and gave them both a big hug too.

"Did you two remain brave through all this?" he asked after he knelt between them in order to see their concerned faces better. He held one in the curve of each of his arms while he glanced back and forth between them.

"Yes, very brave," Amy stated with a firm nod.

Janice's eyes turned heavenward, then looked at her younger sister accusingly. "We both slept right through it."

"Good," Wade said, trying not to chuckle aloud at Amy's immediate pout. Amy was clearly not fond of the idea of having missed all the action. "At least someone around here got some sleep last night."

He then stood again, but continued to rest a hand on each girl's shoulder when he returned his attention to Callie. His blue eyes glimmered with obvious appreciation while his gaze feasted at the sight of her.

Smiling shyly, she was suddenly very glad she had taken the time to change into a clean dress, then brushed and styled her hair into a neat, but becoming twist high on her head before returning back downstairs to join the girls in the parlor for their Bible readings. She would have hated for him to see the way she had looked just a few hours before. It might have caused him to give a second thought to marrying her.

"So what did you find out?" Stretch asked, unable to hold back his questions any longer. "Where's the sheriff?"

Wade glanced at Stretch's concerned face, then at the concerned faces of the other men who had come in earlier and had not been with them when the two men had ridden out from town with a report of two burglaries in town, both needing the sheriff's prompt attention.

320

"I'm afraid there was a little trouble in town last night. The sheriff and his men had to leave shortly after sunup to go see about it. He's coming back, though, sometime this afternoon. In the meantime, because it is possible the men came down off that ridge onto my land, he wants me to ride over to Twin Oaks to see if any of my men happened to notice anything suspicious last night. Then he wants me to send a group of men out to ask the neighbors similar questions."

"Well, if he's been gone since just after sunup, what have the rest of you been up to all this time?" Stretch wanted to know, his face drawn into an immediate frown. He was clearly put out at having been made to wait all this time.

"Been burying the dead cattle," he told him. "And after lunch, I want to get the rest of the cattle herded into that pasture like I mentioned before. In fact I want all the cattle we can find rounded up and brought into the main pasture as quick as possible."

"What about your cattle? You want them brought in too?" Andy asked, rubbing his dimpled chin thoughtfully.

"Yes, there's no time to try and separate mine from Mrs. Tucker's. We'll have to bring them all in together. Then when I ride over to Twin Oaks to see what my men may have seen or heard, I'll have them gather up all they can find on my side of the fence line and put them in the pasture there behind my house. Then we won't have as much area to have to keep such a close watch over, and neither will my men."

"But what if those men who shot at us try to set fire to the vacant pastures once they figure out we are no longer guarding them?" Jim asked, remembering the fires they had already had.

"After the rains we've had recently, a fire won't be nearly as dangerous as it once was. If we detect smoke, we will hurry out and fight the fire as best we can. But until something like that indeed happens, we need to center our efforts on the pastures where the cattle will be. And of course on the houses."

Wade stuffed his hands into his pockets when he turned back to Callie, his expression even more grim than it had been. "How is McKenzie?"

"He's still alive," she told him, though that was about all she really knew. Lowell had not yet come back downstairs from his nap, and she had not returned to the kitchen to ask for a report from Lucille, who was keeping a close watch on McKenzie. "He was shot four times. Two bullets went straight through him, but the other two had to be cut out of him. He's weak, but last I saw, he was resting peacefully. And Lowell is still here, in case something happens."

"How's Ed?"

"Ed's fine," she assured him. "Lowell said Ed would probably be very sore for a few days, too sore to do any heavy lifting again, but that he should be up and around soon enough, probably by this afternoon. Won't be any keeping him down once his medication has worn off."

"You're probably right," Wade muttered, nodding that he fully agreed. Then his expression lifted. "So, when do we eat? We are starved."

A loud muttering of agreement rose from the men, who until now had stood silently by. They had missed breakfast, and had no intention of missing another meal when they did not have to.

Shortly after a quick lunch of fried ham and steamed potatoes had been served, then eaten at a voracious rate, all the men except Manuel and Jim rode back out to round up the cattle from the outer pastures while keeping a cautious eye out for more trouble.

The two who had been ordered to remain behind quickly made themselves comfortable on opposite verandas with a loaded weapon in one hand and a tall glass of cool lemonade in the other.

Half an hour later, the four men who had been out in

the pastures to stand guard while Wade and the others had come in to eat their lunch, rode in for their own quick meal, then disappeared into the bunkhouse to catch some sleep.

Though he had waited at the house until those four men had ridden in, Wade left shortly thereafter. First, he rode out to see that everything was going accordingly. Then he returned barely long enough to tell Callie he was headed on over to his place to see if anybody there had noticed anything out of the ordinary. At her insistence, he promised to stop off and get one of her men to ride over to Twin Oaks with him, just in case the troublemakers were still somewhere nearby.

Before returning to his horse, he took the time to pull Callie into his arms once more while out on the back veranda where no one could see then, and kissed her gently. While still holding her close, enjoying the feel of her tender curves next to his strong, hard body, he tried to reassure her that everything would eventually work out for the best. He then hurried to remind her how very much he loved her, and how as soon as they got the troublemakers out of the way once and for all, they could direct their energies toward winning the girls' acceptance of him — enough so they could finally hope to be married.

But his reassuring words cheered her very little.

"Wade, I'm so afraid that something terrible is about to happen to you," she said, nearly in tears when she reached up to touch his unshaven face adoringly. How dearly she loved that handsome face. With tears reflected in her golden brown eyes, she stood on tiptoe and placed a tender kiss first at one corner of his mouth, then the other. "I don't think I could bear it if you were to in any way be hurt."

"Nothing is going happen to me," he promised her, though he was not certain it was a promise he had any way of keeping. "You just be sure nothing happens to you, or the girls. Keep that pistol loaded and at your side.

I'll be back in a little while." Then he kissed her again, this time drawing her body even harder against his, still hoping to reassure her somehow, and at the same time needing to hold her as close as humanly possible at least once more before he left.

"I'll be waiting for you," she assured him when he finally pulled away. One of the tears that had been brimming in her eyes fell onto her cheek as she looked at him then.

Wade smiled and tried to swallow back the emotions gathering in his throat. Gingerly, he reached out and pushed away the tear with the side of his thumb. "Be sure that you do."

When Wade then rode away, leaving her standing forlornly on the small veranda at the back of the house, he glanced back and waved to her one last time. He quickly tried to memorize the beauty that so easily touched his heart. Then, after he turned back around in the saddle to face forward again, he slipped his hand into the front pocket of his trousers and felt the two metal objects he had found, but had yet to reveal.

Though he would indeed stop and ask Stretch to ride with him to his ranch—in order to appease Callie if nothing else—he planned to go from there to his father's place alone. If there was any danger awaiting him at the Rocking W, he did not intend to drag anyone else into the middle of it. He would face his father and his father's men alone.

Chapter Twenty

Because Wade had taken the time right after lunch to slip upstairs unnoticed, and had asked Lowell if he might see the slugs taken from McKenzie, he now had one of them in his possession and was more than ready to put it to use.

Though it had disappointed him greatly, he was in no way surprised to discover one of the two bullets had been a .44-40 caliber. So had one of the bullets he'd dug out of the dead steers just before he'd given the order to have the animals buried. Now he had two such bullets, which pretty well confirmed his worst fear—since the .44-40 caliber was still uncommon in this area. He personally knew of only one man who had a rifle that shot .44-40 ammunition. His own father.

Only last year, the man had bought one of those new English-designed lever-action rifles that fired the .44-40 caliber instead of the more common .44, which the more popular Winchesters and Henries used. His father had clearly boasted to him about how his new rifle was a rarity in the southern United States, and even had gone as far as to explain how he'd had to order the special brass-tipped ammunition directly from the company that manufactured the rifle itself. That meant the bullet he'd found in the steer and the one the doctor had dug out of McKenzie's chest in all likelihood had come from that very same rifle.

Wade was furious. So furious, he stayed at Twin Oaks

only long enough to find out if any of his men had seen anything that would make his suspicions even more conclusive. After learning none of them had seen anything, even though they had kept an especially close watch once they had heard the gunfire coming from the direction of the Circle T, Wade instructed Stretch to organize a group of those men to ride to a few of the neighbors' houses to see if anyone else might have seen something helpful.

Then, without telling Stretch or any of his own men just where it was he was headed, he climbed back onto his horse and rode off alone, fully prepared to confront his father again. Only this time he had more to go on. Feeling he had an advantage at last, he planned to make the man stop his evil deeds by threatening him with the strongest action he could think of at the moment. Blackmail.

When Wade finally rode into the yard only twenty minutes later, he noticed immediately how many of his father's men were there, standing outside in small groups, watching him cautiously while he traveled slowly through the yard.

Normally, on a Sunday afternoon, most of his father's men would be inside the bunkhouse, sleeping off their revelry from the evening before, or lazing about on the porch at the back of the building playing dominoes or a few hands of poker, betting away what money they had left from their Saturday pay. Usually, about half of the men did not even make it back from their weekend in town until sometime early Monday morning, either because they were married with faimilies to take care of or because they had gotten far too drunk to make the trip back any sooner.

Why then were most of his father's men not only there, but outside, fully dressed, and talking in groups as if waiting for something to happen? He hated to guess.

Next he noticed how, although none of the men was actually armed at the time, several had rifles close by, as if they expected trouble. A few stared angrily at him when he neared the house, while others quickly looked away the moment he glanced in their direction, as if unable to look him in the eye.

One of the men, a tall, burly blond, had his shirt sleeve rolled nearly to his shoulder and wore a thick bandage around his arm. There was a trickle of blood seeping through. Wade wondered if the injury was possibly a bullet wound, and was tempted to veer over and ask the man, though he was certain he would get no straight answer. He was clearly being viewed as an intruder at the moment.

"Wade? What are you doing here?" He heard Evan even before he had turned back around to find his stockily built half-brother standing on the front veranda, with arms crossed defiantly and his legs braced for trouble. Wade did not fail to notice that Evan had a handgun strapped low on his hip. He was glad to feel his own handgun weighing heavily on the side of his own thigh.

Evan's thick brows dipped low over narrowed hazel eyes when he took a step forward. "Have you forgotten that just yesterday Father told you not to bother coming back here? Have you already forgotten? You aren't at all welcome here any more."

"I've come to see him about a matter I feel is very important," Wade answered, intentionally vague with his response as he climbed down from his horse and began to loosely tie the reins to a nearby post. If he came across the need to get out of there in a hurry, he wanted to be able to free his reins with a single jerk. "Where is he?"

"He doesn't want to see you," Evan told him with strong certainty.

"That's too bad, because I sure as hell want to see him," Wade muttered, and began to approach the house with long steady strides.

"He's resting," Evan stated. His voice came out low with warning while the muscles in his forearms flexed rhythmically beneath his rolled up shirt sleeves. "Don't disturb him. Whatever you have come to say you can say to me first. Then I'll decide if he needs to hear it or not."

"Oh, yes, I remember," Wade responded with strong sarcasm. "Yesterday you told me he was not well thinking I would not bother to say what I had to say to him then. But that was yesterday, and it really matters very little to me at the moment. I plan to speak with my father no matter what you have to say. And I plan to speak with him now."

This time Evan did not move away. With a face hardened from pent-up rage, he continued to stand with his legs braced, blocking the doorway. He uncrossed his arms and put them at his sides. His fingers flexed, prepared to react to whatever was to happen next. "You'll have to get by me first."

"I don't see that as a problem," Wade muttered just before he lifted his left hand in readiness to shove his half-brother aside the moment he reached him. But he was not so foolish that he dared take his right hand away from his pistol in order to do so. For the first time ever, he sensed a real danger in Evan, and intended to remain extremely cautious of him.

"Wade, you are no longer welcome here," Evan restated as he tensed the muscles in his legs and shoulders, bracing himself for Wade's blow. His hazel eyes darted from Wade's angry face to his lean, strong body, to where his right hand remained ever so close to the jutting handle of his ivory-handed pistol. His eyes widened, then narrowed again. "Go home, Wade."

"I fully intend to. Right after I've said what I have come to say—to Father." With the ease of a man fully intent on doing exactly what he'd come to do, Wade pushed Evan briskly aside and marched into the house. Turning to watch for whatever retaliation Evan might have planned for him, he moved his hand even closer to his pistol, until his thumb touched the handle itself. He then asked, "Where is he?"

Evan had reached for his handgun, exactly as Wade had

328

expected him to, but had wisely decided against actually pulling the weapon from its holster. Still Evan's eyes bore angrily into Wade while he looked from where his older half-brother's right hand still hovered above his pistol to where Wade's glimmering blue eyes slowly narrowed, as if urging him to try it. Barely a moment later, Evan's gaze left Wade's intent expression and traveled higher, to focus on something further down the hall.

"What is it you want with me?" Walter demanded to know from the third step of the wide, gleaming stairway at the far end of the hall. "I thought I told you yesterday to stay away from here."

"And nothing would have pleased me more," Wade said as he turned, placing his back to the wall, where he could see his father yet at the same time keep a wary eye on Evan. Though his own anger had grown to overwhelming proportions, until it virtually boiled inside of him, Wade was able to speak in a calm, rational voice. "I want to talk with you about something very important. And I think you'd be foolish not to listen to what I have come to say. *Very* foolish."

"And you want to speak alone, I suppose," Walter said, coming closer. His expression remained stern, but he did not yet display the anger he had shown the day before. Instead, he appeared almost curious to hear Wade out.

"Yes, Father, alone. What I have to say can and maybe should be kept between the two of us," Wade told him. His gaze flickered briefly to his father's concerned expression, then back to watch Evan, who remained tense, ready to spring into action. Wade shuddered inwardly at the raw hatred now so clearly evident in his half-brother's narrowed eyes. He knew it would not be at all wise to turn his back on Evan at that particular moment, and sought to get rid of him before he might have to do so. His nostrils flared slightly when he spoke to him then. "And since I would indeed prefer to speak with Father alone, if you don't mind, Evan, I'd appreciate it if you'd just step outside for a few minutes and give us a little privacy."

Evan's shoulders tossed back indignantly, but before he was able to respond, Walter intervened.

"There is no reason for him to leave. This is his home, too," Walter quickly reminded Wade. "You are the intruder here. But if you really think you need privacy, you and I can talk in my study." Then he turned to walk ahead of him.

Wade followed cautiously, paying close attention to any sounds behind him, ready to drop and fire if he decided he was being drawn on. To his relief, the only sound was Evan's angry voice calling out to his father. "I'll be right out here if you need me."

This time Wade took a few seconds to carefully close the door behind them before turning back to his father. Only after the door was closed did he discover his father had his back to him.

"What is it you want?" Walter asked while he crossed the room, already headed for his liquor cabinet. In the place of the elaborate glass decanter he had shattered against the wall the day before sat a plain glass whiskey bottle, already more than half empty. Quickly, he pulled the cork out with his curled forefinger and began to fill his glass. This time he did not offer Wade a drink.

"I'm here to give you a message," Wade began, walking over to the cabinet himself so he would not have to speak too loudly. He did not want Evan to overhear anything they had to say. Though he felt certain his father would fill his half-brother in on all the details as soon as he was gone, for now he wanted Evan to suffer not knowing any of what was being said between them.

"A mesage? From Tucker's widow?" Walter asked just before he took a long first drink. When he had drained half the contents of the glass, he asked, "Has she finally come to her senses and changed her mind?"

"Hardly," Wade muttered. "No, this message is from me."

Walter set the half-empty glass aside and turned to face his son squarely. With his thick brows lowered, as if warning him to be careful of what he had to say, he asked, "And what might that message be?"

"Just this." He extracted one of the bullets from his pocket and held it out in the curve of his palm for his father's inspection. "Two of Callie's men were shot last night during that senseless raid along one of her back pastures. This bullet was taken out of one of the workmen's chests. I know it is hard to tell at a distance, but if you'd care to examine it carefully, I'm sure you'll notice how unique this bullet really is."

Walter's hazel eyes grew wide while he stared at the bullet. Then he glanced first at the window, then at the door, as if frantically searching for a possible excuse and hoping to find it in his own surroundings. His entire body tensed.

"Did the man die?" he finally asked, blinking rapidly while his gaze continued to dart nervously about the room.

"Not yet," Wade told him as he curled the bullet into a tightly closed fist and withdrew it from his father's sight. Carefully, he studied his father's reactions.

"Just what do you plan to do with that?" Walter asked, pausing long enough to swallow hard.

"For now, keep it. But if as many as *one* more head of Tucker cattle dies, or if there is *one* more unexplainable mishap on Circle T land, I will not hesitate to turn the bullets over to the sheriff, along with a detailed explanation about where they were found."

"Bullets?" Walter asked, having caught the fact he had used a plural.

"Yes, I have more than one of these. And they will end up with the sheriff, as well as all the other evidence I have been collecting against you," he told him, running his bluff as far as he could. And a bluff it was, for all he really had was the bullets, which in all honesty was not

331

much.

Although he was not aware of anyone else in the area owning one of the new English-designed rifles, he was fully aware that there could be others he simply did not know about. He just hoped his father would not realize the same thing. He did not want him to figure out exactly how flimsy his proof really was. As of yet, he had nothing that would truly hold up against anyone in court—if it ever came to that.

"You certainly were quick to decide I'm guilty," Walter shouted angrily. His face reddened, then went instantly pale as he curled his hand into a tight fist and pressed it hard against his chest. He struggled to get enough breath to vent his sudden rage, and shouted out in a raspy voice, "How dare you come back into my home issuing even more threats against me, condemning me for someone else's crimes without as much as a single thought for my innocence!"

Wade felt an odd prickly sensation in the pit of his stomach while he watched his father's body tense until the vein in the side of his neck stuck out and his eyelids became so taut they made his eyes look like they had started to bulge right out of their sockets. He had never seen his father quite that angry.

Suddenly, Walter began to slap at his own chest with the tightly curled fist. It was as if his rage fought to take his own breath away. His face grew contorted from intense pain.

"Father?" Wade stepped forward, but did not know what to do for him. He reached out and put a hand on Walter's shoulder. "Father, calm down. We can talk about this rationally. All I'm asking is that you stop tormenting Callie. I won't turn the evidence over to the sheriff unless I have to."

Walter closed his eyes and continued to gasp for air. His chest heaved wildly while he tugged frantically at his shirt with his other hand. Several buttons popped off and clattered to the floor.

"Father? What's wrong?" Panic filled Wade's heart.

"Get me to the doctor," Walter gasped just before he folded forward and slowly collapsed to the floor. Only a second later, he lay unconscious at Wade's feet.

Horrified, Wade burst out of the room like a madman. He found Evan still standing just down the hallway, barely a foot inside the front door, peering cautiously at him. His right hand moved immediately to rest only inches above his gun.

"Evan, send someone for the doctor. Quick. The doc should still be over at the Circle T. Tell him to hurry. Pop has collapsed."

He was totally unaware he had reverted back to the term he had always used for his father in his childhood, back when his mother had still been alive and before all their personal differences had begun.

Evan's eyes widened with instant concern, "Collapsed?"

"Yes, send someone to get Doc Edison!" Wade shouted, then spun around to return to his father's side. Quickly, he gathered him into his arms and, though his father weighed nearly as much as he did, managed to carry the unconscious man up the stairs and into his bedroom. While he worked to tug off Walter's boots and remove his suspenders in hopes of making him more comfortable, Evan came bursting into the room, immediately trying to shove Wade aside.

"What happened? What did you do to him?" Evan demanded to know. His gaze jerked back and forth from where Walter lay unconscious to where Wade stood hovering over the bed.

"I didn't do anything to him," Wade told him, trying to keep control of his anger, for his father's sake. But deep down, he knew that was a lie. He was fully responsible for his father's collapse. He had driven the man to it. Guilt washed over him, making him feel sick right down to the pit of his stomach. His misery was overwhelming. Again

333

Evan tried to push him away, and this time he let him.

"Father? Father? Craig and Eric have gone for the doctor. Father? Can you hear me?" Evan called out, leaning over and feeling Walter's cheeks with his trembling hands. "He's cold!"

Wade's heart came to a stop while Evan fearfully reached for the base of Walter's throat to feel for a pulse. When he obviously found one, he slowly released the breath he'd been holding.

Suddenly, he turned to glare at Wade. "You did this to him. "You—the son he always hated."

The words struck Wade like a board across his chest, making him take another step back.

"I'm the only real son that man ever had," Evan went on to say, his face filled with rage. "Though I was never fortunate enough to ever be allowed to bear his last name, I was the only real son he ever had. I'm the one who stayed by his side no matter what he did. Me! Not you. And I want you to know that if he dies, if that doctor does not get here in time to save him, I'm the one who will inherit all he owns. Not you. I get everything! Do you hear? He has arranged it so I get everything he owns and you get nothing! Absolutely nothing!"

"I expected as much," Wade responded with an aching heart as he pulled his gaze away from Evan's furious face to look down on his father's bloodless features. When he turned his shoulder to his half-brother in order to get a better view of his father, tears began to burn his eyes. How helpless he looked lying there, his chest barely moving, his lips flexing spasmodically, as if in response to the pain that still must be inside of him.

Evan became even more enraged the moment Wade had turned away from him. Angrily, he reached out to grab the shoulder that had been so suddenly presented to him, then shoved it around to force Wade to face him again. "Don't you dare turn away from me. I'm not finished talking to you yet. I want you to know everything. I want you to know just how much he loved me and not you. I want you to know how as soon as our father was able to get the Widow Tucker to sell out to him, he planned to give *me* the Circle T as a special gift for all the loyalty I've shown him through the years. Once he was able to make that stubborn woman finally give up all that Tucker had ever held dear, he intended to hand it over to *me*. Do you hear me? He planned to give you nothing. But then you don't deserve anything, do you?" Evan's mouth tightened against his teeth. "Not a damn thing!"

Wade stared at him, astonished over what his half-brother had just revealed to him. His father did not even want the land for himself. He just wanted to take it away from Callie and the girls because of some sort of personal grudge he still felt against Matthew Tucker. Even though Matthew was dead now and able to cause him no further harm, his father still sought to get even. He then wondered if his father had stepped up his campaign against Callie because he—his own son—had chosen to help her. Had his becoming involved only served to make him angrier? Wade felt another wave of guilt wash over him.

He also felt disgusted—disgusted to realize it was purely his father's hatred that had driven him to try and force Callie and the girls to sell the Circle T—no matter what he had to do to accomplish it. No matter who he hurt.

"Get out of here," Evan said, quickly reclaiming Wade's attention. "Get out of here right now! Before you cause something worse to happen."

"No, I plan to stay," Wade responded immediately. Even though he had just learned the worst about his father, he still planned to stay by his father's side until he knew the man would be all right. He would not leave until he had another chance to speak with his father, and apologize for having caused his collapse and try to explain. He had not meant to bring his father any physical harm. He'd only wanted to make him stop.

Barely twenty minutes later, Lowell Edison entered the

house, then bounded immediately up the stairway. By the sound of his boots on the thick wooden stairs, he was taking them two at a time as fast as he could. Wade called to him to let him know which room to go to, unaware the doctor might already know from previous visits.

"What happened?" Lowell asked only seconds after he had burst into the room and found Evan and Wade standing on opposite sides of Walter's bed like a couple of warring roosters, with Walter lying still unconscious between them.

Wade opened his mouth to explain about Walter's collapse, but Evan interrupted before he could speak. "I think it's his heart again, Doc. Only this time it is much worse."

This time? Wade wondered how long his father had suffered heart ailments. He felt guiltier still to know that he had not even suspected his father had such problems. Lowering his gaze to the floor, he stepped back and allowed Lowell more room at the bedside to examine his father.

"Wade, grasp his shoulders and lift him up off the bed a second," Lowell instructed as he reached for one of the pillows at the opposite side of the bed not already being used to support Walter's head. "I need to get this up under his back to raise his chest a little, to take some of the pressure off his heart."

"I'll do that, Evan said quickly, and reached over to grab Walter's shoulders before Wade could. He shot Wade another harsh look of hatred while he pulled the man up high enough to allow the doctor to slip the pillow into place beneath him.

"Hand me my medical bag," Lowell then said, bending over Walter's body to immediately begin his examination. Carefully, he lifted Walter's eyelids and studied the pupils, then reached for his neck to feel for a pulse.

Wade was closer to where Lowell had left the leather bag, and was able to comply before Evan could make it around the bed. He then watched, with a heart that felt as if it was made of lead, while the doctor snatched the bag open, unrolled a white linen cloth, took out a large hypodermic, then quickly filled it with medicine he kept in a small vial with a bright yellow label.

"What are you giving him?" he asked.

"Strychnia. A thirtieth of a gram," Lowell told him, as if unaware Wade might not know what strychnia was or exactly how much a thirtieth of a gram might be. He frowned when he bent beside Walter's pale body and injected the medication. When he was finished, he bent closer, sniffing the air above his patient. "He smells like whiskey. Has he been drinking again?"

Evan glanced at him guiltily. "Can't keep him from it. He says it helps him feel better."

"It may dull some of the discomfort, but it does not help him at all. I told you both that he was to stop drinking. Whiskey stimulates the heart. He doesn't need that," Lowell scolded, and quickly laid the hypodermic aside to feel again for a pulse at the base of Walter's throat. "The old fool! Does he think he's indestructible?"

Wade frowned when he became aware just how familiar Lowell Edison seemed to be with his father's illness. He wondered why the doctor had not bothered to mention anything to him, but chose to wait until he had finished treating his father before he actually asked for the explanation.

"He ordered me not to tell anyone," Lowell told Wade matter-of-factly while he continued to study Walter's coloring and bent down to once again feel for his pulsebeat.

Evan jerked his gaze away from his father to look at Wade, his eyes still glittering with anger. "He didn't *want* you to know. He didn't think you deserved to know."

Wade fell silent. The ache in his heart grew until it consumed his entire body. All he had ever wanted was to somehow make his father love him again, to somehow regain his respect—though he had never understood what

337

he had ever done to cause his father to turn against him in the first place. Knowing he had failed to make any progress at all toward that goal over the past few years cut deep into his very soul.

When Lowell straightened again and noticed how much Wade was suffering, he reached out and grasped his shoulders in a friendly gesture. Looking directly into his eyes, he tried to explain. "Wade, there really wasn't much to tell anyway. There's only been two other attacks that I know anything about, and they were very minor in comparison to this. Still, I warned him. I warned him to take it easy and stay away from whiskey and tobacco. I warned him that he would develop a serious heart problem if he didn't. But evidently he didn't listen to me."

Wade closed his eyes for a moment, knowing how his father had always had a bad drinking problem, then took a deep breath. "How serious is it? Is he going to die?"

"I can't really say," Lowell answered with a regretful shake of his head. "I'll stay to give him another shot in an hour if he hasn't awakened, but after that I'll have to get back over to the Circle T to check on Mr. McKenzie."

"What?" Evan shouted, hurrying around the bed to confront the doctor. "You'd leave him like this?"

"Not for long," Lowell assured him. "But I do have another patient in just as critical condition as he is. I'll have to divide my time between them both until one of the two finally starts to show some improvement."

"No! I won't allow it. You can't leave here until we know Father is going to be all right," Evan shouted, and reached out to grab the doctor by his shirt front.

"Evan, leave him be," Wade said in warning.

"Not until he promises to stay until Father is completely out of danger," Evan replied, still shouting. His lips compressed into a fine white line while he twisted the doctor's shirt in his hand, drawing him closer.

"Evan, if you can't keep calm, then I'm going to ask that you leave this room," Lowell stated, remaining cool and

338

rational. His gaze fell on where Evan's hand continued to twist at his shirt. "Right now, your father needs to rest in a quiet atmosphere more than anything else. He sure doesn't need to have someone in the room bent on causing such a disturbance."

Wade reached out and squeezed Evan's hand until the pain forced him to release the shirt. "Evan, if you don't calm down and leave the doctor alone, I will remove you from this room myself."

Evan turned his anger on Wade. "Why don't *you* get the hell out of here? You are the one who doesn't belong here. He doesn't want you here. And he sure as hell won't want to find you still here if and when he wakes up."

"I'm staying," Wade said with finality. "Might as well get used to that idea right now. I am not leaving here until I know he's going to be all right."

"Would one of you please get me a pitcher of cool water?" Lowell asked, turning his back to the both of them and bending over his patient once again. "I'd like to bathe his forehead and neck with a cool cloth."

Evan hurried to be the one to get the water, pausing in the doorway just long enough to issue a final warning. "Doc, just see to it that Wade keeps away from my father while I'm gone. I don't want him even touching him."

"Just get me the water," Lowell responded with a tired shake of his head. "Or should I go get it myself."

"I'm going."

Finally, Evan's footsteps were heard hurrying down the stairs to do what the doctor had asked. After a moment, Lowell turned to Wade, his expression full of concern.

"You do understand why I can't stay here with your father for very long, don't you?" he asked, looking at Wade for some indication that he understood.

"Of course. McKenzie's life is at stake too. Just, please, do whatever you can for him," he asked, glancing down at his father's pallid face. Though he in no way approved of his father's recent actions against Callie, he still loved the

339

man and wanted a chance to talk with him about everything he had done lately. He wanted to understand his
father's motives. He wanted his father to understand his.

"I will. You know I will," Lowell said, then reached out
to pat Wade's slumped shoulder reassuringly. "I'll do
everything that I can medically. But I think I should warn
you, there's a very real possibility your father may never
come out of this. There's a chance he is dying. What pulse
I can find is weak and irregular. There is a very real
possibility he will never wake up. He could slip away from
us at any time."

Wade closed his eyes against the resulting flood of pain,
then knelt at his father's bedside. Not caring that the
doctor stood over him, watching, he bent forward to take
his father's hand in his. Sadly, he spoke aloud what was in
his heart.

"Pop," he said, his voice so weak it could barely be
heard. "Please, don't die. Not yet. Not until we have had a
chance to talk. I want to be able to tell you how sorry I am
for causing this. I want a chance to express exactly how I
feel toward you—how very much I still care."

He bent forward and pressed his forehead into the side
of the mattress, still holding his father's hand. Morosely,
he wondered for what must be the hundredth time where
he and his father had gone wrong. How he wished things
had never become so strained between them. How dearly
he wanted to make amends, to somehow clear things
between them and start over.

Suddenly he was aware of Evans footsteps coming back
up the stairs at a frantic pace. Quickly, he stood and wiped
some of the moisture away from his cheek. Strangely, he
felt no shame for the emotional outburst he had just
displayed. He had a feeling the doctor was the sort of man
who understood.

While he continued to gaze down at his father's expres-
sionless face, he reached up and dashed away all trace of
the tears trailing down his cheeks, then spoke to Lowell

softly. He did not want his words to carry out into the hall.

"When you get back to the Circle T, tell Callie where I am. Explain to her I won't be back there until . . ." That was all he could say. Turning away, he walked over to the open window and gazed out at the bright green pastures beyond. His shoulders tensed while he fought to get his emotions back under firm control before Evan re-entered the room.

"I'll tell her," Lowell promised, watching Wade for a moment. Then wearily, he ran his hand over his unshaven jaw just before he turned to wait for Evan to appear in the doorway with the pitcher of fresh water he had requested.

Chapter Twenty-one

Wade remained by his father's side throughout the night, with Evan constantly in and out during that time. Though there continued to be open hostility between the two half-brothers, they kept their emotions within certain boundaries by refusing to get close to one another. Through an unspoken agreement they were able to restrict their anger to the sharp, penetrating glares cast at one another from across the room—but only for their father's sake.

Lowell Edison too was in and out, trying his best to divide his time fairly between his two patients. By morning, he appeared too exhausted to continue, yet he did. Wade worried about him, but realized until one of his patients began to improve, the doctor had no time to rest. Wade wished there was something he could do to help.

But there wasn't. There was really nothing any of them could do. Lowell had already given Walter all the medication he dared, and had explained how it was mostly in God's hands now.

Before he had left the last time to make yet another trip to the Circle T to check on McKenzie, Lowell had again cautioned Wade to be prepared for the worst.

Shortly after dawn, the footfalls of two horses were heard clamoring into the dooryard. Evan was again in the bedroom, seated rigidly in a chair on the opposite side of Walter's bed from where Wade sat, slumped forward with his elbows planted on his knees and his steepled fingers pressed against his forehead.

"I hope to hell that's the doctor coming back," Evan muttered. "He's been gone long enough." Glowering, he rose from his chair to see if it was indeed the doctor. Moments later, when he turned away from the window to look back at Wade, his face registered even more anger than it had before.

"It's the doc all right, but this time he's brought Tucker's widow with him," Evan stated in a tight voice. The muscles in his jaw worked furiously while he strode determinedly across the room toward the door. "I wonder what the hell *she's* doing here."

Aware of Evan's intention to cause more trouble, Wade quickly rose from his chair and hurried after him, catching him by the shoulder before he reached the stairway.

"Leave her alone, Evan. She's probably here because she is concerned. Some people are like that. You just leave her be. She's suffered enough at the hands of this family." For the first time, Wade wondered how much Evan might know about all the terrible things his father had been up to recently. It occurred to him that Evan might have played a vital part in some of it. Realizing that, he became more cautious of his younger half-brother, and more determined to keep him away from Callie.

"Suffered enough? The hell she has," Evan stated, jerking his shoulder away from Wade's grasp, then turning to glare at him. Now that they were in the hallway away from their father's room, he obviously felt it was all right to raise his voice. "She hasn't even seen the beginning of what it is to suffer. Not yet. But if she dares to set one foot inside this house, she's going to find out what suffering really is. I'll see to that. If she wants trouble, I'll sure as hell give it to her."

"I said to leave her alone," Wade stated again. His nostrils flared and every muscle in his body tensed. Both hands curled into fists at his sides. How dearly he would love to smash a fist into Evan's snarling face and send him reeling to the floor where he belonged.

Evan stared angrily at him a moment, then glanced down

343

at the pistol Wade still wore on his upper thigh. He was undecided as to what he wanted to do next, and the muscle at the back of his clean-shaven jaw pumped rapidly while he considered the situation further.

When the knock finally sounded at the front door, he jerked his glance toward the stairs. His eyes narrowed again as a decision was made. Quickly, he turned on his heel and stalked off toward the stairway—his hands also curled into tight fists which swung stiffly at his sides when he walked. He too still wore his handgun, though high up on his hip.

"Evan, where are you going?" Wade wanted to know, ready to physically restrain him if necessary.

"There's work to be done. And I'm the only one who can see that it gets done," Evan shouted in response, never bothering to pause or look back until he had started down the stairway. "Father would want me to keep things going around here, and that is exactly what I intend to do. We've got a hay crop to get in." The hand resting on the bannister tightened. "You can go ahead and let her in this house, if that's what you want, but you'd just better keep her away from me."

Gladly, Wade thought as he hurried to follow down the stairs.

Callie approached the front door with extreme caution. Having seen the hate-filled stares of the men milling about in the yard, she realized she was not exactly welcome, but then she had not really expected to be. Lowell had already knocked once at the wood frame along the side of the wire-mesh outer door and, after having received no response, had raised his hand to try again. Her stomach knotted with nervous apprehension while she waited just a few feet behind him for whatever would happen next.

"I'm back," Lowell shouted, raising a hand to peer through the mesh into the darkness within. Still having received no verbal response, he then took it upon himself to open the door and step inside.

Callie, on the other hand, had not yet gathered the courage she needed to actually enter the house uninvited, and stood outside the open doorway, holding the mesh door back with her hand and peering inside. She was carefully debating her next move when she noticed someone coming down the wide stairway at the far end of the hall. Though she did not recognize the first man, her heart leaped into rapid motion when she saw Wade following only a few feet behind him. Suddenly aching with want to touch him, to be with him, she took a tiny step inside where she could get a better look at him. She ignored the angry glare of the other man.

Appalled by Wade's disheveled appearance, she fought the sudden urge to run to him, to throw her arms around him and try to comfort him somehow. Though she had expected to see the two days' growth of beard on his cheek and the rumpled appearance of the clothing he wore, she had not expected to see him look quite so worn, so completely haggard. Deeply carved, dark semicircles beneath his eyes let her know right away he had not slept. It pained her to see how very much he was suffering because of everything that had happened in the past couple of days, especially over Walter's unexpected collapse. Suddenly forgetting her earlier hesitation over entering the house uninvited, she hurried forward toward him.

Evan paused at the foot of the stairs to glare at her as if he planned to accuse her of something. But in the end, he chose to turn toward a door at the back of the house, and left without as much as speaking a word to anyone.

Callie chose to disregard the man's rudeness, having already guessed who he was by his obvious resemblance to Walter Barlow. She had already heard what a hothead Evan Samuels was known to be. By ignoring him, she hoped to avoid any more trouble with the Barlow family, at least for now. Instead of watching while Evan stalked out of the house or listening to the way his boots stomped across the veranda outside, she went straight into Wade's awaiting arms, glad to discover he did not plan to shut her out as so many men might in a similar situation.

"I was very sorry to hear about your father," she told him just before she closed her eyes and pressed her cheek against his chest. Though she did not particularly care for Walter Barlow as a man, and though she knew the truth about the man's relationship with Wade, she did not like the thought of anyone teetering so close to death—especially when that someone meant so very much to Wade. Whatever touched his heart touched hers, and at that moment it felt as if her heart was breaking. "Is he any better?"

Lowell had continued on past them, but paused on the stairway to listen for Wade's answer.

"No change," Wade said with a glum shake of his head, pressing her close, finding comfort in the simple act of holding her. "No change at all."

Lowell then resumed his climb up the stairs at a much more hurried pace while Wade and Callie slowly pulled apart, then followed. When they moved to climb the stairs together, Callie stayed close to his side, allowing his arm to weigh heavily on her shoulder while hers curved and rested lightly behind his back.

"Are you all right?" Callie asked once they had finally topped the stairs and started down the hallway toward the door through which Lowell had just disappeared from their sight.

"I'm fine," Wade assured her, but in a voice so tired, it did not sound at all convincing.

"Is there anything I can do?" How she hoped that there would be. How dearly she wanted to do something to help ease the obvious pain he suffered. Her heart twisted painfully at the sight of the dark misery on his face. At that moment, she would give practically anything to see another of his heart-stopping smiles.

"There's nothing anyone can do at this point," Wade answered sadly, repeating what Lowell had told him earlier.

At the moment, Wade's expression looked like that of a small child, a small forlorn child who did not know where to turn for help, or even if he should. Callie dearly wished he

346

would turn to her. But he did not. Though his arm tightened around her shoulders, he continued to hold his emotions just out of her reach.

When Callie and Wade then entered the bedroom, they found Lowell already bent over Walter's prone figure, first checking his pulse, then lifting the pale eyelids back one at a time to peer at his pupils.

"Is there any improvement?" Wade asked as soon as he and Callie had come to stand beside him. Carefully, he watched each movement the doctor made and studied his different reactions, hoping to discover the man's thoughts. "Is he any better at all?"

Lowell did not answer right away. Then his face drew into an expression that caused Callie's heart to thump hard because she was not sure if it was a look of mere professional concern or something closer to open fear. Again she felt Wade's arm tighten around her shoulders.

"I'm not positive, but I think his heartbeat is a little stronger," Lowell said, though still frowning while he leaned forward to press his ear directly against Walter's chest for a moment. His eyes widened and a glimmer of hope entered his otherwise tired expression. Quickly he reached for the cloth which still lay on the table next to the tall porcelain pitcher and dipped it into the water. Then, as soon as he had squeezed out the excess, he bent over again and bathed Walter's neck and brow. "Walter? Walter Barlow? This is Dr. Edison. Can you hear me?"

The room went deathly silent while everyone waited for any sort of response. But there was none. Lowell tried again. "It's Dr. Edison. Can you hear me?"

Again there was no response, and Lowell's hopeful expression fell. Reaching for his medical bag, he muttered, "I think it's been long enough now that I can give him another injection."

Callie and Wade stepped back and watched while Lowell hurried to do just that. They waited again for a show of response. There was none.

Slumping his shoulders, Wade turned away, leaving Callie

alone, aching to touch him again. Resuming a stance at the window that was now becoming very familiar, he refused to watch any longer.

After Lowell tried a few more times to get Walter to respond to his voice, he put the wet cloth aside and joined Wade at the window.

"You know I hate to leave again this soon, but McKenzie's starting to run a fever and talk out of his head. I really need to get back there right away. But I'll try not to stay gone too long."

"I understand," Wade assured him, though he never took his gaze from the distant pastures to actually look at the doctor. "You do what you have to do." The muscles along the side of his face jumped reflexively beneath his unshaven cheek while he fought to stay in control of his emotions.

"I'm very sorry, and I wouldn't go if I didn't feel I had to. I'll be back in a couple of hours," Lowell promised before he turned to put his things back into his medical bag. "Do what you can to keep him comfortable until then. Even though he's still partially dressed, make sure you keep him well covered with that sheet. We don't want to risk his catching a chill while his condition is this weak." He glanced again at Wade, only to find his back still to the room. He looked then at Callie and shook his head sadly.

Wade waited until Lowell was nearly ready to leave the room before asking what was obviously foremost on his mind. "What do you think, Doc? Is there any real hope left?"

Though he listened carefully for an answer, Wade never bothered to turn away from the window. He looked so vulnerable, standing there with his shoulders drawn, but his strong chin held so high that Callie's heart went immediately out to him. It was agonizing to watch him suffer so quietly like that.

"As long as there is life, Wade, there is hope," Lowell told him, but when Callie's gaze moved to lock with his and he was aware Wade could not see him, he shook his head sadly, to warn her that although there might still be a shred of hope

348

to hang on to, it was highly unlikely Walter would survive. Callie closed her eyes against the resulting stab of pain. She knew Walter's death was going to hurt Wade deeply.

"I'll try to remember that. Thank you," Wade answered, still not turning away from the window. "And thank you, Callie, for coming. I appreciate your concern and I hope you understand why I won't be able to return to work just yet. I can't leave him like this. I have to be here in case he does wake up, I've got some things I feel I must say to him. There's just so much I still want to tell him. Things that should have been said a long time ago."

"I understand. And I'm not leaving just yet," Callie told him quickly, then moved to put her arms around him again. Pressing her cheek against his back, she tried to keep back her tears. She wanted to be strong for Wade's sake, but it crushed her to see him hurting like that. It made her feel so helpless. Desperately she tried to force the emotional waver out of her voice, but did not fully succeed. "If it is all right with you, I'd like to stay for a little while."

Though Wade did not turn around or answer her, he reached up to place his hand warmly over where hers rested just below his collarbone. He did not speak again for several minutes, and his slow, ragged draws for breath explained why. Only after he had watched Lowell ride off in the direction of the Circle T yet again did he move away from the window. Though Callie wanted to hold on to him a moment longer, she allowed him to gently pull away from her.

"He's dying," he stated simply when he walked back over to the bed and looked down. "He's dying and I may never get the chance to clear things between us." Then as if he'd forgotten she was there, he sank slowly into his chair again and stared sadly at his father, bewildered by what he should do next.

Callie stayed with him for a while longer, although she did not try to break into his lost thoughts in any way. It was enough to simply be with him.

Taking the chair directly across the bed from where he sat

349

staring forlornly at his father, she watched Wade with a trembling heart. His only movement was to occasionally blink or swallow. There was no noticeable eye movement, no body movement. It was as if he had entered into a world of his own, and she allowed him to be in that world without any disturbance from her.

"I'll come back this afternoon," she said softly when the time finally came she should go. Over an hour had passed since her arrival, and Wade had remained silent for most of that time. Slowly she stood to leave. "I wish you'd try to get a little rest before then. Surely there's someplace around here where you can lie down and get some sleep."

Wade's eyes lifted to hers, but he still did not speak. It was then she saw the thick sheen of tears in his eyes. Trembling inside, she walked over, knelt, and pressed a gentle kiss to his temple. Though she really wanted to stay with him, she knew he needed to be alone. He needed to be able to release some of his sorrow and much of the deep frustration he felt, and she knew he would not feel comfortable doing such with her still in the room. It was just the way men were. Women sought comfort in times of distress, but men did not.

"I will be back," she promised again just before she softly walked out of the room, aware his gaze had returned to his father even before she was fully through the door.

When Callie did return late that afternoon, she brought with her a large stoneware jar of the thick, beefy stew Lucille had made for supper. Though she knew Lowell had visited the Rocking W twice more that afternoon, and planned to return as soon as he dared break away from McKenzie yet again, she decided not to wait for her personal escort as she had before.

Worried that Wade was not eating, after having missed so many meals already, and afraid Evan would not offer him a decent meal even if he did have appetite enough to eat, she chose not to wait for Lowell at all. She went on alone shortly before dark, determined to see that he ate. But because she did have the food basket and a fresh change of clothing for him, she decided to take the buggy instead of riding over on horseback like she had before.

When she approached the front door again, this time with the basket hooked over one arm and Wade's clothing tucked under the other, she felt another cold twinge of apprehension, and as she topped the steps and found the door securely closed, she realized why.

Though this time there had been fewer men outside watching her when she drove into the yard, she did not have Lowell with her to help her actually get inside. She worried that Evan or someone equally as hostile would answer the door and refuse to let her enter. The way Wade had been when she left, she knew he might not have even heard her arrival; and if he hadn't, he would be totally unaware she had returned. When she then raised her hand and knocked, she prayed she would not be turned away before she was allowed to see Wade.

To her relief, the small woman who came to the door was pleasant. Though she did not speak English very well, Callie had learned enough Spanish from Manuel to get the idea across to her that she was there to see Señor Wade. It was not until she was inside, headed for the stairway with the woman several feet behind her, that Callie met any real resistance to her presence there.

"What are you doing back here?" Evan asked when he marched out of a nearby room to confront her. It was clear by his tone, he was not at all pleased to find her in his father's house again.

"I'm here to see Wade. I've brought him something to eat," she told him, arching her shoulders enough to let him know she meant business. It irritated her to notice how well groomed and completely rested Evan appeared when Wade had looked so bedraggled and fatigued the last time she saw him. Obviously Evan had slept, but had not bothered to offer Wade the hospitality of a bedroom.

"He's eaten," Evan informed her, his manner very cocky while he tilted his head to one side and stared at her as if she fully repulsed him. He crossed his arms angrily and flared his nostrils enough that Callie noticed. "Carlotta took him some soup just a little while ago." He then looked at the small woman who had answered the door and had been on her way into another room until she had heard her name mentioned. She turned to look at him expectantly.

"Good, I was afraid he hadn't eaten," Callie responded, feeling awkward at the hateful way Evan looked first at Carlotta, then at her. Never had she seen such open hostility before. "How is your father? Is he any better?"

"What do you care?" Evan asked with a derisive snort, then shifted his weight to one leg.

Rather than respond to a remark clearly meant to start an argument, Callie began to move away from him, toward the stairs. She breathed a startled gasp when he reached out and grabbed her by her arm, just beneath the short puffed sleeves of the blue cotton dress she wore. Once he had secured his grip, he jerked her to a sharp halt. "I don't recall having given you permission to go up there."

"Well, if I must have your personal permission in order to see Wade, then I ask that you please give it to me." It took all the restraint she had not to sink her teeth into the stubby hand that squeezed hard into her flesh. Though hearing him cry out with pain would please her no end, she knew she would gain nothing by such a show of rebellion. Still, she continued to glower at him with all the fury that raged inside of her.

Evan hesitated. He glanced at her angry expression, then at the ceiling overhead, before finally agreeing. "All right, you can go up there. But don't stay long. Do you hear me?"

"I'll stay long enough to check on Wade," she assured him, then glared pointedly at where his hand still gripped her tender flesh painfully. "Then I will leave."

Reluctantly, Evan released his hold on her. His lips tightened against his teeth. "Just see that you do."

Callie hurried on upstairs, not only eager to get away from Evan Samuel's penetrating gaze, but just as eager to see Wade again. When she entered Walter's bedroom moments later, she found him still seated in the chair beside the bed, slumped forward and staring morosely down at his father's motionless form. On the table beside him she noticed a small bowl of soup, still full. Beside it lay a saucer with a large piece of bread. Though Carlotta had indeed brought him something to eat, he had not bothered with it. The spoon still lay on the folded napkin beside the bowl.

"Wade?" she said, and quietly moved closer. Tremors filled her heart. How dearly she loved this man. "Wade, are you all right?"

As if startled by her presence, he jerked his head around to stare at her. He blinked in an effort to bring his dismal thoughts back to the present. "Callie, what are you doing here again so soon?"

Motioning to the basket on her arm with a slight sideward nod of her head, she smiled. "I've brought you supper. And a change of clothes."

"Supper?" he asked, then glanced at the clock over the mantle across the room. Because the bedroom was filled with dark evening shadows, he was unable to see the actual time. "It was nice of you to think about me like that, but I'm not really hungry." His gaze quickly returned to his father. "I'll eat later."

Callie was not sure if it was a good idea to force him to eat at such a time, but she worried for his health. She had not thought it possible he could look any worse than he had that morning, but he did. The curving shadows beneath his eyes were darker, more profound, making his sun-browned skin look oddly pale in comparison. "No, Wade Barlow, you will eat right now. While I watch. That way, I'll know you have eaten and won't have to worry as much about you." She tensed while she waited to see if he intended to argue with her.

Wade smiled, looking at her once more. His expression was tired but grateful when he nodded. "All right, I'll eat."

Relieved, Callie quickly went about pouring a large portion of the still-warm stew into the bowl Lucille had packed, then handed it to him before he changed his mind. Because it had already begun to turn dark outside, which cloaked the room with deep, depressing shadows, she took the time to light the small lamp which stood on the bedside table before searching for a place to sit. The chair she had sat in earlier had been moved back away from the bed.

Hoping to take his mind off of whatever dreary thoughts had plagued him only moments earlier, she pulled the chair across the room until it rested next to his and began to speak of whatever cheerful things she could think of while he prepared to eat.

"You'll be pleased to know that Amy has taken it upon herself to be Ed's personal nursemaid and that he is doing much better," she told him, smiling with satisfaction when she watched him dip his spoon into the thick stew and raise a hearty amount to his mouth.

She waited until she had actually seen him swallow before going on. "And you'll never guess who came by to see about Ed yesterday afternoon. Nadine Leigh. Seems she found out about his injury and was unable to stay away. I think there's a budding romance there." She grinned. "A romance between Nadine and Ed. Who would have ever guessed?"

It pleased her to see an interested raise of his brow. "And now that Ed's feeling a little better, he's decided to see to it everyone keeps working while you are gone. And even though he doesn't take a watch himself, because he doesn't like to be very far away from McKenzie for too long at a time, he does see to it there are men guarding the cattle at all times. So you don't have to worry about anything like that. He's taking very good of care of things at the Circle T. And your foreman, Rebel Johnson, said to tell you he also has things under control at your place." She tried not to let it show in her expression how, in all honesty, she no longer believed the cattle were still in any real danger.

"Glad to hear it," he told her after he swallowed a second large bite. He then glanced down at his father, who looked so deathly pale in the small island of light cast by the one lamp, and asked, "Did the sheriff ever come back by?"

"Yes, but he didn't have any more information than he did the last time you spoke to him." And at this point, she was not too sure she wanted the man to find out anything

354

more. With Walter lying on his deathbed, she really saw no point in proving his guilt—because once he was dead, the terrorizing incidents would stop and they could finally get on with their lives. And even if he lived, she felt certain Wade would be able to convince him to leave her alone. She had a feeling that was why Wade had come to see his father in the first place—he had finally had enough and had decided to confront his father face to face.

"How is McKenzie?" Wade went on to ask, breaking into her thoughts just before he looked back at the bowl in his hands and took yet another large bite. Though he had not expected it, he found he did still have an appetite, and realized it felt good to have food in his stomach again.

"Better, I think. At least his fever is down and he's not talking out of his head as much anymore."

"That's good," Wade commented. Then he asked, "What exactly does he say when he talks out of his head?"

Callie smiled sadly, knowing if McKenzie died, he would easily be forgiven for his rantings; but if he lived, he would be ribbed mercilessly for some of the things he had said while under the influence of his fever. "He cusses at Ed mostly. Evidently, he knows Ed was shot and is angry with him for allowing such a foolish thing to happen, as if Ed had had any choice in the matter. I guess he doesn't consider himself even more a fool for having rushed out into the open and gotten himself shot four times, which is far worse than hiding in the bushes and getting shot once."

Wade paused to think about that.

Callie was glad to see his thoughts on something other than his father's predicament, and hurried to tell him more. "McKenzie also claims that as soon as he can get all those chickens to stay off of his chest, he's going to go after the men that shot them. Singlehanded if he has to."

"Chickens?" Wade's brows rose with interest.

Grinning, Callie shrugged and nodded. But before she was able to tell him any more of the ridiculous things McKenzie had said while in his feverish stupor, she noticed a strange movement. It had come from the direction of the bed. Her expression became one of hopeful disbelief. Walter's hand had flexed. She was certain of it.

Wade had noticed the movement too, and quickly set his bowl aside. A mixture of breathless expectation and his own strong fear to believe drew his face into a mask of uncertainty.

"Pop?" he called out, his eyes trained on the hand, watching carefully for more movement. "Pop, can you hear me?"

Callie's heart refused to beat while she too waited for the hand to move again. It did. Ever so slightly. Her breath caught in her throat.

Eagerly, Wade called out to him again. "Pop, can you hear me?"

The man's lips moved, but no sound came forth. Anxiously, Wade stood and leaned over him, bracing himself against the bed with one hand and feeling his father's cheek with his other. Walter's eyelids twitched slightly in response.

"Pop? Are you awake?"

Again Walter's lips moved, but this time there was a deep, gurgling sound. Finally, his eyes came open. At first, he stared at the ceiling, then slowly, he brought his gaze down to focus on Wade's face.

"Son?" he finally said, then attempted to smile. The action had been such an effort, only part of his face lifted.

"Pop! You had us so scared!" Wade said, blinking back the moisture which had suddenly collected in his eyes. "How do you feel?"

Walter lay perfectly still for a moment, as if trying to assess his own health, then tried to smile again. With a mouth that seemed not to want to cooperate, he answered, "I feel like hell."

Wade smiled. "That's understandable. You look like hell."

Walter tried to chuckle, but the sound came out a deep, throaty gurgle.

Callie watched Wade take several deep breaths, as if trying to keep control over a sudden burst of emotions before they managed to get away from him. The tear that trickled shamelessly down his face touched her deeply.

"Wade?" Walter's voice was a little stronger now, which gave Callie a stronger sense of hope.

"What is it, Pop?"

"Wade, I'm sorry. I'm very sorry. I never should have done it. Any of it. Never." He lifted a trembling hand toward Wade's face, but it fell back to the bed before he could actually touch him. He closed his eyes with frustration upon discovering he did not have the strength.

Thinking his father meant he was sorry for what all he had done to Callie, Wade turned to where he could see both his father and Callie before he answered with a reassuring smile. "Father, please, let's not talk about any of that now." Lifting the fallen hand, he gently pressed it to his cheek. His voice trembled when Walter then looked up at him gratefully. Suddenly, he understood how very important their touching must have been to him. "Pop, we can talk about all that later."

"No, I have to. I have to talk about it. Now. I may not get another chance." Walter Barlow clearly understood the seriousness of his condition.

Wade's smile gave way to a look of pure horror. "Don't talk like that," he insisted. "You'll have plenty of other chances to talk about it."

Tears filled the old man's eyes, and his entire body began to shake uncontrollably as if he had suddenly become afflicted with palsy. "Wade. I'm so sorry."

With her own tears blinding her, Callie stood to leave the room. This was a conversation that should be held in private.

"Who's there?" Walter asked suddenly, blinking profusely and staring in her direction.

Aware she was in the shadows, where he was unable to easily see her, she took a deep breath and spoke out loud enough so he could clearly hear her voice. "It's me, Mr. Barlow. Callie Tucker. I came by to see how you were doing. You've had us all pretty worried."

357

"Widow Tucker?" he asked, as if not quite believing she was there. Then slowly he began to rock his head from side to side, his voice full of misery. "Worried about me? Child, I don't deserve your concern. I don't deserve anyone's concern."

"I'm sorry, sir, but I just don't see it that way," she told him. She pressed her eyes shut long enough to clear her vision, only to find the discarded tears quickly replaced with more.

"No, I'm the one who is sorry," Walter responded, jerking his hand away from Wade as if he suddenly felt he didn't deserve to be touched. He turned his face away from them and stared off into the shadows of the room. "Wade, I want you to believe that I never meant for anyone to die."

"No one has died, Pop. McKenzie is still alive," Wade assured him before he reached out and took his father's trembling hand into his once again.

But as if he had not heard any of what Wade had just told him, Walter continued. "Please, believe me. If I had known she would kill herself, I never would have done it. Never."

Wade's expression hardened as his eyes rose to meet Callie's startled gaze.

Walter's face twisted with remembered pain. "Please, son, you have to believe me. I had no idea she would kill herself. None."

Chapter Twenty-two

Immediately Wade realized his father had spoken of Matthew Tucker's first wife, and was at first too stunned to speak. Slowly he pulled his gaze away from Callie, who was clearly as startled as he was, to look back at his father's troubled expression. His stomach knotted with unbearable apprehension. His father *had* had something to do with Beth Tucker's death. But what? So little was known about why Beth Tucker had committed suicide. What did it have to do with his father?

Certain he did not want Callie to have to hear any of what his father was about to say, he spoke quickly to stop him before it was too late. "Father, not now. We can discuss this later."

But the man was determined to make his confession. Seemingly oblivious to the harm it might do, he continued. "No, Wade. Let me speak. I've got to explain. I've got to make you understand why I did what I did. You have to know what I was going through. Your mother was in love with Matthew Tucker. She always had been." His face revealed the strength of the agony that gripped him while he continued to stare off into darkness. "Can you imagine what it was like finding that out?"

"Pop, don't," Wade said, then reached out to still the man's lips with a light touch of his fingers; but the action went unheeded.

"I guess she must have loved him long before she ever

359

married me. What I can't understand is why she even bothered to marry me, if she was so in love with him. Why would she do that?" He rolled his head to look at Wade again. His mouth appeared distorted with the confusion and pain that held him perfectly still while he waited for Wade to answer him.

"No, she didn't. Mother loved you," Wade stated adamantly, believing it with all his heart. Though he had been very young, he well remembered the affection his mother had always shown his father. That affection was real. The love was real. How could his father doubt it?

"Maybe she did love me a little. But she loved Matthew more." Tears again filled his eyes and his voice slurred slightly when he continued. "It's true. When she got the fever so bad — just before she died — she started to babble about certain things. It was then she revealed the truth to me."

"That she loved Matthew?" He still did not believe it.

"Not only that, but that you are Matthew's son and not mine."

That struck Wade like a blow to his stomach. The pain was clearly revealed in his stunned expression.

Walter searched that stunned expression sadly. "It's true. Her words were disjointed, and she was delirious with the fever, but it was clear enough that she wanted to confess her sins before she died. She wanted me to forgive her for her betrayal. Over and over, she kept asking for that forgiveness. And over and over she would call out Matthew's name. And your name. She loved you very much."

"And she told you I was Matthew's son?" Wade asked, horrified his father actually believed such a thing.

"She made that very clear. You are Matthew Tucker's son. Not mine. Can you imagine how that made me feel? How much it hurt to look at you and see so many of Matthew Tucker's traits? To see his eyes? His hair? His mouth?"

Wade's stomach knotted with realization. Suddenly, it started to make sense to him. Suddenly, he understood why his father had begun to turn away from him shortly after his mother's death. Why he had begun to find fault with everything he did. And especially why his father had become even more intent on hating Tucker and see to it the man suffered at every turn. Suddenly, all the missing pieces fell properly into place and all his father's actions began to make sense.

"Wade? Don't you see? Don't you see how I felt? I was overwhelmed by her shocking confession, I didn't know what to do. I wanted to get even. I had to get even. So, in a fit of bitter fury, I decided that the best way to get even with what Tucker had done to me through my wife was to do something equally as bad to him, through his wife. Through Beth."

A deep, restless shame shadowed Walter's eyes. "I wanted to see Tucker's happiness brought down in shambles, just like mine was. Though it took a lot of effort, I was able to lure Beth over here with the pretense of having grown tired of the feud between us. I told her I wanted to find a way to patch things up with her husband, how I was tired of fighting all the time. While she was here, I suggested a toast to a happier future, and saw to it that she drank a little too much. You know how women can be when they have had too much to drink. Especially a woman not used to drink. I was then able to lure her into this very bedroom, where I began to charm her into my bed."

Walter paused. His face grew more contorted with painful memories. "Though she was reluctant right from the start, I managed to seduce her out of her clothes, and it was not until I was ready to finish what I had started that she seemed to understand what was going on and showed any real resistance. But I was too far along with my ploy, too dedicated to getting back at Tucker. I forced her to finish what we had started. She screamed and tried to fight, but I took her anyway."

He pressed his eyes closed from the guilt he felt when he admitted the rest. "I raped her brutally. Then told her exactly why I had done it. I told her I had done it to get even with her husband for what he'd done to me."

Wade closed his eyes too, trying to shut out the images that had come forth, but found that impossible to do. Grimly, he listened to rest of the confession, wishing he didn't have to, yet, like Callie who stood mutely beside him, he was unable to do anything else.

"But Beth was not a strong woman. She could not live with the guilt she must have felt over what had happened, and killed herself that very same night. And because she wanted Matthew to know what she had done was because she loved him, she left him a letter expressing her feelings, her devotion to him, and told him she could not live after having allowed such a disgraceful thing to happen to her. Oddly, she didn't actually name me in the letter, so Matthew could never be sure I was the one who had raped her. How she must have loved him. It's not fair that he should have had two women so deeply devoted to him." He opened his eyes and looked toward Callie's dark form, still cloaked in gray shadows. "No, there were *three* women, weren't there? Three women so deeply devoted to him. Why is that?"

Callie knew he expected an answer from her, but her throat was too swollen with emotions to respond. Tears spilled down her cheeks.

Walter looked away, staring at the ceiling but seeing only the bleak images in his head. "Beth Tucker's death has haunted me ever since. Though I never felt any remorse for the pain Matthew had to endure because of it, I never forgave myself for being the one responsible for her death. The one responsible for taking the mother from those two little girls. Even though I had no earthly idea it would end like it did, I was clearly responsible."

His mouth quivered uncontrollably as huge tears rolled passed the deep curves of his temples and disappeared into his tousled hair. His expression became more strained, his voice more emotional, when he spoke again. "I loved my wife very much. I loved Eleanor with all my heart. She meant the world to me. But she made a mockery of my love, of our entire marriage, by being in love with Matthew all those years." His voice grew gradually weaker, his words disjointed. It was becoming extremely hard for him to speak, but there seemed to be so much he wanted to say. "She married me. But she loved Matthew. And you, son. You look so much like . . . him. I'm very sorry. I was a fool. I never should have treated you like I did. I should have held on to you. For as long as I could."

Callie felt all weak inside when she sank back down into her chair. Though she had intended to leave, she had not been able to, and now she understood why. She could not keep Matthew's secrets any longer. She had to tell Walter the truth. She could not let him die thinking his wife had not loved him when the woman had actually been very *deeply* devoted to him.

But did she have that right?

Suddenly, she knew why Matthew had gone to the trouble to write down all his terrible secrets, all the assorted details of his life, both good and bad. He had never truly intended to take those secrets to the grave with him. He had wanted someone to know. Deep down, he had wanted to make things right by leaving the information behind where it could all eventually come out.

"No, Mr. Barlow, you are wrong. You are so very wrong. You're wife loved you dearly," she said, her voice startling them both. It was as if they had somehow forgotten she was there.

Wade looked at her curiously, but Walter closed his eyes and moaned, "She loved him and not me. She died with his name on her lips."

"No, she did not love him. I don't know why she spoke his name, unless it was out of some misplaced feeling of guilt or maybe out of anger. Your wife never loved Matthew. But Matthew loved her. He fell in love with her long before you two were married. It crushed him when she chose you over him, but even so, he could not make himself stop loving her."

"Matthew told you this?" Wade asked, obviously finding it hard to believe the man would admit to such a thing.

Callie looked directly into Wade's eyes. "In a way, yes.

363

You see, Matthew kept a journal for most of his life. A special diary where he wrote down most of his innermost feelings. In this diary he expressed his love for your mother again and again. And even after she ended up choosing to marry your father instead of him, Matthew never gave up hope. Just so he could be near her, he bought the land that adjoined the ranch your father had purchased just before the wedding. Matthew was determined to remain a part of Eleanor's life, if by nothing else than being her neighbor."

Callie paused to take a deep breath, and realized how deathly silent the room had become. The only sounds heard were Walter's raspy breathing and the faint ticking of the clock from the direction of the fireplace. Running her tongue nervously over her lower lip, she glanced from Walter back to Wade, then continued. "About a year later, as I understand it, your father and your mother had a terrible argument in which your father had said some terrible things to your mother."

"A grave mistake," Walter muttered, rocking his head back and forth from the memory of it.

"Yes, it was," Callie agreed, looking at him with a sudden feeling of compassion. The poor man had lived for years believing the worst of lies. "It was a very grave mistake. Just because she asked you to stop drinking as much, for your own good, you became very angry. You then told her you were leaving her to find a woman who could really love you and would accept you the way you were. That must have hurt very deeply." Callie knew if she'd had to hear such words from Wade, it would be devastating.

Walter pressed his eyes shut and his entire body began to tremble again, but he listened for her to finish. So did Wade.

"As I understand it, you told her you wanted a divorce so you could find someone who would not try to make you into something you were not. That crushed Eleanor, and right after you left — maybe even partly because the argument had been about your heavy drinking — she decided to open one of your whiskey bottles and drink herself into oblivion. It was while she was so very inebriated and so emotionally weakened that Matthew happened by. In his diary, he claimed that he had started out just wanting to comfort her, but once he had her in his arms, he couldn't stop himself He took advantage of her drunken misery and just before she passed out, he made love to her—even though it was your name she called out again and again. And it was only the one time."

Walter's eyes slowly opened. Tears continued to run in steady streams down the sides of his face, soaking his hair and his pillow. Still he listened.

Callie leaned forward to touch his wrist lightly. "When she woke up the next morning and found herself still in Matthew's arms, she realized what she had allowed to happen. She told him to get out and never to come near her again. And she meant it. He tried to see her again, but she wouldn't let him. Three weeks later, you came back and the two of you patched things up. A few months later, she began to show her first signs of pregnancy."

Callie fought to keep back her own tears. "Matthew suspected from the beginning, but when he finally confronted Eleanor, she denied the child was his. Even when Wade started growing up to look so much like him, especially in his eyes and hair, she continued to deny he was the father. Matthew was forced to watch his son grow up from a distance. He secretly wished that one day he would find the opportunity and the courage to tell Wade the truth, but could not bring himself to do that to Eleanor. If she had wanted Wade to know, he knew she would have told him herself. But she never did."

She glanced again from Walter to Wade. Her heart went out to Wade, whose horrified expression revealed his pain and confusion. How she wished he could have learned of his parentage in some other manner. Sadly, she looked back at Walter, who lay waiting for her to continue, which she did. "Matthew lived with a secret longing that one day Wade would find out the truth and come to him. He hoped Wade would eventually take over the Circle T—running it proudly as his son. He explained in his writings how he had nothing

365

but admiration for his son, yet lived with the agony of seeing only apathy in the young man's eyes — eyes so very much like his own."

"He suffered?" Walter wanted to know. "He suffered because she would not admit the truth to him?"

"Yes, he suffered greatly. Don't you see? Eleanor did love you. She loved you so dearly, she was willing to keep Matthew's son from him all those years. It was because she loved you as much as she did that she wanted you to be the boy's father, to raise him as your own. If she had truly loved Matthew in any way, she would have at least admitted to him that he was the father so he could know for sure."

She paused long enough to give him time to think about that before telling the rest. "Matthew suffered for the rest of his life. Every time he saw Wade from a distance, he suffered. Every time he saw the hatred in Eleanor's eyes, he suffered. It was because he knew he had destroyed any chance of ever having Eleanor's love — though he continued to hope for it and dream about it — that he felt driven to turn his energies toward becoming a successful rancher, and so obviously rich. He wanted Eleanor to rue the day she ever chose you over him. His only drive in life became making Circle T the biggest and the most prosperous ranch in all of Northeast Texas. It was not until he met Beth that he found any of what was missing from his life. She filled some of the void that not having Eleanor had left him with. Though he still coveted and lusted after Eleanor, he did truly come to love Beth for the good and caring woman that she was. Her death did indeed hurt him deeply."

Walter trembled harder still. His tears began to come so rapidly, he could no longer blink them away quickly enough to clear his vision. His left hand curled into a tight fist while his right hand twitched randomly at his side. "That is the truth, isn't it? Oh, my God, that *is* the truth. Eleanor never really betrayed me. Never in her heart. And that's what had hurt the most. Thinking she had betrayed me. I had no real reason. No reason to do what I did to Beth Tucker. I feel so guilty. I can't bear it. God, I'm so sorry for what I did. If only I had known. If only. The truth. If only."

"Mr. Barlow, I also want you to know that Matthew was basically a good man with a kind and loving heart. He made a terrible mistake, that's true, but he suffered dearly for that mistake," she quickly added as much for Wade's sake as Walter's. "And he was a noble man. Even though he knew he was dying, he did not attempt to tell Wade of his true parentage, though he left the information at hand should it ever be needed. It's sad really. Matthew had a son he could never claim, not and still feel good about having done so. In the end, all he really had to live for were his two daughters. They were the reason he advertised for a wife. He wanted to be sure someone would take care of those daughters after he was gone. I'm deeply grateful I was the chosen one. He gave me so much more than I had ever hoped to have. And not only was he generous to me with money, he offered me something I had not had since my grandparents died nearly six years ago — he offered me kindness. He took me out of an almost slavelike existence and treated me like royalty. In a way, he handed me back my self-respect and put the fire of life back into my soul. I'll be forever grateful to him for that."

Wade studied her with a solemn expression. "You never told me any of that."

"You never really asked. Besides, my past is not something I really like to talk about."

Walter interrupted them, his voice noticeably weaker. Desperately, he fought for the breath he needed to continue. "I was wrong. I thought she loved Matthew. I really thought. So wrong. So sorry. And Wade. I-I. Pushed him away. Such a fool. Sorry. Ver-y sor-ry. Forgive. Me." He then turned to look at Wade, his face a display of true agony. Suddenly his body tensed so hard it brought his head up off the pillow. He cried out against the pain which had seized him, then only a second later he fell limp. The hand curled into a fist at his side slowly opened.

Wade's eyes grew wide with concern as he brushed Callie's arm aside and bent directly over his father. Gently, he reached out and shook his father's shoulders in an effort to wake him. "Pop? Are you all right?"

Waves of panic filled him when he bent closer still. "Pop, don't die yet. Don't die until I've had a chance to tell you how much I love you. How much I have always loved you. It doesn't matter that I came from someone else. You are the man who raised me. You are my real father. Please don't die. Give me the chance to explain how I feel. There's a lot we need to talk about. So much that still needs to be said."

Callie circled to the opposite side of the bed and felt for a pulse first in his wrist, then at his throat. There was none. Though his body felt warm to the touch and tears still dampened his pale cheeks, Walter Barlow was dead.

"Wade," she said softly, wanting to say something to console him but unable to think of the right words. Instead she reached out and placed her hand gently on his shoulder.

Unable to bear the sudden onslaught of pain in his near-exhausted state, Wade began to weep uncontrollably for the loss of his father. He wept at the realization he had lost all chance to tell the man how very much he loved him, how all he had ever wanted was to somehow regain not only his love but also his respect. He wept for the realization that his father had turned against him, had begun to find nothing but fault in him, because of who his father was. Not because of who *he* was or anything he had done. Had that been revealed to him sooner, had the secret been made known, he could have done something to patch up their differences. All that he wanted to say now could have already been said.

For a brief moment, he blamed Callie for the pain he now felt. She had known the truth and had kept it from him. If only she had told him. If only he had known. Angrily he jerked her hand away from his shoulder and glared up at her. Valiantly, he fought to regain control of his grief, not wanting her to witness any more of it.

"Wade, what's wrong?" Callie asked, her words so strained they did not sound like they had come from her mouth. Suddenly, the fear that clutched at her heart was so strong, so painful, she wasn't sure she could bear it.

368

"You knew. You knew everything, but you didn't tell me." His face hardened with the fury that had quickly consumed him.

Callie's eyes grew wide, clearly revealing the painful apprehension slowly twisting its way inside of her. "I didn't know how to tell you. I wasn't even sure it was my place to say anything. Please, try to understand. Please, don't be angry with me. I love you."

Then just as suddenly as his anger had struck him, it melted. Knowing how foolish it had been to blame Callie for any of the problems between him and his father, he curled his hands into tight fists and tried to control their sudden tremors — but found himself unable to.

His voice was barely above a whisper when he finally responded, "I know."

Weakened from an onslaught of emotions so great he could keep hold of them no longer, he gave up the inner battle and bent over his father's now-lifeless body, again sobbing openly.

All Callie could do was weep with him. Share his sorrow. Hope to eventually help him get over the pain and the frustration he now felt. Hope to somehow help him overcome the tragedy of having lost his father before they were able to make things completely right between them. If only Walter had lived a few minutes more. If only Wade could have had the chance to relieve his heart of so many of its burdens.

Several moments passed before Wade was finally able to gain control over his emotions again. Eventually, he was able to stand, and once he had, he walked calmly to the window. His voice sounded strange — worn beyond physical endurance — when he spoke again. "Callie, I hope you will understand, but I really need to be alone for a while. I need time to think through some of the things I just learned. I need time to come to terms with all of it."

"Of course. And I do I understand," she told him. Not only had everything been a shock to him, he probably felt awkward from having wept in front of her the way he did.

369

Men considered tears such an obvious sign of weakness. "I'll come back tomorrow."

Quickly, she moved toward the door; but just before she reached out to grasp the knob, she heard him call out her name again.

"Yes?" before she responded, pausing after she had opened the door but she actually had passed through.

"I guess you should tell Lowell, there's no need for him to hurry back over here now. Tell him he needs to devote all his time toward saving McKenzie. There's nothing more he can do here." Wade's shoulders looked weighted down and his expression revealed the depth of his misery when he turned to look at her. "And I guess you'd better ask Carlotta to try to find Evan and tell him to come up here. Don't tell her why. I think it would be better if I told him."

"I will tell her, on my way out," she assured him. But because she wanted to give Wade more time to get better control over his emotions before having to face Evan with their father's death, she waited five minutes out in the hallway before actually going downstairs to search for the housekeeper.

Wade was glad it took as long as it did for Evan to come to his father's room. The extra time gave him a moment to prepare for the altercation he knew was only minutes away. Now that Walter was dead, there was no longer any reason for the two to restrain the ill feelings that had been slowly mounting between them. No amount of shouting or accusations would disturb their father now.

Struggling to keep his tears in check and the pain in his heart at a minimum, he remained at the window, looking out on the land which was so familiar to him, yet not really seeing any of it. Reluctantly, he waited for the sound of Evan's boots in the hallway outside the room. When he finally heard them, only seconds after Callie's buggy had pulled away, he turned to face the doorway, prepared for the worst.

370

"What's wrong. Why did you send for me?" Evan wanted to know as he stormed into the room. But when his gaze fell on his father's pale, lifeless form, he knew. With a look of pure hatred, he turned to Wade and virtually trembled with rage while he flung his accusations. "You did that to him. You killed him. Just as sure as you took a gun to his head, you killed him."

Wade shook off the pain Evan's words had caused and responded in a low, rational voice. "I did not know he was ill. No one ever told me he was having heart troubles. Had I known, had anyone thought to tell me, I would have approached him differently."

"About what?" Evan demanded to know. "Just what was so important? Exactly what was it you had to talk to him about?"

"That no longer matters," Wade answered, truthfully. Now that his father was dead, it no longer mattered what his transgressions had been. He would atone for them to a far greater power than any on this earth. It would serve no purpose to reveal his father's sins. Why try to destroy everyone's opinion of a man already dead?

"It matters to me," Evan responded angrily. Moving to stand directly in front of Wade, he crossed his arms defiantly. His lips puckered into a tight, fine line to reveal the depth of the hatred he felt. "Just what was it you said to him that caused his collapse. What was it you felt was so damned important you had to speak with him alone?"

"I told you, it no longer matters," Wade repeated firmly. "What matters now is that we make arrangements for his burial. We need to have a coffin made. We also need to notify the sheriff. We also need to let his friends know."

"I'll see to all that. You've done quite enough already!" Evan's fury was so great, he continued to shake visibly. Tiny white bubbles began to form at the corners of his mouth, and his eyes narrowed menacingly when he shouted, "I want you to get the hell out of this house."

"Not yet. Not until after he's been buried next to my mother," Wade stated adamantly. "I'm staying here until after the funeral."

"*Your* mother. And why shouldn't he be buried in town next to *my* mother?"

Although he knew it was only going to enrage him more, Wade answered calmly, "Because he was married to my mother. He never even bothered to marry your mother, not even after my mother's death."

"That doesn't mean he loved her any less," Evan declared, his shoulders trembling with yet more rage. "He loved her enough to create me, didn't he?"

Wade thought about that and now understood, mainly because Evan's birthday was little more than a week behind his own, that Evan had been the direct result of that argument between his father and his mother. His father had left looking for someone to prove his manhood with, and obviously thought he had found just that in Evan's mother. "I don't think love had anything to do with it."

"Get out!" Evan continued to shake violently, his rage out of control, while he jabbed his finger in the direction of the door. "Get the hell out!"

"No. I'm staying until I've seen to it my father is buried in the family cemetery next to my mother." Wade's own anger had started to edge its way into his voice, though he tried his best to control it. With eyes that gleamed with pure determination, he continued, "And there's nothing you can do to stop me."

"We'll just see about that," Evan said, then spun on his heel and marched out of the room.

Torn between staying at his father's side and chasing after Evan to make sure he did not cause any more trouble, Wade stood in the middle of the room, running his thumb over the jutting edge of his pistol handle. In the two days he'd been in that room, he'd not once bothered to take his gunbelt off. He realized now it had been an act of self-preservation. He had kept the gun on because, deep down, he had understood what a true danger Evan presented.

Stalking immediately out of the room, he went downstairs to his father's study to search for the will. Although he knew none of his father's belongings had been left to him, he felt certain he would find something to verify the fact his father had wanted to be buried on the Rocking W. Even if his father had held doubts about his mother's love, he was certain he still would want to be buried on his own land.

When he arrived downstairs, he discovered Evan already seated behind the huge oak desk rifling through the drawers one after another, scattering papers everywhere, obviously in search of the same thing Wade hoped to find.

"We'll just see how long you stay after I've found Father's will," Evan muttered, glancing up only long enough to be sure it was Wade who had entered the room. "Once it's made clear he left me in authority, left me everything he owned, I can legally order you off this place. Then if you try to come back, for *any* reason, I can have you arrested for trespassing. Try again and I can have you shot."

"You would deny me the right to be at my own father's funeral?" he asked, knowing Evan had no idea of his true parentage. He knew that if Evan ever became aware Matthew was really his father, he would find a way to use that against him too.

"Unless I decide to have the funeral in town—in which case I can't possibly keep you away—yes, I will deny you that right. And I can do it too. Just as soon as I've found that will," Evan told him.

Wade's anger became so intense, he came very close to bounding across the room and jerking his half-brother out of that chair in order to squeeze the very life out of him. It took all the self-restraint he had to stay where he was. "Have me arrested then, because I'm coming to his funeral, whether you have ordered me off this place or not."

"We'll see," Evan said, never pausing in his frantic search. "We'll see how big you talk once I've found that will and it states how I'm to have full authority around here."

Wade stood paralyzed with indecision. Although he wanted the will to be found and any burial requests honored, he knew Evan spoke the truth. Once the will was read and declared legal and binding, Evan would have the au-

373

thority to put him off his father's land. Even if he could find a way to have the legal declaration delayed until after the funeral, he would still be barred from ever visiting his parents' graves again. That realization drove through him like a knife and made him wish more than ever he could destroy Evan. He had to take a step back in order to keep from following through on the sudden impulse.

When Evan's frantic search of Walter's study brought forth no will, he began to grow panicky with his bewilderment. Wade had stayed in the room, near the doorway, but had not helped with the search, and did not follow when Evan bounded out of the room and back up the stairs to resume his search in Walter's bedroom.

Wade could hear things crashing to the floor overhead, and knew Evan was tearing the room apart in his efforts to locate the will. Meanwhile he calmly began to take the books off his father's shelves one at a time and leaf through them, remembering how his father used to hide what he called his emergency money between the pages of particular books. It stood to reason, he might have done the same with his will.

Hoping to find the will first and be assured there were indeed burial requests, he quickly and systematically went through every book in the room. When the search resulted with the discovery of only a small amount of cash and several photographs he had not known existed, he sat down to try to think where else his father might have placed the will for safekeeping. That's when he realized his father's lawyer would have a copy.

A few hours later, when Lowell came by to make sure Wade was all right and to offer his sympathy to both sons, Wade took him aside to speak with him privately. Aware Lowell would not be returning to town himself, with McKenzie still so ill, he asked the doctor to have Callie send one of her men by the lawyer's office the following morning to request he bring his copy of the will out to them as soon as he possibly could. Lowell assured him he would pass along his request, and left shortly thereafter.

Evan did not give up his frantic search until almost dawn, when the fact that the lawyer would have a copy finally occurred to him too, and he announced to Wade his intentions of having the lawyer's copy of the will brought out immediately. He was startled to learn Wade had already made arrangements for the lawyer to do just that.

"Well, don't think that changes anything," Evan retorted. "Just because you have decided to be cooperative isn't going to change one damned thing. The moment that will is read and that lawyer verifies how it is legal and binding, you are going to be ordered out of here. In fact, if I wasn't so eager to see your face when that will is finally read, I'd see you out of here right now."

Holding back his anger, Wade made no comment. Instead he went quietly back to his father's bedroom to spend what time he had left at the Rocking W with the man he had finally come to understand and with his memories of the happier times they had shared — before his mother's untimely death.

Chapter Twenty-three

The rain started shortly after midnight. Wade sat alone in the dimly lit room, mentally sorting through everything he now knew about himself and his father—whom he would always consider to be Walter Barlow. Though he clearly understood Matthew Tucker's blood ran through his veins, it was Walter Barlow who had raised him, taught him, and loved him—at least until his mother had revealed the awful truth upon her death. And it was the Barlow name he still proudly bore.

Oddly, he held no hard feelings toward Matthew Tucker for what he had done. The man had acted on a reckless impulse that had been spawned from the strong love he had felt for Wade's mother. Though Wade in no way condoned what Matthew did, he understood how it could have happened. It was the same sort of impulse that had brought him and Callie together the first time. He knew from personal experience the overwhelming power of such love, and also understood how very much Matthew must have suffered as a result of his impulsiveness. In a way, Wade felt Callie was right. Matthew had indeed behaved nobly by keeping his mother's secret, even after her death. Matthew had never been a bad man, just a misguided one.

And though what had happened did not actually anger Wade, it did sadden him. He realized the bitter heartache and the deep feeling of guilt his mother must have lived with. She had been forced to bear the very same shame that had caused Beth Tucker to kill herself. How hard it must have been. It amazed Wade she had loved him at all, since he was a child born of such a grave mistake. But clearly, the only real and lasting love he'd ever known had come from her — until he met Callie. He was extremely grateful for Callie.

Wade regretted having been so quick to judge Callie for having kept Matthew's secret from him. He knew her well enough to understand that she would never do anything to deliberately hurt him. She was not the type to deliberately hurt anyone.

Wade smiled, remembering how easily she had again proclaimed her love and how worried she had been over his anger. He found comfort knowing she really did love him. Her actions and her kind words had shown him just how very strong that love had become. He knew he could turn to her whenever he needed her and she would be there for him — just as his mother had always been there for him. Theirs was just that sort of love. The sort to last a lifetime.

Therefore, he was not at all surprised when Callie arrived early the following morning, only hours after the rain had stopped. She brought yet another set of clothes for him. Unaware he might be prevented from attending the services, she'd stopped by Twin Oaks to get his best suit for the funeral. Her thoughtfulness touched him more than he could ever express in mere words.

"Thank you," he told her simply as he accepted the clothing, then quickly led her by the hand into one of the little-used side parlors, which was actually a small hidden extension of the main dining room. He wanted to get her out of sight before Evan returned downstairs from helping Carlotta prepare Walter's body for Wednesday's burial.

Wade knew if Evan saw her, he would demand she leave immediately, if for no other reason than to establish who was to be in charge at the Rocking W. And knowing Callie's stubborn streak, such a demand would result in a heated exchange of words that was best avoided at the moment.

"You saved me from having to make a trip home," he told her while he quickly placed the clothing on a sideboard out of the way.

"I hope it's the suit you want to wear. The black one was the only one Rebel and I could find that seemed appropriate," she told him, frowning while she studied his haggard appearance. Clearly, he had yet to get any rest. "But then you haven't even bothered to put on the clean clothes I brought you yesterday."

"I know," he said, smiling tiredly as he rubbed his stubbled chin. "Nor have I taken the time to shave, and I really should."

"And you should try to get some sleep. You really do look dreadful," she told him honestly.

"Thank you," he said again, and his smile deepened. It felt good to smile again. It had been so long since he'd had any reason to, he'd begun to wonder if he remembered how.

"Oh, Wade, I'm sorry. I really shouldn't have said that. It's just that I do so worry about you," she told him, taking a tiny step in his direction as if testing his reaction. She wanted to comfort him in some way, but only if he was willing to accept her comfort.

"I know," he said softly, then held his arms wide. "Come here."

Callie went into his arms eagerly, blinking back the moisture that burned her eyes. She had so wanted to feel his arms around her. "Oh, Wade, I love you so much. I want you to know that."

"And I love you," he told her softly before he brought his parted lips down for a desperately needed kiss.

Callie tilted her head back and responded with a soft moan when his mouth took hers in what turned quickly from a gentle, caring kiss into one of deep, demanding passion. Her pulse quickened in response as she leaned into his embrace, molding her body to his. How wonderful it was to be in his arms again, to feel his strength surrounding her. It had been so long since their last kiss — so very long.

Hungrily she pressed closer. The strong feel of his lips

378

once again against hers sent her senses reeling. The stiffness of his whiskers gently brushed the sensitive skin of her face, which made her that much more aware of him and left her face feeling tingly and alive.

"I wish there was a way we could be assured our privacy," she whispered when he finally broke his mouth free of hers. Her heart thudded wildly against her breast when she considered what they could accomplish if only they were left alone. How dearly she wanted to make love to him, to comfort him in the only way she knew how.

"Ah, but we can," he told her, smiling mischievously while he continued to hold her close.

"How?"

Slowly he released her, then took her by the hand. "Follow me."

Stepping ever so quietly, he led her through a small door into an adjoining parlor, then turned to quickly jam a metal door bolt into place. Pressing his finger against his lips in caution, he then crossed the room and carefully bolted the only other door to the room.

"Now no one can get in," he said with an ominous lift of his brow when he again turned to face her. "And you, my dear, cannot get out."

"I can work a doorbolt," she reminded him, matching his coy smile with one of her own.

"You wouldn't dare," he growled, already headed in her direction, his brow notched with clear warning.

"Or I could simply toss those drapes back and escape through one of the windows," she added, nodding speculatively as she pretended to gauge the distance. But she made no effort to actually do so. Instead, she moved forward to meet him halfway. "Or I could take you in my arms and show you just how very much I love you."

"I prefer that third choice," he admitted, laughing softly when they came together in the middle of the darkened room. "You don't know how I've ached to hold you again. I feel like it has been a lifetime."

"I don't want to hear it," she said, leaning forward to

379

place a tiny kiss at the corner of his mouth.

"Why not?" he asked, returning the favor in kind. His breath fell softly against her cheek, sending a tiny array of shivers down the delicate skin along her neck.

"I'd much rather you show me than tell me," she said, bending to kiss the opposite corner of his mouth. Her brown eyes grew soft with her love.

"Oh? You want a demonstration, do you?" he asked, then moved to take her lips in a maddeningly passionate kiss. Her lips parted naturally beneath his, allowing him to further sample her sweetness. Callie moaned, meeting his tongue with the tip of her own.

Wade had been denied such pleasure for too long, and his emotions thundered through him with a dangerous force. Hungrily, he devoured kiss after kiss, while Callie met his passion with the vehemence of a woman in love. Her heart soared to dizzying heights. She held nothing back. She was his, body and soul.

Slowly, though never relinquishing possession of her mouth, Wade began to release the buttons that held her outer garment to her. One by one, they opened for him, until finally he had reached the last one. The garment slackened away from her skin, allowing him room to enter. Eagerly, he slipped his hand between the material and the delicate skin along her back and shared the warmth of his touch.

Tiny bumps of anticipation sprang to life beneath her skin as she felt him ease the dress from her shoulders, then drop it to her waist. Another tiny tug and the garment slipped to the floor. Petticoats, shoes, stockings, and chemise soon followed, until she stood gloriously naked before him. He yearned to take the pins from her hair and let it fall freely past her silken shoulders, but knew she would not have time to repair the damage.

"You are exquisite," he said, bending forward to taste the slender curve at the base of her neck. His warm breath gently caressed her ivory skin, sending a floodtide of sensations through her.

Callie moaned again her pleasure as she slowly brought

380

her hands around to begin working with the many buttons that bound his shirt to him. In his impatience, he began working with the trousers. Soon he too was just as gloriously naked as she. She embraced him then with a love so strong, and so overpowering, it brought a rush of tears to her eyes.

For a long moment, they simply held each other, their bodies meshed. But Wade's passion became too great and his need to possess her too strong. His mouth sought her lips once more. With growing urgency, his hand moved to gently press against the underside of her breast, teasing and taunting until he was ready to claim it with the whole of his hand. When his fingers fell across the hardened tip, a bolt of white-hot desire set Callie ablaze. Her legs grew weak from the onslaught and she leaned against him.

Callie trembled when he gently lifted her naked body into his powerful arms and carried her the short distance to the couch. The trembling was not from any fear, but from the desperate need she felt for Wade. Fire burned inside her, raging out of control, and only Wade had the power to stop it.

Wade buried his face into her neck and breathed deeply the now-familiar scent that was Callie as he gently laid her on the plush couch. His tongue came out to tickle the sensitive lobe of her ear before he moved to join her.

Reveling in the hardness of his body against hers, Callie pressed herself closer to him, molding against him. Wade's lips quickly reclaimed hers, and his hands again explored the many curves and planes that made up her body. It thrilled him to touch her. Callie gasped when again his fingertips found the sensitive peak of her breast. She bit her lips in order to restrain a cry of sheer pleasure when the desire grew to such a passionate strength that she was not sure she could stand waiting for fulfillment any longer.

With mounting urgency, Wade moved to once again become part of her. Callie responded fully, until finally they reached that ultimate moment of ecstasy. Once fulfilled, Wade fell back against the pillows he had not bothered to remove from the couch, his energy spent, and for a long moment they lay there, content in the aftermath of their love.

A dull thud overhead brought them quickly back to the dim world of reality that surrounded them. They dared not enjoy the stolen moments a second more. Worried Evan might come downstairs at any time and discover the two of them locked away inside the main parlor, they hurriedly grabbed up their clothing and began to redress. They both feared he would try to use their innocent display of love against them if he were to find out. Callie let out an audible sigh of relief once they were both again dressed and the necessary repairs done to her hair.

"Now do you believe I love you?" Wade asked, as he quietly slipped across the room to unbolt the door.

"How about one last reminder before opening that door?" she said, smiling up at him with demurely lowered lashes.

"Whatever the lady wants," he said, agreeable as he again went into her arms, his head already bent to reclaim her lips in yet another long, embroiling kiss. But the rattling sound of a carriage as it approached the house at a leisurely speed brought them suddenly apart.

"I wonder who that could be," Wade said, still a little dazed by the sheer power of the emotions that had so quickly overtaken him yet a second time. While trying to steady himself, he went to the window hoping to catch a glimpse of the vehicle before it rounded to the front of the house, where it would be out of his view. "I wonder if it could be Thomas Ewing, father's lawyer."

"Lawyer?" Callie responded curiously. "You don't suppose he has come expecting to go over your father's will so soon. Surely not before the family has had a chance to get over their initial feelings of grief."

"If he has, it is at my request," Wade admitted. Then, while they headed back toward the door opening out into the hallway, he explained how worried he was about where his father might end up being buried and why.

The moment they stepped out of the darkened room into the lighted hallway, he turned to her and added, "I already know I'm not going to inherit anything. Father told me weeks ago, in no uncertain terms, that Evan would be the one to inherit everything upon his death. Still, I honestly believe there will be burial instructions included in his last wishes. Although I suspect the lawyer would make those wishes known if it appeared they were not going to be met, it simply is not a chance I wanted to take. Having the will read now is the only real way I can be certain Father will end up buried out there beside my mother."

Heavy footsteps crossed the veranda only moments before there was a sharp knock at the door, which was still closed due to an unseasonably cool morning. But before Wade and Callie reached the door to open it, Evan came bounding down the stairs, taking them three at a time in his haste.

"I'll get that door," he stated angrily, and hurried down the hallway toward them. "Get out of my way."

Callie was no longer used to such discourteous treatment, and her chest rose with sudden indignation when she turned to face Evan. Her long silk-trimmed skirts swished at her ankles when she did. She was more than ready to tell him what she thought of his rudeness when Wade's gentle prodding at her side made her choose to clamp her mouth shut and quietly step aside with him.

"There's no point making matters worse," he whispered, and put his arm around her waist to somehow reassure her. Or maybe it was to calm her anger.

It did both.

How dearly Callie wished she could have had someone like Wade at her side back during the time she had lived with her cruel step-aunt and her selfish and incredibly spoiled step-cousins. It certainly would have made those five long years more bearable. Suddenly she realized how long ago that seemed, but in reality it had not quite been three months since. Even when she tried, she could hardly recall her step-aunt's scowling face, and that amazed her. It felt now as if those years in her life had actually been nothing more than a bad dream, one very *long* bad dream. But now she was awake. Now she had Wade. She felt the burst of anger toward Evan slowly slip away.

Together, Callie and Wade stood off to the side of the entrance and watched while Evan opened the door and greeted Thomas Ewing with a hearty handshake and a broad smile.

"I'm sorry we had to call you out here this soon after Father's death, but we were unable to locate a copy of the will, and because of decisions that really should be made right away, we needed to know Father's final requests."

"Perfectly all right," Thomas responded with a compassionate smile. "Actually, there was a reason you couldn't find a copy of your father's will. He had no copy of it. That last time I was here, he asked me to make a few changes in his previous will and together, we worked out a whole new will. I believe he then destroyed the first one. But by the time we had worked out all the details he wanted to include in this new will, I didn't have time to make my own copy. I had to take the copy we worked out together back with me so I could have my wife write out my copy. And because Jane has been terribly ill lately, she was just recently able to get my copy made, which is why I couldn't bring them out here sooner. But rest assured, I have brought them both with me today, and I will leave the original here when I leave."

"Well, that certainly explains why we couldn't find it anywhere," Evan said with a beaming smile. He glanced at Wade with a triumphant expression and then asked the lawyer, "Say, wasn't it about six weeks ago when you were here last? About the time Father discovered Wade was working for Mrs. Tucker over at the Circle T?"

Thomas looked at the two half-brothers curiously. "Why, yes, I guess it was about six weeks ago."

"Wonderful," Evan stated, rubbing his hands together while he turned to escort the lawyer in the direction of Walter's study. Just before entering the room, he turned back and noticed both Wade and Callie had followed. His smile suddenly dropped. He looked pointedly first at Callie, then at Wade, and scowled. "I don't think *she* needs to be here for this, do *you?*"

"Yes, I do," Wade responded in a low, meaningful voice. "She happens to be my future wife and I think she has every right to be at my side through this."

Evan's hazel eyes grew wide with astonishment. "Wife? You're going to marry her?" Then his expression turned snide while his gaze swept Callie's ample figure, aptly displayed in the fitted bodice of the dark gray dress she had chosen to wear. "But of course. You found out you couldn't get your hands on your own father's place, so you decided to see what you could do about getting your hands on the Circle T. And look what else you will be able to get your hands on besides."

Callie bristled, but was able to remain quiet while Wade responded as calmly as he could under the circumstances.

"Obviously you have forgotten. I already have my own ranch, and have had for several years. Not only is it a place I put together all on my own, it happens to be a place I am very proud of. Why would I want someone else's ranch? What would that prove? No, if you must know, I am marrying Callie because I happen to love her. Something I doubt you would understand, so there really isn't much point trying to explain it to you. I'd really be wasting my breath. But, I would appreciate it if you would refrain from making such calloused remarks concerning her," he said, his expression stern, but in control. "Now, if you don't mind, let's get on with the reading of the will. As you yourself said, there are decisions which need to be made."

Callie felt deeply proud of Wade, remaining so very calm in the face of clear adversity. It amused her that he could keep his wits about him no matter how badly Evan goaded him. And as a result, he had clearly put Evan in his place without as much as raising his voice. What delighted her even more was to realize he still planned to marry her, even after learning of the secrets she had kept from him. He had even gone so far as to announced their plans openly. That made it all seem more official somehow. She could hardly wait to marry him.

A pleased smile tugged at her lips when Evan then spun about and marched angrily into the room. Because Evan had been unable to argue whether Wade might truly be in love, he was clearly irritated.

"Are you ready to go in?" Wade asked Callie, interrupting her thoughts. He indicated the still-open doorway with a slight wave of his hand.

"Yes, of course," Callie responded with far more bravado than she actually felt. She braced herself with a slow, deep breath before preceding Wade into the large, book-lined room that Evan and the lawyer had already entered.

Though she dreaded the next few moments, because she knew how painful they were going to be for Wade, she would see them through. She would remain by her future husband's side no matter how heartbreaking the outcome of the reading became. Although she would not openly comfort him in front of the others for fear of humiliating him in some way, she would do what she could to show him all the love and support possible.

"Please, remove your firearms and hand them to me," Thomas Ewing said in a very businesslike manner while he extended his hand to accept the weapons. Then once he had both the handguns safely in his possession, he made a sweeping gesture toward the chairs closest to him and asked that they all have a seat, just before he stepped around to the far side of the cluttered desk and sat down himself.

After taking the time to place the weapons inside one of the lower drawers, he quickly adjusted his eyeglasses and frowned at the disarray before him. The desk was covered with papers, books, and small boxes — some open, some not. Slowly, he began to clear a small area in front of him to place his satchel, then proceeded to take out an unbound scroll and rolled it flat before him.

Wade and Callie sat in a pair of black upholstered chairs that stood side by side, only inches apart. They both faced the huge monstrosity of a desk. Though Wade had been

386

forced to remove his hand from her waist when they sat, he quickly lifted her hand into his the moment she had adjusted her skirts and made herself comfortable. Whether it was a gesture meant to comfort her or bring himself some measure of comfort, Callie was not sure; but she was certainly glad to have the personal contact to sustain her through whatever was about to happen.

Meanwhile, Evan ignored the matching black upholstered chair just inches to Callie's left. Instead, he dragged another chair that had rested against the far wall across the room into a position beside the desk, which would allow him to watch the lawyer while he read the will and still be able to keep an eye on Wade and Callie. Clearly, he wanted to witness the pain on Wade's face when it was announced Walter's older son was to get absolutely nothing of his father's estate.

When he settled into the chair, there was a pleased smile on his face. "Well, let's get on with it."

Wade's grip tightened around Callie's hand when the lawyer helped himself to a swallow of the drinking water from the desk service before he began to clear his throat in preparation to speak. Aware the time had come, Callie looked away to the half-opened window where a pair of pale blue drapes billowed in the cool, early morning breeze. She tried her best to calm her hammering heart. How she dreaded what was about to happen. Suddenly she was reminded of the day Matthew's will had been read and how devastated his children had been to hear his final words. Tears filled her eyes when she glanced back at the lawyer.

Leaning stiffly forward in the huge desk chair, Thomas Ewing adjusted his wire-rimmed eyeglasses one last time, pressing them as high up on his slanted nose as they could go. Then his pale green eyes began to dart quickly across the paper while he read aloud Walter's final will and testament.

To everyone's astonishment, and to Evan's total bewilderment, Walter did not leave him everything, as expected. Instead, Wade was to receive nearly everything. With no explanations given, Evan was left with a set—but tidy—sum of money, a small section of good land along the southern-most area of Walter's holdings, and his pick of fifty head of cattle, but that was all. Other than two other requests which asked that a friend of the family and one of Walter's longest-employed stockmen be given personal items he felt they would appreciate having, Wade was to inherit all else.

"That can't be right," Evan shouted, coming out of his chair with such force the chair fell backward and clattered to the floor. Angrily he jerked the will right out of Thomas Ewing's hands in order to see it for himself. With eyes narrowed, he looked at the lawyer accusingly, "Why, this document isn't even signed! What kind of trick are you trying to pull here?"

Stiffening at having his integrity clearly questioned, Thomas took his eyeglassess off and glared at Evan. His mouth grew taut against his teeth with barely restrained anger. "That, Mr. Samuels, happens to be *my* copy. Of course it has no signature. I was never able to get it back here in time for him to sign it. But I assure you it reads exactly word for word the same as the original, which does indeed have his signature, as I told you. I do happen to have that one with me as well."

"Then why didn't you read from it?" Evan asked, still not wanting to believe it could be true.

"Because my hand came across this one first and I really did not think it mattered from which I read aloud since I planned to leave Wade the original."

"Wade? Why Wade?" Evan demanded to know. He was so angry now the veins in his forehead stood out while he waved the rolled document before him as if brandishing a weapon.

"Because he is the main heir. And because he is Walter's *legal* son. A son, I might add, that Walter was extremely proud of and had fully forgiven for whatever transgressions he had once believed had been committed against him." Though there was anger on Thomas's face, his tone remained professionally calm.

"Why, you," Evan said, his voice practically a growl when

he suddenly began to advance on the elderly gentleman, who flexed his shoulders proudly and stood his ground.

Callie felt Wade's grasp on her hand grow ever tighter, until it was almost painful to her fingers. Then suddenly, he let go and moved with lightning speed to stand between the two men, confronting Evan with the power he now had. His face still revealed some of the awe he felt, but at the same time was brimming with determination.

"Evan, ironically enough, this is now *my* house, and I'd appreciate it if you would not treat a guest in *my* house with such discourtesy." Though there was no smile on his face, Wade clearly took great pleasure in saying what he had to say. "Now, I will allow you to stay here as my guest for a few days, until all the provisions of the will can be met, and until our father has been properly buried — as long as you behave yourself. But as soon as that tract of land Father indicated has been put in your name and you have selected your fifty head of cattle, I'll want you out of here. Since I am not as cruel a man as you seem to be, I will allow you to visit Father's grave each year on the anniversary of his death, and I'll allow you to come here for any business reasons you may have, but other than that, once you have gone, you are not to set foot on the Rocking W again."

Evan became so consumed by his fury that he tore the lawyer's copy of the will in half, then wadded it into a crumpled heap and threw it at the floor, where it hit with such force, it skidded across the room and bounced off the far wall. "Something's wrong here. Very wrong! You don't deserve this place. You don't deserve any of it. How could he do this to me? How could he leave me with nothing after all I did for him? After all I went through?"

"I'd hardly say that ten thousand dollars, three hundred acres of good land, and fifty prime head of cattle is nothing," Wade commented dryly, feeling no pity for Evan whatever. It was more than most men had after working a lifetime to get ahead.

"No, Evan, in all honesty, you've come out of this set for life." Wade tried to sound casual, and in complete control, though he was still just as stunned as Evan himself seemed to be over the fact his father had chosen to leave over eighty percent of all he had owned to him—the son who was not really his son. Of the two, Walter Barlow had chosen the one who had actually left him, moved out in order to make his own way.

Tears of joy filled his heart over the realization his father *had* loved and respected him after all. The lawyer himself had said the man had forgiven him. Despite the fact he was helping Callie hold on to the Circle T, and despite the fact his father had known he was really Matthew Tucker's son—born of Matthew's blood—he had cared enough about him to forgive it all and, in the end, had wanted him to have practically everything he'd worked so hard to establish.

Wade felt so much like crying aloud his happiness that it took all the self-control he had not to. He needed to remember the seriousness of the situation at hand. Evan's anger was not to be easily dismissed.

Aware of Wade's elation, Callie came forward to stand beside him, fighting back her own tearful emotions. She had to cross her arms over her stomach to help still the fluttery butterflies that had surfaced there.

Evan glared at her, then at Wade. His nostrils flared, more evidence of the fury burning inside of him. "To hell with you! To hell with all of you!" Then suddenly he bounded out of the room, slamming the door behind him with such force a small portrait of a mother and child broke off the wall and crashed to the floor.

Reverently, Wade walked over to rescue the painting, and carefully examined the shattered frame. Quietly, Callie followed.

"Your mother?" she asked, glancing over his shoulder at the beautiful woman with shimmering brown hair and large, oval-shaped blue eyes. But even before he had the chance to answer, she knew the woman had to be Wade's mother. There were too many similarities between them, everything from their coloring to the curving shape of their smiles. Callie also saw why Matthew had fallen so deeply in

390

love with her. Eleanor Barlow was as truly beautiful as Wade was handsome.

"That's me with her," Wade admitted, smiling slightly as he handed the canvas to her, allowing her a closer look at the small dark-haired boy with crystal blue eyes. "Don't ask me about the little sailor suit I have on there. It's something I don't like to talk about."

Then, as if unable to hold back his joy any longer, he swept her into his arms and swung her around and around, laughing aloud. "He left the place to me. He *did* care. Despite it all, he cared enough to leave me practically everything he owned. He loved me. He honestly loved me. He left this place to *me*."

Callie laughed with him, sensing it was not as much the fact he had inherited most of the Rocking W as it was that he had been the one chosen to inherit it. In the end, Walter Barlow had come to realize just how important his relationship with Wade was, and had sought to rectify their differences in the only way he knew how.

Without letting go of the portrait, she threw her arms tightly around Wade's neck and hugged him close, releasing him only long enough to reach up with her free hand and wipe away the tears blurring her vision. It felt wonderful to see Wade happy again—to know his self-esteem had been fully restored and his worst fears laid to rest. His father had loved him, loved him dearly, and had proven it through his will. Wade would not have to suffer the rest of his life wondering what, if anything, Walter Barlow had felt for him. It was now very clear.

Callie left the Rocking W shortly after Thomas Ewing indicated he wanted to go over first the burial plans, then some of the different provisions and implications of the will with Wade. It was Ewing's duty to see that Wade did indeed relinquish to Evan Samuels, Mrs. Pyle, and Marcus Taylor the items which had been clearly specified for each.

Callie did not mind being excluded from the conversation. She was too eager to return to the Circle T, see if the girls had gotten a good start to their day, and tell Lucille all the wonderful news she had. Because the news she had to bear was so very good, she did not mind having to leave Wade so soon, but promised to return later that afternoon. Her heart hammered at the thought of what it would be like when she returned. They would finally have a chance to be alone together. She could hardly wait.

She could also hardly wait to announce how at long last, Amy would be allowed to go out and ride her horse to her heart's content, and Janice could go into town and order the new dresses she had wanted to buy before school started that very next week. Now that Walter was dead and that part of their troubles clearly over, she could allow the girls the freedom they dearly wanted and not have to worry for their safety. She too could go into town again with no worries. She would finally be able to start rebuilding all that Walter had destroyed before his death. It was a great weight off her shoulders to know the troubles were behind them. She wasted no time heading home.

"Come on, boy. Get up," Callie called out repeatedly. To her frustration she could not seem to get the lazy horse to trot fast enough, and did not think she could bear having to wait any longer. She was too excited. Their worries were over at last. It was not until she had nearly reached home that she decided to make one little side trip.

Eagerly, she turned down the narrow, grassy carriage drive which cut through a thick span of woods and eventually led to the small fence-enclosed cemetery atop a high sloping hill—only a few hundred yards from the northwest boundary of the Circle T and not too far from where all the shooting had occurred days earlier. Though she did not intend to stay long, she wanted to take a brief moment to visit Matthew's grave. She was not sure he would be able to hear what all she was bursting to tell him, for she was not sure what went on after one's death, but she had to at least try. She wanted to tell him how, at long last, Wade knew he was Matthew's son.

She felt Matthew would want to know that before her death, Eleanor had finally admitted the truth, albeit without actually knowing she had done so. Matthew was indeed Wade's father. There were no doubts about that now. And Wade now understood he was Matthew's son, and had not shunned the idea the way Matthew had always feared he would. She also wanted to tell him how, now that Walter was dead and all their troubles with him, she and Wade would soon be able to get married like they had planned.

Matthew should know that, just as soon as the girls came to fully accept the idea, she and Wade would finally be husband and wife. Wade would then have a major role in running the Circle T just as Matthew had always dreamed, though he would never become the outright owner because of the way the will had been written. But that mattered little. What mattered was that the two of them would soon be working side by side in an effort to make the place prosper once again. Together, they would see to it Matthew's small dynasty was fully restored and in good order when the time came for Janice and Amy to take over.

Too happy at the moment to notice the chill that lingered in the dark shadows surrounding her, Callie began to hum to herself while her carriage bounced along the narrow, wood-lined roadway. She knew that once the road left the thick woods, passed through the small wooden gate, and entered into the open area ahead, there would be sunshine again. And as soon as she had driven a few hundred yards into the pasture, she would be only a short walk from Matthew and Beth's final resting places. Then she would tell Matthew all that he longed to hear. And she would tell Beth how brave her daughters had been throughout the whole ordeal. It would please her to no end to tell such happy news.

As she continued along her way, Callie was too wrapped up in her own true joy—too overcome with the fact the Circle T's troubles were finally over and another of Matthew's dreams was going to be fulfilled—to take notice of any sounds but those of the birds singing overhead. She never noticed the rustling sound made by another horse as it moved restlessly through dense woods alongside her. Nor did she recognize the rider who sat atop the tall, black animal — not in time to consider any possibility of escape.

Chapter Twenty-four

Wade was furious, but realized there was nothing he could do about the situation. If the men were determined to leave, there was no way to stop them.

When he had stepped outside to walk with Thomas Ewing to the small shaded area where he left his carriage, they had immediately discovered most of the men were outside, busy loading their personal belongings into saddlebags or tying them in packs onto the backs of their horses. Having learned the unfairness of Evan's fate from Evan himself, just before he rode out, they were all angry at the injustice and all hurriedly prepared to leave. All but one.

"Just where do you men plan to go?" he asked, hoping they would see how it made better sense to stay where they were.

Mark Lyons, who had worked at the Rocking W barely a year, chose to be the spokesman for the group. "Some of us plan to continue working for Evan. We plan to help him get his own place started. Others aim to hit the road and see if they can find similar employment elsewhere, in other counties, or maybe even further out west. I hear there's land for the taking out there."

The rest of the men nodded their agreement.

Only one man out of all the sixteen working at the Rocking W had chosen to stay, and that was Marcus Taylor, a man who had been with his father since long before Evan had ever come to live there. And apparently Marcus was the only man who held any loyalty to Walter's memory.

After futilely trying to convince even a few of the less adamant men to stay on, Wade eventually gave up. They were far too angry to be dealt with just yet. He knew only too well how Evan could twist certain facts to suit himself, and realized he needed to give the men a cooling-off period. For now, all he could do was let them go and hope they would not go far.

Too emotionally drained to cope with their childish behavior at that particular moment, Wade left them while they still worked at getting their gear together. Trusting Marcus to see none of them took a notion to steal him blind, Wade retired to his father's study to help himself to a tall glass of his father's finest whiskey and to try to figure out what he should do next.

There was so much he needed to think about. There were many emotions yet to be sorted through. Though he still felt grief-stricken over the sudden death of his father, he was proud to know the man had indeed cared enough about him to choose *him* to carry on in his stead. But now that all the workers but one had quit, just where did that leave him?

It left him the brand-new owner of the Rocking W with only one man and one housekeeper to help him work the place. It also meant he would not have as much time to take care of his own place, and even less to help Callie with the Circle T. He wondered then just *how* helpful Ed Grant had proven to be over the past couple of days. Was he actually helpful enough to permanently be put in charge? Would he be able to make sound decisions if made foreman of the Circle T? That's what he would really need: three good foremans, one for each place, so that all he would have to do is oversee the work that went on at all three.

If it was not for the fact a small strip of Circle T divided his place from his father's, he could eventually hope to combine those two operations. Maybe he could convince Callie and the girls to sell him that small strip of land. He'd pay top dollar for it. But then again, he didn't want Callie to think he was taking advantage of their feelings for one another. And he knew how important it was for her to eventually be able to turn the Circle T over to the girls in exactly the same — or even better shape than it was in when she took over the responsibility of managing it. No, he would have to consider each place as separate from the others.

Wade next wondered if eventually he would be able to talk a few of those men outside into returning once they'd had a chance to cool down. If not, he wondered how much trouble he would have finding a whole new work crew. Or would he have to temporarily divide the men who worked for him at Twin Oaks, and possibly take the new men Callie had just hired at the Circle T, since she would not be needing them anymore, not with the trouble finally over?

The more he thought about the situation, the more it angered him to realize that those men had, in the end, been more loyal to Evan than they had been to his father's memory. Some of his father's men had worked there for years, and he felt certain his father had paid and treated them fairly. But then, there was little he could do about that now. Evidently, Evan had found a way to misplace their loyalty and there seemed to be no changing their minds.

Evan.

Wade felt a cold feeling of apprehension creep into the pit of his stomach when he remembered how furious his half-brother had been when he had lit out of there. It felt like someone had spilled a tall bucket of ice water into his bloodstream, making him feel cold and heavy inside. He wondered where his angry half-brother had gone after having riled all the workmen so successfully. He also wondered what sort of trouble he might be planning next. Although the lawyer had assured him there was nothing Evan could do to legally turn the will around, Wade felt certain he would try to do more than simply take his work crew away from him.

Evan would not give up without some sort of a fight, not after all those years of groveling at his father's feet. Wade just wished he knew what it was Evan might do to attempt to rectify what he obviously saw as a gross injustice. If he could somehow anticipate him, he might know ahead of time the best way to deal with the man.

Dismally, he wondered if his father had known what a hornets' nest he'd be stirring up by leaving Evan so little and him so much. He wondered if he had understood exactly how hurt and angry Evan was going to be. He smiled when it dawned on him that his father must have known exactly what he was doing, but had not cared. In the end, his father had wanted *him* to inherit most of what he'd worked all his life to put together, not Evan. His father had obviously felt he would be able to handle any retributions Evan might attempt, and it was that faith in him that mattered most. His mood lifted.

Settling more comfortably into his father's desk chair with yet a second glass of whiskey, Wade drank a toast to his father's innate wisdom, then pushed aside all thoughts of the past in order to mull over the many possibilities the future now held. Now that he had possession of the Rocking W, Callie could not possibly believe he wanted to marry her in order to somehow get possession of the Circle T away from her and the girls. In all honestly, he would have more than he could presently handle with just his place and his father's to tend to. She would have to realize he was marrying her solely because he loved her, because he wanted to spend the rest of his life with her — with her and Matthew's two daughters.

His stepsisters.

"Oh, my word." Wade thought about that for the first time. Janice and Amy were actually his stepsisters. And he and Evan were no blood relation at all. Now *that* was a comforting thought, and deserved a second toast. Chuckling aloud, he refilled his glass and did exactly that, toasted the fact he and Evan were in no way related by blood.

He then leaned back again and smiled at the thought of what Janice and Amy would say if they were to find out he was their half-brother instead of Evan's. He was certain it would dampen their more ardent feelings toward him, but would it somehow turn them against him when he needed their acceptance the most? He was never sure what to expect with those two. Should he and Callie bother to tell them the truth at all? It was something he needed to discuss with her very soon. Callie would know what to do when it came to those two girls. After all, she had once been a little girl herself.

Suddenly, he wondered what sort of childhood Callie had led. Judging from the comments she had made just before his father's death, the past few years had not been happy ones for her. She had come there hoping to escape that past — not out of some inner desire to trick a dying man out of his money. He felt guilty for ever having accused her of such a thing. Knowing her the way he did now, he could see he'd been a fool to ever believe anything like that. He felt he should apologize to her when he saw her that afternoon.

Just the thought of seeing Callie again made him feel all warm inside. How odd that just thinking about her brought such a smile to his face. Eagerly, he closed his eyes to be able to envision her more clearly. Beautiful, headstrong Callie Tucker. A woman of such contradictions. Sometimes, she seemed as vulnerable and helpless as a little kitten; but at other times she was so fiercely independent, so strongly determined, she reminded him more of a young tigress. A hellcat! He chuckled as he recalled the passion she had for making love.

"Callie Tucker." He spoke her name reverently. Callie was the only woman ever able to steal his heart. And the only woman he had ever wanted for his wife. He could hardly wait to marry her. Still smiling, he quickly lost himself to thoughts of what the future might be like, a future shared with such a beautiful and vibrant woman.

Hours passed, and in that time horse after horse was heard leaving as the men left their jobs behind, but Wade chose to pay little attention to them. Let them go, if that's what they wanted.

"I'll not beg them to stay," he said aloud, his jaw hardening at the thought. "If they want to go, let them."

But rather than let his anger get the better of him, he chose to continue dwelling on the happier aspects of his future. But eventually noises from upstairs brought Wade away from his thoughts. Aware Carlotta must still be busy getting Walter ready for burial, he felt a sudden resurgence of sadness. Having just indulged in thoughts of what their children would be like, Wade became suddenly aware Walter would never know the joy of those children — he'd never know the happiness of bouncing his grandchildren on his knee.

Afraid he was about to lose control of his emotions again, Wade slowly rose, ready to return his glass and the remaining whiskey to the cabinet. He'd had enough to drink. Though he had wanted to dull the sorrow he felt somewhat, he did not want to hamper his ability to think. Not when there were so many decisions facing him.

It was when he turned back from the liquor cabinet that he glimpsed his father's gun cabinet near the opposite end of the wall. Suddenly, he felt drawn to it.

Reflecting back to the many times he'd seen his father fling back the glass doors, then hurriedly grab up a rifle or a shotgun from the ornate, hand-carved rack inside, Wade reached in, took out his father's favored rifle, and held it in his hands. Although he knew it was the same rifle his father had used on his attack of Callie's back pasture only three days earlier, he pushed the thought aside and tried to remember instead the day his father had first shown the weapon to him. Such enthusiasm.

Turning the fancy rifle in his hands in order to study its handsome workmanship, he could not help but wonder if McKenzie was any better. He then tried to envision his father angry enough to knowingly use the weapon against another man — but he was unable to imagine it. Even though he now knew the bitter reasons his father had hated Matthew so, he still could not see his father being able to actually pull a trigger against another man.

He fought yet another rush of tears while he lightly fingered the intricate carvings along the rifle stock. Well remembering how especially proud his father had been of his prized firearm, he felt it odd that it had not been cleaned since its last use. Wade thought that was unlike his father, who always took exceptional care of his firearms, and decided to take the time to clean it himself, knowing it would have pleased his father immensely. Then, to show that all the anger and hatred which had raged between his father and Matthew Tucker was now dead and could finally be laid to rest, he planned to have the weapon buried at his father's side.

Carefully, he laid out the cleaning rod, the soft rags, a small bottle of bluing, and the tiny spouted can of gun oil on his father's desk. It was after he had begun to clean away the dusky remains of burnt gunpowder and dust that he first noticed the faint scent of wood smoke.

Though the temperature outside had never warmed as it should for a day still late in August, and had caused him to eventually close the window again in order to keep the odd chill out of the room, it was certainly not cool enough to warrant a fire. He wondered what was burning and why. He had not ordered anything burned, and the scent was too pungent to be coming from the cookstove.

Panic had already begun to grip him when he rushed to the door, eager to search out the source of the smoke. Having earlier taken the time to carefully close the door behind him to assure himself uninterrupted solitude, he reached for the latch to reopen it and discovered the metal handle felt oddly warm to his touch.

He pressed a hand to the door, and discovered it too felt warm. The smell of smoke seemed much stronger on that side of the room. Suddenly, he was aware of the faint crackle and hiss of burning wood. The sounds seemed to come right through the walls.

The house was on fire.

Again, Wade reached for the door handle. He had to get out of there.

To his mounting horror, when he tried the latch, it pulled down as it was supposed to, but the door itself refused to budge. Someone had either locked it from the outside or had jammed it somehow. Or maybe the intense heat from the fire had sealed the door shut. He yanked harder. Still it did not open. He was trapped.

Fire!

The smell of smoke grew increasingly stronger, and for the first time, he noticed tiny tendrils of a blue-gray cloud curling through the tiny keyhole. Barely a moment later, smoke began to seep through the tiny crevices along the sides and at the base of the door. He stepped back, filled with panic as he realized the fire was very close and had already filled the main hall with smoke. In his mind, he visualized the entire hallway already engulfed in flame. If the fire had started in the kitchen, then over half of the house was probably on fire. Even if he was somehow able to get the door to open, he doubted he would find a way to escape.

He next thought of Carlotta trapped upstairs and of his father's body. He wanted to get them both out. Knowing his father's bedroom was directly over head, he began to shout at the top of his voice.

"Carlotta? Carlotta! The house is on fire. Get out!"

Though he was not sure she could understand him, for she spoke very little English, he listened for at least a response to her name. He wanted to know exactly where she was. But there came no response. Had the fire already consumed the upper floor?

He tried again.

"Carlotta!"

Aware the only way out of the study would be the small window which opened out onto the side veranda, he hurried to open it. To his further horror, he saw that the entire veranda was already shrouded with hungry flames. The window cracked suddenly from the intense heat, causing him to jump back. His heart pounded furiously inside him as smoke began to pour into the room.

Wade stood temporarily stunned, staring out at the angry wall of fire edged with black smoke. Suddenly, he realized how quickly the fire had spread. *Too quickly.* One minute there was barely the faint scent of smoke to warn him, and in the next minute his was completely surrounded by a raging fire. While he studied his situation further, he noticed how the core of the spreading flames outside the window seemed to follow a definite path across the veranda floor.

A kerosene trail. The fire had been deliberately set. Someone was out to kill him. And maybe out to kill Carlotta too.

Evan.

It had to be.

Chapter Twenty-five

Callie could hear muffled noises somewhere in the fog-shrouded distance — noises that pulled at her from the aching void that engulfed her. Someone was close by. She tried to wake up and call out for help, but her eyes felt too heavy and the murky haze that surrounded her would not clear. When she tried to speak, she felt her lips move, but her words came out nothing more than a low, guttural moan. Her heart hammered violently inside her like tiny waves splashing against some unseen shore, but still she was unable to pull herself out of the darkness.

"About to wake up, are you?" she heard a voice ask. It was not a friendly voice. Suddenly, fear lashed at her. She remembered what had happened — every horrifying detail. She remembered how he had chased her, had dragged her to the ground, and hit her with something. What she was unable to remember was why. She could remember the violence, but not the reason for it.

"Evan? Why?" she tried to ask, but her voice was still too weak, far too raspy to be understood. She wanted to try again, but she just did not have the inner strength to do so at that moment. She barely had the strength to stay conscious.

"What did you say?" Evan wanted to know. She could tell by the shadow that fell across her that he had bent over her to better hear her reply. Her heart beat even faster when she realized just how close he really was. Did he intend to hurt her again?

Forcing her eyes open at last, she tried to focus on the face that loomed over her in order to judge the danger, but it was no use. Her vision was nothing more than a mixture of gray blurs. She was in pain, but unable to pinpoint exactly where it was she hurt the most. Suddenly she began to shiver from the cold that penetrated her entire body from the hard, damp surface which lay beneath her. She tried again to speak, but the blurred vision began to fade and, although she fought to stay awake, she slowly slipped back into the dark realms of oblivion.

When she awoke again, the pain was worse. She could now tell the worst injuries were at the back of her head and along her right shoulder. The shoulder pain she could live with, but the other was unbearable. It felt as if her throbbing brain wanted to literally burst her skull apart.

Remembering once again what had happened, how violently Evan had attacked her, she tried again to open her eyes. When she did, she discovered everything seemed a little less hazy. This time she was better able to make out her surroundings. She could tell there was a lamp—no, a lantern, a workman's lantern—hanging nearby, bathing her with a dull yellow light. She blinked a few times in an attempt to clear her vision more, and it helped. The shapes around her came better into focus, but it still seemed as if she gazed through a thin veil of tears. Judging by the way her eyes burned and her head ached, she decided she probably was gazing through her own tears. She blinked again. Better still.

Valiantly, she struggled to overcome the strong sense of panic trying to take firm hold of her heart. She knew she needed to keep her wits about her. She then wondered just where she was and how long she had lain there unconscious. More importantly, she wondered where Evan was and how long he had been gone.

Carefully, she listened for any sounds which might indicate his whereabouts, but heard none. All she heard was the pulsating rush of her own blood as it surged through her ears.

Her next thought was of escape. But when she attempted to move her hands in an effort to push herself into a sitting

405

position, she discovered her wrists were bound together. So were her ankles.

Though she tried, she could move neither. Whatever Evan had used to bind her was too strong to break by mere force, and it felt painfully rough against her skin. She tried to see just what it was that held her, but the attempt to raise her head sent such a sharp stab of pain along the back of her skull, she immediately gave up the effort.

For several moments she lay there trying to adjust to the pain, all the while wondering what she should do, what she possibly *could* do. She could tell she was inside of some sort of building, but her vision was just now clearing enough to see anything clearly.

Slowly and carefully, she risked yet another stab of pain as she rolled her head to one side to better investigate her surroundings. Rough-hewn lumber made up the walls that surrounded her. There were no windows to admit any light into the room other than the soft glow of the one overhead lantern. She had no way of knowing if it was day or night.

Tools, garden implements, wire, and rope hung on large metal hooks far over her head, clearly out of her reach. Several chemically treated posts lay across a sturdy shelf, also out of her reach. Large wooden boxes stenciled "Clyde Kennedy's Reinforced Wire" were stacked in the corner, almost to the ceiling.

Against her cheek, she felt the cold, hard earth, and realized she lay on a dirt floor. Turning her head further, until she saw the floor itself, she noticed bootprints all around her. In several places she saw dark splotches of blood — her blood. Her injuries, especially the one to her head, must be more serious than she had at first thought. She wondered then how much blood she had lost and if she was still bleeding. Would she have the strength to remain standing even if she could?

She had to try.

Aware she was in a small supply shed of some sort, she tried to locate the door. She needed to find a way out of there before Evan returned. She rolled her head to face the opposite direction. For some odd reason, her head did not hurt as much when she turned it to the left as it had when she had looked off to the right.

Focusing on the small, planked door standing just beyond the lantern's direct light, she noticed a heavy metal bolt, obviously used to secure the door from the inside. It seemed an odd precaution. Most sheds had locks only on the outside, to keep intruders out while no one was around. Obviously the owner of this shed felt the extra precaution was necessary. And if the shed belonged to Evan, she could easily understand such an unnecessary precaution. After all, she'd already come to the conclusion the man was crazy. Crazy enough to try to kill her. She had to get away.

She studied the huge metal bolt long enough to see that it was slipped back, out of place. Aware how, for it to be in place, Evan would have to be in the room with her, she felt a moment of relief. It meant he must be somewhere outside. But then she already knew that. The room was far to small and the contents too sparse to hide a person of any real size. Of course she was alone.

But for how long? she wondered.

Again, she tried to sit up, and despite the severe pain pounding against her skull like a hammer striking repeatedly at a nail too stubborn to budge, she managed to bring herself upright into a sitting position. She pressed her eyes closed until the fierce pain began to subside a little. When she opened them again, she was able to see that her wrists and the ankles of her boots had been bound with rope. Hemp rope. The kind used to make temporary restraints so strong they held even the wildest animals captive.

Still fighting a blinding pain, she tried again to work her hands free, but discovered she could not. Not only was she bound at the wrists, but her hands had been secured to her body by another rope which circled her entire waist.

She then tried to free her feet and realized, with a little determination, she might be able to slip one of her feet out of its boot — thus freeing herself enough to make a run for safety. Biting hard into her lip, she pushed down on her right foot while she tugged hard on the other, twisting her ankle in tiny circular motions when she did. Slowly, she was able to free her left foot. And with her right foot still stuck in her boot, and the additional boot still tied to it, she turned her efforts to standing up.

Tears again filled her eyes when the pain at the back of her head became so great she felt she could no longer bear it, but she had to get away before Evan returned. She had never seen such hatred in any man's eyes. He was completely mad. She was certain of it. And she was also certain he planned to kill her. Though she could not clearly remember words to that effect, she had seen it in his eyes.

To save herself, she knew her only hope at the moment was that he had not bothered to lock the door when he left—that he would allow his insanity to make him careless. But then again, even if she did get outside, she would still have to deal with the fact he might be out there somewhere, waiting for her.

Gritting her teeth against the piercing pain which now felt a part of her, she pushed her elbows outward, then rolled over, putting her weight on both the outer curves of her forearms and her knees. With a strength she was no longer sure she possessed, she was then able to push herself upright and, eventually, was on her knees in the middle of the dirt floor. She paused only a moment to steady her spinning head before rocking back and pushing herself the rest of the way to her feet.

Her pulse continued to thud painfully against the back of her head, but her pain was no longer important. Hurriedly, she moved toward the door, then paused to listen for any movement outside the small shack. Hearing none, she stood on tiptoe high enough to be able to get the hands still tied at her waist up under the small wooden latch which held the door closed.

Carefully, she lifted it, until the board which was attached on the outside slipped up out of its cradle. She was relieved to discover the door unlocked, and prayed it would not be because Evan waited for her outside. Slowly, she eased against the door with her shoulder and, as it creaked open, she was grateful to find it still daylight outside—though it was clearly very late in the afternoon and would soon be

408

dark.

Once the door was open and she could see some of the surrounding area, Callie paused again to give Evan the time to react should he actually have been close enough to hear or see the door open. When nothing was said to stop her, she took her first step forward to get a better look at the area around her.

To her surprise, she was completely surrounded by woods. She had expected to be out in a pasture somewhere. What was a supply shed doing out in the middle of the woods like that? And on whose land? Where was she? Suddenly, she smelled smoke, but was unable to determine where it was coming from. Then almost as suddenly as she had noticed the smell of smoke, it was gone.

With no way of knowing in what direction she should run, Callie stepped even further away from the shed to judge her surroundings better still. She peered off into the dark shadows of the woods and saw nothing but more woods. Nothing but more dark shadows lay in the distance. Then she noticed a worn trail leading toward the front of the shed off to her left. Aware that would be the path Evan would take upon his return, she turned to leave in the opposite direction.

Hampered by the fact her hands were still tied and the empty boot was still attached to the inside of her other boot, and kept getting in the way of her stockinged foot, she hurried as best she could off into the woods. She had wanted to put as much distance as possible between herself and that shed before Evan's return, but was still well within earshot when she heard the rapid approach of a horse somewhere behind her. Her heart slammed hard against her chest when she realized Evan had already returned and was about to discover the door to the shed open and her missing.

"Oh, please, no," she cried aloud.

Panic gripped her soul while she ran blindly through the darkening woods. She tried her best to run faster. The underbrush tugged at her skirt and tore at the stocking on her left foot until the bottom of it was in tatters and her tender flesh was exposed to the many briars and sharp, broken twigs which covered the ground. To her growing despair, the trees and bushes that surrounded her seemed to grow thicker the deeper she ran.

Limping as much from the pain of her exposed foot as from the fact the boot still on her right foot put her slightly off balance, she continued to run as hard as she could.

Somehow, she continued to put one foot in front of the other. Even though she felt the strength slowly slipping out of her, she was determined not to give up.

"If only Evan had stayed away a few minutes more," her brain cried out as she forced her aching legs to continue to carry her weight forward. The ropes around her wrists tore at her tender flesh; her shoulder throbbed from some previous injury; and her lungs burned. "If only he had stayed away. Just fifteen minutes more."

Suddenly, Callie saw a clearing through the trees ahead, and despite the rapid approach of dusk, she could also see a well-kept post and wire fence. As soon as she managed to get over that fence, she would finally be out of the dark woods, out of the briars and broken twigs that tore at her feet. Maybe then she would be able to figure out just where she was. Maybe she could find a way to get to Wade before Evan could get to her. She knew Wade would protect her. She would be safe then.

The sound of someone or something crashing through the woods behind her caused her to hurry more. Evidently Evan had discovered the direction she had taken, but then as much noise as she made tramping over the dead twigs and leaves, he would have had to have been deaf not to notice the direction she had taken. Fear that bordered on panic caused her to glance back to see exactly how far behind her he was. She wanted to know if he possibly had her in sight yet. When she turned to catch a glimpse over her shoulder, she stumbled on a rotting limb and fell forward.

With her hands still bound at her waist, she could not reach out to block her fall, and her shoulder hit the ground with a hard jolt. White-hot pain shot up and through the back of her head, bursting in a wild explosion against her skull. She cried aloud, but immediately began the struggle to get back on her feet, only to discover she no longer had the strength. Her legs felt numb and her arms were too weak. In the distance she heard the crashing noises coming ever closer.

When Evan caught up with her, Callie still lay on the ground trying to force herself up and sobbing aloud because her own weakness would not allow it. She had heard his rapid approach, and had heard him angrily call out her name, but there was nothing she could do about it. Absolutely nothing. Though her mind still screamed for her to get up and run, before it was too late, her body refused.

"Thought you could get away?" she heard him ask just before she felt the sharp blow to her ribs. She nearly passed out from the resulting pain.

"Thought you could save your miserable hide by running away?" he demanded to know, and kicked her again.

This time the pain was too great, and Callie fell gratefully into the peaceful darkness that reached out for her — aware of little more than the sardonic laughter that trilled to the tops of the trees.

When Callie awoke again, she was not only bound securely at the ankles and wrists, Evan had stuffed a foul-tasting rag of some sort into her mouth. Though her head still hurt, and her ribs now ached when she tried to move, she was able to see her surroundings clearly enough to know she was back inside the same shed as before.

Rolling over on her side, she bent forward and glanced down to look at the rope that now held her ankles tightly bound, only to discover it was not a rope at all. He had removed her boot and bound her feet with wire. When she tried to tug one of her feet loose, the wire cut immediately into her flesh. When she then tried to free her hands, she discovered they were still held fast against her waist by rope. At least she was able to push the rag out of her mouth with her tongue, but knew it would do her little good. She was too far into the woods for anyone to hear a call for help. Besides, Evan could still be nearby. Perhaps right outside. Preferring he not know she was awake just yet, she chose to remain quiet.

Frantically searching for a way to help herself, she glanced at the many items around her, as if by doing so she might come up with some wonderful plan for escape. But she realized as long as she was bound at the wrists and ankles the way she was, her situation was hopeless. It was then she noticed the metal scythe hanging on the wall. If she could find some way to knock the curved blade off the two hooks holding it in place, and send it tumbling to the ground without falling on her, she might be able to use the sharp edge to cut herself free.

It was the only hope she had, and she clung to it fiercely. Biting into her lower lip in an effort to fight the pain caused by the cutting wire, she began to inch her way toward the wall. Once there, she hoped to lift her legs high enough to push up on the long wooden handle that dangled down, and free the blade.

Slowly, and painfully, she continued to work her way across the dirt floor, until she lay directly beneath the scythe. She prayed that the implement, once freed from its hooks, would not come down and bury its curved blade into her heart. The wire burned white-hot into her skin as she raised her legs and tried to kick the tip of the handle. Her toes came within inches. She must kick higher.

Gritting her teeth against the pain, she closed her eyes to concentrate on kicking up as high as her legs would allow, when suddenly she heard footsteps outside. Praying Evan would stay away just a few minutes longer, she thrust her legs upward again, but again they fell scant inches from their goal. Then she heard the clatter of the wooden latch and the eerie creak of the door itself. It was too late.

"What in the hell are you doing in here?" Evan demanded upon entering the room. "What are you doing over there?" Then realizing exactly what she had hoped to do, he laughed that high-pitched laugh of his as he leaned his rifle against the wall, then stepped further into the room, not bothering to close the door behind him. But then why should he? Where was she going bound up like a pig for slaughter?

"You never give up, do you?" he asked as soon as he had his laughter better under control.

"Not when I have so much to live for," she replied, ready to bargain with him for her life if necessary.

"What have you got to live for?" Evan wanted to know, still chuckling softly when he walked over and took the scythe off the wall to examine it more carefully. "If you mean Wade, I'm afraid I have a little bad news for you."

Callie's heart stopped beating.

"I'm afraid Wade has met with a little accident," Evan went on to explain. Gingerly, he ran his fingertip over the sharp edge of the curved blade as if to test its sharpness. Suddenly, he seemed mesmerized by the shape of the metal tool.

"What have you done to him?" Callie didn't as much as take a breath while she waited for his answer.

Evan blinked once, then knelt beside her, still holding the scythe in his hands. With a smile that sent chills of icy panic through Callie, he reached out with one hand and jerked her into a sitting position, slamming her back hard against the wall. Callie fought the resulting pain and looked at Evan's cold, hate-filled expression with an answering hatred of her own.

"And what makes you think I had anything to do with his accident?" he wanted to know. He glowered at her a moment longer, then suddenly burst out laughing and leaned forward until his face was only inches from hers. She felt the heat of his breath against her skin.

Callie pressed herself as hard as possible against the wall, hoping to put even a fraction of an inch more distance between them. The rank odor of wood smoke and perspiration clung to him, making her stomach reel. It took all the powers of concentration she had not to retch in his face. In an effort to calm her churning stomach, she took a long, deep breath, only to be assailed by the putrid stench even worse.

Her voice trembled when she spoke. "Please, tell me what you have done to Wade."

"You sure are a pretty little thing, aren't you? Too bad you had to go and fall in love with the wrong man. But then you never got the chance to fall in love with me, did you? And that's partly my fault. Had I known you were this pretty, I would have come by and paid call on you myself," Evan said

413

as he reached out to roughly caress her trembling cheek with the sweaty curve of his palm.

"Please. Tell me what you have done to Wade," she tried again. Her fear for Wade became so great, she did not think she could bear not knowing what had happened another second.

"Killed him," he responded with a light shrug of his shoulders as if it was a matter of little consequence. His eyes glimmered with satisfaction when he spoke again. "I guess you could say I sent his burning soul straight to hell."

Callie closed her eyes against the bitter anguish his words had caused her, then opened them again, determined not to believe it. He was only trying to frighten her more. "That's impossible. How? How did you kill him?"

"How is not quite as important as the fact that I did indeed kill the man. In fact, I think I'll let you die wondering just how I did kill him. Yes, the thought of that suits me just fine." He leaned back and returned his attention to the long, curved blade of the scythe still in his hands. "But then again, maybe watching you suffer while I tell you all the gory little details, one by one, would be even more satisfying."

Callie felt a deep, driving pain, then a sudden numbness when she came to realize from his expression that he spoke the truth. He had indeed killed Wade. Her wonderful, golden-hearted Wade.

"Why? Why did you kill him?" she wanted to know. Her pale brown eyes were wide with horror and her whole body began to shake uncontrollably with a combination of both grief and rage. "What could you possibly have to gain by killing him?"

"What did I have to gain?" Evan asked, as if he could not believe she was that incredibly stupid. "Don't you see? Now that Wade is dead, that leaves me as the only next of kin. I can inherit everything. In fact, I am now the proud owner of all of the Barlow holdings, which is the way it should have been to begin with. I finally have everything that is owed me. Too bad the house had to go, though. I liked that house and I really would have liked living there the rest of my life; but then again, I now have plenty of money to build myself a new

414

house even grander than that one. Or maybe I'll just live in Wade's house for a while, since it's now mine too."

Evan's words echoed in her mind. *To bad the house had to go? To bad the house had to go?* Suddenly, Callie understood why Evan smelled so strongly of wood smoke. She gasped aloud.

"Who knows?" Evan went on, ignoring her sharp intake of air. "I may even decide to live in Tucker's house. Because, once I've killed you, I am certain I will be able to convince whoever ends up replacing you at the Circle T to finally sell out." He threw back his head and laughed yet again. "I'll own it all. Just like I always planned all these years. I will be the richest, most powerful man in all of East Texas. No one else will even come close. I will finally have everything I ever wanted. And when I do, all the people I meet on the street will finally show me the respect I truly deserve. No one will dare look down on me then. No one will dare call me a bastard son then. They will be too afraid to."

There was such a look of pure, demonic satisfaction on Evan's face that it sent another wave of sickening shivers through Callie. The man was mad, utterly mad. "But what happens when they discover what you did?"

"You mean the fire? There's no way anyone can know I set it. I was careful to see that there were no witnesses. No one else was even around. You see, I sent Carlotta into town. Told her Wade had decided to get Walter a whole new suit to be buried in and how we both wanted her to be the one to pick it out. I told her to have Marcus drive her, then gave her plenty of money to buy two suits if need be. Anything to get her and that old meddler, Marcus, out of the way. Who knows? The blame might even fall on poor Carlotta. After all, she left a fire burning in the stove that just might have gotten out of hand while she was gone. And if no one buys that story, I'll mention that Wade had asked earlier for Walter's pipe and a box of matches. That would suggest to most folks that he accidentally managed to burn the place down himself."

Callie bit down on her lip to keep from crying. How it tore at her very soul to think of Wade burning to death. Or was he already dead before Evan set fire to the place? Was the fire just a way of covering up a crime already committed? "How can you be sure Wade was in the house when you set the fire? How do you know he did not get out?"

"Oh, he was in there, all right," Evan said, smiling deeper. "I heard him call out for the housekeeper. He wanted to warn her to get out of the house. Noble, don't you think? I guess he never noticed she had already left."

"But maybe he got out," Callie said hopefully. Every fiber in her wanted to believe that. "Maybe he got out and is still alive."

"No chance of that. I stood outside—back away from the house in case someone should see the smoke and decide to come investigate. I watched until the house finally started to collapse to make sure he did not come out. Had he somehow managed to get out of that room—which he didn't—but had he somehow gotten out and tried to make a run for it, I had my rifle with me—loaded and ready. The lawyer may have taken my handgun and kept it, but I still had my rifle. And I wouldn't have hesitated to use it if I'd seen Wade come busting out that front door and take out across the yard."

"That's what I figured," came a ready response.

Callie and Evan both looked up in time to see Wade appear in the doorway. His clothing was singed and his angry face streaked with black. In his hand he brandished a three-foot piece of broken limb. Though he still wore his holster, it remained empty. And he had no rifle tucked under his arm.

"That's why I was careful not to be seen and used the smoke trailing off towards the carriage house for cover in order to get away from the house. From there I was able to spot you off in the distance just before you mounted your horse and rode out. I had a hard time keeping up with you, on foot the way I was, since you had had the forethought to let all the horses in the barn loose into the pasture before you set the house on fire. But you were kind enough to leave a nice, clear trail to follow. But then I guess you didn't plan on being followed, did you?"

Evan looked as if he had been confronted by the very devil himself. His grip tightened on the handle of the scythe.

416

"There was no way you could escape. That room was surrounded with fire. How'd you get out?"

"I had no choice but to make a run for safety right through the flames themselves. After breaking all the glass out of the window, I jerked down one of the drapes, doused it with what was left of the drinking water, then threw it over my head and charged across the veranda, right through the middle of all that fire. Though the drapes caught fire, I didn't. And once I managed to get just beyond the reach of the flames, I discovered only the one section of the house was burning. I then re-entered the house through another window hoping to get Father's body out and rescue Carlotta. But when I could not find the woman, I realized either you'd already killed her and had placed her body in the flames or she had left the house before the fire ever started, so I decided to get Father's body and get on out of there while I still could — using all that smoke to cover me."

While Wade explained his escape, Evan's gaze fell on the rifle still resting only a few feet off to Wade's side, aware he had not yet noticed it. Then he glanced at the menacing piece of limb in Wade's hand, and finally at the implement he still held in his own hand. Deciding he clearly had the advantage over Wade, he raised the scythe high over his head and charged like a raging bull.

Callie screamed when Evan brought the curved blade of the scythe down with a resounding blow, missing Wade's shoulder by mere inches. At the same moment, Wade swung the solid piece of limb with all his might, striking Evan sharply in the side.

Evan groaned upon impact, but quickly shook off whatever pain had resulted from the blow as he hurriedly tried to retrieve his scythe from where it had become lodged in the wall. Desperately, he tried again and again to jerk it free, until damp locks of his hair fell carelessly into his face. But when he realized the blade was not about to come loose in time to be of any use to him, he quickly abandoned the implement and made a wild dash for the rifle.

Wade became aware of the danger in an instant, and took another hard swing at him with the piece of limb still in his

417

hands, but Evan was able to jump back in time to get out of his way.

In the follow-through of the swing, the tip of the limb struck a brace in the wall. The resulting jolt tore the piece of wood from Wade's grip. Now defenseless, he too dove for the rifle.

Evan's hand reached the weapon first, but before he was able to get a firm grasp, Wade had his hands on the rifle too. Pulling each other to the ground in their battle to gain control of the only real weapon left, they struggled against each other, stirring up so much dirt in the scuffle Callie could not see clearly enough to know just who had the advantage.

"Wade, be careful," she cried out, trying to peer through the thick cloud of red dust in an effort to tell what was going on. Her heart was frozen with fear.

Rolling over and over in the dirt, with the rifle wedged between them, the two came ever closer to where Callie sat watching with horrified fascination. At one point, it looked like Wade was about to twist the rifle right out of Evan's firm grip, but in the end he was unable to break the weapon free.

The struggle continued until somehow Evan found himself on top, with the barrel of the rifle pressed firmly against Wade's collarbone. Both men quaked from their efforts to move the weapon up or down. Clearly, Evan meant to choke Wade, and rose high above him in his efforts to press the weapon against his throat.

Callie could not stand the thought of it and with a strength born of fear, she rolled forward once, then again, which placed her next to them. Then with all her might, she kicked out at them. Though she wore no boot, the heel of her foot created just enough of an impact to send Evan reeling sideways, giving Wade the advantage at last.

Though Evan did not actually let go of the rifle when he fell, he was stunned enough by the unexpected blow to allow Wade to finally jerk it out of his hands. Once he was in possession of the rifle, it was only a matter of pointing it at Evan's cold-blooded heart and ordering him not to move.

"Don't shoot." Evan cried out, panic-stricken, as he thrust his hands immediately into the air. His eyes were wide with childlike fright while he slowly began to scoot across the dirt floor, using his elbows for leverage, clearly wanting to put distance between him and Wade. "Don't shoot. Please, don't shoot."

"Give me one good reason not to," Wade answered through clenched teeth while he slowly rose to his feet, the rifle still carefully aimed at Evan's heart. The muscles along the sides of his jaws worked furiously when he pulled back on the chamber bolt to make sure the weapon was ready to fire. Once assured, he began to slowly move forward.

Seeing the black hatred in his opponent's eyes, Evan froze, several feet from the door. He then stared at the rifle, horrified.

Wade's finger felt for the trigger while he kept steady aim.

Callie felt her insides buckle with sudden apprehension. "Wade, don't," she called out to him. "Let the sheriff deal with him. Please."

Wade stood motionless, as if he had not heard her. The muscles in his jaws continued to pump in and out while he held the rifle directly at Evan's heaving chest.

"Wade, please. Come untie me." Her heart hammered hard against her breastbone while she waited for his next response. Though she did not champion Evan's life, she dreaded the thought of Wade being branded a murderer. "Please."

Slowly, Wade turned to look at her. For the first time since he'd gained possession of the rifle, he blinked, and she could tell he had finally heard her. Slowly, he brought his finger off of the trigger. She was so overwhelmed with relief, she began to sob openly.

"Please, Wade, come untie me. I want to get out of here. I want to go home."

Wade slowly lowered the rifle to his side. His eyes were still wide with the realization of what he had nearly done when he nodded. "All right."

Callie closed her eyes and slowly released the breath she had held buried deep in her lungs. Wade had terrified her. She felt certain that for one brief moment, Wade had wanted to kill Evan. Her body slackened when she heard Wade take another step in her direction. The worst was over.

When she slowly reopened her eyes to look at Wade, she was horrified to discover she was wrong. It was not over yet. Evan was gone.

Chapter Twenty-six

"Evan!"

Wade was out the door in an instant.

Still securely bound with rope and wire, all Callie could do was sit and wait. And pray. Though she rarely asked God for favors, especially after He had seen fit to ignore her desperate pleas during the years she had been treated as no better than a slave at the hands of her mean-hearted step-aunt, Callie closed her eyes and prayed as hard as she could. Locking her hands together at the fingers and holding them firmly in place, she pleaded with God to see Wade safely through whatever was about to happen.

Outside, she heard the retreating sounds of two sets of rapid footsteps; then she heard Wade's voice cry out in warning.

"Stop! Right there! Before I end up shooting you in the back like you deserve."

The sound of rifle fire only a split second later caused Callie to scream aloud. Her heart sank, knowing that if Wade had indeed killed Evan, he would have to stand trial for murder. And if found guilty, he would hang. She could not bear the thought. Terrified, she cried out his name.

There came no response. Her heart pumped more fear through her bloodstream, chilling her to the very core of her being. Had Evan thought to hide a gun outside? Was it actually Evan's gunfire she had heard?

"Wade? What happened?" she called out again, more

frantic. "Wade!"

Again there was no response, but she still heard footsteps — one set of slow and steady footsteps, in the distance. Then to her profound relief, she heard Evan cry out, "Don't kill me. Please. Don't kill me."

"Don't give me any more reason to want to kill you," Wade responded angrily.

After a brief moment of silence, the heavy sounds of footsteps started again, this time growing steadily louder. Callie was relieved to hear two distinct sets of footfalls. Even if Wade did shoot Evan, he had not harmed him to the point he could not walk. When they at last re-entered the shed and stood where she was able to see them both, she was even more relieved to discover Evan uninjured. Wade could be accused of no crime. The shot must have been a warning.

"Stand over there in that far corner. Face to the wall," Wade told him. His expression remained rock hard, but the moment of intense hatred was gone. Whatever desire Wade might have had to kill the man had passed.

Evan did exactly as told, holding his hands high over his head so Wade would know he could cause no more harm. Evan clearly wanted to live.

Keeping the rifle pointed at Evan's back, Wade took several long sidesteps, then knelt beside Callie. He did not once take his eyes off Evan while he reached inside his trousers pocket and came out with a small folded knife. Cautiously, he began to saw away at the rope which held Callie's wrists to her waist. He warily divided his attention between keeping Evan's face to that wall and freeing Callie at last.

When the rope finally gave way and Callie was able to move her hands and rotate her wrists, she felt a brief moment of pain. Her skin burned where the rope had rubbed her raw, but she smiled, grateful to have her freedom at last. Then, with no further delay, she set about helping him liberate her ankles from the cutting edges of the stiff wire.

"I'm free," she told him just before she tossed the tangle of wire off to the side. Quickly, she bent forward to examine the cuts around her ankles, and then turned her attention to the tender, red whelps that circled her wrists. Her skin still burned, but it felt good to finally be free of her restraints. She sighed aloud with relief. When she attempted to get up off of the dirt floor, she found it harder to do than she had expected. Her left foot was swollen and sore from having run through the woods with no boot, and the bottom did not want to accept her weight. It took a second effort, along with a little assistance from Wade, before she was able to actually get up onto that foot and stand.

Though still a little dizzy from losing so much blood, she held the rifle on Evan while Wade went about tying Evan's hands behind him with the same piece of rope which had previously been used on Callie. Having had her thoughts otherwise occupied for the past several minutes, she was just starting to notice the slow throbbing at the base of her skull again, and could tell it was getting worse with each moment's passing.

"Wade, hurry. I can't stand up much longer," she told him. It did not occur to her that by stating such a thing aloud, she had indicated to Evan she would soon be of little help to Wade.

Noticing the way Evan cut his gaze around to look at Callie, as if to size up her weakened state, Wade hurried to get his hands trussed securely behind him. Then, because there was only the one horse, Wade attached another, longer rope to the one that bound Evan's hands behind him, making a leash which would allow him to keep better control over the man while he walked ahead of them.

After he tested the knot, he gripped the opposite end tightly in his hands and turned to look at Callie. He found her standing bravely beside the open door, trying her best to keep the rifle aimed at Evan as she had been told to do. He could tell how weak she was by the way her arms had begun to tremble uncontrollably, so much so the barrel of the rifle dipped and wavered, rarely held in direct aim.

"Come on," Wade demanded, quickly dragging Evan along behind him by use of twelve-foot lead rope. Though his voice revealed anger, his touch was gentle when he reached an arm out to Callie and led her outside to Evan's horse. He then grabbed her by her waist and placed her carefully into the saddle. Keeping a firm hold on the rope that held Evan his prisoner, he promptly swung himself up to sit behind her.

Firmly, he leaned Callie back against him with one arm while he took the reins in the same hand which held the rope.

"Evan, you have two choices. You can either walk ahead of us and pray I don't decide to run you down. Or I can drag you along behind. But either way, you are going with us," Wade stated in a strong, no-nonsense voice.

In a last attempt at defiance, Evan chose to do neither. Instead, he walked along beside the horse, back just enough to keep his eye on Wade and Callie.

Slowly and carefully, with Wade in command, they set out for the nearest house, Twin Oaks. The going was hampered by the fact Evan was being forced to walk with his hands behind him, which seemed to affect his sense of balance. He stumbled again and again, sometimes falling, sometimes only coming close, but both made the going very slow.

To Wade's dismay and growing frustration, Callie slumped back against him just moments after they had the house in sight. Her grip slowly loosened and, as a result, she nearly dropped the rifle. He was able to keep from losing the weapon entirely by lifting his knee level with her lap, balancing it on his thigh.

As soon as they entered the yard, he wasted no time shouting for help, and was relieved to see several men hurry out of the bunkhouse. Only seconds later, Sam appeared from the back of the house. They were all dressed in their best black trousers and starched white shirts, which was rather peculiar, but Wade did not have time to question them about their choice of clothes.

"We was just coming over to pay our res . . ." Sam started to explain, but cut his own words short when his gaze fell on Callie's battered body. Quickly, he bounded across the yard to meet them halfway. "What happened?" His curious gaze swept from Callie's limp form to Evan's ragged appearance, to the rope that obviously held him prisoner, then back to Wade.

"Callie's hurt. I'll tell you about it later," Wade assured them as he released the horse's reins but kept a firm grip on the rope. Quickly, he wrapped the end of the rope around the saddle horn several times in order to temporarily secure it while he took care of Callie.

"Sam, please, carry her into the house and make her as comfortable as you can," Wade said just before he gently handed her down into his friend's sturdy arms. When he did, the rifle slipped completely out of her grasp and clattered into the dirt. Callie moaned softly when Sam brought her firmly against his chest, but did not open her eyes.

Aware the rifle had landed only a couple feet in front of him, Evan glanced down at it. Frantically, he began to tug at his arms, but in the end realized his efforts to free himself were useless. Wade reached out and gave a hard jerk on the rope, and sent him stumbling backward to the ground, in the opposite direction from the rifle. Securing a tighter grip on the rope again, Wade made certain Evan could not stretch forward and reach the rifle. He then turned his attention first to Sam, who hurried toward the house with Callie in his stout arms, then to the rest of the men, who remained behind to see if they could also help in some way.

"Kelly, I want you to ride over to the Circle T and bring back the doctor. Tell him Callie has been badly hurt and to hurry," he said as soon as he had slid off the horse. Unwilling to give Evan even one inch of slack, he immediately began to wrap the excess length around his hand.

"Rebel, I want you to go into town for the sheriff while I personally stand guard over Evan. When you find him, tell him I may have the man who shot Grant and McKenzie. Explain to him that, although I imagine we could get him to town safely enough, I'd rather not take any chances. I'll hold him here at gunpoint until you get back."

Rebel did not stick around to ask questions. In minutes, he was on his horse and headed into town.

Not about to let Evan out of his sight, Wade picked up the rifle, dusted it off, and pointed it at him.

"Move," he said, then marched him into the barn to the small tack room near the back. After ordering two of his men to guard the outside, he followed Evan and carefully closed the door.

Though the small room had no windows, only ceiling vents, Wade knew when the doctor arrived barely half an hour later. Desperately, he wanted to go inside the house to hear what Lowell had to say. He wanted to know if Callie was any better. But he did not dare leave Evan until the sheriff arrived. He wanted to be certain the man could not escape, knowing that if he did, he would try to harm them again. And this time, he just might find a way to kill one of them. The thought of it not only angered him, but made him exceedingly cautious.

Time crept slowly while Wade waited for some word concerning Callie, and for the sheriff to finally come and take Evan off his hands.

Oddly, during the first half hour, Evan had sat quietly on the floor in the corner staring idly at a jagged tear in his trouser leg, like a lost child. But as more time passed, he began to grow more restless. Finally, he started to talk about his failed attempt to have it all—while continuing to stare, eyes wide, as if fascinated by the jagged hole in his trouser leg. "I came close. I came real close. If only you hadn't found a way to get by me. If only you had died in that fire like you were supposed to. Then I'd have everything. Everything I ever wanted."

Wade refused to dignify such remarks with a reply, and continued to stand, leaning against the door frame, quietly staring at him. Oh, how he wished the sheriff would hurry.

Evan did not blink. Only his throat and his mouth moved while he let his thoughts continue to ramble forward. "I'd not only have the Rocking W. No. I'd have the Circle T too. Just like I always wanted. Everything I always wanted."

While he talked, his gaze became more distance, as if he no longer saw the hole in his pants, though his eyes were riveted there. "It's true. Once I had Callie out of the way, I'd have been able to frighten whoever eventually took over that place into selling out. I know I would. Damn woman. And I wouldn't have had to work as hard at it either. Whoever took over next wouldn't feel such a foolish loyalty to Tucker. It wouldn't have taken near as much for me to scare the rest of those bludgers off. It's just that she's so damned stubborn."

Wade felt an odd prickling sensation in the pit of his stomach. "You? You caused all the trouble at the Circle T?"

"Of course, it was me. Me and a few of the men who worked for us. Men I could trust to keep quiet. I wanted that place. I wanted it real bad. And Father promised I could have it. He told me that all he had to do was get Tucker's widow to agree to sell out and he would be able to buy it for me. He had plenty of money saved up." Evan's gaze rose to meet Wade's, and though he still did not blink, his eyes narrowed until they were only half their normal size. "And after he bought it, he planned to give it to *me*. Because he loved me best."

Wade at first felt weak from the shocking revelation, then began to feel a burning anger grow from the very core of his soul. "You let me believe it was Pop who did everything."

"You believed what you wanted to believe," Evan said. A faint smile curled the corners of his mouth when he considered what he had gotten away with. "Don't blame me for what you chose to believe."

"Don't give me that. I believed it because you wanted me to. You wanted everyone to think he was the guilty one. You used Pop's stationery to write your threatening notes. You even took his new rifle and used it, knowing that if I went to the trouble to inspect the bullets, I'd automatically connect the crime to him," Wade said. His brow drew low over glinting blue eyes at the realization.

"You give me far more credit than I deserve. I used his paper because I didn't have any of my own. And I took his rifle because it was more accurate than any of the others and because of its speed in firing. The part about you finding the bullets and realizing they had to come from his rifle was really just luck." Suddenly Evan's expression brightened. "I just thought of something. Father's will was burned in that fire. And I tore up the lawyer's copy and threw it away. There's no longer any proof I am not the heir to the ranch. And even if I can't convince everyone that I am the one he truly wanted to take over the Rocking W, at least now I can claim an equal share."

427

Wade frowned at the madness of Evan's words. It was clear that Evan's mind was not all there. The man continuously snatched at thoughts that suited him the most, whether they made sense or not. "Evan, the will did not burn in the fire. Thomas took it with him so his wife could write out another copy to keep on file at the courthouse. But even if he hadn't taken it, there are witnesses who can attest to what was written in the will. There's Callie. And there's the lawyer. And you yourself went right outside and told every man who worked with you all about the contents of that will."

Evan's expression dimmed. "I forgot. I guess all I get is the measly bit of acreage the will left me with."

"And that won't do you any good in jail," Wade pointed out, staring curiously at him. Obviously Evan did not understand the true seriousness of his situation.

"They can't put me in jail. There are no witnesses."

"There's me. I'm a witness. And there are all the men who helped you."

"They won't talk because they know they would be putting themselves in jail if they did. And you didn't see me do anything," he stated obstinately. "Besides, I still plan to kill you. It's the only way I can ever get what's mine."

Wade wondered just how he planned to do that when he was now bound at both his hands and feet, and the sheriff due to arrive at any moment. Yet, he knew it would be useless to try to explain any of that to Evan. He had lost any firm footing on reality.

Even after the sheriff had come and he and Wade had hoisted Evan up onto a horse for the ride into town, Evan continued to babble on about everything he would own one day and what he would do with all his wealth.

When the sheriff tugged on the lead rein of the horse Evan rode, which caused the animal to lurch forward and follow slowly, Evan's parting words to Wade proved just how lost his mind really was.

"You'd better take good care of my ranch while I'm away. There had better not be any problems when I get back."

Rather than argue with a man who had rejected all rational thought, Wade shook his head sadly and responded, "There won't be." To himself, he added, "Because you won't be coming back." He shuddered at the thought of what might happen if he did somehow get away and come back for them.

With his head full of all he had learned in the past hour and his heart heavy with concern for Callie, Wade turned toward the house, eager to speak with the doctor. It was then he noticed a wagon had been brought around to the side of the house.

"What's going on?" he asked when Sam hurried passed him with a tall stack of quilts in his arms.

"Got to get the wagon ready for Mrs. Tucker. The doc wants to take her back home so's he can keep an eye on her while he also keeps an eye on Hank McKenzie."

"Is she well enough to be moved?"

"Doc seems to think so. She keeps trying to open her eyes, but just can't quite seem to come fully awake. Doc told me and Cody to get the wagon ready so's she can be transported. Seems McKenzie is still pretty bad off and the doc don't want to waste no more time or effort traveling back and forth between patients—not when he don't have to. He told me to spread these quilts out across the back of the wagon to make it more comfortable for her."

Frowning, Wade turned and hurried inside.

"Doc?" he called out, not sure which bedroom Callie had been taken to. He paused at the foot of the stairs. "Doc?"

"In here," came the response.

Aware the voice had come from the direction of Sam's bedroom near the back of the house, Wade wasted no time getting there.

"How is she?" he wanted to know when he entered the small bedroom only seconds later. Even before Lowell answered, Wade noticed her head and right shoulder were already bandaged. Her right arm had been made immobile by two large strips of cloth that bound it securely to her side.

"Hard to say how she is," Lowell answered, his expression full of concern. "She's hurt her shoulder and has some pretty bad bruises on her chest and stomach, but it's the head injury that has me most worried. I don't know what he hit her with, but she's got quite a bit of swelling. I've given her an injection and applied cool compresses for the moment, but when I get her back home, I plan to put an ice pack on it."

"Ice?"

"To help reduce the swelling. I asked Sam if you had any and he explained you did not normally keep such luxuries. He explained how, because your cellar stays so cool year round, you did not really need to store ice here. But I don't need cool, I need cold. That's one reason I'm so eager to get her back home."

"I see," Wade said morosely. If the doctor truly thought moving her was for the best, he would not argue to keep her there.

"By the way, I hope you don't mind that I borrowed a change of clothes from you. I couldn't go on living in the same set of clothes much longer."

"Huh?" Wade asked, looking down at Callie's pale face, only vaguely aware the doctor had spoken. Absently, he glanced at the dark blue trousers and the pale blue work shirt the doctor wore, and realized what it was he had said. "Oh, yes, fine. Whatever you need. When are you going to move her?"

"As soon as Sam comes back. I'm just waiting for the wagon to be made ready. I already have her ready for travel."

"I want to ride over with you. Then I need to get back over to the Rocking W and see what damage has been done."

"Damage?"

Wade then explained about the fire and how he had been forced to abandon his father's body in the carriage house in order to track Evan down. The thought that rats and other small rodents could easily get to the body made him eager to return.

"I guess I'll bring his body back over here until it's time for the funeral. People are going to want to pay their last respects," he said sadly, then dropped off into a long moment of silence.

Aware of everything Wade had been through over the past few days, Lowell wanted to offer his friend a word of comfort, but was too tired to think of anything really appropriate. Finally, he sighed heavily and rested a reassuring hand on Wade's shoulders. Silently he shook his head, wondering how much more one man could possibly bear.

"I think your friend is about to wake up," Lucille said as she bent over McKenzie and cocked her head to one side so she could better judge his facial expressions.

As if aware of her close scrutiny, McKenzie twitched his cheek, then wiggled his nose.

Spotting the movement, Ed shot out of his chair and hurried to stand on the opposite side of the huge four-poster bed. "Mac?"

McKenzie's eyes fluttered open, and for a moment he stared at Ed as if he was seeing a ghost. He blinked with obvious confusion. "Ed? Is that you?"

A wide, relieved grin slid across Ed's face. "Hell, yes, it's me. Who'd you think it was?"

McKenzie turned his head to stare at Ed from the corner of his eyes. Then he frowned, still confused. "You come back to haunt me?"

"Haunt you? What are you talking about? Of course I'm not here to haunt you. I'd have to be dead in order to do that."

McKenzie lifted one shaggy eyebrow. "You ain't dead?"

"Who, me? Dead?" Ed reached up to touch a hand to his chest as if suddenly he felt it necessary to check. "Hell, no, I'm not dead. Takes more than a bullet in the shoulder to stop me."

A trembling smile lifted McKenzie's heavy beard, revealing the edge of his chipped tooth. "I thought they killed you for sure."

"Nope, you're not that lucky," Ed responded with a tearful laugh, then pulled out the collar of his shirt so McKenzie could glimpse the small bandage he still wore. "I was barely hurt. You are the one we all thought was going to die."

McKenzie's eyes suddenly narrowed. "Is that why you are here? You waitin' for me to kick off so you can get your grimey hands on my new boots?"

Ed laughed louder.

McKenzie wiggled his toes, and his eyes suddenly widened

431

again. "And where the hell are my boots? What have you done with them?"

Just when Ed was about to retort that he had them on, trying them out for size, Lucille quickly announced the truth. "They're safe. In fact, they are over there in the corner all polished up like new."

"They are new," McKenzie muttered. "Only had them a month." He then pulled his suspicious gaze off Ed long enough to look at her. "Thanks for taking such good care of them. They are special made. I appreciate it you polishin''em up for me."

"Oh, but I didn't polish them, Ed did," Lucille quickly told him, before she noticed how frantically Ed had begun to wave his hands in an effort to stop her before she told too much.

"Did he now?" McKenzie turned his head back to get a better look at his friend. "Don't tell me that after all these years you're getting a soft spot in you."

Ed's eyebrows pulled down to form a menacing scowl. "Of course not. It's just that if you did happen to die and I was able to claim them for my own, I'd want them nice and shiny is all. Don't go making it into something it ain't."

McKenzie chuckled, then tried to raise his head off the pillow, but winced when the movement resulted in a dull pain across his forehead. "Damn, what did you hit me with?"

"I didn't hit you with nothing—*yet*. But keep it up, partner, and I just might."

"What did you say?" McKenzie asked, thrusting his grizzled chin out as if daring him to repeat his words.

Ed brandished his fist before him. "I said, keep it up and I just might see to it you fall back asleep for another four days."

"Four days?" McKenzie's eyes narrowed again suspiciously, then he looked to Lucille for verification. "I been knocked out for four days?"

"Yessir, I'm afraid you have," Lucille said with a firm nod of her dark head.

"And you two have stayed here doctoring me like this all that time?" He glanced back at Ed again.

Ed paused as if trying to decide whether or not to take credit for such a noble deed, but in the end chose to tell the truth. "Not exactly. You see, the doctor is here and has been, off and on, ever since you were first injured. It's just that he's in the next room tending to Mrs. Tucker right now."

"Mrs. Tucker? What happened to her?"

Ed's expression hardened. "She's been hurt. Evan Samuels tried to kill her. Tried to kill Wade too. Way I hear it he almost did 'em both in."

"What?" McKenzie responded, clearly surprised. "When did this happen? Why?"

Ed sat down at the edge of McKenzie's bed and quickly filled him in on what he knew about the events of the past several days, though he admitted some of it still seemed a little sketchy even to him.

Occasionally, whenever McKenzie would raise an eyebrow in a clear display of skepticism, Ed would turn to Lucille for verification, but he continued to explain as best he could how Evan had been the one responsible for all the terrible incidents that had happened at the Circle T. He also told him how Wade had at first thought the culprit was his own father, and because of that, had gone to confront the man face to face. He then explained what a powder keg of trouble that had set off, and how Mrs. Tucker now lay motionless in the next room with her eyes wide open but unseeing. And how either Wade or one of Matthew's daughters was always at her side.

Ed shook his head sadly as he finished his tale. "It's like she's already dead, yet she still breathes. She just lies there staring off into nothing. Saddest thing you ever did see. I don't know what those two little girls will do if she don't get better soon. They don't have nobody else to take care of them. No more family at all that I know anything about. Sure as the sun rises in the east, they'll both end up wards of the county. And it's not just the girls I worry about. I don't know what Wade would do either if she was to die. It's clear enough to me that he's in love with her."

"I know," McKenzie muttered. "He's been in love with her for some time now. And I'd bet my new, polished boots she feels the same way about him. It'd be a shame if . . ."

He let his last thought go unspoken.

A low guttural moan welled deep inside Lucille's throat while she tried to blink back the tears that suddenly scalded her eyes. Quickly, she turned away. She did not want the men to see her face as she set about straightening the clutter on the bedside table.

McKenzie and Ed looked at each other, then at her trembling shoulders.

"Excuse me, I got washin' to do," she said suddenly, her deep voice strained with emotion. Then, before either man was able to say anything, she was gone.

Chapter Twenty-seven

The following afternoon, Wade left just long enough to attend his father's funeral, then stop by Virginia French's house to see if she had any pink roses in her flower garden. having remembered a conversation held in the toolshed the very first day he'd started working for Callie he was determined to have a large bouquet of pink roses waiting for her when she finally became aware of her surroundings again.

After his neighbor learned who the roses were for, being the notorious matchmaker she was, she provided him with an armload. Enough so that Lucille had been able to fill three large vases, two of which Wade brought up himself and handed to the girls, wanting them to decide the best places to display them.

Immediately, Janice put the vase he handed her on the table beside Callie's bed, while Amy tried the one she'd been given in several locations before deciding on the tall cheval dresser. If it were placed there, she felt Callie would be certain to see the roses the very moment she began to see again.

"There, now, that makes the room much more cheerful, don't you think?" Wade asked, smiling. Though exhausted, having gone without sleep for days now, he was determined not to let the girls know it. He wanted to remain as strong and cheerful as he possibly could, for their sakes. Not wanting them to know exactly how serious Callie's situation was, he had even gone so far as to shave, and had changed back into his usual work clothes after the funeral. He wanted things to seem as normal as possible for Janice and Amy. "And after Lucille gets through with supper and has brought up the third vase and placed it somewhere over in there, this room is going to look more like a garden than a mere bedroom."

"And when she finally wakes up and sees all these flowers, she's going to think she's died and gone to heaven," Amy stated thoughtlessly. But the minute she realized what she had said — as if by just stating the word she might help make it come true — she covered her mouth with both hands. Horrified, she glanced at Callie to see if she had heard her thoughtless statement. Her blue eyes were wide with unspoken apology.

"That's all right," Wade assured her, blinking back the fine sheen of moisture that belied the smile still on his face. "Her eyes may be open, but she can't hear you. The doctor says she can't hear any of us right now. Besides, you are right. When she wakes up to find all these pretty flowers around her and your two smiling faces, she *is* going to think she's died and gone to heaven."

Huge tears filled Amy's eyes when she slowly brought her hands away from her mouth. She began to tremble all over. "What happens if she does die? She's all we got."

"She's all I've got too," Wade tried to explain. "But you've got to believe she is not going to die. Try to remember, the doctor said her swelling is down and she has no fever. Those are good signs." He did not mention the fact Callie should already have come out of this semi-comatose state by now, or how that worried Lowell Edison no end. They did not need to know that there was a strong possibility Callie could remain the way she was forever. Able to sleep and able to open her eyes, as if awake, but unable to respond to life in any way.

When Amy stared up at Wade with her tear-filled eyes and her quivering lower lip, she looked so much like a little lost angel that his heart went immediately out to her.

Her lips pulled down at the corners. "But what if she does die? Who is going to take care of us then?"

"She's not going to die," Janice said stubbornly, clenching her hands into determined fists and stamping her foot hard.

"But-but what if she does?" Amy asked in a voice so tiny it

436

was almost not heard as she looked back at Callie's lifeless form, at the way she stared off into space with unseeing eyes. "What will happen to us?"

"Nothing," Wade assured her, and moved to take the little girl into his arms. With tears brimming in his own eyes, he lifted her off the floor and held her close. "I won't let anything happen to you."

"You promise? If she dies, will you promise to take care of us?" Amy asked, her words muffled by the soft material of his shirt as she pressed her wet face into his shoulder.

"Of course I will. But Callie is not going to die. She has far too much to live for," he said, trying to relieve some of the child's concern. Silently, he prayed his words would prove true. Because, although he would indeed see to the girls' welfare should the worst happen, he had no idea who would see to his. Who would help him get over his misery? Who would see him through his grief? Then he realized he would need the girls as much as they would need him. He closed his eyes against the pain that filled his heart.

A sharp knock sounded at the door, but Wade's throat was far too constricted at that moment to be able to answer. Instead, he headed for the door to open it with Amy still in his arms. He felt certain it was either Lucille or Lowell returning to check on Callie's condition. But since Lowell had left only minutes earlier to go just down the hall for a much-needed nap, he truly expected Lucille.

The knock sounded again, only louder, before he was able to completely cross the room. With no hand free, he shifted Amy to his left arm, using his hip for partial support of her weight, then reached for the handle. Just before his fingers touched the knob, the knock sounded yet again. Loud.

Closing his hand over the knob, he tried again to clear his throat of all lingering emotion so he could to speak. At the same instant, he heard Janice's soft intake of breath directly behind him. When he looked back over his shoulder to see what had caused the older girl to gasp, he noticed Callie's face was drawn into a tight frown. It was the first facial expression of any kind since the accident. The knock must have penetrated into her conscious thought.

Though she did not appear to actually see any of the things around her, the suddenly tensed expression on her face was her first real response to any form of stimuli. Wade's heart stopped.

"Wade? You in there? It's us, Mac and Ed. Can we come in for a minute?" McKenzie called through the door. Then he knocked yet again. "Hello?"

Callie tossed her head to one side, squeezing her eyes shut because of the pain, then muttered in a weak, groggy-sounding voice. "Come in."

For a moment no one spoke, then everyone spoke. Finally the door opened and Ed and McKenzie peeked in to see what all the commotion was about. When they did, they found Wade, Amy, and Janice on their knees at the side of the bed, each trying to coax Callie into opening her eyes again. Ed and McKenzie looked curiously at each other before stepping further into the room.

"What's going on?" Ed finally asked, when he could not make out what anyone said because all three spoke at once.

Wade turned to face them, his expression joyous. "Didn't you hear her? She talked. She moved her head and she talked."

Ed and McKenzie exchanged glances again, then joined Wade and the girls on the floor beside the bed just when Callie opened her eyes again, this time staring curiously at her strange, babbling audience. She blinked in an effort to comprehend, then muttered, "It's not polite to—"

Her words were cut short by the loud whoops and shouts as Amy scrambled onto the bed and hugged her close and the others threw up their arms with joy, shaking happy fists up into the air.

"What's going on in there?" Lowell called out just moments after he came bounding into the room. His eyes narrowed with a doctor's concern while his gaze darted around at all the unnecessary activity. Finally, he noticed Callie's wide-eyed expression, and came to an abrupt halt in the very center of the room.

"That's a good question, Doctor" Callie muttered with a weak smile while her eyes swept the many jubilant faces in the room. "Seem's there is some cause for celebration." Then her gaze fell on McKenzie. "Mac? How long have you been up and around?"

"Since yesterday," he told her, grinning broadly, then pounding himself lightly on the chest with a curled fist, gritting his teeth at the resulting pain when he did. "I'm as good as ever."

"Actually, I tried to get him to stay in bed a few days longer," Lowell put in, voicing his disapproval. "But he refused to stay."

Ed cocked a half smile. "He can be pretty stubborn when he wants to be—even when he doesn't want to, for that matter. But don't worry. All we are letting him to do is a little woman's work here and there. Nothing that can really hurt him."

Callie wondered where he ever got the idea woman's work was easy, but had no chance to comment.

"Seem unfair, since I feel as good as I do," McKenzie muttered, scowling. "I keep telling them I'm as fit as I ever was, but nobody will listen. I keep telling them Doc did such a good job on me that I'm as good as new. Looks like he did a pretty good job on you too." He finally smiled, showing the edge of his now-familiar chipped tooth. "You're finally back with us."

Callie looked puzzled. "Back? I don't understand? Where have I been?"

"Good question," Wade answered, gazing at her tenderly. "Your body was here, but just where it is your mind wandered off to, I have no idea. It was almost like you were sound asleep with your eyes open. You couldn't hear us or speak to us. You wouldn't even look at us."

"And how long was I like that?"

"Too long," everyone answered, almost in unison, then broke out laughing over the fact they had all responded with the same thought.

"Almost two days," Wade then told her, aware she had been serious about her question and deserved a straight answer.

Callie blinked with disbelief. "Where's Evan?"

439

"In jail, where he belongs. As are three of the men who helped him do some of his dirtier work. I figure as much as the sheriff has tallied up against them, they'll all be in there for a long, long time."

Relief washed over her. "I'm so glad it's finally over, that they are all finally in jail. Very glad." She smiled at Wade in an effort to pass along a silent message only he would understand. Now that all the bad was behind them, they were that much closer to being able to finally get married. All they really had to do now was concentrate on winning the girls' approval. Her heart pounded with hope-filled joy. She closed her eyes to better feel her elation.

Mistaking her closed eyes for rapidly waning strength, Lowell quickly let the doctor side of him take a firm hold on the situation. "All right, you've all seen that she's fully awake again, and you've all had a chance to talk to her. Now clear out. She does seem much better, but she still needs lots of rest," he said sternly, while waving his hand toward the door. "Come on now. Everyone out!"

"No, no, I feel fine," Callie said quickly, and except for a dull pain at the base of her head, she did feel fine.

"Just the same, you need your rest," Lowell stated adamantly, not about to be easily swayed as he lifted Amy up off the bed and placed her feet on the floor beside him.

"But I don't want to go yet," Amy said defiantly when Janice tried to take her by the arm and lead her from the room. "I want to stay right here." Then she placed her hands on her hips and, in a very grown-up voice, added, "If you don't mind, I have something I wish to discuss with my mother."

Everyone looked at Amy with astonished expressions. Wade tried his best to suppress the grin, as did Lowell, knowing it might serve to insult her. But Ed did little to hide the humor he saw in the situation, and chuckled at the little girl's audacity. McKenzie elbowed him to keep him quiet.

"Will you keep your discussion short?" Lowell finally asked, and when the child nodded that she would, he continued to wave everyone else on out of the room, carefully closing the door behind them.

"And just what is so important?" Callie wanted to know, so curious about what the girl had to say and so truly happy over the fact she had just referred to her as her mother instead of her step mother, she temporarily forgot all about the dull, throbbing head pain. Suddenly, she had never felt better.

"I want to discuss Mr. Barlow," Amy said, still taking what she considered her most grown-up stance.

"Oh?" Now she really had Callie's attention. "And what is it you have to say about him?"

"I like him," she stated simply, and with a firm nod that made her thick braids bob about her shoulders.

Callie lifted an eyebrow. "I like him too. But just what is all this leading to?"

Amy's expression grew hopeful. "Do you? Do you really like him too?" Suddenly she bounded forward and climbed back onto the bed where she would be able to see into Callie's face better.

"Yes, of course I do."

"Then ask him to marry us." Her voice was almost pleading.

"What did you say?" Callie could not have been more surprised.

"Ask him to marry us so he doesn't have to be all alone. Don't you see? If he married us, he could be your husband and Janice and I could pretend he was our father. He told me himself how, if you had died, he would have no one left. He also told us how, if you did die, he would take care of us. And I liked the way that made me feel. I liked it a lot. I want him to take care of us. And I want us to help take care of him. After all, he just lost his father, like we did, only difference is he has no one else. At least we had each other. He doesn't have anyone. His only other kin is in jail. He needs us. He really does. And I think we need him too."

Callie could not believe it. Her heart soared. "But what about Janice? What do you think she would have to say about such a thing?"

"She'd love it. She likes Mr. Barlow. She has told me so. She thinks he's every bit as nice as Father was. She even told me that if we ever had to have a new father, she hoped he would be someone like Mr. Barlow," Amy said, her face wrought with determination. "And its not as if he doesn't like us too. After all, he risked his life to save mine. And just look at all the pretty flowers he got for you."

Callie glanced around the room, and for the first time noticed the two large bunches of pink roses. The realization that he had remembered her favorite flower and then gone to such trouble touched her heart.

"So, what do you say?" Amy asked, bringing their discussion back to the problem at hand. "Will you do it? You said you like him, and he likes you. Will you ask Mr. Barlow to marry us?"

Callie reached out a hand to touch Amy's fair cheek, the cherubic cheek of a true angle. "I'll have a long talk with him about it."

"Goodie!" Amy squealed, clapping her hands with glee. "I'll go find him."

Before Callie could respond one way or the other, Amy was off the bed and across the room. Seconds later, she had the door flung wide and immediately began to call Wade.

"What is it?" Callie heard Wade answer, obviously not far away.

Amy barely had time to disappear from Callie's sight. "You need to go in there," she responded brightly. "I think she has something real important she needs to talk to you about."

Moments later, Wade entered the room, his face full of questions. "What's going on?"

Aware Amy had carefully failed to mention just what she wanted to talk to him about, Callie kept her expression serious and gently patted the bed beside her. "Close the door, then come and sit down here beside me. We have to talk."

"What is it?" he wanted to know as soon as he had complied. Frowning, he reached out and pushed a stray lock of her hair away from her face so he would be better able to see her solemn expression.

His sudden touch made it temporarily difficult for Callie to concentrate. It took her a moment to steady her hammering heart. "I-I'm afraid it has to do with our wedding plans."

Thinking the worst, Wade took in a deep, apprehensive breath while he waited for her to continue.

"Wade, I know you hoped that once we finally had who- ever was responsible for all those terrible incidents out of the way, we could pool our efforts and try to win the girls over to the idea of our marriage. You yourself said their approval was the last real thing keeping us apart, and that was true at the time." She paused to give him plenty of opportunity to jump to the wrong conclusion.

"But?" he prompted her immediately, ready to know the worst so they could start working on a way to deal with it. His jaw hardened while he waited for further response.

"But I think you should know, it really is pointless to do that now." She looked away from him, afraid he might see the mischief in her eyes.

Thinking the news so bad she was unable to face him with it, Wade showed all the horror she had expected. "But why? What exactly did Amy say to you?"

"Seems she has already made her decision concerning you and it's a firm one."

"Well, that decision will just have to be changed, firm or not." His voice rose with determination. Gently, he reached out to force Callie to look at him. She must see how serious he was about marrying her.

Still Callie avoided his eyes. "I don't know if you will want to even *try* to change her decision, not when you hear exactly what she has asked me to ask you."

"And what is that?"

"She wants me to ask you to marry us. She seemed very adamant about it." Callie was unable to hold her serious expression any longer, and broke into a wide grin. Her eyes sparkled with the joy that filled her heart.

"Vixen!" Wade growled, and bent forward to pull her close. Though his words were harsh, his smile let her know he was not truly angry with her. "How could you torment me like that?"

"What did I do?" she asked innocently, closing her eyes to enjoy the feel of his strong arms around her. How good his warm embrace felt. Smiling deeper, she snuggled closer. But all too soon, the moment of euphoria was broken when he quickly put her away from him.

"When? When can we be married?" he asked eagerly, his eyes searching hers.

"I don't know," Callie said, and for the first time really gave it some thought. "Do you think there should be a proper mourning period? After all, you father just died."

"I don't think he'd want that," Wade answered honestly. "I think he'd rather I get on with my life."

"But there are other things to consider."

"Like what?" He drew in his brow and shrugged his shoulders as if he could not fathom what those other things might be.

"Like where will we all live? Do you plan to rebuild your father's house? Or do you want all of us to live in your house at Twin Oaks? Or would you agree to living here?"

Wade thought about her questions a long moment before answering. "Although I have no intention of rebuilding my father's house, I do want to keep my own house in good repair so you and I will have a place to go after the girls are finally of age and married. After they both have families of their own, we would just be in the way here."

"Then you are willing to live here?" Callie could not be more happy over his decision.

"For now, yes. I think we should live here. This is the only home the girls have ever known and, in all honesty, it really does not matter to me where we end up—as long as we are all together. That's all that matters."

"And what shall we tell the girls about you?"

"About my being their half-brother? I think eventually we should tell them. But not until they are much older. Until then, I'll be satisfied being their . . ." He paused to think about that. "What will I be? Their step-stepfather?"

"If they can come to think of me as a real mother, then I'm certain they will come to think of you a real father. Until then, you can continue to be their very best friend," Callie said, reaching up to caress his cheek with the curve of her hand. Overjoyed when she looked at him then, she spoke what was foremost in her heart. "I love you, Wade Barlow."

"And I love you, Callie Tucker," he said, smiling proudly at her as he put out his hand and gently stroked her dark hair. "But I do want to make it clear right from the beginning that I don't plan to neglect my own ranch. I fully intend to see to it that my place and my father's place continue to prosper as much as the Circle T does. Even though we won't actually be living there, at least not for a while, I will want to make absolutely certain that I have something worthwhile to pass along to our own children. Though the Circle T will rightfully go to Amy and Janice's children, the Rocking W and Twin Oaks will go to *our* children, and I'll want only the best for them all."

"Our children?" Callie asked, pretending to be surprised he would think of such a thing. "And how many children do you propose we have?"

"As many as you think you can handle," he said with a light chuckle. "Which, knowing you like I do, puts no limit to the size of our family whatever."

"And just when do you propose we start on this large family of ours?" she ventured to ask.

"If it wasn't for your injuries, I'd suggest we get started right away," he said with a meaningful lift of his eyebrows.

A playful grin tugged at his mouth, bringing her attention temporarily to the fullness of his lips and sending a scattering of sensations through her, all which tended to make her feel vibrantly alive and very much a woman.

"If it wasn't for my injuries, we could get started on our family *right away*?" she asked, as if confused by such a statement. Smiling as she lifted her arms out to him, she spoke her next words softly. "And what injuries might those be?"

ZEBRA HAS THE SUPERSTARS
OF PASSIONATE ROMANCE!

LOVE'S BRIGHTEST STARS SHINE
WITH ZEBRA BOOKS!

CATALINA'S CARESS   (2202, $3.95)
by Sylvie F. Sommerfield

Catalina Carrington was determined to buy her riverboat back from the handsome gambler who'd beaten her brother at cards. But when dashing Marc Copeland named his price — three days as his mistress — Catalina swore she'd never meet his terms . . . even as she imagined the rapture a night in his arms would bring!

BELOVED EMBRACE   (2135, $3.95)
by Cassie Edwards

Leana Rutherford was terrified when the ship carrying her family from New York to Texas was attacked by savage pirates. But when she gazed upon the bold sea-bandit Brandon Seton, Leana longed to share the ecstasy she was sure sure his passionate caress would ignite!

ELUSIVE SWAN   (2061, $3.95)
by Sylvie F. Sommerfield

Just one glance from the handsome stranger in the dockside tavern in boisterous St. Augustine made Arianne tremble with excitement. But the innocent young woman was already running from one man . . . and no matter how fiercely the flames of desire burned within her, Arianne dared not submit to another!

SAVAGE PARADISE   (1985, $3.95)
by Cassie Edwards

Marianna Fowler detested the desolate wilderness of the unsettled Montana Territory. But once the hot-blooded Chippewa brave Lone Hawk saved her life, the spirited young beauty wished never to leave, longing to experience the fire of the handsome warrior's passionate embrace!

MOONLIT MAGIC   (1941, $3.95)
by Sylvie F. Sommerfield

When she found the slick railroad negotiator Trace Cord trespassing on her property and bathing in her river, innocent Jenny Graham could barely contain her rage. But when she saw how the setting sun gilded Trace's magnificent physique, Jenny's seething fury was transformed into burning desire!

Available wherever paperbacks are sold, or order direct from the Publisher. Send cover price plus 50¢ per copy for mailing and handling to Zebra Books, Dept. 2650, 475 Park Avenue South, New York, N.Y. 10016. Residents of New York, New Jersey and Pennsylvania must include sales tax. DO NOT SEND CASH.